PRINCES OF ROSEWOOD HALL #1 VAUGHN

PRINCE OF THORNS

ALSO BY E.J. KNOX

the Sinners of Saint Benedicts

Gods & Angels

Princes & Wolves

Men & Monsters

Rivermont Royals

Reign

Rival

Rivermont Royals Reveals

Obsess

Infatuate

Little Nymph

Little Nymph

Little Secret

Immortals of Lionswood Academy

Pawn takes Knight

Knight take Bishop

Bishop takes Rook

Princes of Rosewood Hall

Prince of Dreams

ALSO BY SCARLETT KNOX

the Vampires of Knightsbridge

Monster of Fate

Heaven & Hell Chronicles

Damned if I do

Damned if I don't

Damned if I know

Eternal Academy
Wanged

ALSO BY PIPPA LANGHORN

Love to Hate You

Sexy Siren Shorts
Heat of the Moment

AS ELIZABETH STEVENS

NEW ADULT/ADULT BOOKS

Grace Grayson Security
Chaos & the Geek
Hawk & the Lady
O Lord & the Queen
Rollie & the Rocker
Tank & the Rebel

Loving the Sykes
Caden
Carter
Luther
Oscar
Ashton

MATURE YA/NEW ADULT BOOKS
the Trouble with Hate is…
Gray's Blade
Being Not Good
Popped
the Art of Breaking Up

Accidentally Perfect Books
Accidentally Perfect
Perfectly Accidental

PRINCES OF ROSEWOOD HALL #1 VAUGHN

PRINCE OF THORNS

ELIZABETH STEVENS WRITING AS

E.J. KNOX

Kinky Siren
An imprint of Sleeping Dragon Books

Prince of Thorns
by E.J. Knox

Print ISBN: 978-925928945
Digital ISBN: 978-1925928938

Cover design by Melony Paradise of Paradise Cover Design
http://www.paradisecoverdesign.com/

This one's for Riker.
I promised not to ask, but you know I want to.

CONTENTS

AUTHOR'S NOTE

This is a dark, angsty, contemporary high school bully/enemies-to-lovers, forbidden romance with enough steam to melt your screen. He falls first, and he falls HARD and FAST. This is a crash course in insta-love for both of them. Do not engage in public consumption unless your poker face is impenetrable.

Do not read if you don't like bossy alpha males claiming what's theirs, a nerdy but feisty heroine determined not to fall for a silver tongue, sassy besties, snarky love-to-hate-them side characters, or bad boys with secret hearts of gold.

This story is set in a very bastardised combination of settings. I wanted to use a European school year because I like the timing and the weather better, but I imagine Hammersby Bay being a small (depending on your definition) US town on the coast/a river (like in Oregon, maybe?), and the more specific references of course skew Australian as usual. So, have fun!

This book is written using Australian English. This will affect the spelling, grammar and syntax you may be used to. This might come across as typos, awkward sentences, poor grammar, or missed/wrong words. In the majority of cases (I won't claim it's infallible, despite all best efforts), this is intentional and just an Aussie way of speaking (it took my US beta readers a bit to get used to). I can't say 'the' Aussie way, since we seem to differ even within the same state. Just think of us as a weird mix of British and US vernacular and colloquialisms, but with our own randomness thrown in. I still hope you enjoy it, though!

CHAPTER ONE

My last year of school was looking like it was going to be as epic as all the movies promised it would be. Year 12 screamed 'watch out world, this is Maggie McCallan's year!'

And why wouldn't it? I'd spent the whole summer holidays with Parker Bates. And I do mean *with* Parker Bates. Nothing was official yet, but it was only a matter of time before it was, and I couldn't wait for everyone to know.

The only way this year could get any better would be if I finally fell into that vat of acid or something and got the superpowers that my parents had promised me at birth when they christened me with a name like Magenta McCallan. Because, so far, it was a big fat bupkis on that front.

And, speaking of parents, there was one who wasn't going to let a little thing like my first day of my last year of school pass without making some comment about it. As though he knew I was walking through Rosewood Hall's front doors for the last first time, my phone buzzed in my pocket.

Dad

Good luck! You'll be amazing.

As always. Love you.

Maggie

Thanks, Dad. Love you, too.

See you Friday ❤

Dad

See you Friday. Can't wait ♡

As I slipped my phone back in my skirt pocket, I heard my name called by the boy in question. My stomach fluttered madly, and I had to bite my lip to stop the goofy smile he always gave me; a girl didn't want to look *too* smitten and give away any possible advantage she might have.

But just looking at him, I knew I was. Too smitten. Parker was amazing. He was sexy and sweet and kind and smart. He was the captain of the football team and this year's Head Prefect. With his light brown hair and deep brown eyes, his wide shoulders and chiselled jaw, and a warm, welcoming smile that made his eyes sparkle, he was gorgeous. What he lacked in height, compared to the rest of the team, he more than made up for in speed and talent.

"Hey, Parker," I said with a casual nod.

"How are you?" he asked as he put his arm around my shoulder and kissed my cheek. I felt in pride of place at home beside him.

Because everyone noticed. Noticed that Parker was paying someone – me – the kind of attention you paid them if you were dating them. All our friends and most of the rest of the year knew we'd hooked up over the holidays. It had been kind of obvious. But seeing this… Well, this was the next step, wasn't it? This was the point at which people started to wonder if we were finally exclusive.

I nodded. "I am good. How are you?"

Parker grinned around the corridor as we passed people. There was a very 'yeah, me and Maggie, what are you going to do about it?' sort of vibe to him that made not just my stomach flutter, but my heart as well.

"Much better now I have you in my arms, babe."

Oh, yes. Caitlin did actually do a double-take at that and I felt very self-satisfied about it. She might not have thought much of me, but the Police Chief's son calling me 'babe' meant something to these people. I wasn't just one step closer to dating the perfect guy, but also one step closer to finally being trusted by the people of Hammersby Bay.

But then, Caitlin was suddenly ever so less concerned about the disruption of the status quo and more concerned about being steamrolled as she hurriedly side-stepped. After all, face-planting the nearest doorframe was much preferable to the alternative.

Because there they were. All five Princes of Rosewood Hall. They were nicknamed the V.I.C.E.S. It was an apt name. Not only were they everyone's secret vice at least once, but they were also viciously wicked. They would squeeze you for everything you were – sexual, mental, physical, financial – only to discard you and leave you a crushed, ruined mess at the end of it. They thrived on it. They took pleasure in it. The messier, the better.

And I knew all of them all too well.

They were the kind of guys everyone got out of the way of. Even the nice, popular, Head Prefect kind of guys like Parker. If the V.I.C.E.S. were walking down the hallway, you moved. They were the broken misfits. The brooding outcasts. The dark criminals. But they ruled Rosewood Hall.

They all wore their uniforms in the loosest sense of the word, the style dependant on their individual personalities.

The daredevil racer.

The bareknuckle fighter.

The dirty rich bastard.

The swindling mastermind.

And, simply, the criminal.

Like they weren't all criminals.

They were like the hipper, younger, edgier Breakfast Club. If the Breakfast Club initiation included tattoos, grand theft auto, and killing a man.

The V.I.C.E.S. adherence to the school dress code was almost as loose as their trouser zips, which everyone knew 'fell' multiple times a day. At the back of the oval. In the bathrooms. A deserted classroom. Even in the teacher's lounge, if rumours were to be believed.

I pulled my eyes away from them quickly and focussed on Parker as I pulled him to the side of the corridor and out of their way. The purpose was two-fold. With my back against the wall, I slipped my arms around his shoulders and brought him in for a kiss.

Bless him.

Bless everything Parker was.

Because he didn't hesitate.

He thought nothing of the fact that the Princes of Rosewood Hall were coming in our direction, and I'd chosen that moment to kiss him. He didn't see an ulterior motive. Couldn't believe me capable of one.

Not that I was.

Because I didn't care if the deadly Lord of the Blood Roses himself was stalking the school corridor. Not that I'd be seen dead kissing a boy in front of my father.

Just as I didn't care that a certain Prince of Rosewood Hall was coming along the corridor. I couldn't care less. I just liked kissing Parker. It wasn't like I needed the distraction or anything. But it was. Distracting. Parker was a crazy good kisser. He was crazy good at a lot of things, and I'd enjoyed the both of us discovering *all* of them over the last couple of months.

"Well, that is certainly the way to start the new school year," Parker chuckled as we pulled away from each other.

I ignored the stare of at least one Prince as the five of them passed. I pretended I couldn't see him watching us behind Parker's head out of my periphery. I kept my eyes on Parker's dark chocolate gaze and threw myself all in to where I wanted to be.

"I feel it's always important to start a year the way you intend to finish it," I reminded him. We'd said as much to each other after we kissed at midnight last New Year's Eve.

He smiled at me, big and warm. "I really like that policy, but maybe one more wouldn't hurt? Just to make sure it sticks." It was another thing we'd said on New Years.

I nodded. "I think that's very sensible."

He kissed me again, pressing me into the lockers at my back as his hand ran up my side. My whole body tingled, and I had to stop myself from wrapping my legs around him. When he pulled away the next time, he nudged my nose with his.

Then I had a very good reason to divide my attention as my very bestest friend in the whole world found us. "Good morning!" Clove said happily.

She was my favourite person ever. She was a little taller than me, with bleach blonde hair and incredible green eyes, made even more beautiful by her luscious long lashes.

I let go of Parker and went to hug her. Yeah, we'd spoken not half an hour earlier, but there was nothing like seeing your best friend.

"Good morning," I replied, equally as happily.

I saw the look in her eyes and knew she wanted to say something about seeing Iago – the way she always did – but with Parker there, she refrained. She knew as well as I did that reminding Parker that I got along with one of the Princes might hurt my chances of locking him down.

Parker nodded to Clove. "Morning, Clove." He put his hand on my back and kissed my head. "I'm going to go find Nick. I'll see you ladies at recess?"

I nodded. "Sounds good."

"Bye, babe."

He pressed one more kiss to my lips, then strode off. Clove joined me in following his arse as it disappeared down the corridor. She might have had her clit very firmly set on another, but she was nothing if not supportive of my romantic ambitions.

"So?" she asked.

I shrugged. "So far, so good," I told her.

She huffed. "That's still not a sealed deal."

I laughed. "No. But it's still going in the right direction."

She pointed at me. "This is true."

As we headed towards first lesson, two of the popular girls – Caitlin's friends – bustled up to us, fawning all over me. I knew what it was; superficial more than genuine. They were no doubt on a fact-finding mission. Parker and I hooking up pretty constantly over the holidays was very different to us actually acting all loved-up in the school corridor.

"Oh, my God," Lettie hissed. "You and Parker are *so* cute!"

Gloria nodded. "Couple goals."

I smirked. "We're not a couple."

"Yet," Clove added pointedly. Always my cheerleader.

"Girl," Lettie said with a wry smile. "It's only a matter of time. He's totally in love with you!"

"Oh, *totally*," we heard the satirical, falsetto tones of a very familiar voice.

I turned to find Iago behind me with a cocky half-smirk on his face, his whiskey-coloured eyes shining with all the shit he so loved to stir. At a little over six foot, the guy had this weird K-Pop or anime-esque kind of vibe going on. With his dark grey/green hair brushed back from his face, the numerous piercings, the tattoos climbing up his neck and down his hand, stark against his pale skin. His trousers were always tight, his blazers cropped and embellished with chains and brooches, his nails always painted, and his school bow tie was always undone. He was far more meticulously put together than anyone would expect given his extra-curricular activities involved him beating men unconscious on the regular.

"Did anyone ask you?" I said.

The shit-stirring humour in his eyes only shone brighter. "I don't need to be asked, Mags. This is just the service that *I* am willing to pay for the greater good."

I rolled my eyes but couldn't help the smile fighting to break free.

Iago West was the most harmless of the Princes. On first glance. With the very short list of people he deigned to put up with. Chief among them, so he told me, was me. He took our semi-acquaintance to his very closed-off heart and spent as much time teasing me as actually being nice. As far as boys like him understood the meaning of words like 'nice'. He was, for all intents and purposes, closer to a frenemy than enemy. Almost like the older brother I most definitely hadn't asked for, but who was going to butt his – usually – well-meaning nose into every aspect of my business whether I welcomed it or not.

"Mind your business, *Prince*," I told him.

Lettie and Gloria were watching the exchange with interest. It was times like this that hurt my image with these people. Times that I seemed far too familiar with the criminal element of our school. But, when it came to Iago, I couldn't help myself. He just had this unfailing ability to endear himself to people when he wanted to, and he used it to his full advantage. It was like he could read your mind. He knew your hopes and dreams, and he used them to worm his way into your heart before he ripped it right out of your chest.

It was just lucky that he had no interest in my heart beyond the obligation my blood placed up on him.

He looked to Clove, Gloria and Lettie, spared them the sort of wink that had them giggling despite themselves, then sauntered on his way, leaving me with conflicting feelings as always. It wasn't just the fact that our interactions in the school corridor were a visceral reminder of who my father was, but his parting flirtatious wink also reminded me that there was another heart he acted like he had no interest in, despite the fact it was already his. As much as I wanted them to get their shit together and just see where their mutual obsession went, I also knew there was an almost guaranteed chance that he'd break her heart.

"Did you hear Chief Bates had Maggie and her family over for dinner last week?" Clove offered by way of segue, and I sent her a silent thanks.

Her answering smile told me she would always have my back.

Clove was, in the grand scheme, not the only one who would always have my back. My family would also have my back when it came to trying to maintain my façade of normality in the face of my background.

Although, a lull in the conversation at the dinner table that night made the announcement on the news a very awkward underline to the lack of conversation. "Officers report the perp was a known associate of Hammersby Bay's notorious crime lord, the Blood Rose himself, Blaise McCallan."

The whole room did a great job of pretending the reporter wasn't pinning the blame for this latest murder on the mayor's stepdaughter's dad. The stepdaughter being me. The crime lord being my dad. And all four of us at the table knew that it was quite likely that Dad, or at least his gang, *was* to blame.

"So, how was the first day of school, Maggie?" my stepdad Jonathan asked instead, not even batting an eyelid.

Our family had come to numerous unspoken agreements to make sure the Mayor of Hammersby Bay could claim plausible deniability at every turn. To ensure that I could have a relationship with my father even though he was, indeed, a legitimate crime lord. It was made easier by the fact that Dad's lawyers were impeccable. Everyone in Hammersby knew that he was the uncontested leader of the Blood Rose MC, they also knew that the Blood Roses were responsible for ninety-eight percent of crimes in Hammersby and surrounding towns, but the actual evidence they could provide in a court of law was a different thing altogether.

"Good, thanks," I answered with a smile. "They came in hard, though. We already have our first assignments."

Jonathan nodded. "Treating you like adults now, Mags," he laughed. "I'd expect nothing less."

"Oh, I'm glad they're challenging us. I just wish they'd waited until tomorrow."

Jonathan nodded. "And you'll have them all half-finished by then."

"I'm not *that* big a nerd!" I objected.

Mum and Jonathan shared a proud look. I worked hard at school. For them. Mostly. I kept my nose under the radar. I didn't put a single toe out of line. I followed the rules. I made sure that nothing negative that anyone said about me was more than licentious rumours.

For them.

Mostly.

And a little bit for me.

"Has football training started yet?" Freddy asked. At eleven, my half-brother idolised Parker. Like most of the wider student populace at not just the high school and junior school, but the whole damned town.

I gave him a warmer grin. "Not until Wednesday."

Given the seven-year age-gap, Freddy and I got along pretty well. He was already taller than me. All gangly – unlike me – and glasses – very like me. His love of football far outweighed his ability, at least for now. Parker had promised to help Freddy train so he could go out for the Rosewood Hall team when he got to high school.

Our night went along the same way it always did, with the knowledge of my paternal heritage hanging over us but everyone refusing to let it be a raincloud, but rather a rainbow. Because if there was one thing we all knew, it was that my dad loved me more than anything. Which is why he was checking in again, at the end of the day as I was getting ready for bed.

Dad
How was your day? ♡

Maggie
Good. ♥ How was yours?

Dad

Same old. Bit of a business hiccough, but I did manage to find that recipe for the brownies we talked about last month.

Maggie

Winning! We can make them on the weekend before we watch the movie 😊
I saw the news. How much of a hiccough? Everything okay?

Dad

Sounds perfect. I'll make sure one of the boys picks up the ingredients for us tomorrow.
Everything's fine, darling. Our latest acquisition threatened to go south. We negotiated our way to a win.

It was the closest he'd come to telling me anything about his real day. Like the happy family's side of my life, Dad and I had agreements as well. I wanted to know about his life to the extent that we honestly shared our days with each other, but he didn't want me to know anything about the explicit details. Of course, Dad also knew that he couldn't hide everything from me because, like that night, I saw the news and I heard the rumours.

So, instead of pretending that his life was on the up and up, he always talked in code. Some of that was legally-driven; if he used innuendo and glossed over details, no cop or lawyer could use our texts against either of us. Which meant that he talked about his day like any CEO dad would.

Maggie

As long as you and everyone else is okay.

Dad

Fit as a fiddle, kiddo.

Except the guy they'd killed, obviously.

Before I had a chance to reply to him, a message came through from Parker.

Parker

Party at Nick's Friday. Wanna be my date? 😉

I wasn't usually one to check with Dad before agreeing to a party or not. Mum and Jonathan insisted I run all post-dinnertime plans by them and I had a strict curfew that had been pushed to one AM over the last holidays after some hefty negotiation. I loved that they cared, but it felt pretty stifling all of the time. Dad, on the other hand, encouraged me to go out with friends. I'd had to remind him to impose a curfew on me, but he'd just looked at me hopelessly, shrugged and asked me if three AM was too early.

But there was the matter that we'd made plans that week. So I shot off a text to Dad before replying.

Maggie

There's a party on Friday. Okay if I drop my stuff by your place and then go for a bit?

Dad

Course, darling. Need a lift?

Maggie

I suspect Clove will be playing chauffeur.

Dad

Sounds perfect.

Then it was a message to Parker.

Maggie

Oh, I think I could probably make an appearance. Just so you can say you have a date and all.

Parker

Lol. Sweet. See you tomorrow.

I lay back on my bed with a smile. An official date was yet another step closer to officially exclusive.

CHAPTER TWO

By the end of the first week back, the whole school knew that Parker and I were on the cusp of being an official item, or thought we already were.

We'd spent all week holding hands and kissing and laughing and being vomitably – according to Iago – cute. Parker flattered me and held doors for me. He always found me at breaks. We talked every night, even if we'd spent like all day talking.

And yet… There was still nothing about making anything officially exclusive. But our date was finally that night and I was going to keep seeing that as the next step I'd believed it to be on Monday. Parker was clearly as excited about it as I was.

"You *are* coming tonight, yes?" Parker checked as he walked backwards to his car after school finished for the day. Nick whacked him companionably, teasing Parker for his obvious mooning over me.

I nodded. "Yep. Clove's taking me to drop stuff at Dad's." I pointed my thumb at her over my shoulder, because just in case he'd forgotten who my best friend was. "Then we'll be there."

He smiled and nodded. "Okay. Cool. I'll see you tonight."

I also nodded, biting my lip against a full smile. "I'll see you tonight."

Clove grabbed my arm and we tried very hard to fight our excited laughter as we headed to her car. I swept the plethora of books and receipts and spare jumpers off the passenger seat as I got in. It always amazed me how she ever had any clean clothes; like half her wardrobe was always strewn about her car at any given time.

Dad had offered to buy me a car. Of course he had. But, after a short conversation with Mum, the three of us had decided that maybe it would be better to let the upstanding stepdad buy the car to avoid the speculation it would otherwise induce. And Jonathan had some grand plan he'd wanted to do for my eighteenth since I was about six, so I was going to have to wait a few more months. Until then, Clove was my very willing chauffeur when we wanted to be self-sufficient. I could at least drive her car if it was her turn to drink. Which it was that night, so I'd drive us home.

"Okay, so we drop our shit at your dad's, get changed, eat ALL the food, pop past the Laneway, and then off to Nick's," Clove said as we pulled out of the carpark and made the right hand turn towards the 'wrong side of the tracks'. She said it super quickly, as though hoping maybe I hadn't noticed that bit in the middle.

I smiled. "Sorry. Pop past the Laneway?" I clarified as though I had no idea what she'd be talking about.

She cleared her throat. "What?"

"What?" I laughed.

She rolled her eyes. "Fine. Yes. Pop past the Laneway. Please? Iago made a mention they'd be there and–"

"They're there a lot. That's not news," I teased, but it was all good-natured.

"Okay. I know, but–"

"It's fine," I told her, giving her knee a squeeze. "We can totally go past the Laneway. I'm just giving you shit."

She nudged me playfully. "Like you don't want to go anyway."

I shrugged, all coy. "I don't *not* want to go," I admitted.

I had no issues with the Laneway. In theory. I could easily hold my own. What amused me was that Clove had no hesitation about going. It was funny what one was willing to do to satisfy one's clit– I mean, heart.

When we got to my dad's place, she was the first one inside, as always.

"Hey, Mr McCallan!" Clove called as she walked in. For someone with legal aspirations when she was older, she didn't seem to have a care in the world about just walking on into a known crime lord's house. But then, I guess, to her, Dad was and had always been first and foremost her best friend's dad.

He appeared from the kitchen with a big smile, wiping his hands on a tea towel. "Afternoon, my girls. And what have a said about calling me Blaise, Clover?" Not her name, but he insisted on calling her it anyway, and she loved it.

She grinned at him as she headed to my room to drop her bag. "I know. I know. Sorry, sir!"

I snorted as Dad came to hug me. "How was your day?" he asked.

I nodded. "Good. Same old. You?"

"Same old," he agreed. "Where's this party tonight?"

"Nick Walker's place," I told him.

Dad scrubbed a hand over his chin as he worked out if he knew who that was.

Given that his lifestyle involved drugs, sex and rock and roll to the extreme, he was looking mighty fine on it. At the ripe old age of forty-two, his hair was still a dark auburn with very few signs of grey. Which could not be said for his eyes. Because his eyes were a sparkling slate grey, the exact same shade I'd inherited from him. If only I'd also inherited his less vibrant hair colour, rather than it combining with Mum's strawberry blonde to give me a wicked shade of very red. It was cool, but I stood out a lot already.

"His mum run the auto shop?" Dad asked.

I nodded. "That's the one. Why?" I teased. "You send her some cars to chop up."

Dad waggled a finger at me as the oven timer summoned him back to the kitchen. "You gotta wake up earlier in the morning to learn my secrets, darlin'."

I smiled, knowing it was useless to try to pry anything more out of him. "We'll be back out in a sec," I told him.

"No rush," he called. "I reckon it's got at least another half hour on it."

There was only one reason Dad didn't have a snack ready for us as soon as we walked in the door. Work had got in the way, and he would have been pissed about that. But that was covered by one of Dad's rules; he didn't let anything tarnish the week we had together. That meant he took off his club leader hat the afternoon I arrived and didn't put it back on until I was safely back at Mum and Jonathan's. No matter what else was happening. For the weeks he had me, the Blood Roses were supposed to run themselves. Most of the time, they behaved. As far as anything they ever did could be considered 'behaving'.

We didn't bother changing yet, since we'd just change for the party later. So, still in our uniforms, Clove and I went back out to the kitchen to find Dad frowning at his phone.

"Sorry, darling," he said as he typed out a message, then stuffed the offending device in his pocket.

I shook my head. "All good. Trouble?"

"Nothing you need worry about. Now, who wants nachos?"

Clove threw her hand in the air. "ME!"

Nachos turned into pasta – Dad had drilled into me the importance of carbo-loading before going to a party and drinking – and chats, then Clove and I went to get ready to go to Nick's.

As I fixed the placement of the jewellery at my neck, I could feel her smirking.

"What?" I asked.

"And this outfit has *nothing* to do with me convincing you to go past the Laneway first?" Clove teased as she looked me over.

I huffed fake-indignantly. "Of course not. Parker will be seeing me in it."

"Parker will be seeing you *out* of it maybe," she muttered, sassily.

Which was the hope, but it wouldn't be a wasted effort if he didn't. Especially since we *were* going past the Laneway as well.

Where Clove was in her typical short, halter, floral jumpsuit and massive blush pink heels, I'd gone for the sort of thing I only wore when Mum and Jonathan were at no risk of seeing me; ripped, cropped purple tee with black skirt and my Goth-inspired boots. Flats of course because, even when I wasn't drinking, I gave my lack of height absolutely no advantages. I was way too uncoordinated for heels and far too lazy to put the effort into being good at wearing them.

"You both look lovely," Dad said as we came into the kitchen to say goodbye.

"You'll be okay home by yourself?" I asked him and he gave me a fondly exasperated smirk.

He looked up from the dishes he was cleaning. "Nah, darlin'. I won't know what to do with myself. What with it being such a rare occurrence and all. I sure hope you recorded my favourite stories for me to wile away the time."

Clove laughed. "We'll be back by one."

He shrugged. "Whatever you like, girls. Have a good night."

"Da-ad!" I chastised and he shook his head.

"Mags, if you want to impose a curfew on yourselves, go ahead. But I know you'll be safe, so I trust you to make good decisions." He gave us both a cheeky wink. "They can't be any worse than mine."

I rolled my eyes at his cheesiness, and Clove snorted a laugh as she ushered me out to the car.

The Laneway was packed, like it always was on race nights.

Clove threw the car in park, saying, "I'll be like five seconds. I've gotta get something from Iago real quick."

I smirked as I pushed my glasses up my nose. "Yeah, his cock maybe."

The pink flush that crept over Clove's cheeks was visible under even the meagre light filtering in the car's windows. "That would be great, but that would require him to notice I existed."

I knew for a fact that the Prince of Dreams knew Clove existed.

"Also," she continued as she opened her door, "real quick is not what I had in mind for his cock."

I laughed as I climbed out of the car as well.

"You're coming?" she asked.

I smiled as we closed our doors at the same time. "You think I'm going to pass up the opportunity to watch you go ga-ga all over Iago?"

She huffed as she locked the car and came to take my arm in hers. "Honestly, the guy is heaven."

I snorted.

Heaven was not a word any sane person used to describe any of the V.I.C.E.S. Oh, they were as gorgeous as angels, all right. The five of them. Their voices were like silk and velvet. Their faces could make the Madonna herself weep. But each of them was built for nothing but sin. They'd been born in the depths of Hell and none of them would rest until they'd watched the world burn. Which was a certain kind of sexy in and of itself.

A race was in progress as we exited the carpark. Bikes by the sound of it.

"I'll give you a tenner an hour," some jerkwad leered as we passed him, and I felt Clove tense in apprehension.

"My castration services are at least twice that, soz," I shot back, and he growled.

I lunged towards him quickly and he stepped back as though he thought I was about to go full-on Mad Mary on him. I gave him a saccharine smile and thanked all the deities that growing up as my father's daughter had given me steel balls when I actually needed them.

Clove's arm tightened in mine as she snuggled into me on our way to the pits.

"Oh, hello, Magenta," Clove said, her laugh shaky. "Long time, no see."

"Well, hi," I replied, in my best Southern belle accent. "It has been a while."

"Have I told you lately how much I like Magenta?" she asked.

I smiled. "No, I don't believe you have."

We called that side of my personality Magenta, my full name. She was the person my father's world could make me if I fell into it. She had grit, sass, and could wield a blade far more expertly than even Clove knew. She only came out for very special occasions and Clove was about the only person who knew she existed. She was nothing like Maggie, who just wanted to become a primary school teacher and wear knitted skirts and sweater sets every day.

Which started with a nice guy. Parker for example.

A university degree wasn't going to be enough for our town to see me as anything other than Blaise McCallan's daughter, even if everyone who met me knew I was a nice, hard-working, respectable girl with the bad luck of being born to the leader of the Blood Roses. I was the product of a one-night stand between said leader and an upstanding member of the community six years his junior. Despite the unexpected nature of it all, Mum had still caught years of flack for her life choices. She now only saw him in the rarest of circumstances and, with her eventual marriage to the mayor, she had finally been cleared of anything to do with my father's supposed crimes.

Me? I spent one in every four weeks with him and no amount of assuring people that we didn't go on Daddy-Daughter murder sprees or bank heists could absolve me of the taint of my father's love. Which was ridiculous. He just wanted his little princess – his words, not mine – to have the best in life, otherwise he'd have 50-50 custody with Mum.

So, Parker was my way out. Police Chief's son and the most upright and noble boy that had come out of Hammersby Bay in centuries. Being with him made me acceptable. Which wasn't to say I didn't want to be with him because of him. But liking him had perks that made me overlook certain other…annoyances.

Annoyances that were the very reason Iago was at the Laneway in the first place. I looked for the tell-tale number that heralded said annoyance but didn't see him in the pits.

"Iago!" Clove called over the rumble of engines. Or tried to, anyway.

I elbowed her. "Be more desperate why not."

"Oh, please!" she laughed. "I could literally throw myself on him, stark raving naked, and he'd still not notice I was anything other than wee little Clove."

"We'll make that the omega plan, shall we?" I smirked.

She nodded as she dragged my whole person over to Iago. "Yes. Last resort tactic."

"Last resort tactic," I agreed.

Iago happened to turn and finally saw us, giving us a nod that was more of a kick of the chin in greeting. Were this a race sanctioned by any official body, he would have had a headset and probably a clip board and…that was the extent of my knowledge of such things outside a Pixar movie.

Clove buzzed with excitement as Iago and Stone made way for us to get through to them.

"What are you doing here?" Stone growled down at me as Clove bounded to Iago.

The Prince of Sorrow was a fucking arse. I didn't know how much of it was born of the fact he was a loyal soldier and how much was just him. He wasn't just the criminal; he was a brooding arsehole who seemed to embody every emo kid of the early 2000s put together.

The second tallest of the Princes, he glared at everyone he met with a pale brown gaze. Since his stint in juvie, his brown hair was always shorn in a buzzcut like they'd sent him to some military camp or something. Whatever it was, it certainly hadn't straightened him out. He wore boots, dark grey jeans and a tight-fitting black tee that made his muscles bulge unnecessarily. He had tattoos up both arms, disappearing under his sleeves.

Did I not know that Stone would find himself in a very shallow grave for touching me – and by extension, Clove – then I'd be terrified of him. As it was, he still gave me the willies, but I could hold my own against him and know that he'd do little more than just glare and growl and use his meanest big boy words.

"We're not staying," I assured him.

"No," Stone said, as though he could actually boss me around. I mean, he could if he really wanted.

"We've got a party," I said by way of excuse. Or maybe it was a defence; like, I was totally popular and cool, and I totally had better things to do than hang out with the criminal element.

Stone didn't give a shit either way. His eyebrow rose in the very dictionary definition of 'I don't give a fuck' before he crossed his arms and waited very impatiently for Clove to be done so we'd hurry up and leave.

Unlike Iago, Stone took the whole 'Maggie stays out of this world' decree from my father horrendously seriously. I was sure it stemmed as much from the good little soldier following orders as it did from the fact that he hated me with a passion. Then again, hate was about the only thing Stone *did* with passion. Hate, football, and murder. I would have been willing to bet that the murder earlier that week had been him.

"Clove's just–" I started, as though I had to explain myself to this degenerate, but a huge celebration interrupted me.

"He's only fucking won!" Iago yelled in excitement as he twirled Clove around.

I turned and watched racer 666. He did another full lap of the track before pulling into the pit next to us.

It suited him. The number. He'd raced under it since the first time he'd raced back when he was still riding a freaking tricycle.

Vaughn Saint was the goddamned devil and no mistake. Like the flower our school was named after, Vaughn was a rose. Stunning. Gorgeous. Enticing. Heady. Just one prick and he'll have you bleeding. Apt that he was known as the Prince of Thorns then. The fact he was the unofficial heir to the Blood Rose empire was just icing.

The guy looked good, climbing off a motorcycle and dragging his helmet off even with sweat sheening his body. He pulled off his leather jacket and threw it at some wimpy twat trying to get admission to the Blood Roses by serving Vaughn. Which left him in his tight leather pants and a white tee that was plastered to every single ridge and contour of his very perfectly sculpted body.

Why did he have to be so attractive? In that whole 'bad boy', 'disenchanted with the world', 'look but don't touch' kind of way.

A full head taller than me, he was six-foot-four of rippling muscles, dark brown hair that refused to be tamed at any length, and piercing blue eyes that reminded me of lapis lazuli. He was more trouble than he was worth. Striding through life with a hard glint in his eye, a cocky smirk, and a chip on his shoulder so big it was a wonder it didn't crumble his majestic frame to the ground.

He strode towards us, heedless of the cheers that rang out for him, giving no fucks about them calling his name at the podium to collect his cash winnings, caring about nothing except the fact that he'd seen Clove with Iago, and he knew that meant I was there as well. He didn't stop until he was standing right in front of me.

My breath hitched a little and I swallowed hard as his gaze roved painstakingly slowly down my body then back up. By the time his eyes pinned mine again, there was a cocky mischief in his that glittered. Vaughn wasn't the kind of guy to smile more than absolutely necessary, but there was the hint of a half-smile tugging one corner of his, admittedly, very kissable lips.

"And what is Blaise McCallan's little princess doing at my race?" he purred and I, annoyingly, felt it in places that a voice really shouldn't have any effect. Not like that, anyway.

"Oh, were you racing?" I told him. "I didn't notice." It was my turn to rake my eyes down and up his body. Although given how pleasing on the eyes the package in front of me, that had been a bad idea. I hid it well, I think. "You could do with a wash."

"You offering?" he asked, one eyebrow rising along with his lip. It wasn't a smile so much as a knowing amusement.

I bristled, because that was much preferable to the heat that swept my body. "Don't you have a prize to collect?" I filled my voice with as much disdain, as much unimpressed apathy, as I could.

Vaughn stepped even closer, and I fought the urge to step back and give him the satisfaction of intimidating me.

"Prize?" he said. His eyes dropped to my lips. Lips that, under the pressure, caught in my teeth. I saw that lapis lazuli flash. "I couldn't give a fuck about more money." His voice was so low and deep and… *Oh, boy.*

He took my chin in his large, warm hand. His fingers gentle but firm. It was an act to show his restraint while hinting at exactly what he was capable of if he threw off the shackles of his unparalleled control.

"The next time I win, *Magenta*, I will take my prize," he ran his thumb over my bottom lip, leaving neither of us uncertain about what he meant, "from you."

His thumb was rough against the softness of my lip. The sensation was easy to imagine on every single piece of my skin. My whole body responded – my lips parted ever so slightly like they were going to wrap around him – and I stamped it down furiously.

It was not okay to feel like that about fucking Vaughn Saint. I mean Vaughn-fucking-Saint. No. Either. It wasn't okay to ever put 'fucking' and 'Vaughn Saint' in the same thought, whether 'fucking' was a verb or an adjective.

We both stared at each other, his hand on me, for far longer than we should have. I felt like I was breathing far too heavily, like it was my control that was close to snapping. He didn't seem to have that problem at all.

"Uh, Mags?" Clove said uncertainly. "I've got… I'm good. Shall we go? Parker's probably waiting…"

I took a hurried step back from Vaughn. That cocky humour was burning in his eyes and playing at his lips. "Yes, *Mags*," he said, all growly and delicious. "You'd better not keep the good little boy waiting too long. It would be a shame if someone else…helped you out of that delectable little skirt, wouldn't it?"

He licked his lip sensuously and I felt heat totally sweep my lower half, but I refused to acknowledge any of the other feelings he elicited in me. Instead, I grabbed Clove's hand, said an absent goodbye to Iago, and hurried back to Clove's car.

"Thanks for that," I said as we climbed in.

She shrugged as she started it. "All good. I figured all that sizzling sexual tension could do with an ice bucket. Mr Thorns himself could do with the reminder that you're spoken for."

"Oh, and you're not suggesting I do?"

She grinned at me. "That's up to you. You want Parker, then Vaughn can back the fuck off. But if you want Vaughn…"

She left the end of that hanging and I told myself there was no reason other than giving me shit. There hadn't been any sexual tension between me and Vaughn. He was unnecessarily sexy and gorgeous and could do unspeakably fantastic things to a person's body, I was sure. But I had no interest in doing them with him. I wasn't even thinking about it.

No, there was no sizzle.

And I took that significant lack of sizzle straight to Parker's very capable hands.

VAUGHN: ONE

Playing with Little Miss Redemption was my favourite pastime.

My boss' daughter was the perfect example of a girl who thinks she's got what it takes to play with the big boys. She thought her blood, by sheer birth, made her tough enough to put all of us in our place. Like some tiny little chihuahua puppy trying to prove its worth in front of a fucking full grown rottweiler.

That she was also fucking gorgeous was just icing. She got me hard just by thinking about her. Thinking about the pleasure in ruining Hammersby Bay's golden girl, the proof of their triumph of good over evil. Like they were ever really going to accept her.

And that night had been no different.

I loved the weeks she was at her dad's because she dressed like she could fuck a man up. Don't get me wrong, I loved the sexy librarian look, especially when she bit her lip while those deep grey eyes shone behind her glasses. Fuck, that did things to a guy. Things that would make a stronger man than me lose his shit with lust for her.

But the weeks she'd come from her dad's. Fuck me right, darling.

I'd watched her arse sway away from me under that fucking tiny pleated black skirt. Watched the way her waist rocked, the skin on full display between her waistband and the purple t-shit she had on. While she'd been sassing the shit out of me, I'd had a full view of her cleavage through a rip in that tee and fuck, but I'd wanted to keep ripping it right off that tight little body.

And I was still thinking about it while I was holed up at Kenicki's with the boys later that night. I was still fucking hard, dreaming about her walking in, taking a seat on my lap, and easing the ache she so effortlessly caused in me.

So, I was going to have to take my mind off her. It wasn't usually hard. Not once I'd finished with my prey, anyway. And I saw the perfect girl, dancing alone in the middle of the throng. Pink hair. Tight silver dress. Staggering black heels. She was begging for it.

She was a Monster's girl. I knew she was. No doubt the last one who's had her had done her almost as wrong as I was planning to, and she was at Kenicki's looking for revenge. Starting with fucking a Rose. Well, I was more than willing to oblige.

I drained my beer and slid out of the booth, sharing a knowing smirk with Iago as I did.

"Have fun," he said with a wink.

"Oh, I will," I assured him.

As I came up behind her, I slipped my hands around her stomach. She jumped in surprise, and I felt her body taught in defence at my intrusion. Then she turned and saw my face, and she fucking melted in my arms.

I gave her my most charming grin. "Well, hey."

I saw the effect I had on her in her eyes. Whatever she was to that Monster, she was fucking clueless about what I had planned for her. She thought they lived up to their names? She had no fucking idea how weak those idiots were compared to us. Oh, I was going to fucking ruin her and send her back to them a mess, a mere shell of what she used to be.

I danced against her as I licked my lip and dragged my gaze over her. I could feel her fucking trembling in excitement in my arms.

"My god," I purred as I leant my lips to her ear. "You're fucking beautiful."

She leant into my body. "You're not so bad yourself."

All right. Not a total wallflower. Not that I really expected it. I could work with that.

She ground her hips against mine as she wrapped her arms around my shoulders. I ran my hands up her sides as I nuzzled my nose into her neck. She was almost as tall as me, and I was going to love the things that would let me do to her body.

"Have I just been waiting for you to arrive?" I asked her and I felt her smile.

"I don't know. Have you?"

I nodded against her. "Oh, I think I have, sweetheart."

She ran her hand down my body and felt the bulge in my jeans. Already? All right, then. I wasn't going to draw this out any longer than it had to be.

"It feels even better between your legs," I purred as I ran my nose over her cheek, and she trembled again.

Fuck, this shit was almost too easy. Still, it was guaranteed now, and I wasn't going to pass on that.

"You want to show me?" she asked.

Oh, I could almost like this one.

I gave her a smile as I slipped my hand in hers and started pulling her to the bathroom.

Iago's eyebrow rose in surprise as he looked at me and I tipped one side of my lips in response; I know, quick, huh?

When we got to the bathroom, I pushed her into the stall and closed the door behind us. I didn't mind an audience, personally.

But I never assumed. The majority of chicks did not, and I didn't want to put them off.

As I claimed her lips in mine, my fingers went between her legs. She was fucking dripping for me. Fuck, but this was way too easy. It was almost enough to make me go limp, but then she dragged her teeth over her bottom lip as she looked at me and I was fucking hard again. Not that I was thinking about anyone else with a tendency to do that.

I made quick work of getting her off, then fished a condom from my pocket. She seemed more impatient to get me inside her than I did, and a guy had to appreciate that. Fuck, but she was tight, and a guy definitely appreciated that. Then again, I'd never met a pussy that wasn't, even on the chicks I knew got around A LOT. Amazing things that they were.

This chick responded.

"Oh, my god," she whimpered.

"What did I tell you?"

She nodded. "It feels so good."

It didn't take her long to finish. Her whole body trembled as she came and there was something so much less satisfying about it than if the eyes looking up at me so adoringly had been framed by dark glasses. I shook my head to clear the image and railed this chick harder. Her fingers gripped my shoulders hard as her head fell back.

Well, no need for me to hold on any longer than necessary. She was fulfilling a purpose and I had other shit to do. I pulled out of her and flipped her over to slam back into her from behind. She cried out and that made me cockier than usual. I pounded her. Hard. And, fuck, but she enjoyed it.

By the time I was throbbing in her, her legs were shaking. I felt her walls clamp on me and that was enough to finish the job.

And, yeah, she'd been decent. Enough. But she was still a Monster girl and she needed to be reminded of that fact.

We tidied up and I led her back out to the main bar. As we walked back out of the bathroom, someone snapped a picture of us, and I huffed a rough laugh.

She was clearly surprised. "What the hell?"

From behind her, I wrapped my hand around her throat, and we looked over the people watching us. "You've been branded a Rosette now, sweetheart," I whispered in her ear, then pressed a kiss to her cheek. "You're one of our discards. You think that will make them jealous?"

She shoved me away and I let her. "You arsehole."

"Oh, Trudy, don't take it so personally," I laughed, my eyes hard.

"My name's Chanel."

Sorry, did I ask? I shrugged. "Like I fucking care."

"What is wrong with you?" she asked me.

"Sweetheart, there isn't enough time in the world to go through that list. Now, you take that ruined pussy back to Snowtown and see which of those fuckers is first for my seconds, yeah?"

"What?"

I gave her a cavalier shrug. "I've done you a favour, Trudy. You should be thanking me."

"Thanking you? For being a dick?"

I took her chin in my hand and looked her over as I chuckled, "Oh, sweetheart… What did you think this was?"

She stammered. "I…" She blinked and I saw the tears welling in her eyes. She shoved me away from her again and ran out of Kenicki's.

I waltzed back to the table, rearranging my jeans pointedly as I did.

“Good enough for the show?” Iago asked, a smirk playing at his lips.

“Eh. She got the job done. Satisfactorily.”

“And you?”

I scoffed. “What kind of unfeeling, thoughtless, disrespectful arsehole doesn’t?”

We looked at each other, then spluttered at the same time, “Cairo.”

CHAPTER THREE

Weeks at my dad's place were way more relaxed than weeks with my mum, Jonathan and Freddy.

It wasn't that Mum and Jonathan didn't trust me, but they were also pretty hard on me. They expected amazing things from me. Which, sure, was nice that they believed me capable of awesomeness, but it did lend itself to being stressful. All those high expectations and wanting to live up to them could get really exhausting. And they weren't even that big. Compared to other kids, I knew I had it easy. All they wanted from me was decent grades, enrolment to university, and a safe and upstanding job and life.

In the grand scheme of things, that's all most parents wanted from their kids. Dad wanted that for me as well. What made Mum and Jonathan's expectations so stifling was the fact that I felt so close to letting them down constantly. People like Caitlin and Lettie and Gloria, their parents, half of Hammersby, they were all just waiting for me to slip up. Waiting for me to be anything other than absolutely perfect, faultless, and beyond reproach at all times. It felt almost impossible and was so tiring to be that spotless all the time.

Dad on the other hand was much easier to please. He thought my B average was perfect and more than enough to get into my junior teaching degree, and he knew that any life that wasn't as a

Rose's old lady was as upstanding as it needed to be so long as I was happy. I didn't have to strive to be perfect for him because I was already living the life that he wanted for me.

My lack of car, and Clove living on the other side of town, meant that if Dad didn't pick me up from school, then one of the Princes were temporarily granted permission to be within the same vicinity as me as it was a far lesser evil in Dad's eyes than me catching the bus to Dad's house.

Cairo was on duty that afternoon, and he had Ezra in the backseat chattering away about something I don't think anyone else was really paying attention to. Not that Ezra needed anyone to be paying him much attention to be telling them all about the chemical compounds he was currently experimenting with. For a guy who seemed to be quite literally emotionless, he sure had a lot of feelings about his chemistry set.

By rights, Cairo had people to drive him everywhere and he utilised that a lot. His dad wasn't just a Rose, but his mum was some political heiress – funny what people overlooked when it suited them and there was enough money and legal power to destroy the evidence. But, like all the Roses, Cairo valued his independence and that meant having his own car. But, of course, it was a Porsche. He said it was his mum's choice, but I had to wonder about that.

As we travelled down the straight that separated the classy and criminal sides of Hammersby, Vaughn's bike overtook us. He spared us a glance as he passed, but I couldn't see his face through his visor. He and Cairo shared a short nod, and I couldn't help but feel like Vaughn was checking up on me.

"Fucking get off me," Cairo grumbled to himself as Vaughn's bike pulled into the lane ahead of us. He threw me a look. "You'd better be fucking worth it."

I blinked. "Excuse you?"

"Your old man thinks your babysitters need babysitters. Either your pussy's made of the most virginal fucking Leaver's lace or some shit, or he thinks I'm incompetent."

Ezra snorted. Neither of us bothered to point out that he knew whatever Leaver's lace was, or cared enough to ask what it was. Cairo's point was made.

"Or it's not her old man who thinks you're incompetent."

Cairo growled at him. "You want me to show you incompetent?"

I didn't doubt that incompetence on Cairo's part was probably worse than his competence. I sure didn't want to see his incompetence, thanks.

Ezra didn't care he was baiting Cairo and he kept pushing. "Do you think he's going to escort you the *whole* way to Daddy McCallan's?" he sneered, the teasing thick in his voice.

Cairo's leg shifted and I was fairly certain he was going to slam on the break, drag Ezra out of the car and show him how incompetent he could be. But then Vaughn took the turn towards one of their local hangouts, and Cairo's hands relaxed on the steering wheel.

I knew there was a lot of trust between the Princes. There had to be, the shit they got up to. The shit they relied on each other for. And I could understand Cairo being pissed at the idea Vaughn didn't trust him with me. That anyone wouldn't trust him with me. Lord Blood Rose himself had given the Princes a job to do and they'd do it – and do it well – regardless of how they felt about me. The five of them were equal. For now. And maybe that was part of the problem.

Even Ezra kept his mouth prudently closed for the rest of the journey. Cairo pulled up in front of Dad's and Ezra leant forward rather violently between the front seats.

"Fuck are their bikes doing here?" he asked, looking at the two foreign motorcycles in the driveway.

Cairo looked to me like he wondered if I'd need backup. I grabbed my bag and gave him a terse nod in thanks. "I'll see you tomorrow."

His nod was a lot slower. "Sure. Tomorrow."

"Ciao, Mags," was Ezra's contribution and he'd climbed through to the passenger seat before I was fully out of the car.

They didn't wait for me to get inside. They were gone before the front door was open. I dropped my bag in my room and went looking for Dad.

"–know better than to come here when I've got Maggie," I heard his exasperated voice.

"Dad?" I asked as I pushed my way into his study.

The St Jude twins were looming large, as they and Dad all turned to me. They were the older brothers of he dubbed the Prince of Frost, Ezra St Jude. It was said the whole family were psychopaths. Or was it sociopaths? I always got the two confused.

"What do you want, darling?" Dad asked me, his voice hard and sharp.

It was his business voice. The one he usually left behind on the weeks he had me. Obviously whatever news the St Jude twins brought wasn't of the good variety.

"Sorry, it can wait. I'll leave you to it," I said as I made to slink back out.

Dad sighed and scraped a hand over his face. "No, love. It's fine. These idiots were just leaving."

"Boss, what do you–?" one of the twins started, but Dad silenced him with a look.

"We do not discuss business in front of Maggie, you sorry excuse for an arsehole! I'd get better down the glory hole at Racy Dalys, and most days you can count on it being old Finkle's dog! Now get out of here before I castrate the both of you with the bluntest object I can find."

The twins didn't stay for a second warning.

As the side door – Dad's business door, he called it – banged shut, Dad sighed again.

"Sorry you had to see that, darling," he said, his voice softening by the minute.

To say my father was a hardened criminal was putting it mildly. The stories I'd heard about him, especially during his rise through the ranks of the Blood Roses, would put hair on anyone's chest. Right before they passed out in shock like one of those delicate ladies in old films.

But he hid as much of it from me as he could. I'd grown up knowing who my father was – he would never lie to me – but also knowing that he loved me more than life itself. I was his redemption arc, and he'd be damned if I didn't go on to uni, then a nice stable job, and a house in the burbs, married with two-point-five kids and a dog.

So he kept me separate. The only times I saw any of the Blood Roses covered in blood, or with their weapons out was total accident or poor timing on my part. I never got embroiled in his shady business dealings. I wasn't allowed anywhere near their headquarters or clubhouse or whatever they called it. And there was no way I was allowed to date one. The only reason any of them were allowed to be in a room with me was because Dad hadn't found a way around truancy laws and even the Blood Rose kids had to go to school.

But that didn't mean I didn't get whiffs. It didn't mean I didn't cross paths with any of them. It certainly didn't mean that the Princes of Rosewood Hall didn't seem to feel an affinity – a familiarity, even – with me born of the knowledge that we knew things others didn't. That we were joined by things others weren't.

Even if my father, the leader of their merry band of misfits, kept me as far away from their world as possible, I was still his daughter. My blood still belonged to their world. I had one foot in their world. And the Princes knew it. They knew I was one bad decision away from tumbling headfirst into their – our – world. Like some perverted Alice.

The only question was, who or what would be that bad decision?

The next morning, Iago was driving me to school. He leant against his Lexus, one hand in his pocket as he puffed on his vape pen and acted for all the world like he was completely unaware of the fact that Vaughn sat in his front passenger seat.

Dad kissed my cheek. "Bye, darling. Have a good day."

I nodded. "I'll see you tonight."

"Love you."

"Love you, too."

He settled in to see me to the car.

Iago bowed and pushed off the car as I approached. "Your chariot awaits," he said, taking my hand and pressing an exaggerated kiss to it.

"West!" Dad growled from the front door and Iago shot me a cheeky smirk.

"Boss?" he asked, looking around me.

Dad's hand hovered at the gun I knew was at his back. "Take your hands off my girl and you'll leave here with the right number of holes in your person."

Iago dropped my hand quickly and inclined his head to Dad. "My bad."

"Let it happen again and I'll be saying that to your mum."

I watched the colour pale in those whiskey-coloured eyes. Even though there was absolutely nothing like that between us – and never would be even if Hell froze over or we were the last two people on the planet – he knew better that to stir my dad with his usual level of teasing. Instead, he just opened the door and kicked his head to Vaughn.

Vaughn muttered in his usual grumpy way and unfolded his unnecessarily large frame out of the two-door coupe, snagging Iago's vape pen off him as he did. He got out of my way without getting any further from me than necessary. His trousers rubbed past my skirt. His blazer brushed mine. Those blue eyes twinkled in the morning light as he looked at me through the hair hanging over his face.

Jesus, but he was attractive. Why did he have to be so hot? I'm talking stomach squirming under his intense not-even-vaguely-flirty-but-definitely-antagonistic-and-maybe-even-a-little-murderous gaze as it raked over me. As though he didn't see me in my uniform five days a week. I took a much too deep breath as I tried to stop my heart from racing.

One eyebrow rose like he was daring me to get out of *his* way.

He took a long drag as Iago held the seat forward for me to climb into the back seat, trying to keep as much of my dignity intact and my arse off show as possible.

When I was situated, Vaughn pushed the seat back into place and climbed in, his eyes on Dad. They two of them exchanged a curt nod. Whether it was recognition, greeting, or understanding of one of those unspoken rules, I didn't know. Then Iago was in the car, his music was blaring at all of us, and we were peeling to school.

Dad

If he touches you again, feel
free to christen Mr Bubbles.

Mr Bubbles being the new knife he'd got me as a start of the school year present. As though that was a normal present to give your teenage daughter to celebrate her final year of school. I'd joked that we should give it a name so we could reference it in conversation and the friendly federal agents who monitored our phones could be none the wiser. Somehow, we'd landed on Mr Bubbles, and it had stuck.

I sighed, knowing it was useless to argue with him. The issue with me was black and white to him, because lines could be crossed or blurred to various shades of grey. Dad wasn't taking the chance that some hot-headed young-blooded Rose would seduce me into idiocy and lead me down a life of sin and crime. I liked to think that he was overly fiercely protective of my life goals rather than he actually thought that little of my willpower.

Maggie

That would require me having
him on me.

Dad

I put him in your bag.

Of course, he had.

Maggie

Thanks, Dad.

"He checking up on you already?" Iago asked, humour in his voice.

I took another breath. "Just informing me that I have a knife in my bag if you get handsy again."

"Fuck, Mags," Iago laughed. "Ever since your tits came in, we can't even be friends."

Friends was probably a generous description of what we were now and had always been actually.

Vaughn blew out a very heavy cloud of vape. "Try talking about her tits one more time," he snarled.

Iago threw me one of those shit-stirring smiles. "I'd make a joke about touching them, but I'd worry that Daddy McCallan has her phone bugged."

Vaughn smacked him this time. I tried to hide my smile, but I knew Iago saw me in the mirror based on the way his widened and he quickly changed the subject.

But I was also remembering the last Rose who dared flirt with me, and it made me wriggle uncomfortably in my seat. The guy had been young and new and clearly misunderstood the rules he was supposed to push for acceptance and advancement. He'd taken the rule about me as more of a guideline.

Given he'd been only a couple of years older than us, Dad had assigned the beating to Vaughn. Last I'd seen of the guy, as I'd been carted out of the room as fast as Iago's legs could literally carry me, Vaughn's fist was bloodier than the guy's face. Iago had later vaguely hinted that Stone had dragged the guy out of there and *no one* had seen him again. And that had been the reward for asking me whether I liked the idea of dinner and a movie in the loosest of hypothetical terms.

I couldn't help but look at the back of Vaughn's head, and I didn't rightly know why.

Maybe it was the fact that I couldn't help but wonder what it would be like if Vaughn actually followed through on his threat from Friday night and did kiss me. Because maybe I was supposed to be the sweet, naïve, innocent Maggie, but I knew what prize he was threatening to take from me. And what was wrong with me that I'd thought about it? That the idea appealed to me. Simply on a hypothetical and data-gathering level of course.

The whole thing was hypothetical, though. Vaughn would never really touch me. I was a game to him. A game that got him what he wanted by just watching my reaction when he told me things like he'd take his prize from me.

And, yeah, I was going on about it – in the privacy of my own head – because it had, annoyingly, got to me. I still felt a thrill whenever I thought about it. A thrill that burst in my chest and cascaded to heat and tingle WAY lower down.

I wriggled in my seat again and noticed Iago's eyes were on me in the mirror again. Did he know what was going through my head? He couldn't have. Then again, he wasn't called the Prince of Dreams for nothing.

CHAPTER FOUR

Given that we'd left the mayor's house that night, I was appropriately dressed in my simple, strappy, floral pale brown dress. My hair was half-up-half-down. I would have tucked my phone in my bra, only the mostly-backless nature of the dress didn't really allow for bras. Good thing I thought ahead and got one with pockets!

As Clove pulled into the Laneway, I checked my phone again.

Parker
We're gonna be there about 9.

Maggie
Brill. Clove's just got a thing, so we'll meet you there?

Parker
Sounds perfect. I can't wait to pull you into that booth and put my fingers exactly where you like them.

I laughed and Clove craned over from her seat to read the message. I turned the phone to her so she could see better. I watched as the smile grew on her face.

"Naw, he's trying."

I nodded. "Definitely trying."

"What?" she teased as we got out of the car. "Is that not actually where you like his fingers, Mags?"

I grinned at her as I tucked my phone in my pocket and took her arm. "No." She looked at me in sympathetic distress. "No!" I assured her with the right emphasis this time. "No, that is a *very* good place for his fingers. I just…" I shrugged.

"What?"

"I don't know. Just… Maybe it's sexier when he's not *trying* to be so sexy?"

Clove chuckled. "Wow. Now you're going to complain that he's not trying to be sexy *right*?"

"I cannot help what turns me on," I informed her.

My eyes happened to find racer 666 as he was taking his practice lap. I pulled them off him quick smart. I'm pretty sure she noticed.

"Clove! Mags!" Iago called, waving us over.

Stone didn't have time to disagree with my presence as he was focussed on Vaughn. Iago liked to play head of pit crew, but we all knew who the chief engineer was. Vaughn was plenty good with mechanics – they all were, any machine they drove or rode was like an extension of them – but when it came to race time he was meant to focus on the riding.

Clove practically skipped over to Iago. He watched her with a warm smile until they hugged. I took a more stately pace and found Ezra standing in front of me.

"Well, if we don't have little Maggie in our midst tonight," he said. His words were more aggressive than passive, but his tone was jovial enough that I wasn't intimidated by him. It was Ezra, so I was wary, but not intimidated.

"What gave it away?" I sassed and he grinned. But it never reached his eyes.

His eyes darted down my body. "Might be that desperate attempt to fit in with those wankers, mightn't it?"

I tried not to smile and completely encourage him. "I do fit in with those wankers," I reminded him.

"Of course you do," Iago said as the four of us gravitated towards each other.

"Don't patronise her," Clove interjected, hitting his arm.

He flinched, as though she'd actually done him some harm. "I'm not. I was being sincere! Maggie fits in whenever the hell she wants."

I laughed. "Yeah, sure. Because I haven't spent my whole life trying to make sure they can't fault anything about me."

I saw the sympathy in Clove's eyes and ignored it.

Iago shook his head. "Anyone who sees fault in you is a fucking idiot. You hide it so well," he teased.

I couldn't help but laugh at that. At his attempt to cheer me up.

"Yago!" Clove cried, smacking him again as she dropped the first syllable of his name to make it shorter for reprimand.

He snorted. "What?"

"Race is about to start," Cairo said as he walked past.

Iago nodded to him. "Roger."

By the time I dared look away from Iago and Clove, the racers were taking their places at the start line. Vaughn was climbing onto his bike as Stone frowned at him over something. There were honestly too many options for me to even begin to guess what it might have been.

Stone jogged back over to us, and the race finally started. The roar of the engines vibrated in my ears the way they always did, especially going from silence to something like twenty of the damned things.

Two of the racers who were gunning for the lead were taking stupid chances. Their first victim crashed on the third lap.

"Fucking De Lorenzos," Iago growled.

Clove looked at me, but I shook my head.

The second rider crashed on lap eleven, and forced Vaughn almost to the back of the pack or he risked going with him. My nails dug into the palms of my hands and my heart refused to return to an appropriate rhythm.

Which was made even worse in the last lap.

My heart didn't just try breaking out of my chest, but tried crawling out of my mouth as I watched the bike ahead of Vaughn tip and then skid across the track. Vaughn's bike was heading straight for it. My hand gripped Iago's arm but he, thankfully, said nothing more than his own curse of concern as I chewed my lip nervously.

But the master he was, Vaughn got himself out of trouble and gaining on the two in the lead. It looked like they were going to try to cut him off, but he managed to get between them, and then there was no way he wasn't winning.

"Yes! Yes! Yes!" Iago yelled, jumping up and down as Vaughn closed in on the finish line.

Then Stone had stepped forward, and I saw his eyes narrow. "No. Not now. Hold it. Hold."

Panic clawed at me again. Not now, what? Hold what?

"It'll be fine," Iago said but I heard the note of false bravado in his voice.

My heart hammered.

What wasn't going to be fine?

But Vaughn got across the line and the flag dropped. Then he was off the bike in moments, surrounded by people who started firing fire extinguishers at his fucking bike!

"Sorry, what?" Clove said.

Stone's head twitched like he was pissed with himself. "I should have caught that."

"He's fine," Iago called to him as he ran towards the bike.

Vaughn was walking towards us, and he sure did look fine. And I didn't just mean in the unscathed kind of way. I watched as he pulled his helmet off and it was like goddamn slow motion hit the world. His hair was damp with sweat as he flicked it off his face and passed his helmet to the same wimpy twat who'd been serving him the other week, but his eyes never left mine. He ran his hand through his hair, and I wished that was my hand.

No.

Bad, Maggie.

He was ignoring the rest of the world around us. His focus honed on me until I stopped noticing the rest of them as well. He licked his lip sensuously as he stopped in front of me and stared down at me. I didn't know what he was thinking, but the look in his eyes was heating me up something terribly.

"I told you I'd take my prize from you, Magenta," he purred, and I felt it in those places that voices had no right affecting. I swallowed hard and plastered on all my animosity for him.

"And are you always all talk, Vaughn? Or do you *sometimes* follow through on your threats?"

I knew I was tempting fate. I was tempting him. He'd promised what he'd take from me, and I was standing there in front of him, almost like I was daring him to go ahead do it. Like I actually wanted him to do it. I preferred to tell myself I just wanted to see if he'd follow through on his threats, or if they were as empty as his heart. It had nothing to do with wondering what he tasted like.

And he'd liked it. Vaughn pulled me to him, sparing me one 'show me what you're going to do about it, baby' look. Then his fingers were wrapped around the back of my neck, dipping in my hair, and lips were on mine. It was like something in me ignited. The spark was visceral, and I saw it burst behind my eyes as they closed against his kiss. No. Not against. For.

My goddamn body betrayed me in the most heinous of ways. Because, for one…two…three freaking heartbeats, I gave into it. To him.

I didn't give a shit what he tasted like. Even though it was a 'smoky but sweet and too damn nice' that made something in my chest flutter.

I couldn't care less what he smelled like. And it was that 'heady, little-sweaty-but-somehow-still-sexy' mixed with his deodorant or aftershave kind of all-man musk that filled my nostrils and addled my brain.

I was out of bothers for how he felt. All hard and soft in all the right places. His muscles hinting at the barely controlled power and pleasures they contained that made heat pool in me dangerously.

No. It was the way his lips on mine made *me* feel. Like I was alive for the first time in my life. Like every nerve was awakened. Like a part of my soul, that I'd been previously missing without even realising it, was somehow found.

And it was that that had me finally pushing him away. Yeah, all right, it took me a minute of wallowing in it. A moment of my hand tightening on his jacket before both my hands were firm against his chest and pushing him away.

As he stumbled back, our eyes accidentally locked and I saw the victory in his. Because he knew. Of course he did. He knew that one kiss was all it took for me to forget all my morals and higher ground. Because it hadn't been Parker that made me push Vaughn away. No (almost) boyfriend would have stopped me succumbing to Vaughn's kiss. It was, dangerously, far more powerful than that.

And Vaughn knew it.

He'd felt my response as keenly as I had. I could see it in the way he was looking at me. He saw my outrage and indignity for what it was. Because he'd *felt* it.

I was breathing way too deeply.

He seemed as calm and cocky as usual.

"You could have died!" I spat at him.

Jesus H Christ. Was that literally the first thing on my mind? Concern at a world without Vaughn-goddamned-Saint in it? Do not tell me I was already too far gone for this miscreant, before he'd even kissed me. No. I was just deflecting.

"With a kiss like that waiting for me, I'll always cross the finish line," he said with a smirk, and those blue eyes fucking dazzled.

I scoffed, and even I heard how pathetic it was because I was bloody dazzled by sparkling lapis lazuli. "I will never kiss you again!"

He stepped up close to me. Crowding me. Our clothes brushed against each other like a sensual whisper. That's how close he was. My breath hitched.

He ducked his head towards mine. "Let's see how long you keep that promise, baby."

How was it possible to burn with anger AND melt with desire at the same time. Vaughn was insufferable. Taking what he wanted... But the way he called me 'baby'...

Fuck.

No.

I was not going to be another idiot who fell for a Prince's tricks. The Prince of Thorns no less. The unofficial heir to my father's criminal empire. The empire the good girl – I was expected to be – was meant to have nothing to do with.

But then, if this was a Prince's tricks, I did *not* blame anyone who fell for them. Because dayum, they were good.

He smirked wide when I didn't answer. "How about this? I'll let you make the next move but, after you kiss me again, all bets will be off."

"I've already told you–"

"You will kiss me, Magenta," he said, his voice so low and seductive I almost did right then. "And, when you do, I'll be playing for keeps."

I shouldn't have like that. I should not have liked that. Oh, I really shouldn't have liked that. But I did. I really did. I liked it. A. Lot.

I actually had to shake my head and take a step away from him. If I didn't, I couldn't tell what I might do. I had to take a deep breath before I could trust myself to talk and not sound like I was inviting the whole lot of them to bed. Hell, I didn't even need a bed at that point. I'd go right here–

Jesus...

I looked for Clove, who was still standing with Iago. Her mouth was open in a little 'o' and her eyes had bugged out of her head. I seconded that sentiment. She snapped her mouth shut and I knew we were going to spend the whole trip to the Hut talking about this.

Why the hell had she convinced me to come to the Laneway? I knew why. I was about to go and lose myself in Parker for the night and the wing-woman payment for that was Clove getting to see Iago first.

"Should we go?" I asked her. More like begged. "I feel like we should go." Clove nodded quickly and I look at all the boys.

Except Vaughn. If I looked at him now, I was climbing him like the sexually-charged man mountain he was. "Lovely to see you as always, boys. We will see you at school."

"Going to the Hut later, Clove?" Iago asked and I mentally kicked the fucking lot of them.

I so badly wanted Clove not to tell him our plans. But if she didn't, how was she supposed to eventually get her shot? Ugh. Conundrums.

"Yeah," she answered, all gorgeous and coy. "Yes. We're going…Maggie's meeting Parker."

"My boyfriend!" sort of exploded out of me unbidden and I cursed myself mentally.

I wasn't this girl. I didn't moon over the bad boy biker just because he'd gone and kissed me. It wasn't anywhere close to my first kiss. Each to their own, but I wasn't some clueless, untouched virgin who didn't know what she liked or was so inexperienced that she got swept off her feet by the first guy to show her passion.

NOT that Vaughn was the first one to show me passion!

"Who're you convincing with that one?" Vaughn asked snidely and I no longer had to force myself out of the horny, dazed, bordering-on-smitten haze that had descended over my brain.

Obviously knowing I was considering whooping Mr Bubbles out on Vaughn, Clove grabbed my arm and strongly encouraged me towards her car.

"Oh, I want to kill him," I seethed as we walked away.

Clove laughed. "Yeah, with your vagina, maybe."

I glared at her. "Not funny."

She held her finger and thumb very close together. "A little funny."

I rolled my eyes, released a pent-up breath, and told myself all my annoyance went with it. "He's insufferable."

"He's dead sexy."

Yes, he was. "You are not helping."

She shrugged. "I am helping."

"In what way?"

"In the way that I am going return some of your very sage advice to you; follow your clit."

I huffed a rough laugh. "Parker happens to be very good with my clit."

Clove nodded wisely. "I have quite literally heard," she teased. Yeah. I could get pretty loud sometimes. "But we're talking about *the* Vaughn Saint."

"No. We're not."

She nodded again, more earnestly this time. "Oh, but we are."

"There is nothing to talk about."

"Excuse you?" she said, indignantly.

I nodded. "There is nothing to talk about."

We got into the car, and she grinned at me knowingly. "Parker's sure going to appreciate that burning denial you have going on."

I batted her. "Shut up."

But Parker did appreciate it. We danced and we drank, and we kissed. He even pulled me into the booth and put his hands exactly where I liked them. It was probably about 11pm when the whole Hut went deathly still. As though I knew the cause of it, I turned to the door to see the Princes walking in like they owned the damn place.

"What the hell are they doing here?" Parker huffed.

I shrugged. "Bored with their own stuff?" I suggested.

By rights, there was no reason they *couldn't* be there any more than anyone else should or shouldn't be drinking underage. And there was certainly no way that this 'side of the tracks' could keep them out if they wanted to crash the party.

I put a hand on Parker's cheek and turned him to face me. It took a couple of goes before his eyes stayed on mine. "Ignore them. It's just us."

He smiled and I saw that he was indeed going to ignore the Princes. At least for a while. And I did as well. I refused to look at a certain Prince who would remain nameless. I wasn't going to give him the satisfaction of thinking he'd got to me.

I dragged Parker back to our booth but, before I could lose myself in him, Nick and Jeremy joined us, sliding in across the table. I hid a frustrated sigh behind a smile as they all got distracted talking about football. My eyes did wander, but only enough to watch Iago and Clove's progress.

It didn't take long for them to make their way to each other. They did take their time, like a good half an hour, maybe forty-five minutes, while I semi-listened to football talk and nodded periodically. Clove and Iago looked, for all the world, like maybe it was just lucky happenstance and not at all a very carefully crafted plan on both their parts. They ended up in front of our booth, letting me have a front row seat to their mutual and/or wilful obliviousness.

"Dance?" Iago asked her and she nodded happily before she passed me her drink.

It sloshed a little since she didn't seem all that interested in taking her eyes off Iago. I didn't blame her.

I watched as he took Clove's hand and pulled her into the dancers, feeling like maybe someone's night was going well.

No.

My night *was* going well. I didn't need to remind myself of that. My night was going exactly the way I wanted. I was here, with Parker. I gave zero fucks that Vaughn was dancing with some girl who was probably from Snowtown; she had that look about her. It didn't bother me at all that he had his hands on her arse. I couldn't give a shit that he only took his lips off her neck to look up at me with the biggest shit-stirring grin in his eyes.

With his eyes still on mine, I saw his hand slide down her body. His fingers teased the bottom of her very short skirt before they disappeared between her legs. I watched her back arch, and I knew where they were. He was actually… Huh. And right in front of me?

No.

I didn't care.

I was with Parker and that was endgame.

While Vaughn was still watching me, I pulled Parker to me and kissed him hard. Nick and Jeremy laughed, knowing to make themselves scarce. Parker's hand went to my thigh, and I coaxed it between my legs.

I didn't look back at Vaughn until Parker had me moaning in his ear. As I found Vaughn's eyes across the dance floor, I licked my lip slowly, letting a self-satisfied smirk play across them as I slid my hand down over Parker's crotch.

Vaughn's eyes were narrowed. He was pissed. I could take any number of guesses as to exactly why – jealousy or disgust, chief among them – but I couldn't be bothered. It didn't matter. What mattered was that *I'd* got a reaction out of *him*.

He thought he was the only one who could play the game?

I winked at him as I climbed into Parker's lap and pretended that I didn't see Vaughn drag that girl towards the bathroom.

VAUGHN: TWO

The fuck was she even doing out? She was at her mum's that week. Although, clearly not because, as I pulled the bike in from the practice lap, she was standing in our pit at the Laneway talking to Ezra.

My eyes flicked to Iago, and I saw Clove throwing herself at him again. A fucking sorrier sight I'd never seen. Even *I* knew those two needed to hurry up and just fuck already. Maybe then they'd stop all this disgusting longing from afar and put the rest of us out of our misery.

I understood why Iago kept his distance from her. In theory. The guy was smitten with her, and he was convinced that he'd only get her hurt if he even thought of her as anything more than a friend. I could follow his argument to its logical conclusion and understand why he ended up where he did. But I didn't know why he thought that was the *only* logical conclusion.

"How's it running?" Stone asked and I nodded.

"Good. Fine. Something felt a little off on that last curve, but it sorted itself out on the stretch."

Stone kicked his chin and set to checking over the bike, just to be safe. Given the affiliations of our families, it would be fucking embarrassing to get taken out in a bike crash.

While I went over the Laneway track again in my head – as though I didn't know it better than my own hand – I kept one eye on Maggie. She and Ezra were with Clove and Iago now. Someone – probably Iago – had said something to make her laugh. She wore this huge smile and her eyes shone behind her glasses as she pushed them up her nose subconsciously.

I got a nervous restlessness in my whole body, watching her, and tried stretching out my neck to compensate.

"You've got ten minutes. Marshal wants you at the start line," Cairo told me, his eyes having followed mine. "You think that's a smart move?"

"Do you see me making a move?"

"Forbidden fruit doesn't taste sweeter no matter how much we tell ourselves otherwise."

It didn't matter how much I trusted the guy with my life. He could believe what he wanted, but I was sure that Magenta McCallan would be the sweetest fruit I'd ever had the pleasure of…plucking and no one could tell me otherwise. It was better for everyone if I at least gave them some plausible deniability.

"I've got the hint, Lock," I told him.

"Do you? Because you never were very good at following the rules."

That was rich coming from him. "And you are?"

Cairo put his hand on my shoulder. "I'm not looking for a reason for Blaise to put me out of my misery."

I shook him off. "Neither am I."

"You keep chasing the thrill and it's gonna bite you in the fucking arse at some point. When's the chase gonna be enough, huh? Racing's not enough anymore so you're going after McCallan's girl? What? You want to kiss her? Fuck her? Break her heart? Just break her? She's not just *any* girl, Saint. Blaise will do worse to you than he made you do to that nominee two years ago."

I didn't need to remember how good it felt to have that shitstain's bones breaking under my knuckles. I grinned at Cairo as the marshal yelled my name to hurry the fuck up. "Daddy McCallan's gotta catch me first, mate." I winked at him.

Ignoring Cairo's annoyance, I grabbed my helmet while Stone wheeled my bike over.

"You should listen to him, Saint."

"Don't you fucking start."

We got me in my starting position, and I threw my leg over to rest in the seat.

"Our lives are one thing. She's another."

I pulled on my helmet and straightened my gloves. "I don't need you wankers babying me like I've forgotten who Magenta McCallan is."

"Then quit making threats like you're 'going to claim your prize from her'."

I looked at him in utter shock at the voice he'd put on. "I'm sorry. Was that supposed to be me?"

Humour flashed in his eyes. "Don't be a fucking idiot, Saint. Just go find some other chick to play with."

"And if I want to play with her?"

"Then I'm wearing nothing but a fucking banana hammock to your funeral."

I coughed to cover the snort that tried to escape me. "Undignified and fucking disrespectful. Now fuck off. I have a prize to claim." And I snapped my visor down.

Stone shook his head. He knew better than to keep cautioning me. He knew better than to fuck up my inspiration. If I wanted to think of Maggie to get over that finish line first, he wasn't going to stop me; he wanted me to win as badly as I did.

There was the familiar fire in my veins as I waited for the go. The way my whole body ignited in unbridled, energetic restlessness. My heart pounded, hard and steady in my chest. Death was about ten seconds from staring me in the face and fuck it felt good.

The race started and the shitting De Lorenzos were playing dirty already. Gav and Montrose were pieces of shit and no mistake. But it wasn't until the last lap that they did some real damage. I'd already fallen behind after they'd sent a couple of riders to the ER, but I was making up ground and they did not like that. Shame they missed me and took out Carlos instead.

At the last second, I squeezed the brake and watched Carlos' bike careen past the front of my wheel. My adrenalin spiked and I felt the smile on my face; this was what I lived for. I was safely past him when his bike hit the wall.

Making up for lost time, I pushed my bike as hard as I could. There went that shake in the front left. Once I was over the line, Stone and I would have a whole week to work out what was wrong with it.

Sliding between Gav and Montrose De Lorenzo, it was me and open track ahead. Round that last curve, down the straight, and the prize was mine. I was so close. So, of course, a few metres from the finish line, the rattle got harder. But I'd rather be dead than let that get in my way.

It was mine. This one was mine.

She was mine.

The cocky arrogance surged in me, and it was a better high than half the drugs we'd done in our lives combined. I was fucking unstoppable. I was immortal. I was a fucking god.

The flag went as I crossed the line, and I didn't hesitate to get the fuck off the bike in case it blew, letting it slide away from me.

Extinguishers went off around me – precautions first – as the rest of the racers finished, but I had one fucking goal. As I pulled off my gloves, Stone glared at me as he ran to deal with the bike. We could argue about my priorities later.

I pulled off my helmet and threw it at Nate, raking my fingers through my hair as I locked eyes with her. Hers went wide and I so wanted to know what she was thinking. Did she see the smouldering heat she fanned in me?

The announcer was still calling my name across the Laneway. Cheers were erupting. But there was only one thing I wanted. One thing I was owed. One thing I was going to take. I was going to taste Blaise McCallan's little princess and see if Little Miss Redemption was half as good as being off-limits made her seem.

I stopped in front of her and looked down at her. She was so tiny, and she never wore heels. I had no idea why that was, but all it made me do was picture all the ways I could hold her up, and the only sweat I'd break was based on how hard and fast she wanted me to drill her.

"I told you I'd take my prize from you, Magenta," I said, almost daring her.

I saw defiance flash in her eyes as she looked me over. "And are you always all talk, Vaughn? Or do you *sometimes* follow through on your threats?"

Fuck, but she was a spitfire. Born and bred from and for our side of the tracks, even if her old man had decreed that she was to have no part of our life. Everything about her had me itching to touch her. To have her. To fucking ruin her. And it wasn't just the fact she was forbidden. Though it did make the idea of her sweeter, regardless of what Cairo thought about it, it was her spice that got me hard first.

Fine. She wanted to challenge me. Challenge fucking accepted.

I wrapped an arm around her waist and pulled her to me. My other hand went to her neck, and I brought her face to mine. I stared into her bright grey eyes, like I was daring her to do something about it. And I kissed her. I fucking kissed her.

Except…

That was not how that kiss was supposed to go.

I felt like I'd been kicked in the chest as I felt her lean – not away, but into my body – as I felt her lips part for me, and my tongue swept in to claim hers. Not that she was giving it up without a fight; her tongue fucking came to battle. Her nose pressed into my cheek as she actually nipped my lip. But it was the way her hand tightened on my jacket that really got me.

Then she pushed me away and my whole fucking world had been turned upside down.

Little Miss Redemption wanted it.

She wasn't supposed to want it. I mean, she was supposed to want it. My horrendously cocky ego would have taken a fucking hit if there was a chick that I turned my attention to who said fucking no, but Maggie's kiss had very definitively said yes.

She was meant to fight. She was meant to…

Jesus, I hadn't just won the race that night, but I'd won the fucking lottery, and I knew she saw the victorious conceit in my eyes as hers met them. Panic laced hers. Panic that she'd given the game away. She'd given in.

I wondered what the prissy little boyfriend would think about that.

Oh, and the idea of him finding out I'd just rocked his girl's world with nothing more than a fairly chaste kiss just made me far more proud.

And she was furious. But she wasn't furious with me. Oh, no. She was furious with herself. She was pissed that she hadn't pushed me away because of the boyfriend – I wasn't sure she was even thinking about him now. She'd pushed me away because she'd liked it.

Game-fucking-on, Princess.

Then she went and surprised me. "You could have died!"

Oh, love. I didn't know you cared. "With a kiss like that waiting for me, I'll always cross the finish line."

She scoffed, but it wasn't very convincing. "I will never kiss you again!"

I stepped as close to her as I could get without actually slipping inside that tight little body. "Let's see how long you keep that promise, baby."

Desire pooled in her eyes, but it was at war with how much she hated me and that suited me just fine. Hate me all you like, darling. That only makes it more fun.

I leant my head to her, my nose only just not touching her cheek. "How about this? I'll let you make the first move but, after you kiss me again, all bets will be off."

Like the good little girl she was – supposed to be – she bristled. "I've already told you–"

Fuck, I wanted to know just how bad she really was under that good girl mask. In that moment, I knew she had to be mine. I didn't look too closely at that logistics of that. I didn't give a shit what the plan was. Magenta McCallan was mine and I was fucking having her.

"You will kiss me, Magenta. And, when you do, I'll be playing for keeps."

Her eyes went wide again, and I knew this was a battle I'd already won. Now, it was just a matter of seeing how long she could keep up the pretence. Nothing had ever filled me with such excitement as the game before us. More life. It was a heady rush that only compounded with the rush I was still feeling after racing. And it was all directed at this sinfully delicious creature in front of me.

Seemingly at a loss for words, she stepped back from me as she shook her head. Finally, she pulled her eyes off me, licking her lip somewhat subconsciously as she turned to Iago and Clove.

"Should we go? I feel like we should go," she said, and Clove nodded hurriedly.

Poor little Clove. Unlike Maggie, Clove was actually good to the marrow. There was no mask. No façade. What you saw was what you got. She wasn't ignorant to the darker side of the world, but she felt no need to be part of it. Unless she could be a part of Iago, of course.

Maggie started walking backwards as she nodded to every Prince but me. "Lovely to see you as always, boys. We will see you at school."

"Going to the Hut later, Clove?" Iago asked.

Sound more fucking desperate, why not, mate? God love him.

Clove bit her lip against a full smile and nodded. "Yeah. Yes. We're going... Maggie's meeting Parker."

"My boyfriend!" she said pointedly.

"Who're you convincing with that one?" I asked and she studiously ignored me.

Clove grabbed Maggie's arm and they turned and headed for their car.

I heard Ezra chuckle. "Boss is going to beat you a pretty fuckin' shade of black and blue if he finds out what you just did. Even if it was a joke, he won't care who you are to set an example for the rest of the Roses."

Nodding absently, I couldn't take my eyes off her as she walked away with Clove. She didn't look back. That pissed me off. Why wouldn't she look back? My skin crawled as I waited for just one more look. Something happened in my chest, and I scratched it absently.

"Jesus fucking Christ," Iago muttered. "That's not good." He smacked me. I couldn't pull my eyes of Maggie until he'd hit me for the fourth time. By then, she was out of sight anyway.

"Fucking what?" I snarled.

"Don't do that," Iago cautioned.

I shrugged, deciding that playing dumb was better than acknowledging this new feeling festering in my chest. "Do what?"

Stone crossed his arms. "I warned him."

"As did I," Cairo added. "Literally only an hour ago."

Iago rolled his eyes and shoved me. "You fucking moron."

I shoved him back then held my hands up. "What?"

He shook his head. "Don't fucking 'what?' me. You know what! That wasn't just impulsive bullshit. That was wilful impetuous bullshit."

"You expect to impress upon him the direness of the situation by using big words?' Cairo huffed, probably not even noticing the irony in his words.

"I know what 'impetuous' means, you fucker," I snapped.

"Yeah, you fucking *will*," Iago sighed, pinching the bridge of his nose.

Deciding he needed to stop thinking about where I was planning to put my cock, and start thinking about his own, I gave him an offer he wouldn't refuse, "Who's up for getting pissed at Kenicki's and crashing the Hut?"

I was definitely going to learn even more viscerally the meaning of the word impetuous very soon. And I wasn't the only one who knew it. Kissing Magenta McCallan was meant to be a game. It was supposed to fuck with her.

It wasn't supposed to have fucked with me.

And yet, it did.

And going to the Hut the night after the race and seeing her little *display* had only made it worse.

I couldn't get her out of my head. Just the idea of her gave me a twenty-four seven boner that no number of girls out the back of Kenicki's could satisfy. And believe me, I'd been *very* creative and incredibly thorough; I'd tried them in every possible position, formation, and up to three at once. I'd been so thorough in my experiments that I'd made sure to enact each test more than once. Nothing fucking worked. Even three times the…attention wasn't enough to stop me thinking about her.

By the end of the next week, I was officially obsessed with her. More so than I had been before she'd been nothing more than an idea. Everything in me didn't just itch, it tingled and fidgeted at the lack of her presence. In my lap. In my hands. Against my lips. I was fucking jonesing like I'd had an unparalleled trip on one of Ezra's more successful experiments.

I didn't know if I wanted to love her or ruin her. It didn't actually matter anymore. I just knew I had to have her. I had to find a way to get her to prove she wanted me too. It was fucking depressing, but I was an addict, and I couldn't shake it. Her.

I didn't understand how Iago stuck to it. His thing with Clove. I saw the way he looked at her when there was no chance that she'd see him. How did he keep his fear for Clove's safety outweighing his need for her? His draw to her. His obsession with her. Because I'd kissed Magenta McCallan once and I knew it wouldn't be enough. Maybe that was Iago's trick? He knew once was all it took, and I'd been too fucking cocky to heed his example.

I watched as the Police Chief's wanky progeny kissed her and heard Iago's laugh. I looked at my hand and found I'd crushed the bottle in it. I swigged the remnants of my coffee and screwed the cap back on.

"Fucking shut up," I told him.

He shrugged. "I didn't say anything."

Instead of chucking my bottle in the bin next to our table, I threw it at him instead.

I felt my jaw clench as I saw her laugh at something her *boyfriend* said.

This wasn't me.

This sad sack of ridiculous bullshit. Maggie McCallan was nothing more than a conquest. Any other conquest. My cock might stir only for her now – even if I could put it to good use in any other willing bitch – but that didn't mean this was anything 'special'. That didn't make me jealous, it made me pissed at being blue balled.

I knew the schedule as well as any Blood Rose. It was beaten into us to ensure we didn't disturb his Lordship's happy family's fairytale bullshit. Maggie would be at Blaise's again the next weekend. Which meant she'd be going out.

I had a little over a week to make her admit she needed me as much as I needed her. A week to make her seek me out. A week to make sure she would be exactly where I wanted her.

Let the games begin.

CHAPTER FIVE

When I walked into school that Monday morning, checking my phone to see where Clove was waiting for me, I felt the back of my neck prickle. I looked up quickly, my eyes finding him almost instantly.

Vaughn leant against the wall over in a darkened corner of the corridor, one foot planted back against it as he locked his gaze with mine through the haze of vape smoke wrapping around him. As an image, it did a lot for me.

It also didn't hurt that his uniform was all askew in that 'gives no fucks' kind of way. That 'did I just have sex or am I just ready for it?' kind of way. Half his shirt was untucked next to the thumb hooked in his belt, his tie was loose at his neck, his blazer collar was uneven, his messenger bag hung loosely off one shoulder, and the hair hanging over his face just begged me to come and find out all his secrets. With my tongue.

"Oh, my God," I muttered, looking around as though trying to tell if anyone else was experiencing this, or if it was quite possibly all in my own head. "Dramatic much?"

Iago walked in behind me with Ezra and a Blood Rose daughter called Faith who was not kept half-in, half-out of their world. Faith bumped into me as they passed, sparing me a look that I thought was supposed to be an apology but fell rather short.

As the three of them walked over to Vaughn, he pushed himself off the wall and wrapped his arm around Faith's shoulders. Iago took the vape pen off him and they headed off up the corridor. I watched them go, not sure why I desperately wanted Vaughn to turn around.

What in the hell would that achieve?

Just as I felt Clove companionably run into me in greeting, Vaughn did look back and I told myself my heart didn't skip a beat as his tongue ran over his lips before he ducked them to Faith's ear. Her arm went around his waist, and I frowned. Vaughn's smirk lit his eyes, and then the four of them disappeared around the corner. The breath I released was unnecessarily dramatic.

"If you say we're not talking about him, then I'm going to combust."

I looked at Clove. "I'm not sure what there is to say."

She shook her head. "No. You don't get to do that. I'm living my Blood Rose old lady fantasies vicariously through you now."

I laughed and linked my arm with hers as we headed for first lesson. "Sure. No, we can talk about him. I meant I have no idea where to start."

"Oh." She gave an over-the-top nod. "Gotcha. Different. I'll allow it."

I leant my head to her shoulder.

I had, of course, told her about the little standoff between Vaughn and me at the Hut while she was rubbing her body all over Iago's with zero progress. I'd told her how much my body craved him. I'd also told her there was no way in hell I was risking what was happening with Parker because of it. She was ignoring that last part.

"I'm pretty sure he's on a mission to seduce me," I told her.

"The man is scary when he's single-minded."

"I was going to go with dead sexy," I told her, and we both spluttered a laugh.

"Yeah..." she said slowly. "How long you wanna tell yourself Vaughn isn't like your perfect type?"

I sighed. "As long as it takes for me to believe it."

Clove nodded. "I know..." She paused and I waited for her to decide which way she was going to play this.

She knew as well as I why Parker was endgame. And I did like Parker. It wasn't *all* about social status. That was just the bonus of wanting a guy like Parker over a guy like Vaughn. Parker's pro column was far longer than Vaughn's. Likewise, Vaughn's cons column was a shit tonne longer than Parker's, especially if we counted Vaughn's literal rap sheet.

Clove took a breath, and I could guess which way she was leaning. "I know the plan. I know it makes sense. But..." Another deep breath released before, "Are you sure that there can't be a different endgame? Why can't you have both?" came out in a rush.

I squeezed her am. "Jesus, babe," I huffed roughly as I pressed my face into her shoulder.

"Oh!' I knew she was blushing. "Oh, no. I didn't mean both of *them* at once. I meant the good life *and* the bad boy."

I chuckled. "I know. Don't put that thought in my head either."

She laughed. "Okay. Right. Sorry."

"Babe!" Parker said with a smile.

I pulled my face off Clove and looked at him. "Hey."

He looked between Clove and I. "Hey. You okay?"

I nodded as I went to him. "Fine." I kissed him and he didn't hesitate in responding.

"Well, good morning," he said with a chuckle.

"Good morning."

I slid my hand down over Parker's arse and gave it a squeeze as we walked into the classroom. He laughed, but there was almost something self-conscious and surprised about it. Not that I was paying all that much attention, because I looked behind me and saw Vaughn paused on his way into his own classroom.

I gave Iago next to him a pretty little smile. Iago looked down to hide his as it broke over his face uncontrollably. Vaughn was less amused as I followed Parker in, and Iago pushed Vaughn into their room.

And that was just the beginning of the game.

Because I'd been right. Vaughn was on a mission of seduction. And he wasn't scared to go subtle or like a freight train straight to my clit. We spent the week locked in a battle of wills. Him with other girls, and me with Parker. His fingers trailing mine gently as we passed in the corridor, that smallest touch alone igniting my whole body. That time he 'had' to squeeze past me between lessons and his hands were somehow all over my body and not nearly everywhere enough. Sweltering, lingering glances across any room we happened to be in that made everything heat and tingle in the most pleasant of ways.

Parker had a *very* good week.

All my pent-up sexual frustration had to go somewhere. It made more sense that I directed it at the guy I wanted to be with rather than by myself. But I might have taken it a little far on Thursday when I climbed into Parker's lap at lunch and basically dry humped him while his hands squeezed my arse under my school skirt.

Vaughn found me in the bathroom in the middle of the next lesson. I was washing my hands when he stormed in, locked the door, and strode across the room.

"You think you can make *me* jealous? Vaughn growled.

I mean, I was going to say 'yes' based on the current situation.

"Oh, is that what you've been trying to do to me?" I teased.

He clearly had similar feelings about it as I did. The only difference was that I was far more used to the mask of naïve indifference, to hiding all those sultry feelings of hate-fuelled desire behind wide smiles, big doe eyes, and sweet innocence.

I dropped my lips into a fake pout. "Oh, what's the matter, Vaughn? Did your dastardly plan not work?" At his obvious annoyance, I smirked. "It's not so fun, is it, *Prince*?"

He frowned but rose to the bait. "What's not?"

I bit my lip, all flirty and coy. "When *you're* the one being tormented by someone else having what you…" I groaned softly, "want."

It was meant to be a jibe, an annoyance, just some insult he was supposed to refute and then throw something worse back at me. The problem was, the look that flashed deep in his eyes told me that was exactly it; he was jealous of Parker. Fiercely jealous. He'd tried making *me* jealous by finger fucking that nameless girl in front of me, he'd tried it with Faith and those other girls all week, and it had totally backfired on him when I retaliated with Parker.

My mind went blank, avoiding any thought processes that could tell me something I didn't want to know. My body was more than happy to know it, though. Everything in me fluttered and tingled at the realisation. The possessiveness of him. For me. I wanted it. Him. Wanted to be wanted by him. Wanted to be *had* by him.

And, now I saw that feeling was way more mutual than *just* a game. Oh, I knew a lot of it was still a game, and we'd both play it like it was more war than game. But it wasn't *just* a game.

Not that he was going to admit it any more than I was. "You know you want me," he purred in my ear.

Yes. "I have a boyfriend." My voice trembled annoyingly.

"Is that what you tell yourself?"

To resist Vaughn? Yes. I'd tell myself whatever it took. If it helped, I'd tell him, too. And his irritation over my defiance would be the cherry on top. After all, Parker was endgame. Vaughn was nothing but a bucket load of regret begging to happen. He was a blip on my otherwise perfectly planned life. A temporary distraction. A seduction. A temptation. And I was woman enough to say no to it.

"You really want a cheater, Vaughn?" I teased him. "What's the old adage? Once a cheater, always a cheater? I cheat on Parker with you, and how long until I cheat on you?"

His snarl was feral, and it turned me on. "That will not be a problem," he promised.

I nodded. "No. Because you don't want to date me. You just want to ruin me. Blaise McCallan's little princess. You want her to be as damned as you, as you leave her for dust in your rear-view mirror."

He stepped up to me and the fury near made him vibrate against me. "I don't want to date you," he admitted. "What I have planned for us is far more than just *dating*." His hand snaked around my throat as he ran his nose over my face gently. "I'm going to claim you, Magenta."

My whole body came alive, and I had to stop myself from leaning into him. His whispered promise made my nipples harden against my bra and I thanked anyone who might be up there that it was padded. I didn't need him to lord yet another thing over me.

"You just don't need me to dump my boyfriend to do it?" I spat sarcastically.

He pressed into me, and I felt how hard his cock was against my hip. “You will,” he assured me, and I wanted to say he wasn’t right. “I don’t need you to leave him to claim you, but you will leave him. For me.”

“My father would kill you.”

I saw the acknowledgement in his eyes and there was something that murmured ‘wild abandon’ to me. He didn’t disagree with me. “But you’d be mine.”

A dangerously pleasant shiver spread through every inch of me.

In his voice and his eyes was all the information I needed. Vaughn would claim me and not give a shit about the hell it left in his wake, just like he did with everything and everyone else in his life. He’d do it, knowing full well that my dad would kill him for touching me, for even *considering* thinking about me like that.

I was off-limits.

They all knew that.

Vaughn clearly didn’t care.

He wanted me and he was willing to die just to have me.

It was an easy promise for him to believe, when death wasn’t currently staring him right in the face. But then again, I was very certain that Vaughn got off on the risk of death. He raced motorcycles for money he didn’t need. He got into fights. He drank. Did drugs. Didn’t follow the speed limit no matter where he was. Got up to who knew what other risky behaviour for the Blood Roses – and fun. The thrill of death was quite possibly the only thing his broken soul could still feel, but the idea of him ceasing to exist in the same world as me once again hit me in ways it shouldn’t have.

His sentiment also did more to me than it should have, but I wasn’t going to fall for it.

"I don't need your death on my conscience, Vaughn," I told him, aiming for flippant and hoping I didn't give too much away.

His nose ran over my cheek again. God, he smelled so good. He felt so good. Every nerve ending was waiting in baited anticipation for his next touch, desperate to be the one to feel it.

"Why not?" he whispered. "Would the guilt be so much you'd have to admit you were thinking of me every time he was between your legs?"

I shrugged and pretended I was unaffected. "But it *will* be him between my legs. Won't it, Vaughn? Him making me…" I leant my lips to his ear, "…whimper in pleasure as I cum all over his cock." I dragged my teeth over his earlobe and actually felt him shiver.

I had pull back or I was in danger of forgetting myself. Of forgetting that the whole point here was to push him and poke him and annoy him without touching him. But Vaughn clearly had other ideas. His arm wrapped around my back, and he pulled me to his very hard, lickable body.

"Oh, no, darling," he said. His voice was husky with need, and I felt it fan a burning ember in every single part of me. "No." His chuckle was humourless. "You don't get to do that now, Magenta." His hand slid over my arse, and he squeezed slowly. Heat pooled and I got so damn wet for him. "You want to play? Make the move and I'll play." His other hand went to my hip and slid agonisingly slowly up my body until it came to rest under my breast. His lips dropped to my neck, brushing over me with the barest of whispers. "Take me or don't, baby. None of this half-arsed, teasing bullshit. *Commit* to it."

He nipped at my neck with his teeth before he pulled away from me suddenly. I was so surprised by the movement, that my body swayed after his for a moment. Then I blinked, shook my head, and gave him the glare he deserved.

He was full of amused cheek. "But make sure you really want it," he continued as he walked to the door. He unlocked it and looked back at me. "The next time your lips touch *any* part of me…" He pointed at me. "You're mine."

Then he was gone, and I felt like I could breathe again. I sank against the tiled wall, thankful for its chill. I raked a hand through my hair and took a deep breath.

"Okay, pull it the fuck together," I muttered as I shook myself out and headed back to class.

"I have a plan," Clove said after I'd told her about the bathroom incident sitting in my room that afternoon, and I looked at her with a raised eyebrow. She shrugged. "Well, I figure, if you're in denial, I'll come up with the plans."

I smiled. "I'm listening."

"This weekend. Rizzo's."

I blinked at her. "Rizzo's?"

She nodded. "Hear me out."

"Have I said no?"

"Not yet." She looked at me like she dared me to.

I sighed. "I *am* listening."

"After spending all week undressing you with his eyes, Vaughn expects you to go to Rizzo's–"

"So, give him what he wants?"

She shook her head. "No. See – and this is my brilliance – what he *wants* is to intimidate you into *not* going. He wants to get back the power you've so delightfully taken from him. So, show him you're keeping it."

I thought about her logic. "So… He wins either way. If I don't go, he gets the power. If I do go, I'll be there."

She shook her head noncommittally. "Okay, there's a flaw if you look at it like him winning."

I smirked at her. "Look at it as another situation to show him I have the power."

She pointed at me. "Exactly."

I nodded. "But this time…" I grinned as an idea hit me. "Turn it back on him. I won't make him jealous with someone else – there's no way I'm going to even try to get Parker to Rizzo's. I give him a taste of his own medicine. I'll put my hands all over him. I'll give him a sample of what he could have, and then I'll just walk away." I shrugged. "Easy."

Clove smiled. "Game on, Prince of Thorns."

Excitement fluttered in my chest and my stomach as I thought about it. The only blip on my confidence in my plan was Clove's added, "Are you going to have the willpower to walk away from him?"

I rolled my eyes as I threw a cushion at her, and she laughed.

CHAPTER SIX

On Saturday night, we said goodnight to Dad and headed to Everdale. Our closest town, it was a little under an hour away. It wasn't the kind of place you went for anything more than the occasional football game…or Rizzo's.

No one from Hammersby would be caught dead at Rizzo's. Except the Blood Roses. And that was the exact reason we were there. The Everdale version of a seedier Hut, Rizzo's was the place to go if you wanted anonymity and dark, depraved indulgence. If you wanted a dalliance with a someone you weren't supposed to have a dalliance with. For example.

After the week we'd had, Vaughn would be here. Knowing him and his quest for power, Clove was right; he was half-hoping I'd turn up as well as half-hoping I was too chicken shit to do it. Well, I was going to show him that Maggie McCallan wasn't scared of anything. Least of all whatever he thought was burning between us.

Dad had given my outfit a semi-interested glance, then just smiled and told us to have a good night. Which was a long way from what Iago did when he saw me first. And, based on Iago's reaction, I was going to like Vaughn's.

I had chosen my outfit, after all, to really mess with Vaughn and I was proud of my efforts, even for me. I was in all black. A crossover halter top that showed off more skin than it covered and an equally tight black skirt that only barely covered my arse, leaving plenty of room for movement. I paired the choice with the closest I came to heels; my black knock-off Converse wedges. With those four extra inches of height, I was actually taller than Clove for once. Barely.

Clove, meanwhile, was in a slinky pink, shiny halter dress that was just as short as mine. Then she'd put on her monster heels, and I'd been the short one again. But, oh well.

As we walked into Rizzo's, I was ahead of her. Iago's eyes widened at the sight of me. But it wasn't until he saw Clove that his jaw quite literally dropped as well. I peeked at Clove and saw she was trying very hard not to just eye fuck him from across the room as well.

And why not? Iago was wearing black trousers and a white shirt with a big black cross on the back and the sleeves cut off. His hair was styled so the front had more height than I had ever attempted on mine.

But I didn't much care how good Iago looked because my eyes had difficulty staying off the guy beside him. In dark grey jeans and a deep red tee, his tattoos peeking out of the rolled sleeves and a low v neck, Vaughn looked like all my wildest fantasies come true. As I looked him over, he raked his hand through his hair and the muscles of his upper arm bulged.

Iago smacked Vaughn's stomach, making him turn mid-rake and he froze at the sight of me. Butterflies erupted in my stomach at the burning desire smouldering in his eyes, even at that distance. Vaughn's tongue ran over his bottom lip, and he finally seemed to remember he had his fingers in his hair.

I beelined for the bar and Clove followed, knowing full well the game was afoot.

"He was just about to give up," Iago said with a wry smirk as he helped himself to the spot between us.

I leant deeper against the bar, hoping Vaughn's gorgeous blue eyes were pinned to my arse, and patted the wood absently. "Was he now?"

Iago nodded. "He was convinced you weren't coming."

"How disappointed was he?" Clove asked and I shot her a look.

It seemed the two of them were quite happy to conspire together. "He was a fucking mess before she walked in the door. Now I'm pretty sure the mess is in his pants."

I fought the laugh that threatened to escape. "I'm dancing. Anyone else?"

Clove waited to see if Iago would say anything. When he didn't, she shook her head. "I need a drink first."

Iago inclined his head. "And I need to buy it for her."

It was easier to fight that smirk as I nodded to them. "Sure."

They gave me a smile as I pushed through the people to get to the dance floor. For a Saturday night, there weren't a hell of a lot of Blood Roses on site. Most of the patrons were from Snowtown or, as far as I could tell, unaffiliated.

Even I knew better than to mess with a member from Snowtown, so the first step in the plan – baiting Vaughn onto the dancefloor – didn't look like it was going to said plan.

Then I heard a voice call, "Maggie McCallan!" and turned to find Jason behind me.

Jason was first gen Rose. Older than us but one of the younger ones who hadn't yet properly earned his place. He would do.

"What are you doing here?" he asked.

I smiled at him winningly. "Blowing off steam. You want to help me?"

He grinned and I could see he was a few sheets to the wind already. “That sounds like a sure-fire way to lose me my hands.”

I stepped closer to him and bit my lip. “But who’ll keep me safe from all these Monsters?” I asked with a pout.

His grin grew. “Well, when you put it like that.”

“Nope,” came the growl that coincided with the body pressing up behind me.

I tried to keep my breathing even.

“Blaise would have your fucking head,” Vaughn spat at Jason, still all possessive growl.

Jason gave an awkward laugh. “Blaise doesn’t need to know. Does he?”

“But I know.”

Vaughn’s family had been Roses back before they were Roses. Even without being Dad’s heir, Vaughn sat much higher in the hierarchy.

“Come on, Saint. I didn’t even touch her.”

“You thought about it. You know what’ll fucking happen to you for just thinking about it.”

If possible, Vaughn came up even closer behind me. Between his size and the tone of his voice, Jason would have seen it for the threat it was. Whether he realised that Vaughn would be more than happy to dispense justice for his own agenda without my dad being any the wiser, I wasn’t sure.

Jason’s smile was more of a grimace. “It doesn’t have to be this way.”

“Vaughn, come on,” I said, half-turning.

Vaughn took a step toward Jason, putting his front against mine, and grabbed the front of Jason’s tee. “You want me to forget you even looked at her?” Vaughn asked and Jason nodded quickly. “Then you and your boys get the fuck out of here right now. And if I see you anywhere near her again, I will fucking end you, sanction or no."

Why did I like that? I should not have liked that! Fucking caveman, alpha douchehole bullshit. But, Jesus, it did something for me. It spoke to something deep in my genetic code, or something equally ridiculous.

As Jason ran off to collect up his cronies and get out of there before Vaughn's leniency wore off, Vaughn and I were left standing hard up against each other in the middle of the dancefloor.

When I dared to look into his face, he was glaring at me in fury.

"Oh, sorry," I said sarcastically. "I thought you didn't get jealous."

"Blood Roses don't touch you. Daddy McCallan's rules."

I scoffed. "No. True. And you're nothing if not a staunch supporter and enforcer of the rules, aren't you, Vaughn? I mean you wouldn't possibly think the rules didn't apply to you. You couldn't – wouldn't – do anything to someone who touched me if they weren't a Blood Rose…could you?"

His next words proved both my points for me. "The only one who touches you is me."

Oh, he was all feral possessive obsession and I fully planned to rile him up further to see more of it. To make him give me more of it.

I looked around and pointed at someone I was prepared to pretend wasn't a Monster. "What about that guy?"

Vaughn bared down on me as his hand wrapped around my throat. "You think I waited here the last two nights just to watch you with some other piece of shit?"

I swallowed at the implication of his words. "Oh, you're not *that* shit, Vaughn," I teased, and he growled at me. My clit tingled and I knew there was point at which I'd pushed him *too* far. So I eased off. A little. "Well, what are you going to do about it, then? I'm here now, Vaughn." I lay my hand on his chest and slid it up his body. "Are you going to dance with me, or are you just going to growl at me and prevent *all* my fun?"

His hands went to my hips as we stepped up to each other. His forehead leant down as he gazed at me through his hair. Like he was simultaneously asking me if I was sure about this, and he just couldn't help himself. "Given the choices, I'll dance with you."

I nodded as I slid my hands up his arms and we started moving together. "Sensible choice, Vaughn."

"Possibly the first good choice I've ever made," he teased, and I tried to not to smile and encourage him.

"I'm not sure that's an achievement to be proud of," I told him.

He just smirked as we danced, staring into my eyes so deeply I felt him in my very soul.

"I don't think I've ever seen you in anything but flats," he said softly.

"Oh, because you've seen me dressed up *so* many times before."

"And what does your boyfriend think?"

"Of the shoes or me coming to Rizzo's?" I shot back. He wanted to play? Fine.

He shrugged. "Either." He kicked his chin at me as he demanded, "Both."

"Let me guess," I huffed. "If it were up to you, you wouldn't let me out of the house with this much skin showing or let me be seen dead at a seedy establishment like Rizzo's?"

He leant into me as his hand slipped from my hip around my back. “If it were up to me, you could wear as much or as little as you wanted and go wherever the fuck you wanted.”

“So long as you were there to keep an eye on me?”

“Look, I’d prefer to have my eyes on you for my own perverse pleasure, but you’re your own woman. You make your own choices.”

“And you want to be one of those choices, Vaughn?” I guessed.

He grinned at me as our bodies rubbed together to the music. “Baby, I’m not a choice.” He spun me so my back was against his front and purred in my ear, “I’m fate.”

I wanted to argue with him. I wanted to tell him he was wrong but, for some reason, the words wouldn’t be said. “And what does that make me?”

I felt his smile against my cheek as his hands were hot on my hips. “My fate.”

My heart fluttered and pounded and just had no idea what to do with itself. So I said nothing. I just distracted the both of us by rubbing my arse on his cock and telling myself I didn’t wish it was inside me.

“Do you know what those shoes make me wanna do to you?” he murmured in my ear after a few more songs, and my heart tripped.

I shook my head as my hand slipped up and back around his neck. “No, but I’m sure you’re going to tell me.”

One of his hands slid down and over the front of my thigh to rest between them. “I want to hook your pretty little leg over my shoulder while I fuck you so hard you see stars.”

I lay my hand over his and coaxed it just a little higher. “This leg, Vaughn?”

"Mmhmm," he murmured as he dropped kisses along the back of my neck. "Or the other. Which is stronger?"

Sorry, I was standing during this? Standing on one leg while the other was hooked over his...and he was... Oh, my God. Okay. I could get behind that. I mean, *he'd* be behind me...

Our hands inched further up my leg, and I felt his smile against my neck. "Do you like that, baby?" I was nodding before I could stop myself and his other hand wrapped softly around my throat, pulling me against him. "Yeah, you do," he purred, and I should not have liked the proud approval in his voice. "The idea of my cock deep inside you. Fuck, I wanna feel the way you quiver on it as I shatter you."

My thighs pressed together, our hands still between them and his smile widened before his teeth grazed over my neck.

"Are you wet, darling?"

Again with the nodding.

"How wet are you?"

God, it was a bad idea, but I couldn't help it. I dragged his hand further up until he got the message and trailed his fingers over my inner thigh agonisingly softly until they found the heat of my centre. He rubbed over my clit so softly and lazily.

I leant my head back on his shoulder as I ground my arse against the thick, raging length in his jeans. While he stroked between my legs, his other hand blazed fire across my stomach, making it break out in butterflies. Goosebumps chased over my skin. My heart raced.

And all I could think about was my leg over his shoulder...

Okay, so maybe I wasn't strong enough to walk away from him after all.

"Don't read anything into it," I told him as I spun in his arms.

Then, before he could query or comment, I crushed my lips to his. I felt his victorious smirk for a mere moment before it fell, like the victory itself wasn't what was most important here – not anymore – as he deepened the kiss. He wound his arms around my waist, and mine wrapped around his broad shoulders.

This. *This* was what a kiss was supposed to feel like.

Blossoming warmth spread through my body, radiating from my chest. Every nerve felt alive. Rejuvenated. I tingled everywhere, from the tips of my fingers to the heavier throbbing in my clit. Energy ricocheted between us, not that there was a lot of space for it, and it told me one thing; Vaughn was it.

Vaughn was the one to make me feel alive.

Vaughn was the one my heart beat for.

Vaughn was, quite simply, the one.

But it would be a cold day in Hell before I ever told him any of that. We couldn't be together, even if we wanted to be. He was everything that my father – that I – didn't want my life to be. He was a Blood Rose. My father's all-but declared heir. He was about as far away from my ambitions of a clean and good life as I could get. Not even taking into consideration the fact my dad would kill him for touching me.

So, being together? Not a thing that could or would ever happen.

But Jesus.

Kissing him, I didn't give a shit.

My arms wrapped around him tighter. My body pressed to his. His hand dropped to my arse, and he gripped me hard. It was so damned sexy, and I know I moaned against his lips. That only made him squeeze me harder, and I liked that even more.

When we finally pulled apart, we just took a moment to look into each other's eyes. Whatever I found in his, I was sure that he found it in mine as well. That certainty I'd felt? The very rightness of it all? He'd felt it too.

Then, I saw the arrogant charm flash in his eyes. He licked his lip as though he was still savouring me before he said, "You're mine now, Magenta."

VAUGHN: THREE

Ha.

Ha!

She'd fucking kissed me.

She'd slid my hand up her leg and kissed me.

She wanted me. She was dripping for me. And then she fucking kissed me.

I was on top of the fucking world, regardless of the glare she was giving me.

"I told you not to read into it," she huffed.

I smirked. "And I told you, the moment your lips touched me again, you're mine."

She took a couple of steps away from me, then stormed back to poke me in the chest. "You can't just go around claiming people!"

I shrugged. "I think I gave you plenty of warning, darling. You knew what you were doing. Are you angrier you gave in to me or that you 'cheated' on your 'boyfriend'?" And yeah, I layered on as much sarcastic snark as I could just to push her buttons.

Fury rippled over her face, and she just looked fucking sexier. "Maybe I'm just pissed that you're a poor winner!" she snapped.

My smirk grew. "You're crowning me winner? My commiserations to the Police Chief's wankstain."

"I am *not* leaving him for you!"

I chuckled as I closed the distance between us again. “Maybe not tonight, Magenta.”

“Maybe not ever!”

“Why?” I teased as I took her chin in my hand. “You don’t need to worry about your reputation, darling.”

She spluttered. “My reputation? You think I’m worried about my reputation?” Her eyes went wide as though maybe she’d just realised that was exactly what she was worried about.

“No one could blame you being unable to resist fate, Magenta.”

“Ooh!” she huffed, and I wondered what choice words she was bottling up. When she didn’t say anything more, I realised that she was actually at a loss for words.

So, I decided to hit that final button. “And my woman would never cheat on me.”

She actually slapped me so hard my head whipped sideways. As I looked back to her, I gave her my biggest smile.

“Kinky, darling.”

Her finger was in my chest, and she was leaning dangerously close to me. “You think you know anything about my kinks, Saint?” she sneered. “You wish you knew half of them.”

I nodded. “Yes, darling, I do.” I wrapped my arm around her back and pulled her tight to me to whisper in her ear. “And I can’t wait to show you all of mine.”

I felt the small tremor that ran through her as she pulled away to look at me in surprise. But nestled in the surprise was heat. So, like the cheeky bastard she made me, I ducked forward and pressed a kiss to her lips. For the space of just a couple of heartbeats, she kissed me back. Hungry. Needy. So damned sexy. But, when she realised her hand was slipping up around my shoulder, she pushed me away.

Her eyes raked over my cocky grin, and she frowned as her jaw clenched in utter fury.

"You insufferable arsehole!"

"Oh, love," I chastised. "I've no doubt you could *suffer* me just fine."

She took a deep breath. One step towards me with her mouth open. Mouth snapped shut and a step away. One more step towards me with her finger jutted at me. Then she scrunched her face in annoyance and stormed off.

I took my own deep breath and rearranged the aching rod in my jeans as I watched her arse sashay away from me through the crowd. "Fucking hell," I muttered to myself.

She didn't stop until she got to Clove and Iago. They'd found a booth, and she dropped in beside them.

"Poor choice, love," I said to myself as I strode over, casual as you please, and took the seat next to her, boxing her in.

Maggie pushed against me. "What are you doing now?"

I looked to Iago and Clove as though I had no idea why she'd be pissed at me. "Also sitting with our friends. Did you want me to get you a drink first, darling?"

She crossed her arms and slunk in her seat while I exchanged humour with Iago and Clove. I knew Iago would always be on my side of this battle, regardless of what Daddy McCallan would do to me if he knew what game I was playing with his only daughter. But I was surprised by Clove's support.

I gave her a wink. "Not going to tell me to keep my hands to myself?"

Clove hid her amusement as Maggie turned her glare on her best friend. "I don't berate anything consensual," was Clove's very diplomatic answer.

I gave her a nod. "Thank you."

"Oh, don't thank me. You still have to convince her."

"I am right here," was Maggie's interjection as she sat up violently, leaning on the table towards Clove. "And I don't need convincing. There's consensual and then there's regretful."

"And then there's denial," Clove added.

Iago and I snorted as Maggie's glare deepened.

"How many drinks have you had?" Maggie accused her.

Clove shrugged. "Many?" she suggested as Maggie rolled her eyes. "You said you were fine to drive!"

Maggie nodded as she sat back again. "I am fine to drive. Driving's not my problem. You siding with these idiots is my problem."

"I've told you," Clove insisted. "I'm not siding with them; I'm siding with your clit. And your clit wants–"

"OKAY!" Maggie said very loudly as she sat up again, throwing me a guilty look, and I felt fucking victorious. "Enough talk about my clit. I think I could do with that drink now." She turned a very pointed, furious glare on me.

I nodded. "Anything for my lady."

I saw her jaw twitch at how close I was to referring to her as something more serious than we would probably ever get the chance to be. I almost convinced myself that I saw longing in her eyes, but then she'd cleared her throat and was looking at Iago.

"Can you pick me up on Monday, please?" she asked him.

As he pretended to think about it, I scooted closer to her, put my hand on the seat behind her, dipped my lips to that spot where her jaw met her ear and pressed a kiss to it. I felt her breath catch and I saw the goosebumps chase over her skin. I felt the way she started to lean into me before she caught herself and slid away just enough to make her point.

"What do you want, baby?" I asked her with a grin.

She turned to me and our noses bumped. “Cola.”

I nodded. “Your wish is my command.”

She was not afraid to maintain eye contact as she huffed, “Then I wish for you to back the fuck off.”

I scrunched my nose at her. “Sorry, darling. You can’t wish away love.”

I saw what my words did to her by the look in her eyes. “I don’t lo–”

“Drink?” I asked the others quickly and I felt her anger emanating from her.

Iago gave me a look like he expected her to fucking shiv me right there, and Clove was busy grinning into her own glass.

“Beer,” he said.

Clove nodded. “Me, too.”

I inclined my head to them and slid out of the booth. While I waited at the bar, I watched Maggie lean across the table to the others. She looked pissed, confused and exasperated. Exactly where I wanted her. But I couldn’t afford to let her think too much about this. It had to be instinct. It had to be impulse. If her head came into it, she’d keep fighting what she felt.

But I also couldn’t push her too hard or she’d fight simply to spite me. Which, look, got me hard as well. It would also, if I didn’t play it right, meant she just walked. The game would be over and we’d both lose.

When I got back to the table with the four drinks, I kept my hands, my eyes and my tongue to myself. I felt her burning beside me. As a rule, I wasn’t into this negging bullshit. You went after what you wanted without tearing her down to get it. Hot and cold was a shitty way to show you were into someone. But I did my best to ignore Maggie outside anything other than polite conversation. If polite involved swearing like a sailor and talking about all manner of dirty things just so we could see Clove blush harder and harder the more drunk she got.

Maggie and I both needed the cooldown. Sexually and argumentatively. There was only so many harsh words we could sling at each other without causing irreparable damage and I wasn't anywhere near ready to give up yet.

It was after one when Clove's ankle rolled on the way to the bathroom and Maggie was climbing over me hurriedly to get out of the booth. Despite how much I wanted to make some innuendo out of it, I knew it wasn't the time. Clove needed her.

"Okay, I think it's time we got you home, miss," Maggie said as she tucked herself under Clove's arm.

They both wobbled and Maggie huffed.

"Why heels?" she muttered as she tried to keep her balance.

Iago was up in seconds. "I've got her. Where are you parked?"

Maggie let Iago pick Clove up, who giggled and cried, "My knight in shining armour."

Iago smirked at her. "Thanks for pointing out how sweaty I am" he joked, and she pressed her face to his shoulder as she giggled again.

I rolled my eyes, happening to catch Maggie's eye as I did. We shared a look that said 'yeah, they're both idiots'. Then she seemed to make some realisation as she chewed her lip and looked away from me.

"Uh, we're out the front," she said as she started heading for the door.

I looked at Iago, heavily suggesting that they take a second to themselves before following and hurried after her. About halfway across the parking lot, I caught her hand. She turned to me but didn't pull away from me.

"What, Vaughn?" she huffed.

I licked my lip in frustration. I had no idea. I was acting on that instinct I wish she'd just give into instead of letting her damned head get in the way. "I'll pick you up on Monday," was what I went with.

I saw her hesitate. Her mouth opened, then closed. Then she chewed her lip again.

"Please?" I was not above fucking begging her if I had to.

The Princes were allowed near her for the purposes of chauffeuring her. It was the one time I could guarantee alone time with her, and it be sanctioned. Provided one of the other twats didn't beg a ride from me as well.

Finally she let go of her lip, nodded and sighed. "Fine. Yes." She nodded again as I fought my smile. "Yes, you can…" She looked up at the sky like she was praying for patience before gently pulling her hand from mine. "I'll see you Monday morning, Vaughn."

I nodded to her. "Okay. See you Monday."

Iago and Clove appeared beside us, and Maggie helped him get Clove in the car.

"You are playing a fucking dangerous game," Iago muttered as he stepped back to me.

I watched Maggie get into the driver's side of Clove's car. "No one saw us."

"You don't know that."

Maggie started the car, then gave us both a companionable wave goodbye before driving off.

"I do," I told him. "I spent all fucking night finding a reason to send Roses home. Jason was the last one."

He scoffed humourlessly. "Yeah, because Frankliln's gits aren't likely to rat you out."

"If they even recognised me, the chance they recognised her is minimal."

"That's not nothing."

"I can't fucking help it!" I snapped, then took a breath and ran my hand through my hair as we watched the car drive off. "I can't help it, West. I'm fucking…"

"Gone for her?" he suggested.

I nodded. "And I can't be like you. I can't just pretend she'll be better off without me. I'm not that strong."

"I don't know what you're talking about," was Iago's quiet answer.

I huffed my own humourless breath. "Yeah. 'Course you don't."

"So, what's the plan?" he asked, clearly desperate to change the subject. "You what? Got her to kiss you and now what? What the fuck does that prove?"

"It proves she wants me, too."

"And the fact she has a boyfriend doesn't bother you at all?"

I grinned at him. "Not when she wants me."

He shook his head. "Mate, this is the most fucked up way to start…" He waved a vague hand at me, "…whatever the fuck you think this is going to become."

"It doesn't matter what it is," I told him honestly. "I'm hers and, before Blaise kills me for touching her, I'm gonna make her mine."

"That's still not a plan! Are you gonna find yourself a friar and get married in secret? Knock her up? I don't understand what you think you're going to achieve."

I shrugged again. "Me either."

Iago nodded in exasperation. "Oh. No. Good. Great. Just fucking great. I'm risking death by aiding and abetting you, and you don't even have a plan."

"Fuck, if you're going to be so dramatic, I'll make a fucking plan," I muttered.

"Oh, yay. What's your plan going to be then? You convince her to leave her boyfriend and the two of you run away together?"

"It's better if she doesn't leave him."

Iago scoffed incredulously. "Excuse me? What the fuck?"

I sighed. "There's no way I get out of this alive, West. Not if she's mine. Blaise will find out. It's what he does. And if he doesn't, maybe I'll go ahead and tell him."

"Why the fuck would you do that?" Iago's voice rose at least one octave in the middle of that sentence.

I swallowed. "So she still gets the life she wants to live. She gets that with him."

"Oh, my fucking God. Who's dramatic now? I would like you to acknowledge my impeccable willpower in not pointing out how whipped you must be to be putting quite literally your own life over her happiness."

"Very noble of you not to mention it." I whacked him, and he whacked me back.

We exchanged a few more rounds before he scrubbed his hand over his jaw.

"Fuck," he breathed. "Okay. Fine. If we're going all in, we're going all in. How are we doing it?"

I ran my hand over my jaw again. "The playoff game."

"What about it?"

"That's as far as I've got."

Iago growled in frustration and actually stomped his foot like he was trying really hard not to punch me. He took a deep breath and turned a look of utter serenity on me. "We need to work on your planning skills."

So, we went inside, found a booth and did just that.

An hour later when I sat back down after visiting the little boys' room, he showed me a text chain on his phone.

Clove
It's Mags. Home safe. Thanks for tonight.

I
Ta. Want me to tell V? 😉

Clove
Fuck. Right. Off.

I
I'll give him your love 😘

Clove
Be my guest. Declare my everlasting love to him.

I
Really?

That was the end of the chain and I looked to Iago more desperately than I should have.

"And?" I snapped.

His grin nearly earned him a slap, but he took his phone back and then showed me a different chain.

Maggie
I am not having this conversation on Clove's phone. It will confuse her to no end.
If you want to meet the pointy end of Mr Bubbles, be. My. Guest.

I

Our little secret. You like him, don't you?

Maggie

I like being fucked absolutely raw too, but that doesn't make it good for me.

I

I did not need all that information.

Maggie

Then be more careful what you wish for.

I

Okay, I'll try.
I wish for you to admit you love V.

And that was it.

"She said 'too'?" was his offering.

I dropped my head onto the table. He patted the back of it, and I batted his hand away. "Don't fucking patronise me."

"I'm not. It's called sympathy."

"Empathy," I corrected him just a little spitefully, knowing this was probably how he'd felt every day for the last like four years.

"Empathy," he agreed so softly I was sure I wasn't supposed to have heard it.

CHAPTER SEVEN

I should have known that after Rizzo's, Vaughn wasn't going to play fair.

He picked me up every morning from Dad's and he drove me back home after school. Just him and me in his black GT, much to Ezra's annoyance since Cairo was in one of his moods, Iago's car was in the shop, and Stone was busy with football practice before their big playoff game on Friday night.

So it was a good twenty minutes twice a day with the hulking form of the sexiest man alive sitting next to me. And we both knew how that made me feel.

Especially after he always held my door open for me, finding some excuse to touch me as I got in. A hand to steady me. 'Accidentally' standing in the way. 'Oh, I forgot to move that off the seat for you, let me move it and whoops I copped a feel of side-boob on the way'. Where 'copped a feel' was a sensual caress that left me breathless.

At school, he was no longer trying to tease me with other girls. If anything, it was the opposite. None of his energy went to anyone else but me. I told myself I didn't feel anything about that, but even I knew I was lying.

That morning, Vaughn had rung the doorbell and hung back with Dad as I got into the car. I saw them do some complicated handshake thing that ended with their arms around each other,

Dad's hand on Vaughn's head. I watched Dad say something to Vaughn and, when Vaughn pulled back, there was a hint of a smile playing at his lips. He nodded, gave Dad a fist bump, then headed to the car.

"Hm," I mused as he started the car. "Dad sure does believe in you. Like you. Take you into his trusted confidence. It's almost like he doesn't know that you broke his number one rule."

"It's almost like don't want him to know either," he replied, just as sarcastically wondrous.

I scoffed. "So now I can't be forgiving, it must be because I'm into you?"

He shrugged. "You're more than one thing."

"I'm with Parker. I'm going to uni. I am going to live in East Ham and be a primary school teacher and have nothing to do with Rose life! Where exactly do you think you figure in that plan?" I had no idea why my heart twinged.

He licked his lip like he was keeping his choicest words to himself. "Exactly whose life are you living, Magenta?"

I blinked. "And what is that supposed to mean?"

"Are you actually living the life you want to live? Or the life the stuck-up fuckers of East Ham want you to live just so they can deem you failed, and all will feel right in the world because people couldn't possibly be any more than what their birth makes them."

"Oh and I suppose you know all about that. You who are *so* much more than your birth, Vaughn. Right?"

"Whose point are you trying to make?"

I huffed, crossed my arms, and slouched in the seat. Damn him starting this while we were driving and leaving was not an option. "I don't know. But what is wrong with wanting a life that follows society's laws and morals?"

"Absolutely nothing. *If* that's what you want."

"Well, I don't want to be a murderous, drug dealing psychopath!"

"We're not all murderous, drug dealing psychopaths. Plenty of old ladies–"

"OH!" I cried, shutting him up. "Oh, no. You are not just about to suggest that Blaise McCallan would ever let his little girl be someone's old lady? I know you're not that stupid."

"Tell me something honestly, Magenta."

I looked at him, scared of what he's ask. But I nodded. "Fine."

"Is that his rule because he wants to keep you pure and untouched by our criminal ways, or is it just because he wants to protect the life that he *thinks* you want?"

My arms tightened around me as I looked out the window. I knew which answer I wanted to be true. And not just because it would make me less off-limits to a Rose. Theoretically of course.

"You looking for a loophole, Saint?" I huffed.

"Not at all. I knew well before I kissed you at the Laneway that made my life forfeit. I just hate to see you busting your balls for those arseholes when they will never truly see you as one of them. You will always be Blaise McCallan's daughter. Even if they forget for a while, they will turn on you the first chance they get if you let them."

"Parker's not like that."

"They're all like that."

"And you're not? Judging me for my life choices and wanting to be a good person?"

"I judge you for living a lie," he said, and I felt it like a kick to the gut. "You don't accept yourself, so how do you expect anyone else to accept you?"

I felt weird. Annoyed and defensive and called-out and pissed off and vulnerable and attacked. "So you're prepared to die just to fuck someone you don't accept?" I snapped.

He sighed. "Magenta, there is no world, no life, no future now where you are not mine. For who you are, not who you pretend to be." He shook his head, then said more to himself., "Then again, if you didn't, maybe I'd have seen it sooner..."

"Seen what, Vaughn?"

He shook his head again. "Nothing, Maggie."

He seemed reluctant to say more and I didn't think I really wanted to know what it was if *he* was reluctant to talk about it.

We were almost at school when my phone went off.

Freddy
Tickets are booked for Saturday afternoon, and Dad said we can have the car.

Mags
Sounds perfect. But I expect my date to pay for the Freezes.

Freddy
I've been saving up ALL month! Unless you want cherry. I'm not paying for that.

Mags
Cherry is the only good flavour!

Freddy
I'm not buying you that.

Mags
Then I'm not buying you Funzone tokens.

Freddy

You can have cherry.

"I *know* your boyfriend isn't texting you," Vaughn said lazily, as though we hadn't been sitting in sudden silence for the last ten minutes.

"Boyfriend?" I said absently as I replied to Freddy then blinked. "I mean, what about Parker?" *Real smooth, Maggie.*

"You never look like that because of him."

I wriggled in my seat. "Like what?"

"Actually happy."

I cleared my throat. "I was organising a date," I told him honestly.

"Oh, how formal of you," he teased, affecting a snooty air. "Will you take the horse and buggy?"

I was distracted by Freddy's reply. "Freddy's not keen on horses."

Vaughn shot me a look of surprise. "Freddy?"

Fuck. I mentally rolled my eyes at myself. "Yes. I was organising a date with Freddy."

"Freddy?"

"My little brother."

"I fucking know who Freddy is."

"Then what exactly surprises you, Vaughn? Or are you just disgusted some of us play happy families for more than one week a month?"

The glance he gave me as he turned the corner was unidentifiable. "I *like* that it was just your brother putting that smile on your face."

"You...? You like that it was–?"

"Contrary to popular belief, Magenta," he interrupted, "I'm a big fan of the truth. I like it. I give it whenever possible." He pulled into the school parking lot. "I'm going to be honest with you and the truth is, yes, I'm fucking glad it was just your brother that made you smile like that."

My eyes narrowed as he found a park. "Why?"

He turned off the car and grinned at me cheekily. "Because it proves me right."

I huffed. "Fine. I'll bite–"

"Fuck. If only."

I glared at him. "–Right about what?"

"Right that the Police Chief's premature ejaculate isn't right for you."

"Oh, and you think you are?" I scoffed as I picked up my bag. My hand was on the door handle when he replied.

"I know just the thought of me makes your heart race. I know that every time you bite your lip, you're thinking about me between your legs or trying not to smile at me. I know it doesn't matter if I'm right for you or not because you still want me more."

I was angry enough that I didn't want to argue with him anymore. I didn't need him telling me things I already knew and was studiously ignoring. The whole point was to ignore them, not have the source of all my dirtiest fantasies rub them in my goddamned face!

So, I picked up my bag, got out of the car, slammed the door terrifically satisfyingly, and stalked to the school building, fully ignoring Iago as I passed him.

"What the fuck did you say to her now?" he laughed to Vaughn behind me.

"Maggie's got a very complicated relationship with the truth," was Vaughn's cocky-arse response. "She doesn't like to hear it."

I barrelled into the building, leaving them to laugh it up.

Vaughn could act like pursuing me was fine. Iago could be supporting him all he liked, but the fact was; Vaughn would die if Dad found out. At least one guy had probably died for a lot less. So the Princes might have been able to laugh and joke and act like this was any other seduction, but it was the whole situation that was complicated.

As I headed up the corridor, I saw Lettie all over Parker and it did a lot to take my mind off Vaughn. Two seconds sooner and they might have been kissing for all the distance between them. Parker saw me, grinned tightly, and pushed Lettie away from him. As she stepped back, she rubbed her finger over the corner of her mouth, and I mentally rolled my eyes at her inanity.

Parker pushed his way between the others to me and, after my conversation with Vaughn, my smile was forced.

"Babe, there you are."

I nodded, glaring at Vaughn as he 'innocently' brushed past us on his way to his locker. "There was traffic."

Parker's eyes followed Vaughn for a moment, then looked back to me. "Oh. Okay."

"I'm not surprised," Lettie said. "East Ham is the *only* place to be. You know that, Maggie."

She was all passive-aggression and I wondered how long I'd been ignoring it. Had it been there on the first day of school when she and Gloria gushed about me and Parker? Or was my conversation with Vaughn playing on my insecurities and making me overreact?

I gave her my best smile. "Sure is." Patting Parker's arm, I told him, "I need to find Clove. I'll see you later?"

He nodded and leant in for a kiss, but I turned my head at the last minute, looking down at my phone like that had been the reason I'd turned away.

Giving them all another very forced, saccharine smile, I hurried off. Vaughn was up the corridor, like he'd been watching me. And the absolute cocky amusement in his eyes told me he knew why I'd really turned my head.

He was hovering at a corner next to a cleaning cupboard. So, on my way past, I pushed him around the corner and dragged him into the cupboard before shutting the door.

"This you giving in, love? I hope you've got your funeral dress dry cleaned."

I was so pissed off with him that absolute drivel poured out of my mouth. Drivel, lies, and something I hadn't once thought about. Ever. "No, Vaughn! Not happening! You're just going to have to live to a ripe old age and watch while I go off and marry Parker!"

Marrying Parker was apparently so far off my radar that my stomach actually tried rebelling against the idea. Like it knew I never wanted that. Ever. The thought of marrying someone else, meanwhile...

He squeezed my chin in his hand, his nose dug into my cheek as he growled in my ear, "Magenta Saint suits you far better than Maggie Bates, love."

My heart did that thing again. The thing it had done in the car just before when I'd basically told him that he had no place in my life.

And now that someone had said it out loud, 'Maggie Bates' did kind of make me sound like a tragic spinster in an Austen novel. Or worse. Not that I needed another reason to know that being with Parker wasn't the right choice anymore. After all, it wasn't *reasons* that were stopping me from ending whatever was happening with Parker, it was fear.

My hand tightened on Vaughn's shirt at his chest as I pressed my body against his. "You proposing to me, Vaughn?" I sassed.

His hand still on my jaw, his other one slid up my leg and coaxed it around his hip. I wrapped it around him, holding our bodies close together. He gripped the flesh of my upper thigh – more arse really – hard, his fingers digging into me in a way that had heat pooling right where he was nestled against me.

"Would you like that? Me begging you to be mine?"

I pulled back only enough to look into his eyes. "It wouldn't be the first time."

I saw the snarl ripple through his eyes. The fury. The barely-contained need to force me to submit to him. My world was shadowed. His was pitch black.

"Ask me nicely and I might give you what you want, love," he purred against my lips, and I fought the need for more. Fought the way my body tried to follow his when he took them away.

"I have a boyfriend," I reminded him, while reminding myself that a white lie never hurt anyone.

"So you say." A cocky mischief lit those deep sapphire pools as he thrust against me. "But you don't want him."

"I don't want *you*," I lied. He let me push him away from me. "I won't walk away from something good just for a chauvinistic player." I took a step towards him and ran my finger down his chest. "You just want what you can't have, baby."

"And what about you?" he purred.

"What about me?"

"You call the little snitch your boyfriend, but what promises has he made you? Because I would promise you the world, *baby*."

Damn him. Damn Vaughn Saint and whatever cursed vagina he crawled out of. Because holy shit. Lines like that were in serious danger of working on me.

"You gunning for Iago's title, Vaughn?" I said snidely.

A snarl chased a grin over his face. "Oh, no, love. You deserve the world and I'll fucking give it to you. No dreams. No empty promises. Just everything you could ever want."

I mean, it sounded amazing, but I had to remember he was the goddamn Prince of Thorns. "There's a flaw in your logic. How does your death figure into that? I can't want you *and* want you dead, can I?"

I think that was the first actual smile I'd ever seen on his face. It was small and it was cocky as sin, but it was still a smile. "That's just it. The best of both worlds, Magenta. You get to have me – spend the rest of your boring suburban life knowing you were the last thing I ever wanted – and then you're rid of me. Your precious little snitch none the wiser as to that good girl mask you wear being total bullshit."

I had to argue with him because otherwise I was scaling him. "It's not a mask and it's not bullshit," I snapped.

There went another smile as he stepped back up to me. Crowding me. So close. But not close enough. "You want them all to believe you're some sweet innocent little princess, Magenta, but I know the truth of what lurks in your heart. In your soul."

"And what exactly *does* lurk in my soul, Vaughn?"

His fingers slipped around my neck, so very softly. My nipples tightened and my clit throbbed. "You are so much better than them. You are strong. You are fierce. But you hide it all away for their approval. You don't owe them shit, baby girl. They should be begging for yours." His nose pressed into my cheek as he whispered in my ear. "You don't apologise to them. They apologise to you."

My hand went to his chest, but I wasn't pushing him away. My fingers gripped the material of his shirt tightly as my face nuzzled into his. He leant right into me as well.

"Why are you doing this?" I whispered, my eyes closed like I could pretend this was all a dream and that made it okay.

"I told you, if you kissed me again, that I'd be playing for keeps. You're mine, Princess McCallan. Even if you want me only half as much as I want you, you know it's true." My eyes opened and locked with his as he said, "You feel it, too."

My heart swelled and clenched and fluttered all at once. I didn't know how much longer I could – wanted – to resist him. Honestly, I'd never really *wanted* to resist him. But it had been the right thing to do. It had *felt* like the right thing to do.

All I felt now was that what he was saying was true. I'd known it since I'd kissed him at Rizzo's. Since he'd kissed me at the Laneway, to be honest. My clit throbbed for him. My heart beat for him. My body longed for him. It was so wrong that it was starting to feel right.

As I reached up to him and closed the distance between us, I said not at all believably against his lips, "I have a boyfriend."

His lips brushed mine as he replied, "I don't fucking care."

"If I kiss you again, what will you think that means?" I asked him, feeling slightly breathless.

"I think it means you want me, baby, even if you're pretending otherwise."

This whole thing would be way easier if he didn't see right through me. "And what's the punishment?"

I felt his smile against his lips and that lapis lazuli sparkled. "Depends how hard you want it."

I frowned. "Last time, you said I'd be yours. Will you take the next one as acceptance of your proposal?" I sassed.

"The next one, baby?" he teased.

I mean, our lips were touching with every single word between us. Based on his last rules, this would count.

"Hypothetically," I argued.

He grinned against me as he full on just picked me up and coaxed my legs around his waist. "Oh, hypothetically?" he teased.

"What are you doing?" I breathed, my heart pounding.

Ever so gently, he pressed me against the door and thrust. My whole body came alive.

His lips dipped to my neck. "What do you want me to do?"

My hands gripped his shoulders as my head fell back against the door. He thrust again.

"Do you want me to put you down, darling?"

I couldn't speak. I couldn't breathe. I couldn't do anything but give myself over to him in the moment. My hands slid into his hair as he thrust against me again.

Just as his lips were trailing up my cheek, just about to touch mine, the bell for first lesson rang and I realised what in the hell I was doing. I pushed against him, and he dropped my feet gently to the floor.

I was breathing heavily but, this time, I wasn't the only one.

"You want me," he said.

I looked at the door, hearing mass movement behind it. If we left now, people would see and people would talk.

"Fine," I spat, as much to stall for time as I knew there was only so long that I could lie about it when shit like this kept happening. "Fine, Vaughn. I want you. But some of us can say no to the things that aren't good for us."

"Can you walk away from your addictions, darling?"

My breath caught. "Who says you're an addiction?"

His fingers brushed under my chin as he looked down into my eyes. “Takes one to know one, baby.”

I swallowed hard and I knew that was all the answer he needed.

“Give me one chance,” he begged.

“For what?” I asked.

“For us.”

My heart fluttered in my chest, but it fucking tried jumping out of my throat when a knock came at the door.

Vaughn wrapped his fingers around my wrist. “Please?”

The knock came again. Vaughn swore and ripped the door open.

“What?” he snarled at Iago.

Iago poked his head in and almost looked disappointed by the decency going on. “Clear. She won’t want to be any later than necessary.”

“Fucking…” Vaughn sighed, scrubbing a hand over his chin.

I picked up my bag that had dropped at some point in our altercation and slipped out of the cupboard.

“Maggie!” Vaughn hissed. “Maggie, that’s not a no!”

I could only say ‘no’ to him so many times in one morning. So, I turned back to him and bit my lip pointedly. If he was so sure he knew what that meant, then he could guess what my answer was.

CHAPTER EIGHT

The rest of that week, Parker was in his usual pre-game pep, which conveniently meant that he hadn't noticed I'd been a little absent and distracted. He was on top of the world, and he didn't even suspect that I might not be there with him.

"Tonight is going to be epic, babe," he said as he wrapped his arms around my waist.

I nodded to him. "Totally epic." *Jesus, that was wanky.*

"I've got permission from Coach for you and Clove to ride with the team."

Yay, an almost hour-long bus trip with some post-match sweaty teenage boys. My dream date. But I smiled. "Great. Thanks."

He grinned at me. "Fuck. Tonight is going to be epic!"

I tried to be excited. But then, was he just referring to the game? Or was he going to ask me to be official tonight? We'd already fucked, so it wasn't like that first was on the table. And that, I realised, was the main hindrance my usual ability to fake excitement over football just then.

Was Parker going to make it official tonight?

While I was his preferred hook up and we were heading towards monogamy, I knew he'd had a few other hook ups since it started looking like we'd become a real couple. So I hadn't felt all that guilty over Vaughn.

So why did I feel guilty over Parker? Like I was cheating on–

"Oh, shit."

I didn't realise I'd spoken out loud until Parker gave me a confused smile and a, "What's wrong?"

I forced a warmer smile. "No. Nothing. I just realised I think I left my charger at home."

He laughed like he thought I was stupid. "You can use mine."

I nodded. "Of course. Cool."

But it wasn't cool because I'd just realised that I had a very glaring issue.

I just... As nice as Parker was, and skilled and attentive and amazing, he just wasn't really registering on my radar anymore. I liked him, but I liked… No. I didn't like Vaughn, I just wanted him more. But giving into that… Giving up a future with Parker for something that had no future? That seemed insane. More than insane. It was just plain stupid.

There was only one thing for it; get over Vaughn. However I had to do that. Get over Vaughn and then give it a real go with Parker. If nothing had happened with Parker and I by the end of the holidays, then I'd just flat out ask him to make it official for him. I was a strong, independent woman, I could totally be the one to start the conversation.

"I need to go to my locker," I told him. "I'll see you later?"

He nodded and leant in for a kiss. I gave him one absently, smiled on total autopilot and then headed for my locker. Clove was waiting for me, and she gave me a smile as I wandered over.

"You good?"

I shrugged. "I have made an admission to myself I'd rather I hadn't."

Her eyes went wide with excitement. "Oh, yes?"

I looked at her as I pulled open my locker, then set about looking for my book. "Don't you start."

"Why are you acting like it's a bad thing?"

"Because it's not a good thing." As though I knew what was on her mind, I added, "If you say it'll be good for my clit, I'm walking away."

"What's Kenicki's?" Clove surprised me by asking as I rifled in my locker.

"Uh, it's a joke among the younger Roses. It's what they call their hang out. It was named to rival Rizzo's." I paused and looked at her. "I'm not supposed to know about Kenicki's. How do you know about it?"

She held up a piece of paper. "This fell out of your locker. I read it."

She did her best to look sheepish, not that I cared. Clove and I didn't have secrets. And it wasn't like the note was folded or stuck down. There was no attempt to keep its secrets.

Kenicki's. Tonight. I won't read into it. V

How could three sentences – seven words – say so much?

No, I wasn't supposed to know about Kenicki's. But Vaughn specifically mentioning it was his way of reminding me he knew I wasn't as innocent and naive as I was supposed to be. It may have even been a reminder that he was okay with it. Well, he'd be the only one.

He knew tonight was the big football game and, as Parker's potential future girlfriend, I should be at *his* after party at the Hut. The Blood Roses kids and their closest compatriots would be having a rival party, and their parties were always held at Kenicki's. If I went to Kenicki's, Vaughn knew that would be me choosing him over Parker. Even if it was just for one night.

Which made the last sentence annoy me even more. He wouldn't read into it? There was no way I was going to Kenicki's and it meaning nothing.

And why hadn't he said anything in the car that morning?

"He's offering you a free pass!" Clove hissed excitedly.

I started nodding, then frowned. "What's a free pass?"

"You know," Clove said. "One night only of whatever you want him to do to you, and then you can pretend it never happened."

"In my dreams," I scoffed.

There was a very pointed pause before she hissed, "So? Are you going to go?"

"The Rams are playing the Storms tonight, though," I reminded her.

She rolled her eyes. "So?"

"It's a playoff game." Whatever that meant. I didn't give two shits about football, but I could pretend for Parker. "In Everdale…"

She shrugged. "I am not seeing the problem. We're on the team bus there. We cheer – yay Rams – and we come back to go to the party at Kenicki's."

I looked at her. "You're coming, too?"

"Duh. Of course, I am."

Now I had two conundrums. On one hand, I could never take away a chance for Clove to hang out with Iago and there was no way I was letting her go to Kenicki's without me. On the other hand, could going to Kenicki's do what I'd just decided needed doing? Would it be what I needed to get Vaughn out of my system and get over him.

Of course, the timing was…awkward. Parker and I hadn't talked about it, but I knew the expectations as well as anyone.

Then again, if we hadn't talked about it, maybe Parker wasn't expecting anything?

I bit my lip. "I'll think about it."

I was still thinking about it as Clove and I went to find some seats as the teams warmed up that night. Iago had found us and in no uncertain terms told us that we would be sitting with him.

I would have argued, but I realised that it was not negotiable. And it didn't take long for him to confirm exactly why that was.

"Fucking Monsters," Iago muttered as we pressed through the throng of people.

"Who are the Monsters?" Clove asked him.

"The Monster Aces. Rival club," I told her. "Like Stone and Cliff are Blood Roses, half the Storm are Monsters."

Iago shook his head. "Fucking football. Bringing the Blood Roses and Monsters to 'neutral' territory. Neutral my fucking arse. Everdale should be Blood Rose territory, and I don't fucking care what pissing Grant Franklin has to say about it."

I shared a humoured look with Clove, then realised she didn't know who Iago was talking about. "Franklin is the head Monster."

"Ah." Clove nodded.

"Not that you should know any of that," Iago said, but I saw the humour in his eyes telling me he certainly didn't give a shit.

I shrugged. "It's difficult not to pick some stuff up."

He shook his head. "Your old man would kill me if he knew you knew that stuff."

"Dad would kill you for sitting with me at a football game," I pointed out and he inclined his head.

"Touche, ma'am."

“Why *are* you sitting with us?” Clove asked. Iago and I shared a look. Clove nodded. “The Monsters?”

Iago nodded as we took our seats; him, Clove, me. Vaughn was sitting in front of us with Cairo and a couple of other Roses. Ezra was behind us with a guy I was pretty sure was called Campbell and another Rose I only knew by sight. And to my right, yet another Rose took a seat. Although, I probably wasn’t supposed to know any of them either.

I hadn’t been to an away game against the Storm before. I knew all about them, but I barely went to the games when they were at home if I could avoid it. And it didn’t take a genius to work out that the Monster Aces had the Blood Roses on edge. Clove and I being flanked by nine of them and all. And those were the ones I recognised.

“Was the protection detail Dad’s idea?” I asked as I leant over to Iago.

“Not quite.” Iago’s eyes darted to Vaughn almost guiltily, and I couldn’t help but follow them.

My eyes narrowed in question when they returned to Iago and he gave me a ‘so, what?’ shrug before opening Clove’s bottle for her and passing it back while diving headfirst into conversation with her like he wanted to avoid talking about Vaughn’s possessiveness.

“I heard you were undecided about Kenicki’s,” Ezra said as he leant down to me.

I was a little surprised that all the Princes seemed to know Vaughn had extended the invitation to be honest.

I gave him a wild shrug. “I can’t see why I’d have a reason to go to Kenicki’s over The Hut.”

It pleased me to see Vaughn’s shoulders tighten at my words, but he otherwise ignored me.

"Oh, come on, Mags," Iago whined. "We throw a wicked party, and you know we're gonna have the good shit."

I smirked at him. "I don't care what kind of shit you have. I'm more concerned about the calibre of people," I teased, and he laughed.

"Oh-ho! Oh, you're fucking in for it now. You goddamned snob, Maggie McCallan. *We* are your *people* and you're going to do us dirty like that?"

He wanted to throw down? I could throw down. "My people?" I said, trying to school my smile under the guise of our play-fight. "You're common criminals."

Ezra tutted. "Darlin', there's nothing common about a single one of us."

Iago nodded as he put his hand on his chest solemnly. "We're born of only the purest felonious stock."

Cairo spared him an icy look. "Some of us, anyway," he drawled, and I bit my lip against laughing at him.

Cairo was not the kind of guy you laughed at unless you wanted to hurt. And not in a good way.

The Prince of Agony was the torture guy. Not that I was supposed to know that. At least, I'm sure I wasn't supposed to know it was more than just rumour. But, where Vaughn left you bleeding and Iago promised you the world before ripping it out from under you and Ezra went through life completely emotionless and Stone was the killer who'd do it for the sheer enjoyment, Cairo was the one they called in for information. Or, at least, that was what they were training him up to be.

Even with only one foot in the seedy underbelly of the Roses, I knew that these boys – as deadly and dark as they were – were still only shadows of the pitch black they would be in a few years' time. When they'd been not just trained and initiated, but fully immersed in the life. They were bad now, but they would only get worse – or better, depending on how much value you placed on their proficiency.

When it came to pain, Cairo was already a master. Physical. Emotional. Mental. He wielded words as expertly as weapons to bring you exactly what his moniker promised; agony. And his speciality was leaving as little trace as possible. You wanted to send a message? Send in Vaughn or Stone. You want no one to know you'd intercepted a message not intended for you? Cairo was your man.

"Come on," Iago pressed, nudging Clove. "Tell her she has to come."

Clove nodded at me as she sipped her drink. "You do because I'm going, and you can hardly let me around the hooligans alone. All sweet and naïve and innocent that I am." Clove knew who she was – loved who she was – and I loved her all the more for it.

I shook my head. "I said I'd think about it!"

"So think about it as a 'yes'," Iago laughed.

I shook my head. "Maybe."

They spent the rest of the game trying to convince me. Even Cairo seemed to feel obliged to get me there. Probably only for Vaughn's sake, but he did it anyway.

Sometime in the third quarter of the game, Iago took an exaggerated bow at me. "Okay, let me try this again. I wish for you to come to Kenicki's with us tonight."

"MAGGIE!" I heard Parker calling. By the sound of it, he'd been calling for a while.

I turned from Iago, a smile still on my face at his ridiculousness. But it dropped at the sight of Parker's furious expression. He waved his arms at me in a 'what the fuck?' kind of action. I gave him a return 'what do you mean?' and pretended I had absolutely no idea why he'd be pissy.

"Oh, are you in trouble now?" Iago teased and I only elbowed him once Parker was distracted by his coach again.

"Shut up," I told him.

"Come to Kenicki's," Iago said. "You want to get chewed out all night for not giving a shit about football, or you want to spend all night getting 'chewed' out..." He winked and I rolled my eyes.

"Yeah, I don't think chewed is what you want going on there, Dreamer."

"Oh, Mags," he laughed, and it was full of amused sympathy that had me blushing. "Honey. Has Mr Police Chief Wannbe Poser *never* used his teeth on you?" He leant towards me like the next bit was a secret. "Because I know someone who knows how to use them *very well*."

My eyes darted to Vaughn in front of us. He was sitting with his head bowed with Cairo. But, as though he knew what Iago was saying, he turned back to look at me with a cocky heat in his eyes as he dragged his tongue over his lip.

I didn't doubt that Vaughn did know how to use his teeth – among many other things – very well. I'd only had them on my neck in the barest of hints and I knew I wanted more.

But that was decidedly not the point.

I cleared my throat and looked to Parker to find him glaring at me.

Between his displeasure and the ideas of Vaughn's pleasure... It was weak but I knew what my choice was. I held up my hands and smiled. "Fine. Fine. Kenicki's it is!"

There was an unnecessary cheer that rang out among the Roses around us, which coincided quite conveniently with Stone slamming into one of the Storms. The guy went down and did not get up. The whistle blew and Stone was eventually sent off. We watched him stalk off the grounds and through the tunnel to the changerooms.

"Fuck. Illegal tackle. Shall we go?" Iago said to those around us.

"Anything to beat this fucking traffic," Cairo muttered.

The Princes escorted us out of the stadium, and we waited for Stone at Ezra's pick up. There was a bike on the back, and I suddenly realised that they only had one car between the five of them.

"Uh…we can just get the bus back?" I suggested.

Iago looked at me. "You want to be stuck in a bus with Mr Pissy for an hour?"

Yeah, no. Not so much.

"How are we all going to fit?" Clove asked.

Iago kicked his head at Vaughn. "He's got his bike."

"That's still six in the car," I said.

Iago looked at me like I'd missed the fundamental point. "Someone's riding with Vaughn."

My heart thudded and my mouth went dry. "Who?"

"None of the boys," Iago said with an apologetic shrug. "Is it gonna be you or Clove squashed in the back between me and Stone?"

Well, if those were the options, I knew what my answer would be. Take away Clove's chance to have her body pressed against Iago's? Not something I could do, even to avoid riding on the back of Vaughn's bike. I sighed and held my hand out to Vaughn. I wasn't allowed around their world, but I knew the drill.

"Give me the fucking jacket," I grumbled.

His shit-stirring grin rivalled Iago's as he shucked his jacket off and passed it to me. I knew the deal about wearing a Roses' jacket, but I ignored it as I pulled it on. I also ignored it as I realised it was still warm from his body heat. That it still smelled like him. I resisted the urge to bury my nose in it as I zipped it up.

"Mags on the bike?" Stone asked as he wandered over, his duffel over his shoulder.

Iago nodded. "I kinda didn't think about that when we left. Coach gonna miss you?"

Stone shrugged. "Coach can get fucked."

Iago nodded. "Fair."

Stone threw his duffel in the pick up's tray and helped Vaughn get the bike down. Vaughn pulled on his helmet and passed a spare to me.

As he climbed on, I looked the bike over. They'd all seemed concerned about it at the Laneway the other week, and I wondered if they'd fixed whatever was wrong with it.

"It's not the same bike," Vaughn chuckled, and I looked at him quickly.

"It's not?"

He shook his head as he held his arm out to help me on, a smirk playing at his lips. "Can you really not tell the difference?"

I pulled the helmet on and climbed onto the seat behind him. "Why would I be able to, Vaughn, when Dad likes to pretend that I don't even know what a motorcycle is?"

"Remind me to show you the difference sometime," he said, and I felt his humour rumble through him.

Something else rumbled through *me*. Excitement. Apprehension. Nerves. And something warm and bright that snuck into my chest at the idea that he wanted to spend more time with me, that he wanted to show me his world and share what was important to him.

I went to push it away, then remembered tonight was my free pass. If I let myself enjoy Vaughn and the way he made me feel for this one night, then maybe I could wake up tomorrow and be over him.

VAUGHN: FOUR

I didn't fucking care what Iago's thing was. Keep his distance because he was so far gone for her? How did that even work? How in the hell did he do it? And how had he done it for *years*?

It had been four weeks – four fucking weeks! – since I'd kissed Maggie, and I couldn't do it anymore. I couldn't watch her with that idiot. Not without taking my chance. I'd planned it all out to optimise that chance and, so far, it was going off without a hitch. The major details at least.

She'd sat with Iago during the game, and he'd successfully distracted her from it to the point the idiot got well pissed off. She was coming back to Hammersby with us and then onto Kenicki's. She'd chosen me over the shithead, even if she wanted to tell herself it was just for tonight. She'd left Clove in Ezra's car and was currently wrapped around my body on the back of my bike, wearing my jacket.

I knew this *would* only be a one-time thing if I played this wrong. I had one chance to make her see that wasn't all this was.

So, against my better judgement and my usual preference, I took the roads slow and steady. The engine didn't go a single click over the speed limit, and the corners were taken lazily. It didn't help that, with every corner, Maggie's arms tightened around my waist, and it distracted me to no end. But I refrained from taking them faster or tighter just to make sure I got the response out of her. There would be plenty of time for having her react to me, and I much preferred she was getting pleasure out of it.

Ezra drove behind us, giving the impression that I was leading the way, so we all arrived together. As was the plan. As far as Maggie and Clove knew it. It was in fact not the actual plan, and it was coming time to enact the next stage.

We were coming up on the Overlook, so I waved to the car behind us and pulled off. Ezra and Iago waved at me out their windows as they drove past. I pulled the bike up, flicked the kickstand, shut the engine, and took off my helmet.

"What are we doing?" Maggie asked.

I swivelled to her as I pulled my phone out of my pocket by way of explanation. Looking down at it, I was actually surprised to see a message had come through. But it was just fucking Iago.

Iago
No glove, no love, mate ;P
BUT you really want your first time to be at the fucking OVERLOOK? Talk about a fucking cliché, you adorable wanker.

I rolled my eyes as I said to Maggie, "Thought my phone was ringing. Was just a text," and shot off a reply to the idiot on the other end of the phone. At least my stalling tactic hadn't been a total fabrication after all.

Vaughn
Fuck off. I will take your commentary when you sort the blue ball situation in your own pants, yeah?

How's having her tight little body hard against yours in that fucking tiny backseat?

Iago

That was uncalled for, sir.

And having yours wrapped around your whole body and knowing you can't do jack shit about it?

"Work?" she asked softly.

I looked up at her and found her checking her own phone. Her face twisted in a frown as she scrolled like she'd missed a lot of notifications. I could guess what – or who – was to blame and I wasn't fucking having him fuck this time I had with her. If I had one night to convince her, I was making it count, damn it.

She slipped her phone into her pocket with a sigh. I put my finger under her chin and tilted her face to look at me. "Don't think about him tonight."

"And when *do* you suggest I think about him?"

I looked into those beautiful, angry grey eyes and wondered how in the hell she'd got under my skin with nothing more than a kiss and a few defiantly sassy words. But there she was. "Don't think about any of them. Don't think about their expectations. Or what they want for your life."

Her eyes narrowed but she didn't pull away from me. "No? Should I think about *your* expectations? What *you* want for my life?"

I spun myself around in the seat to face her and pulled the helmet off her head. "No. Yours."

I saw her swallow hard as she searched my eyes, something similar to panic in hers. But her knees pressed against mine and her hand went to my arm where it hung over her thigh, holding the helmet by her foot. She chewed her lip like she was thinking, her eyes never leaving mine.

I leant into her gently, my other hand sliding slowly up her other thigh. Her tongue ran over her lip and the grey of her eyes went liquid silver with desire. "I think," I said as I kept my lips just out of reach of hers, "it's time you did what *you* want to do, Magenta."

Her body swayed forward like she was after my kiss, and I shifted to maintain the minute distance between us. I saw the frustration light those steely greys. "And you think I want to *do* you?" she challenged.

"We both know, baby, that the feeling is mutual." My hand was at the very top of her thigh, under her skirt. I tipped it to half-cup her arse and I squeezed firmly.

My eyes were planted on the way her teeth would not let go of her lip. But I felt her wriggle, like she was trying to press her legs together against whatever I'd elicited there. I fucking loved it. The way I made her squirm as she tried telling herself there was nothing between us.

I trailed the hand on her thigh back over her whisper soft skin. My thumb dipped next to the heat at her centre and her breath caught. "Ask me nicely and I might give you what you want, love…" I purred as I leant closer to her.

She didn't fight me. Didn't argue. Didn't make a big show of pretending she didn't want me. This time, she closed the gap. Her hand ran up my arm and into the base of my hair. Her fingers closed around it tightly, making it pull, as she kissed me deeper. Fuck, but it was the sexiest thing I'd ever felt. Her leg hooked around mine, so her knee was hugging my hip, and I actually dropped her helmet in favour of taking her waist in both hands.

Maggie McCallan kissed me like the fucking world was ending.

Even that very first time, she'd responded to me in a way no one ever had before. The other week at Rizzo's, it had been even better. And at the Overlook on my bike? I'd never been kissed like that before.

It was like we both knew this was it. This was the practice lap. We get this right and there was a very real chance that we were taking home the prize when it came time to the real race.

Maggie unzipped my jacket and took my hand to lay it on her breast, all without breaking our kiss. I squeezed tightly. Maybe too tightly. But then her back arched into me as she sighed in pleasure. I was hard for her in seconds. But then, I'd been constantly hard for her for weeks. This fucking gorgeous creature with the sweet and innocent outside and the hardarse sexy inside that got my motor revving.

She wrapped her arms tighter around my neck, cradling my head with her forearms and bringing her body closer to mine. Her glasses pressed into my cheek but, if she didn't care, neither did I. I ran my hands firmly down the sides of her body until I found the top of her thighs and fuck but I loved having them in my hands. I slipped my hand over the top of her leg again, teasing her. I felt her hips rock for more.

Her wanting me to touch her didn't even feel like a victory at that point. It felt like a fucking honour. I didn't want to own her anymore. I didn't want to ruin her. She'd kissed me fucking once and I was the one ruined. I was the one owned. This wasn't about dominating her – outside whatever might get her off – but just being with her. And I had no qualms admitting that to anyone…except her old man or anyone who might rat us out to him.

She paused and looked into my eyes. There was some hesitation in her, but she was breathing hard, and I hoped it was just because she wasn't used to voicing out loud the kind of thing I really hoped was on her mind.

"I want you to touch me, Vaughn," she said, breathless and desperate.

Something ran through me that I'd never felt as I brushed my thumb gently over the inside of her pelvis. Her hips bucked and I saw her eyes narrow as she glared at me.

"I suppose 'asking nicely' to you is me begging?"

I knew it was all part of the game between us. I knew that, and I certainly wasn't going to say 'no' if she was going to beg me for it. "Beg me, Magenta," I dared her.

"Touch me, Vaughn," she moaned. Fuck, but her voice was this low, pouty, sultry tone that would have been indecent in any other situation. I knew she was exaggerating, but I still strained against my jeans. "Please, Vaughn. Touch me. I want to feel you." She pressed her tits hard against me.

Jesus, game or not, I would never be able to say 'no' to that. But I could tease her. My hands tightened against her skin. "But I *am* touching you, baby…"

I saw the snarl ripple through her eyes. "None of this half-arsed teasing, baby," she threw back at me. "Commit to it."

One hand on the back of her head, I crushed my lips to hers, but she wasn't waiting any more time for me to give her what she wanted. She put her hand over the one on her thigh and slipped it right on up into her panties. Fuck, she was wet. My fingers trailed over her clit, and she actually bit my lip as she sucked in a sharp breath.

"Do. Not. Tease. Me. Vaughn," she growled as she pulled on my hair, and my cock sat up and paid attention.

"Yes, ma'am."

I fucking throbbed for her. Literally ached to know what she felt like wrapped around me. I wasn't going to stick my cock in her – yet – but I had a decent substitute. For her.

I started with one finger and I fucking melted as I felt her relax around it as she leant her head to me with a groan of pleasure.

"Fuck, you're tight," I breathed as she rolled her hips.

She was tight, but she was so fucking lubricated it was easy as to slip a second finger into her and it was hard not to blow my load at the way she reacted to it. My thumb pressed against her clit as I pumped her, and I felt her breath catch again as she bit her lip. She stared right into my eyes as she rocked in time with my rhythm, and I had never been more turned on in my life.

She leant forward to kiss me hard. When she bit me, I got the message and thrust into her harder. Faster. She nodded her approval as she almost squeaked, "Mmhmm," at me. "Mmhmm, just like that, Vaughn…"

Well, if that's what she wanted, who was I to say no?

She kissed me hard and deep, her hands roaming my body as I finger fucked her on the back of my bike. Iago could tell me it was fucking cliché to hook up at the Overlook but, with her body writhing under mine, I didn't fucking care.

She nodded as she whimpered, "Yes, Vaughn. I'm gonna cum. Yes. Please, baby."

Was I not already as far gone for this woman as it was possible to be, that would have done it. Yeah. That would have… Her total abandon in the heat of the moment. Unfiltered. Unrestricted by the constraints she put on herself to make her 'respectable' to those people. She was achingly beautiful, and I was totally addicted to her.

I kissed over her neck, trailing down as she leant back. I pulled her top and bra down and sucked hard on her nipple.

"Fuck," she moaned, arching further into me.

When I nipped the sensitive flesh of her breast, her hand fisted in my hair like she was afraid I'd stop. She cried out and her whole body wrapped around mine at the same time she was clearly trying to relax and let me mercilessly pleasure her.

Her hips ground against my hand as I pumped her harder. She was all breathy moans and wanton carnality. She sat up again, her lips finding mine as she clawed my arms. Her movements against me started getting more erratic and her breathing got shallower as she held me tighter.

I felt her contract on my fingers, her whole body tensing, as she pressed her face to mine and groaned, "Shit, Vaughn… Don't stop."

She shook as she came, and my hand was drenched. Not the insane torrent you saw on a porno, but enough for me to know I'd hit the perfect spot. And the first time, too. My woman had just squirted on my bike and it was the fucking sexiest thing that had ever happened to me.

She leant into me, breathing hard, and gave a self-conscious chuckle as she fought to get her breath back. "I've never... That hasn't–"

I tilted her face to mine. "It was so sexy."

A touch of pink crept up her cheeks behind her glasses before she pushed them up her nose. "It was?"

I nodded as I slowly slid my fingers out of her. She watched, eyes wide and cheeks flushed as I sucked the two middle ones. "So. Fucking. Sexy."

Her cheeks heated even further as she looked down. I coaxed her to look at me again before claiming her lips with mine.

"You are everything," I murmured against her kiss, and I felt her hands tighten on my leg in response.

One hand crawled up my body. She gripped my shirt hard and held me to her as our kiss deepened. Her tongue battled mine and she wasn't afraid to use her teeth at the perfect moment. I trailed kisses down her cheek to her neck.

"We should probably make a move," I told her. I sounded regretful and resigned because I would have much rather stayed there all night and make her cum until she couldn't take it anymore.

Her hand slipped to my crotch and, when she looked into my eyes, she looked almost drunk on the pleasure I'd just given her. She darted forward and nipped at my lip again. As she pulled away, I went with her; there was no way I could ever get enough of her.

"*That* is less easy on a bike," I told her, ruefully.

"But not impossible…?" she asked, looking up at me through her eyelashes.

I couldn't help but smile. "Clove is about two seconds away from calling you to find out where you are. I guarantee it. If you want to tell her what just happened then, by all means, we can take our time."

She grabbed my shirt again and pulled me to her so she could reach up to my ear. "You assume I won't be giving her all the sordid details later anyway." Then she dragged her teeth over my earlobe, and I instinctively wrapped my arms around her and bent my head to her shoulder.

"God, you're fucking something else, darling…" I breathed and realised far too late what my tone was actually saying to her. I'd never used the 'L' word in my life except as a semi-teasing nickname for her. My tone had just definitely suggested I was about to break it out now.

At the unbidden and unmistakable emotional desire in my voice, she pulled back to look at me. I saw some of the lusty haze lift from her eyes as they softened. The way she was looking at me made my heart tingle in my chest. My breath hitched. The air around us was full of unsaid things. But they were all in my favour. I might not have planned to get her off on the back of my bike at the Overlook, I certainly hadn't planned to almost tell her I loved her, but both those things were definitely helping my cause.

She chewed her lip as she nodded. "Yeah. I guess we should meet the others, huh?"

I was both relieved and annoyed by her decision. I wanted her all to myself, but I also knew that this had to work outside of physical pleasures. I needed to spend time with her. She needed to spend time with our people. And being around those people would help me keep my hands – and my cock – to myself so she knew this wasn't all physical.

Back on the road, there was something different in the way she held me. She wasn't just holding on around my middle for dear life. Her hands were splayed on my chest and my stomach, and she leant into me in a way that wasn't just fear of falling off, but because she wanted to be close to me.

When we got to Kenicki's, the others were hovering around outside waiting for us. Iago threw me one of his patented shit-stirring grins and I rolled my eyes at him. As Maggie was climbing off, I pulled my phone out of my pocket.

V

What's her size?

Clove saw the message and looked at me quickly, frowning.

Clove

Weird brag to your friends?
And how did you get this number?

V

I have my ways.
I want to buy her something.

Clove

Of course you do.
If it's sexy lingerie, I feel obliged to inform you she has VERY specific tastes. Plus she's got that covered 😜

Okay. Well, I definitely needed that image to fuel the already rock-hard cock in my jeans that was unlikely to see any relief in the foreseeable future. Not.

V

It's not lingerie, but good to know.

Clove

What is it then?

V

I'm not telling you.

Clove

Why not?

V

You'll tell her and I want it to be a surprise.
What size is she?

She gave me a wide grin that could stir almost as much shit as one of Iago's. Fuck, but those two were far more suited than even either of them realised.

Clove
12

V
Thanks.

As I put my phone back in my pocket, I looked at Maggie where she was talking to Iago, a bright smile on her face. She turned it to me, and I watched as her teeth caught her lip like she was remembering our stop at the Overlook. I crooked an eyebrow at her and ran my tongue over my lip. I could have sworn she blushed again, before she busied herself with taking off my jacket.

Iago came over to me as Clove caught Maggie's attention.

"How did it go?" he asked as we watched the girls conferring. Were they debriefing already as well?

I shrugged. "A gentleman doesn't kiss and tell."

"Good thing you're not a gentleman then."

I smirked. "A gentleman doesn't make her squirt and tell."

Iago's head actually dropped back as he chuckled. "Fuck. Lucky bastard."

I gave a rough laugh as the girls made their way over. Maggie held my jacket out to me uncertainly and I took it from her, making sure the brush of our fingers lingered. She caught her lip again and looked down as she cleared her throat.

"Are you fuckers ready or am I going dry all night?" Cairo called.

"No one said you had to wait!" I told him.

He shook his head before storming inside, Stone and Ezra following.

"Ready?" I asked Maggie.

She plastered on one of those smiles she gave the idiots. I was about to reprimand her for it, but I realised it wasn't for me when she gave me the truth. "Not really, but I want to be."

My heart did that thing again as I tried not to hope that was code for whatever was happening between us. Instead I climbed off my bike and nodded. I wrapped my arm around her as the four of us headed inside. As Iago opened the door, I kissed her temple and let go of her, knowing it might be a while before I could safely touch her again. At least the way I wanted to.

CHAPTER NINE

Vaughn let go of me and the nerves flooded in. But they weren't the kind of nerves I had around the East Ham kids. I knew I wouldn't measure up, and the freedom from expectations was actually liberating. I was excited nervous.

I still had to force myself not to grab Vaughn's hand for support. I reached out for Clove's instead and I was sure Vaughn chuckled like he knew.

He pulled the door open and held it while Iago, Clove and I went in. As he stepped in behind me, he gave my arse a quick tap. I turned to him and he gave me a cocky wink that had me biting my lip as much because he seemed to think it was a message between us as anything else.

Kenicki's was large and dimly lit. Much like the Hut but, where the Hut was all modern and bright, coloured highlighting, Kenicki's was old school. Big, wooden bar. Pool tables under low lighting that were the brightest in the whole place. A row of booths around the walls, some other tables off to one side and a big area for dancing next to a stage on which an *actual* live band was playing.

"It's like the Bronze!" Clove hissed to me in excitement, and I smiled.

"The Bronze meets biker bar," I added.

"Maggie McCallan?!" I heard someone yell and Iago took half a step in front of me.

"What?!" someone else exclaimed as a whole bunch of people looked towards the door.

I felt Vaughn take a step closer behind me.

"Was this a bad idea?" Stone asked.

Then someone called out, "PRINCESS MCCALLAN IN THE HOUSE!!" and the whole place erupted in an obviously drunken cheer.

"First drink's on me, McCallan!" came another call and, with the excitement passed, the majority of attention left us once again.

Vaughn chuckled, "Nope," in answer to Stone.

"Dance, Mags?" Iago asked and I blinked at him in surprise.

"What?"

He leant in close to me. "We're going to need to share you to avoid suspicion."

"You watch how much you're sharing, West," Vaughn warned him, and I heated all over at the possessive growl.

Iago gave him a very unimpressed, withering glare. "Mags is like a sister to me. I don't like this any more than you do." Then he looked at Clove. "You're next on my dance card, darling." And winked at her.

She blushed and nodded furiously. I hid a laugh as Iago grabbed my hand and pulled me to the dancefloor. I snuck a look back to Vaughn, who was doing a very good job of pretending not to care I wasn't holding *his* hand.

Iago pulled me into the middle of the group, and I was amazed at how relaxed I felt. These kids didn't care who I was, that I was there, or what I was doing. They either completely ignored me in favour of what – or who – they were doing, or they gave me grins.

Like they knew I was being a little naughty, but good on me and they'd keep my secrets.

"What happens at Kenicki's stays at Kenicki's," Iago told me, wryly, as we danced.

"I thought they'd hate me being here," I said. "I thought they'd whisper and glare and see me as the interloper."

"You are like royalty to these people," he said with a scoff. "Like a goddess come down from the Heavens themselves to grace them with your presence. A princess come to celebrate with the commoners. They look at you here, they see you pushing the boundaries we live to push, and they love it. Even if it took you a while."

I shook my head. "You lot are so dramatic."

He grinned. "We're a lot of things once you stop being a snob and get to know us, Mags."

Something ugly hit me. "Is that really what you think of me?"

His eyes were soft as he looked me over. "Not me. Never me. I understand." I pretended I didn't see his eyes dart to where Clove was dancing with Vaughn. "You needed to be separate. We didn't exactly facilitate civility."

Iago had always facilitated civility, even if it was the annoying but beloved older brother kind, but I knew he was trying to make a point, so I decided not to correct him. "It doesn't hurt that your reputations aren't actually all that exaggerated."

He smirked. "No. I guess not."

"I couldn't stay separate and *not* hate you. Hate everything you are and what you stand for."

He nodded. "I know that. He knows that. Now."

I sighed as I looked over to Vaughn and Clove. She was laughing. He was smiling and shaking his head.

"What has he told you is happening here, Iago?" I asked.

Iago was clearly not ready for that question. "Uh...?"

"It's not rocket science. It's not a fucking trial. The rest of the Princes obviously know there's something going on between us. So what has he told you to convince the four of you to risk life and limb?"

He looked me over and, for a split second, I thought I saw pity in his eyes. "Is there no one you'd do anything for?"

"Freddy. Clove," I said instantly.

Iago nodded. "Saint didn't have to tell us anything. We all tried to stop him in our own way, and nothing could persuade him." He shrugged. "That's all we needed to know."

"But he's told you something."

"Of course, he's told me something. I think he's batshit insane, but I can grant him his last request."

"My dad doesn't have to know. It's one night, Iago. One night and I walk away."

He inclined his head. "How long are you gonna lie to yourself, Magenta? Because you're the only one who believes you'd rather be that prissy little princess than be one of us."

I blinked. "Excuse you?"

"I'm excused. Have you seen yourself since you walked in? Since you climbed onto his bike? You don't have to be a criminal or a Rose to be with..." He paused like he'd realised something he'd rather not. But he took a breath like there were more important things. "With one of us. To be happy."

I swallowed hard. "My dad will kill him."

Iago nodded. "Maybe. Maybe all it would take to save his life is the word of one little princess?"

"I can't take that risk..." I whispered, barely audible above the music.

He sniffed. "I get that."

Then, as though to shake the melancholy that had fallen over us, he spun me out. I landed, laughing, in Ezra's arms. So, I danced with Ezra for a while. Then Stone. Then Cairo. With Clove. With no one particular as we all jumped around.

I felt the most free I think I had in my entire life. It didn't matter if anyone was judging me or not. I didn't care about anyone outside my bubble. I couldn't remember the last time I'd smiled that much in public.

Around it went between chatting and laughing and drinking. For hours. I even danced with a few random Roses, while the Princes stayed close.

When I finally found myself in Vaughn's arms, his face was neutral, but his eyes shone warmly.

I slid my arms around his shoulders. "I was starting to think you weren't going to claim your share," I said as I reached to his ear.

His arms tightened around me. "I thought I had my share at the Overlook?" he sassed.

"Oh, so you're not interested in seconds?" I teased.

"Darling, I want it all. But having it all tonight just seems greedy."

I smirked. "Greedy or strategic?"

"How is it strategic?"

"Well, isn't this your big chance? I'm not sure exactly what you're trying to achieve here, Vaughn, but if *I* wanted to succeed, *I* wouldn't be holding back."

"You came all over my bike and you think I'm holding back?"

Yeah, I had done that, and I hadn't stopped craving more of his touch since. My whole body zinged and tingled in the most delicious anticipation at the very memory, let alone the hope he'd do it again.

I shrugged, all faux-coy. "I don't know, Vaughn. I don't know what you're capable of. What you can do. How can I, if you don't show me?"

His arm tightened around me again as he sucked his teeth and looked around. He locked eyes with Iago, and something passed between them. Iago nodded and Vaughn bundled me out to his bike.

"Where are we going?" I asked.

He dipped his lips to my jaw. "Somewhere I can show you what I'm capable of," he growled, and I laughed.

He threw me his jacket again and I juggled it in my hands. "I know protocol," I started.

"But?"

"But I'm just supposed to picture you getting skinned alive if we crash?"

There was the smallest wince in the corner of his eye. "It's best not to think about that."

"But I–"

He pressed a kiss to me so lingering I almost forgot what I was arguing with him about. "I'm very glad you care, love, but I will be fine tonight. I promise."

I looked up into his eyes. "Promise?"

He nodded. "Promise." I sighed as I pulled his jacket on, and he bit his lip as he looked me over. "I could fucking get used to this."

"To what?" I asked as I picked up his spare helmet.

"You. This. Everything."

My heart caught, and I really liked the way that felt. Parker had never made it do that before. It felt like nerves and shyness and certainty and hope all at once. I'd felt it on the back of Vaughn's bike at the Overlook earlier that night when he'd said I *was* everything. And again when I'd heard the emotion, surely unbidden, in his voice a few moments later. I felt it just thinking about it.

"You're so sure about this – me – that you're willing to risk not just your life but the other Princes' lives as well?"

There was a flash of guilt in his eyes, but he stamped it down. "There are easier games to play, Magenta. Easier chicks to play them with. I get why you might not believe me, and I don't know how to convince you except to keep putting my heart out there and hoping you might meet me even halfway."

"Your heart?" squeaked out of me and he nodded.

"You told me not to hold back, baby. So I won't. My heart is in this, as short-lived as that might make me. I just want to enjoy the time we can have. I'd rather love and lose than not love at all."

I didn't want to go too deeply into everything surrounding that statement for fear I'd plunge headfirst into something I wasn't quite ready for. So I teased him instead. But I did it as I pulled the helmet on, and hopefully he'd realise that I *was* at least ready to start the conversation.

"You're quoting Tennyson?"

He shrugged and played nonchalant, but a smile tried to break through. "It's a good line, damn it. It's go hard or go home time, Magenta. I'm not gonna half-arse this." He put on his helmet and climbed on his bike. "We going hard or going home, baby?"

I climbed on behind him and wrapped my arms around his waist. "Let's go hard, baby."

I felt his chuckle as he revved the bike and tore out of Kenicki's parking lot. Although, I was sure that 'tearing out of there' had more to do with my inexperience on the back of a bike than it did the actual speed Vaughn rode.

I leant against him, enjoying the feeling of him and the rumble of the bike under us and the breeze against my skin. I took a deep breath and felt properly content, like that was exactly where I was supposed to be.

Vaughn took us a little South out of Hammersby, finally pulling off the smaller back roads onto a property that lay along the river.

"Where are we?" I asked him once he'd cut the engine.

He helped me off then climbed off as well. "Before my mum fucked off with..." His head twitched and he winced as he took his helmet off. "Dad bought this place to build us all a home." I wasn't quite sure what to say to that, but he continued. "Dad comes down maybe twice a year to keep it from completely overgrowing. But otherwise, it's basically abandoned."

I took off my helmet as I looked around and put it on the bike. The moonlight glinted on the water and the leaves of the trees, across the swathe of grass Vaughn had parked on.

"It's so beautiful," I said.

He came up behind me and wrapped his arms around me. "I've always loved it here, but I've never really had a reason to come here."

"And I'm a reason?"

I felt him shrug as he pulled away again. "Where else am I guaranteed to have you all to myself for more than five seconds without worrying someone's going to see us?"

"I think the Overlook was more than five seconds."

He smiled as he went over to the bike and pulled something out of the storage. "Just wait until I've got six, darling."

I laughed out loud. He turned to me in pleasant surprise and I pressed my lips together in embarrassment.

He shook his head. "Don't do that, Maggie. Not with me. I'm not them. I want nothing but the truth from you, no matter what that is."

Vaughn certainly wasn't them.

Iago's words at Kenicki's played in my head as Vaughn shook out a picnic rug on the grass. That the Princes knew what this – whatever it was – meant to Vaughn. Vaughn's own words about easier games. I couldn't shake the feeling that whatever was happening between us wasn't just a passing fancy. The feeling from Rizzo's washed over me as I watched Vaughn drop onto the rug.

Vaughn was it.

But all we had was tonight.

Vaughn lay back, putting an arm behind his head. "Whatever you're thinking, baby. Stop. Not tonight. We can either deal with it or ignore it tomorrow."

I resolved to do just that and sat on the blanket beside him. "Just how much of tonight did you plan, Vaughn Saint?" I asked him.

He laughed as he grabbed hold of me and pulled me onto his body. I gasped in surprise but couldn't help laughing as well.

"Very little gets by you, does it, Magenta McCallan?" he said.

I smiled down at him, liking the way his body felt under mine. The way he felt between my legs. I told myself that was just his jeans button hard up against my clit.

"How much, Vaughn?" I pressed.

He sighed as he rolled us over, nestling between my legs proper and fuuuuck but it felt perfect. "You really want to know?"

I nodded. "I really want to know, Vaughn."

I watched his eyes roll, then he dropped his lips to my neck and told me between kisses, "You on the back of my bike. The stop at the Overlook." He huffed a laugh and his breath chased goosebumps over my skin before he headed down my body. "But I was just planning to talk."

"Talk?" I spluttered, then he lifted my tank and nipped at my stomach playfully and I sighed as I melted back against the rug.

"Yes, Magenta. Talk. Tonight was supposed to be more than just physical." He kissed down passed my belly button and my hands went to his hair. "*Someone* seems to have different plans."

"Well," I said, trying to affect a lofty, nonchalant air. "One could argue that we've talked enough."

Vaughn looked at me through his hair as his hands ran up my thighs slowly. "Talked enough or argued enough, Princess McCallan?"

"You've got one night to show me what this could be, and you want to waste it on words, Prince of Thorns?"

His fingers gripped the waistband of my pants, and he coaxed them down my hips. I wriggled to help him get them off me. "Is that why you're with the priss? Is he that good?" There was a chuckle in his voice that was missing from the intensity of his eyes.

I sat up, putting my fingertips under his chin. "I thought we weren't thinking about him?"

Vaughn's jaw clenched. "I'm trying, but it's difficult not to remember you're going back to him tomorrow."

My breath caught and I know he saw it. Something passed over his face as he searched my eyes.

"*Are* you going back to him tomorrow, Maggie?"

He saw the uncertainty in me. I know he did. Because I couldn't say no. I couldn't say yes to him, but I knew one hundred percent that the answer wasn't 'no' anymore.

"Show me what you've got, Saint, and I'll think about it."

He growled playfully. “Your wish is my fucking command, love.”

He gently pushed me back down into the rug as he disappeared under my skirt. He pressed a kiss to my upper thigh. Then the other. I bucked my hips impatiently and I felt him chuckle. Then he had both hands on more arse than hips, holding me tightly, as he ran his tongue through my folds. I wriggled both for more and away from too much, but he held me tightly as he sucked hard on my clit.

“Shit,” I breathed as my back arched off the rug.

One of Vaughn’s hands slid up my body and squeezed my breast. Tight. God, it felt good. Two fingers of his other hand slipped inside me, and I realised I hadn’t known the meaning of good before then.

I knew I shouldn’t compare them, but it was impossible to completely ignore the thought that floated through my head that Parker might have been good, but he did not measure up to Vaughn. In any respect.

Not that I was thinking about that for long, because Vaughn seemed hellbent on showing me just how he didn’t hold back. He had me screaming his name with what felt like very little effort on his part but, unlike some other people, he didn’t stop at once. He kept going until I squirted again. Twice in one night when I hadn’t even realised that I could do that at all.

“Fuck, you even taste good.”

I smiled as I tried to get my breath back. “What do you mean ‘even’?”

“I mean...” I felt the smile against my leg as he planted a kiss on it. “...that you smell good...” Another kiss. “...you feel good, and...” one more kiss. “...you fucking taste good.” He dragged his teeth over the sensitive flesh of my thigh and my back arched off the ground again.

I breathed, "Shit. Iago–"

Vaughn knelt up quickly, grabbed my hips and yanked me down so his face was hovering over mine. "Fucking, what?"

I smirked at the possessive disbelief on his face. "Iago warned me about your teeth."

He relaxed again. "He fucking did, did he?"

I nodded. "He was sure I'd enjoy it. I wasn't convinced."

Humour lit his eyes. "And what's the verdict?"

I wrapped my arms around his neck. "Iago was right," I told him before kissing him hard.

I lost track of how long we were there, snuggling on his blanket – which I was very sure had been part of his elaborate plan which I couldn't even be mad at. I lost track of how many times he made me cum before I finally convinced him to let me return the favour.

But eventually I realised it was already half three in the morning and I sat up quickly.

"Shit, I should not still be out."

Vaughn sat up next to me and dropped kisses on my shoulder as he righted my bra and tank top. Of course, it might have been as much a ploy to touch my boob as being helpful.

"Let's get you back, then."

"Not going to try to convince me otherwise? Extend your one night?"

I felt his smile as his lips trailed up my neck. "Nope. I've already had far longer than I thought I would. And, if I deny your wishes, then I don't deserve another chance." He pulled himself up and held his hands out to me.

I finished tidying my top up and I looked up at him for a moment. “You think you’re getting another chance?” I teased him before taking his hands and letting him pull me to standing.

He wrapped his arms around my body. “I hope for another chance. Your choice.”

I bit my lip as I searched his eyes. “I’ll let you know,” I promised.

The smile lit those eyes, but he kept his expression as neutral as possible. “Sounds good.”

We got back onto Vaughn’s bike, though I wasn’t allowed my pants back, and he took me home. He surprised me by stopping a couple of streets away.

“What are you doing?” I asked him as he killed the engine.

“Dead giveaway if there’s a bike in your street, isn’t there?” he said.

I realised he was right, and I really should have thought about that. “Right.”

He smiled, took my hand and we walked the rest of the way to Mum and Jonathan’s house. As we got to it, I started for the side gate.

“Back door?” he asked, and I nodded.

“The safer option if I’m hoping to get in unnoticed,” I said.

“Fair.”

He was still holding my hand. Both of us seemed reluctant to let go.

“You should get in.”

“I should.”

“Night, love.”

I took a deep breath and reached up to press a quick kiss to his lips. He swayed after me as I pulled away. His eyes were closed with a smile on his face as I said, “Good night, Vaughn.”

He inclined his head before he opened his eyes, took a very noticeable step backwards and slid his hand out of mine.

I didn't want to leave him – to end our one night – but I had to. Neither Mum nor Jonathan had texted or called so they probably hadn't noticed I wasn't home, but I was seriously pushing my luck. I took a couple of steps backwards, just wanting to see him for a few more seconds.

Then I took a deep breath and turned to force myself inside before I lost my nerve.

But…

"Maggie?" Vaughn caught my hand and I stopped.

"Vaughn?"

"Thank you."

"For what?"

His fingers played with mine. "For tonight. For giving me a chance."

"What exactly *did* you think it would achieve?" I asked softly.

"Do you really not know?"

I searched his eyes as I took a step closer to him. My heart tingled and my stomach fluttered. I desperately tried to not chew on my lip.

Yeah. I knew. And I really like it.

"Dad would kill you," I said gently as I cupped his cheek.

He leant down towards me until his lips brushed mine as he said, "Worth it," before kissing me so damned tenderly.

I tried to be unaffected by that. But there was no denying there was something heady about someone willing to die for you. There was a small part of me who still had to question if it was just a game, but there really were much easier ways for Vaughn to get himself killed if that was the objective.

I could see him pursuing this for a short time, if that's all he wanted. But not this long. The Princes played plenty of games, but there were much more satisfying games to play than the one Vaughn and I had been playing.

I felt myself smile against his lips before pulling away slowly and gently. I lay my hand on his chest and then my head followed.

"I should go inside. I am so late."

I felt the chuckled rumble through his chest. "Okay. I don't want to get you grounded or anything."

"Oh, really? Why not?"

"Because it's officially holidays, baby, and I was hoping you might like to spend some of them with me."

I took a deep breath before pushing away to look at him. Based on the look in his eyes, he knew what I was thinking. He knew my answer to that next chance; hell, yes. But were either of us bold enough to say it?

He pressed a quick kiss to my lips before stepping back. "Text me."

"I don't have your number."

"I'll send it to you."

I grinned and shook my head as I walked back towards the house. "I'm not gonna ask."

"Plausible deniability is a wonderful thing, darling."

"Goodnight, Vaughn."

He inclined his head. "Goodnight, Magenta."

I hurried through the side gate and to the back door, punching in the code to unlock it. As I slid the door closed again, I heard a noise behind me. Turning guiltily, I saw Freddy sitting at the kitchen island with a bowl in front of him.

"What the hell are you doing up at four AM?" I hissed, locking the door.

He almost comically slowly shoved a spoonful of cereal in his face. "What are you doing sneaking in at four AM?" he asked through a very pointed mouthful.

I looked in the vague direction Vaughn would have gone in, wondering if that was the rumble of a bike engine in the distance. "Uh… What's your silence going to cost me?"

"You drive me to school when you get your car."

I blinked. "That really it?"

He shrugged as he shovelled more cereal in. "I'm going through the 'mum and dad are super embarrassing stage'."

"More embarrassing than your big sister?"

He nodded. "My big sister is the lesser of two evils."

I smirked. "Okay. Deal. Thanks."

"No worries."

"Night, Fred. Love you."

"Love you, too," he mumbled through more cereal.

As I slunk up to my room, I thought about the lesser of two evils. I thought about loving and losing versus not loving at all. And I made a decision: no more lying to myself. No more denial.

I didn't want to be with Parker. I didn't want to make things official with him. And I was certainly no longer thinking about that life that being with him could give me.

I wanted Vaughn.

V

Goodnight 🩶

Maggie

Night 🩶

CHAPTER TEN

After Friday, there was no more ignoring it or denying it. Vaughn had his claws in my very soul and no amount of reassuring myself that we didn't have a future would get them out. It wasn't like I could be *with* Vaughn even if – though? – I wanted to, but it *was* time to tell Parker whatever we were doing was over. Past time.

The Prince of Thorns was in my head, my heart, my dreams, my very soul. I thought about him every waking moment. He haunted my dreams every night. His hands digging into my skin as he pulled me close. His voice in my ear and his breath against my neck.

And that wasn't fair to Parker.

I spent all weekend trying to get hold of him and failing. He didn't answer my texts or my calls. I tried him on DMs, and I even emailed him!

All I'd been able to say was vagueness along the lines of;

Maggie

Hey.

How's things?

How was the Hut?

What's up?

What have you got planned for the break?

Is everything okay?

Which it CLEARLY wasn't.

Can you talk to me?

Let's talk about it.

Because I didn't really know how I was going to end things once I got hold of him.

Finally, we bumped – somewhat strategically on my part – into each other at the Hut on Monday night, and I convinced him to slip outside with me for a moment.

"What, Maggie?" he asked, pretty damned hostile.

I'd convinced Clove to borrow her car for this? Jesus. "Look, I'm sorry–"

"Sorry?" he spat. "What happened? You were supposed to be there!"

I blinked. "We never talked about–"

"We didn't have to! You knew you were meant to be there. It's expected."

All right, I was feeling a little pissy with him now. "Expected? How was it expected?"

"Oh, come on. You know what's going on here. You were supposed to be by my side."

"Parker, we made each other no promises. You didn't ask me or even tell me what you wanted for Friday. I didn't owe you anything!"

"Owe me? I think I'm owed plenty, Maggie."

Excuse him? "Clove and I–"

Parker's laugh was as far away from humoured as it could get. "Like I fucking care what – or who – you were doing. I spent the whole night sharing Lettie with Nick."

I mean, ouch. And it was obviously intended to ouch. I knew we weren't exclusive, but there was a difference between not making each other promises and shoving other girls in my face to try to make me jealous or to hurt me.

That made this whole thing ten times easier; it wasn't just about choosing Vaughn now; it was also about choosing my fucking dignity. "You know, Parker. I think we're better off as friends. Maybe not even friends."

His eyes narrowed. "Is there someone else?" he asked, and I wasn't sure I imagined the slight note of pain in his voice.

A small part of me crumpled at the idea I was hurting him like this. But I couldn't not do this. I already should have stopped lying to myself earlier and just done it. So, no matter how hurt he was or how he lashed out because of it, I could deal with feeling awkward and guilty and uncomfortable.

But, Jesus, what did I say to that?

My mouth opened and drivel came pouring out. Flooding, really. Flash flooding. "Yes…and no. I mean, someone else made me realise that, as much as I want to be the girl for you, I don't think I am. Or will be." To say nothing of his current behaviour. "But there isn't anyone else. Like that. I'm not going to be dating anyone else tomorrow or anything. If that's what you're…asking." My verbal vomit finally slowed to a trickle, then stopped.

I was sure my answer hadn't been the one Parker was after.

"I'm sorry," I blurted out.

"Sorry that you're so fickle that you'd dump me just to sleep with another guy?" he snarled, but nothing about it was sexy.

It was feral and angry, but not primal like Vaughn. Definitely not sexy. It was something else. It was twisted and dark in an acrid and terrifying kind of way. Like passing a bare window or mirror at night after watching a horror movie. Hairs on the back of the neck prickling. Danger in the most undelicious of ways.

"Parker, it's not like that. And we were never really dating," I breathed, wondering who in the hell this was and how he was making me so honestly scared of what he'd do next.

"No?" he sneered. "What is it like?"

I was so taken aback by the look in his eyes. "What if it was, Parker?" I asked suddenly. "Would it be better for me to cheat on you?"

"It would be better for you to be loyal to your boyfriend!"

Um. Okay. Delusional double standards much? What about sharing Lettie with Nick not three nights ago? "Oh, I'm sorry! I'll just have better control over who I fall for in future!"

"You fell for him?" he spat.

Well, fuck. Yes. "No!" This was not going to plan. "I didn't fall for anyone." Shit. "Else!"

Well, didn't I look innocent as all get up? Not that there was any reason to feel that way. But I still did. It was ingrained in me to try to make these people like me, to please them. Even if Parker was looking more and more like a guy I didn't even recognise, and I was feeling less and less bad for ending things with him.

I had to remind myself; how was I the bad guy here? I mean, other than letting Vaughn kiss me, and letting him flirt with me, and then kissing him, and maybe – okay, definitely – flirting with him back? But that's why I was ending things with Parker before they really got serious! Because, despite my best intentions, I liked Vaughn, and I couldn't keep stringing Parker along like I was a decent person.

"I don't believe you," Parker said. "You're seriously dumping *me* just to fuck some *loser*? I'm the fucking Police Chief's son! Head Prefect. The most popular guy in school."

Excuse him? "Modest, aren't you? You don't even know who it is!" burst out of me and I actually clapped my hands over my mouth.

"So, there is someone else?"

I shook my head and peeled my hands off my face. "It shouldn't matter, Parker. Your reaction's shown me that you're not the guy I thought you were, so I'm just glad I'm doing this now."

"I'm the guy I've always been, Maggie. You're the one playing at acceptable when all you'll ever amount to is the illegitimate daughter of a shady criminal."

His head whipped back just as pain burst in my knuckles. It took me a second to realise that the two were connected.

Parker looked back at me and there was blood streaming out his nose. I looked at my knuckles and saw they were bleeding. Or maybe it was his blood. They certainly hurt like a bitch.

"You fucking whore!" he spat.

Blaise McCallan's little princess held her own. "You fucking entitled prick," I shot back.

His hand flew back, and I prepared for the hit. If I couldn't catch his arm, I wasn't going to give him the satisfaction of even flinching. But yes. I caught his wrist and the utter fury in his eyes, the tight clench of his jaw, the hard line of his mouth, made my blood run cold. But Magenta wouldn't flinch.

"You're not better than me, Parker," I said, my voice ice cold. "You just get everything handed to you on a fucking velvet pillow whether you deserve it or not. But you don't deserve me."

I threw his arm back to him and walked away, wiping the blood off my aching knuckles as I did.

My heart pounded and my stomach fluttered uncomfortably, ready for him to run after me. I didn't know if I thought it more likely that he'd hit me or beg for me back. I mean, I expected the former but, if he really was the guy that I'd thought he was, then the latter was still possible. After all, if he was that much of an entitled twat, who was to say he didn't feel entitled to keep me with him against my wishes?

But he did nothing. Nothing that concerned me anyway. He didn't say anything, call after me, try to text me, or come after me. He just let me walk away.

And, as I did, I couldn't believe I'd really thought he liked me. That he respected me. Had he always thought I was no better than Blaise McCallan's daughter? Had I been some social experiment? Did he laugh with everyone behind my back? Or had that just been the knee-jerk comeback from a guy with hurt feelings?

Whatever it was, I was glad I was out. I'd tried doing the right thing – admittedly maybe a little too late – and it had blown up in my face anyway. Apparently, nothing would have been right for Parker except me staying with him until I died, no matter if I ever loved him or not.

So, I was going to do what any sane person would and go straight to Vaughn for my revenge. Or maybe my reward. I wasn't sure yet. But I'd ended things with Parker for a reason, and I'd be damned if that reason didn't do its job and make me feel better about my life choices in the only way I was interested in just then.

I was angry. I was horny. I was frustrated, in more ways than one. And I needed a distraction. A release that was going to make me forget my problems. What better distraction to compliment my mood than a hate fuck?

Although, I was being honest with myself now. And, to do that, I had to admit that I didn't hate Vaughn. Anymore. I hated how much I wanted him. I hated how much that complicated just everything. But hate was not what I felt for *him*.

I was, though, still incredibly pissed off.

I knew for a fact that Vaughn's old man was currently on a job for my old man. I also knew his mum had high-tailed when he was barely a year old, he had no siblings, and he didn't bring hook-ups home. So, if anyone was home, it would be Vaughn. Alone.

Walking up to the front door, the nerves hit, and a part of me hoped no one was home.

A big part.

I could have told anyone who might be interested – Clove – that I *had* knocked and – oh, no, what a pity – no one was home.

But I knocked like Magenta would have.

Vaughn pulled the door open in nothing but a goddamn pair of low-slung tracksuit pants. A full six-pack on display. The few tattoos he'd had time to get since turning eighteen. Or earlier, how was I to know. A smattering of hair disappearing from his belly button down to untold pleasures.

Goddamn.

I'd come here for one thing, and I was even more determined to get it now.

"Magenta," he said, his voice full of surprised humour. "To what do I owe the pleasure?"

I pushed the door open further and stormed inside. "Trust me, the pleasure will be all mine," I told him as I slammed it behind me.

He was all snide victory in the face of my anger. "I thought you had a boyfriend?"

"Not anymore."

That sinful smirk danced over his lips as I pushed him into the wall. "This you admitting you're mine, then?"

I did a very poor imitation of his annoyed growl. "This is me refusing to cheat on a good, kind, decent guy. A guy who deserves me far more than you do."

I mean, lies, but Vaughn didn't need to know that the guy who was supposed to be my knight in shining armour turned out to be way more shitty than Vaughn ever was.

"Yet it's still me you're about to give your body to."

In my annoyance, I hated that he was right. It was bad enough that he'd made me end things with Parker. It was bad enough that I was proving him right. I didn't need him to be even more right.

I shoved against him, more than prepared to do the dance, get the anger out of the way before things became more serious. "This is me admitting you make me crazy. Admitting that I need you to have me once before I lose the rest of my goddamned mind so I can go back to my life of sweater sets and nursery songs."

He was clearly done with me being in charge. He slid out and around me easily, pressing my front into the wall where I'd just had his back. His hands went to my body, clearly already thinking about the fastest way of removing my clothes.

"You can wear those sweater sets home to me every night for all I care. You can spend your days singing nursery songs. Someone will need to know what to sing to our kids to chase away the nightmares."

His fingers dug into my skin and my nipples responded. My clit responded. My whole damn body responded.

"Dad would kill you before I had a chance to move in with you," I told him. One of us needed a reminder that there was *no way* we'd get to kids – plural.

His body slammed mine into the wall. "You want to move in with me, love?" He thrust against me, and I had never wanted anything more.

“I *want* to get over you,” I lied.

He ran his nose over the shell of my ear. “You want to be on top, you just have to ask.” Then he nipped my earlobe, and I melted back into him instinctively.

“I don’t care how you have me, Vaughn, so long as you fuck me hard and make me forget all my problems.”

As he snaked my hand in his, he said, “Oh, I’ll do more than that, Magenta…” Then went to push it against the wall by my head.

But that was the hand I’d just punched Parker with, and I couldn’t help the small hiss as my knuckles protested. Vaughn was on the other side of the hall in a second, his hands up like he wasn’t about to risk being caught with his hands dirty.

I shook my head, trying to indicate he wasn’t in the wrong, as I cradled my hand. I suspect he realised that, whatever the problem was, he couldn’t have caused it.

He stepped back to me, crowding me comfortingly with his body as he took my hand gently in his much bigger ones.

“What did you do, love?”

I blew a strand of hair out of my eyes in frustration. “I punched Parker,” I admitted, not sure if I actually did want Vaughn to know that Parker wasn’t as good as I’d made him out to be, or if I just thought Vaughn might think more of me if he knew I had a badarse streak. Not that either of those reasons were good ones.

I felt Vaughn’s humour as he looked my hand over. “Why did you punch him?”

“He wasn’t very complimentary,” was the answer I went for.

I felt Vaughn nod. “I see. Did he hurt you?”

The possessive protection that rose in Vaughn’s voice made everything in me tingle and flutter in what had become a very pleasant way when I wasn't having a mini tantrum. But I was still angry with Parker.

"He tried," I said through gritted teeth.

Vaughn slid his hand over my stomach. "Fuck, you're fierce," he breathed as he trailed his nose over my face. "It makes a man wanna marry you right here."

"Marry me?" came out an embarrassingly breathy whisper, and all – most – of the fight left me. The fight against Vaughn, at least.

He nodded. "Whose ring did you think you were wearing while dressed up in those sweater sets, darling?"

"Maybe they should call *you* the Prince of Dreams," I huffed a humourless laugh. I had to be numb or what I did feel was going to be more dangerous than me turning up to his house for what I was sure we both knew was going to happen next.

"Iago wants to believe he can't have his picket fence *and* this life. I know my destiny, Magenta. I can want something, take something, even if I know I'll never really have it. I can want you, even knowing it might be the last thing I ever do."

"You would seriously give up your life for this?" I asked, hiding in denial and defiance as my emotions threatened to overwhelm me for a moment. "For what? The chance to fuck me out of your system?"

His hand gripped my throat. "I would risk my life for you. To be with you, yes. But if you think you could ever be out of my system, you're wrong."

I searched his eyes, but I didn't know what I was looking for, let alone if I found it. "What do you want from me, Vaughn?"

He seemed far more content with whatever he found in my eyes. "You, Maggie. Just you."

I licked my lip as I tried to work out my response to the utter sincerity in his voice. I didn't know what I should say to convey what I felt. I was still scared of what I felt, even if I was trying not to lie to myself about it anymore. So, I opened my mouth just to see what came out.

"Why did you kiss me?"

He knew what I meant, and he did me the courtesy of a straight answer for once.

"Because I wanted to fuck with Blaise McCallan's little princess. I thought I'd mess you up, make you want me instead of that simpering idiot–"

My defence was instinctual. "Parker is not–"

"Yes. He is. But," he continued pointedly, to avoid my next outburst, "I ended up messing with myself more."

Vaughn ran his hands up my sides as he pressed into me. The nose at my jaw was sensual. Everything about him was the perfect combination of soft and hard. And not just the fact his cock was hard.

He was both tender and domineering. Reverent and demanding. I felt like he wanted to worship me and utterly destroy me in the best possible way.

"One kiss and you were all I could think about," he groaned, his voice husky and low. "Oh, I already wanted to fuck you. *You* got me hard as much as the idea of what fucking you meant to the Blood Roses, to Hammersby, to your dad. It got me off, knowing I would be the downfall of Little Miss Redemption."

Had I not wanted – needed – to know where this was going, I'd have pointed out that he thought an awful lot of himself. As it was, I kept my mouth shut.

"But you fucking got to me. Me. The boy they broke. The boy they crushed. The man they trained to crush everything for them.

I didn't – don't – just want to fuck you, Magenta. I want all of you. I want to give you everything. And I will die to have you."

"And what about me?" I heard myself whisper. Not a fight, just an actual question.

"What do you mean?"

"What do I do once you're dead? Go back to my life like we never existed? My reputation ruined. My dad probably unable to look at the great disappointment I'd become? And the one person who was supposed to make it all worth it, just gone? And why the hell are you smiling?!"

Because as I talked, Vaughn's smile widened. Victory shone deep in those flashing blue eyes. His grin was so big, I was starting to worry he was about to disappear into thin air on me.

"What?" I pressed.

"You said 'we'."

"What? No, I…" totally had.

How could his grin grow? "You said 'we existed'. This isn't a one-time thing, love. And you know it."

I blinked, trying to find a way out of this certainty we'd fallen into without lying. But I couldn't backtrack *and* be honest. I did know this wasn't a one-time thing. Whoever Vaughn was and whatever we were, this was somehow way beyond a one-time thing, and had been for a while.

"Can something that hasn't even happened be a one-time thing?" I sassed, feeling a smile warm in my eyes.

"You're here. You came to me. You dumped your boyfriend and turned up at my door. This is happening."

"I'd heard you didn't bring girls home," was the joke I made to try to diffuse the intensity between us. It only served to increase it.

"I'm willing to die to be with you, love. I'm more than happy to bring you home."

I looked into those beautiful lapis lazuli pools, took a deep breath, and finally told the truth to both of us. "Then I'm giving you another chance, Vaughn."

Those blue eyes sparkled so bright as he nudged my nose playfully with his. "You're giving me another chance?" he teased, because we both knew what I was really saying.

"I want *you*, Vaughn," was the admission and agreement that we both needed to me to make. "I need you."

"I'm yours," he said as he picked me up and kissed me deeply.

My legs went around his waist and my arms wound round his neck as he carried me to his room.

"How long have I got?" he asked between kisses.

"How long do you need?" I teased.

"Baby, all night is barely going to be enough for all the time I wanna make up for."

I smiled against his lips. "Mum and Jonathan think I'm at Clove's tonight. She'd rather I be satisfying my clit."

He chuckled roughly and it warmed me through. "I can definitely help with that."

He kissed me hard before throwing me on his bed. As I bounced, I watched him half-turn to his door to close and lock it. As his muscles moved, the bleeding rose that took up most of his back shifted. Dad had one just like it.

As Vaughn stalked back to the bed, he pointed at me. "You?" he said, and I nodded eagerly. "You, Magenta McCallan, are mine."

A thrill ran through me as he climbed onto the bed and over me.

“There is going to be nothing slow about this, baby. Not the first time. I am far too keen and I’m sorry about that, but you drive me crazy.”

He lifted my knee around his hip as he lay over me and trailed his lips across my cheek, my jaw, my neck.

I held onto him tightly as our bodies pressed together. “I don’t care. I need you, Vaughn. I need you now.”

“Fuck,” he breathed, then pulled me to sitting and made short work of pulling my top and bra off.

His lips never left mine, even as he coaxed me back to lying down and he got rid of my pants and skirt before ripping off his track pants. He only moved away from me long enough to grab a condom. He knelt between my legs and pinned my eyes with his as he rolled it on. He stroked himself as those eyes raked over my whole body, leaving blazing heat everywhere they landed. And oh, my god, it was the sexiest thing I think I’d ever seen.

Then he planted one hand by my head as his other hand went to my clit. His fingers teased me, and I squirmed pleasantly under him. His grin was all self-satisfaction as he rubbed me fast but lightly. The pleasure built in me quickly.

“I thought this was going to be–?” I started but was interrupted when my back arched off the bed as I came hard. “Shit,” I breathed.

“Fast enough, baby?” he teased before he claimed my lips with his.

“Yeah,” I huffed a laugh. “Yeah. Fast enough.”

His fingers stroked me gently as his tip teased my entrance. Butterflies had officially escaped my stomach and were rumbling around my whole body madly.

“That, on the other hand…” I said pointedly and he laughed.

"I'm not ramming you the first time, love. Not straight away anyway."

God, why did I like the sound of that so much? "Oh?"

"Oh," was the only answer he gave me as he started easing into me.

I saw why he hadn't wanted to ram me. "Oh…" I breathed as I made myself relax around not just his girth but his length as well.

Damn it. He felt so good.

"Oh," he chuckled in agreement as he dropped kisses over my neck, which helped me relax even more.

Once he reached hilt, he pulled back again straight away. Thrusting in and out of me slowly and steadily as I got used to the incredible feel of him.

His lips found mine again and our kiss grew more frenzied as his pace increased. My hips met his thrust for thrust. His hand gripped my waist so hard it almost hurt, but it hurt so good, joining the jolt of pleasure he was growing within me again with every thrust.

My hands ran over his back, his shoulders, into his hair. I couldn't help pulling it a little as my orgasm got closer.

"Vaughn…" I breathed. "Vaughn. Yes. Right there. God, yes. Make me cum."

He pounded me faster. Harder. Lifting my leg up so he drove in even deeper. The angle was… Jesus. I came hard and felt the telltale sign of my new party trick all over his cock.

He groaned in such an appreciative way I felt it all the way from my heart to my clit. "Fuck, I love that," he moaned, and I felt him tense. "Jesus, Maggie," he breathed as he came.

The hand on my waist gripped me harder and I loved it so much. That line where pain could become pleasure. That proof of how crazy I drove him. How he couldn't help himself. It made me so much more sure of this.

It didn't hurt that he was officially the best sex of my life. And I didn't shy away from the fact that what I felt for him probably had a hell of a lot to do with that.

Vaughn thrust a few more times, getting slower and lazier as he did, then kissed me deeply as he slid out of me. A weird little disappointed almost-whimper escaped me as he did, and I saw the cocky victory in his eyes.

"Trust me. I'll be ready for round two very soon."

He got up to deal with the condom and I watched again as the tattoo on his back almost danced with his movements. It was weirdly beautiful. Kind of mesmerising. And there had always been something about tattoos that had been really sexy to me. Tattoos on Vaughn? It was like my Kryptonite.

"Are you going to put my leg over your shoulder next?" I teased him as he lay back down next to me.

He smirked and shook his head almost self-consciously, like he was almost regretting say those words to me. Or maybe just the fact I wasn't afraid to hold them over him. "Tell you what. You wear those shoes for me again and I'll show you just how hard I can make you squirt on my cock."

Shit. That sounded good. It sounded so good. I decided that maybe there was a reason to learn to walk in heels. Then again, I didn't have to walk in them, did I?

VAUGHN: FIVE

"This doesn't solve the problem, Vaughn," she said as she snuggled against my chest. "That *really* didn't solve the problem." She sighed both contentedly and in annoyance.

"What problem?" I asked with a smile, and not just at the change of topic. Fuck, I hoped she was going to wear the shoes for me again, though.

She put her hand under her chin and leant it on me to look at my face. "The fact we can't be together."

I looked at her innocently. "And remind me why it's a problem that we can't be together?"

Her eyes narrowed fiercely as she pushed against me and huffed, "If you're about to tell me you've been playing me all this time, you'll–"

I wrapped her against me so she couldn't get away. "What are you going to do?" I teased. "Give me a shiner to match your ex?"

"I'll break your nose like I broke his, then leave you to bleed in my wake," she threatened and I fucking swooned.

Hardening again already, I was convinced I'd never get enough of her. She was absolute perfection, and she was all fucking mine. All I had to do was not fuck it up and she'd stay mine.

"Fuck," I groaned, as I pulled her over to straddle me and pressed her down against my cock. "If I hadn't wanted you before, consider me yours, love."

I thrust against her, and she leant down over me to lean her chest on mine. I ran my hands up her body, then back down to cup her arse.

"So," she said slowly. "We've established that we want to be together. Despite all the reasons we shouldn't, we do."

"And exactly what are the reasons?" I teased seductively.

"You're a bully, a criminal, you stole me from…another guy, you're violent and dangerous and a total degenerate." The way she paused, I knew she didn't think much of her ex-prissy wanker anymore. I tried not to gloat about it, but I also wanted to smash his stupid face in if he hurt her.

"Darling, you're describing all my best qualities. What's the problem?"

She tried not to smile at my cheek. "The main one owns your arse and I spend one week in every four with him."

Oh, yeah. That problem.

I nodded as I thrust against her again. She rolled her hips back, and we fell into a rhythm as we rubbed together. My hands on her hips to push her into me harder and, based on the way she moaned, she loved it as much as I did.

"Well, what do you propose?" I whispered in her ear as I reached for another condom.

I pulled her up to run my tongue over her slit as I put the condom on. She gripped my bedhead and sighed as the pleasure grew in her. Fuck, that was sexy. When I had her back in my lap and she was looking into my eyes, she said to me, "I don't have a proposal. Maybe the answer is that this *is* a one-time thing after all?"

Fuck. That.

No.

Nope.

I was not accepting that as an option.

"You're telling me that, after that – after this – you could walk away? Because I don't plan on letting you go, baby girl. I told you that I'd claim you…" I lifted her slightly and then, in one thrust, filled her. Fuck, it felt like coming home. "And I'm fucking keeping what's mine."

One of my hands pressed on her lower back, the other on her upper back as I thrust sure and strong and steady, like I was punctuating every word. She pressed her face into my shoulder.

She seemed to hesitate, like she was thinking. Then finally, she reminded me, "But no one can know." As much as I hated it, at least one of us was still thinking straight.

"Can you keep a secret, Magenta?" I asked, knowing exactly how far I'd go for her.

Her arms wrapped around me tightly as she rode me. "You want to date me in secret?" she sassed.

I slid my hand down her body, so they were both holding her tight against me, and pushed deep inside her almost punishingly.

"I told you, Magenta. I'm not going to *date* you. You are mine and I am yours. What we are is much more than *dating*."

"You want to date me in secret," she repeated, but it wasn't a question this time.

She was going to play it like that? Fucking… Fine. Whatever it took. I'd told her no lies. So she'd get the truth. Trust her to force me to say it. I rolled our bodies to get her underneath me. I was still inside her as I looked down at her carefully.

"If that's what it takes, yes." My agreement was the most begrudging thing I had ever heard, and I knew she was the one feeling victorious this time.

She hugged her leg around my hip higher and I thrust hard, sending pleasure shooting through me. Her back arched against me, and a breathy moan escaped her. I very much understood the sentiment.

Laying over her, I held her leg up and back as the other hand braced beside her head. I drove into her over and over again until she was clawing my back and moaning in my ear. I was a dead man for touching her, but not keeping her now would kill me. I knew what she was to me and there was no way I could ever let her go without losing one hell of a fight.

"If you want me to date you, darling, I'll date you," I told her. "Dinner. Movies. Roses. Monogamy. It's yours and you can call it dating if you want, but we both know that's not all this is."

"Shit, Vaughn," she moaned, and I felt her cum hard. Not a gusher that time, but I'd had one that night, so I wasn't going to complain or worry about my performance.

I was still far too excited about finally being inside her that it didn't take me long to finish either. I was seriously going to have to work on getting my stamina back so I could fuck her like she really deserved.

We held each other tightly for a moment, kissing lazily, before I got up and got rid of the condom. I cleaned up and wrapped it in a tissue, then chucked it in the bin by my bed.

She moved over and ran her fingers over the tattoo on my back. I shivered as she hit all the right nerves but leant back into her touch. As she shifted to kneel behind me, she slipped her hand over my shoulder, and I took it before kissing the inside of her wrist gently, then wrapped her arm around me tighter.

"So?" she asked, kissing my shoulder.

"So?"

"What do we do next?"

"Well…" I kissed her arm. "How do you feel about anal?" She snorted a laugh and I turned to face her. "I know what you're asking, baby. What do you want to do?"

She looked me over, her teeth chewing on that bottom lip in the way I'd become so damned fond of. "You really think you can do secret?"

I scoffed. "Aside from five of our closest friends knowing exactly what's happening, yeah I really think I can do secret."

She smiled. It was wide and beautiful and took my goddamned breath away. I hadn't seen her smile nearly enough in the almost lifetime I'd known her, since our paths had invariable crossed when we were just little kids despite all Blaise's precautions. I vowed right then to change that. I'd give her a reason to smile every day if I had to, so long as her life was full of real happiness and freedom. She deserved no less.

"You don't want to get on the closest roof with a megaphone and tell the whole world that Magenta McCallan is yours?" she teased, and there was no doubt that I was in love with her.

I pulled her into my lap. "Of course, I fucking do. And I'm not afraid to face the penalty for being with you, darling. You're more than worth it. But I would like to be with you as long as possible. So I think the rooftop declaration might need to go on the backburner."

Her smile was just as big, but her eyes were so soft as she looked me over and breathed deeply. She slipped her hands into my hair, curling it around her fingers as she searched my eyes.

"What are you thinking, love?" I murmured as my nose nudged hers.

"Everything. How utterly surprising and amazing and wonderful this feels. It's… It's you and me. The undeclared Blood Rose heir and the mayor's stepdaughter. Criminal and supposed golden girl. And it just feels…" She took a breath.

"Right?" I finished for her, and she nodded slowly.

"So right."

My heart actually warmed and did a thing that could really only be described as fizzling or tingling. I felt like the Grinch, convinced it grew three sizes. It was one thing to be arrogantly, defiantly sure that she felt the same. It was another to have her confirm it. It was yet another to believe it beyond cocky conceit.

"Vaughn, I…" she started, then paused like she wasn't sure what to say. Or maybe she wasn't sure how to say it.

"What?" I coaxed gently, my heart tripping over itself in excitement at what I hoped she was going to say. Should I say it first?

She grinned like she was embarrassed or nervous and dropped her head to my shoulder. I wrapped my arms around her tightly.

"Want me to go first?" I asked her, trying not to smile so hard my face might break. When I felt her nod against me, I couldn't help it. "I think I love you."

She sat up so quickly I had to hold on more tightly or she was going to fall off my lap. "What?" she squeaked.

Oh. Well, fuck. Was that not what she was going to say? "Uh…"

She blinked quickly. "No!" burst out of her and I was feeling less good by the second. She shook her head and put her hands on my arms. "No. I mean, it's not that I don't… Um… I just wasn't expecting that." She breathed in, smiled, and said, "I really do think I might love you. I'm not really sure what else this could be. I just…wasn't going to say it yet and risk scaring you off."

I looked into those gorgeous grey eyes for a moment, trying to decide if she was just covering or not. But all I saw was sincerity. At least, all she was showing me was sincerity.

"I'm risking death by being with you and you think throwing around the 'L' word is going to scare me off?"

She shrugged. "I don't know. It's just all very sudden. What if that made it too real and you freaked out because I was suddenly too clingy?"

My God, she was even more adorable than I'd thought she was. But we were seriously going to have to work on her self-confidence. She did not deserve to let anyone make her second guess anything about herself, let alone the truth about what she felt.

"Everything about us is sudden, baby. Do you think that means it's not real?"

Her arms tightened around my shoulders. "It feels real to me. So real it's almost scary, but I don't want to let it go."

"Then cling as much as you fucking want, darling. Don't hold back and don't let go."

Her breath caught in her chest as her lip caught in her teeth. "Don't hold back and don't let go," she breathed before crushing her lips to mine and claiming whatever tiny piece of my soul remained that hadn't yet belonged completely to her.

We fell sideways on the bed, but our kiss just grew more frenzied. It was a near thing to grab another condom before she pulled me inside her. And God how I loved the way she arched into me and dug her nails into my back as I did.

I didn't know when my dad would be home, but he'd probably be too tired to bother with anything other than going to bed. If he came home at all. If I wanted to make sure he stayed too tired to bother with anything other than going to bed, I was going to have to keep Maggie a little quieter, but I figured I could coax at least one more scream of pleasure out of her before I had to worry about that.

So, I did.

Waking up next to her the next morning, even with her hair tickling my nose, was more than my wildest dreams. But before I could let her leave my room, I checked to see if my dad was home.

Dad was Blaise's right-hand man. There was a very large chance that Dad would kill me in Blaise's stead for the slight. And as much as I was being honest about my willingness to die for her if I had to, my preference was not to.

I found him passed out face down on his bed, still in his boots and jacket. Both were splattered with blood, and I hoped it wasn't all his. Blaise wasn't usually one to send anyone home with a seeping wound, so McTavish would have patched him up before letting him head home. It was all stuff I could deal with once he'd slept anyway.

I slipped back into my room and found Maggie looking for her panties. I raised my eyebrow at her, and she gave me a withering glare.

"Seriously?" she whispered.

I grinned. "No. Not really. I think they're over there?"

She looked down the side of my bed and nodded, flashing me her arse under her skirt as she bent over to pick them up.

"You are testing a man's patience," I told her pointedly.

She turned to me with a winning smile. "Well, isn't it lucky the man owns this arse, and he can have it later." Then she added, "*If* he's a very good boy."

Fuck, I loved her. "'Good' isn't really in my vocabulary, baby."

She shrugged as she pulled on her panties. "Well, isn't it lucky that you being good doesn't require you being *good*?"

I watched as she found her shoes and pulled them on. "You got a thing for the bad boy, Magenta McCallan?" I teased and she gave me a smile that also told me to fuck off and stop teasing her.

"A thing for *one* bad boy," she corrected me as she stood up.

"I am very pleased to hear it."

She came up to me, slid her hands up my chest and over my shoulders. "Don't get cockier, Vaughn. I'm not sure I could take it." She winked at me, and it fucking undid me.

I couldn't help but laugh. "God, you really are something else, but if we want this to be more than a one-time thing, you are probably going to have to leave now."

Maggie nodded. "Ah. Yes. Okay. What are you and the boys doing today?"

I looked her over. "Why?"

She shrugged. "I thought you wanted to spend some time with me these holidays?"

"Really?"

"Why not? You want to spend time with me, and you want to prove to me this is more than just physical. Two birds, baby, one Stone." Her eyebrows jumped at her joke, and I groaned.

"Oh, that was… Wow."

"Are you rethinking this now you know my terrible taste in jokes?" I teased.

I shook my head and wrapped her against me tightly. "After all, you used to have terrible taste in guys, but we fixed that."

Her mouth dropped open in surprised and she batted me playfully as she smiled. "Rude!"

"True," I corrected her, and she nodded begrudgingly.

"True. But what if my taste in jokes is less easily fixed?"

I lay my finger under her chin and tilted her face up. "Then I'll love you anyway."

I saw the emotion flood her eyes and I felt it mirrored in my chest. "You really will, won't you?" she asked gently.

Fuck it hurt. It hurt to know that I'd shot myself in the foot when it came to her. I wasn't surprised she didn't fully trust me. My past behaviour wasn't exactly conducive to showing a history of relationship trustworthiness. I'd prided myself on my ability to love them and leave them. I knew what they said about me. I knew why I was the Prince of Thorns. I left them bleeding, they said.

And, until Maggie, I'd been very okay with that. Gone out of my way to live up to my reputation. I wanted to leave them dying for more. It satisfied my ego, and it freaked out the fucking East Hammers who put up with us because they were too scared of us to do anything about it.

But now there was Maggie and all I wanted was to prove to her I was fucking in this. Risking death for her went a long way, I knew. I chased death as often as possible, got a rush out of cheating it. I got high off that feeling of invincibility it gave me. Actual death was totally different, though, and I got the feeling that Maggie knew that.

It just wasn't enough to remove *all* doubt.

"I really will, Maggie. And I will gladly spend the rest of my life proving it to you."

She reached up to me. "I don't think it will take your whole life."

I smiled. "I'm very happy to hear that."

Her grin went wry. "It might, though, take all holidays…" The note of cheek in her voice had me even harder, but fuck she needed to go if we were going to have the holidays.

"You've got yourself a deal, darling. But if we're going to have–"

She nodded. "I know. I'm going. I'm not at all thinking of how quick and quiet I could be."

I leant my head to hers. "Fuck. Later. Okay? Text me. Tell me when and where and I'll be there."

Her lips teased mine and I groaned.

"Please, baby. My restraint is hanging by a very tenuous thread as it is."

I felt her smile before she pulled away. "Sorry. Okay. Food court at Everdale. One o'clock?"

I nodded as I ushered her out of the room. "Yes. Definitely."

"And bring the GT."

I felt my eyebrow rise. "Oh?"

She shrugged, all coy as I pulled open the front door. "I've always wondered how small the backseat really is."

I leant on the door frame as she started walking down the front path. "The front is plenty big enough," I assured her.

She bit her lip and I almost thought I'd made her rethink this with a reminder of my past, but then I saw the smile in her eyes, and I knew she was just thinking about my front seat. God, she was amazing.

"Everdale. One," I said, and she nodded.

"Everdale. One."

Then she climbed into Clove's car and headed off.

"She's fucking worth it," I told myself.

It wasn't really a reminder. It was more surprise. Surprise that I was lucky enough to be in this position. Lucky enough that she was mine and even luckier that I was hers.

I went about making a coffee, knowing there was no way I was getting back to sleep now. Despite the very little sleep Maggie and I had got the night before, I was too excited to sleep now. Coffee was going to have to do. I was on my second mug when Dad rolled into the kitchen and dropped at the table.

"Mornin'," he growled. We were both nothing if not gravelly morning people. Mine was still wearing off, through lack of sleep for the most part.

I nodded to him as I drained that second mug. "Coffee?"

"How many have you had?" he asked as I got up and made them.

"Why? A guy can't just vibrate naturally?"

Dad snorted as he scrubbed hand over his face, looking like it was taking some effort to stay awake. "Usually I'd ask if it was a girl, but I know better with you. You win big last night?"

I sniffed as I tried to school my expression. "Yes, I did." Which wasn't a lie. I won the fucking biggest.

"Congrats. You take those De Lorenzo fuckers out finally?"

"Sure knocked them down a peg," I said as I sat back down and slid his mug over.

"Fucking good for you, son." He nodded to the mug as he wrapped his hand around it. "Thanks."

"What time did you get in?"

Dad shrugged as he drank. "I don't even remember. Nearly dawn, I think? You stay in last night?"

I nodded. "Yep. Yeah. Quiet one."

He nodded as well, somewhat absently. "Good. We all need a fucking quiet night once in a while." He hung his head back against the wall behind the bench seat that ran around our kitchen table. "Life can't be all drink and drugs and women and racing, mate."

"I think I might agree with you," I told him, and I saw his eyebrows rise in surprise. Pleasant surprise.

"Oh? You sure there isn't a girl?" he teased.

I huffed a rough laugh. "Why? That the only way I'm gonna grow up?"

Dad leant his elbows on the table between us and pinned me with a serious stare. "You're already grown, Vaughn. The Roses make a man grow early and no mistake. But there's grown and then there's being responsible for someone else. For their life, their happiness and coming home to them. Joke all you like, but you think you're ready for that?"

"Were you?" I countered.

He shook his head as he leant back again. "Fuck, no. Your mum made me nut up fast. Maybe too fast. Maybe that's why it didn't last. Maybe that's the only reason it lasted as long as it did. I always wondered if she'd fallen as hard as fast as I had. Turns out she didn't."

He wasn't bitter about it. Anymore. It was just a part of life. I was the one who was still bitter that she'd left and never looked back. Never so much as left me an explanation or tried to reach out with one since. She'd just walked out the front door one morning and not come back, and the next Dad heard she was shacked up with some arsehole in Snowtown.

But then Dad finished with the same thing he always did when the topic of my egg donor came up. "Not that it matters, because I got the one thing that does."

I gave him a smile. "Thanks, Dad."

He gave me a nod over his mug. “But I’m fucking serious, son. One day you’re gonna have to nut up. Whether it’s a woman, a man, a kid, a friend. You get a free pass to be an idiot while you’re young, but every day you’re getting just a little bit older.”

I nodded, not having the balls to tell him that I was pretty sure today was the day I nutted up. Ironic. “I’ll keep that in mind.”

“Do that while I get us some more coffee,” he said with a smile, giving my hair a ruffle as he got up.

My parents were a siren. Flashing lights. A warning to me that Maggie and I were too hard and too fast. I knew that. I wasn’t that fucking stupid. But I had no doubts that she was as powerless – as all in – as I was. And the first sign she wasn’t, then I’d let her go. I’d fight to the literal death to be with her. Against everyone. But if she didn’t want me anymore, then I’d lay down arms. Her happiness was everything.

And the timing of it all was fucking perfect, because I got a call later that morning to say that her present was ready to pick up.

“Sorry, darling,” I said to myself as I got dressed to meet her. “No GT today.”

V

I'm taking the bike.

I

Did it come in already?

C

Fucking load of wank.

E

Are we all taking bikes?

S

Everdale will love a pack of Blood Roses descending on them.

I was going to ignore Cairo's cynicism. It wasn't his fault they beat the mean into him far deeper than the rest of us. We were pretty doubtful about Ezra's ability to feel *anything*. Cairo felt, but the only thing he could really feel was pain and anger, and the satisfaction he got inflicting it on other people. Everything else was dulled.

V

Is five REALLY a pack?

C

You want the focus to be on spending time with your woman, I'd advise against.

I

I'll drive then.

E

Nope. I'm not squashing in anyone else's backseat. We'll take the pickup.

V

Yours or Daniels'?

S

I'm easy.

E

Let's do both in case West sacks up and decides to hijack one of them.

I laughed as I picked up the rest of my shit and headed out of the house.

CHAPTER ELEVEN

So, despite what I'd told Parker, I *was* actually kind of dating someone else the next day. But I wasn't going to feel bad about it. Not after what he'd said – whether he'd been hurt or not – and not when the butterflies in my stomach, as I waited to meet Vaughn, told me that I'd made the right choice.

Clove and I sat at one of the tables in the food court at Everdale, keeping an eye out for anyone we might know from Hammersby. The East Hammers would never head North unless it was for a football match, and the Blood Roses only ever came to Everdale to go to Rizzo's and bait Monster Aces into another battle in the turf war.

So, unsurprisingly, we didn't see anyone we knew. I did see a few Monster Aces, obvious when you knew to look for the double ace that was their standard. I thought it probably better not to point them out to Clove, who was blissfully unaware that I might have accidentally organised front row seats to one of those turf battles.

"Your life is like a literal movie," she sighed as she fiddled with her straw.

I smiled. "In what way?"

"You're the illegitimate daughter of the Lord of the Blood Roses." I winced slightly at the word Parker had thrown at me. "Sorry. I meant that in a good way. Let's call you 'forbidden fruit' instead." Feeling a little less sour, I gave her a nod and she quickly moved on. "And his heir is risking his life to date you in secret. It's so swoony!"

I snorted. "I don't know that I'd call it swoony." I would. "But I do feel lucky."

"Who would have thought that Vaughn Saint could actually fall in love?"

"I don't know that I'd say he was in love."

"Then you would be the only one. Do you remember what he did to Danica?" she asked, changing the mood drastically and I doubted it was anything more than just her thought process.

"I would prefer not to," I said wryly.

Clove smirked. "He's not going to do that to you." I nodded absently and she said, "You don't believe me?"

I shrugged. "I believe you. I believe him. But there is a flicker of doubt when I remember what happened to Danica."

"It wasn't *all* his fault…" she said softly, and I gave her a short nod.

No, Danica's death hadn't been *entirely* Vaughn's fault. And no one could really pin the blame on him. Certainly not in a court of law anyway. But it didn't take a genius to work out that Danica had only got fully wasted at that party because she was upset over what he did. His actions were the reason she then went on a massive rant at everyone there in anger and false bravado. And the subsequent embarrassment was what had her climb in the car and drive away. All culminating in her crashing and being pronounced DOA.

"I know. They were all her choices. But it's not like she's the only one he's ruined."

"She's the only one who died. Although, there *was* that one who ended up committed."

"That we know of," I reminded her.

"Are you second guessing?"

I sighed and dropped my head on the table. "Weirdly, no. Does that make me an awful person?"

"I think I'd call you whipped rather than weird."

I scoffed. "So, no different to the rest of them?"

"Very different to the rest of then. You whipped him."

"He probably wishes."

"Maybe an idea for your first anniversary?"

I laughed just as Clove elbowed me hard, and I looked up to see all five of the Princes walking through the food court. They were not hiding their affiliation in any way, and I rolled my eyes before quickly trying to work out if there were any Monster Aces in the immediate vicinity.

I knew enough to know that, strictly speaking, public places were off-limits for anything more than rude words and slung insults; the less witnesses and evidence you could give the cops and lawyers, the better. I also knew – intimately – what Roses like Vaughn thought about things that were off-limits.

Watching them walk towards us, with no one around to really judge my ogling, I could really look at them. I could look at them and wonder how in the hell five so very different people were so close. They looked like some eclectic 90s boyband or pop group or something; there was one to cater for everyone. So long as everyone's type skewed various degrees of bad boy.

Ezra raked a hand through his hair, glancing to one of the shops to his right. The chain on Iago's trousers swung as he licked his lip. Vaughn rearranged his jacket, flinging his elbows wide. Cairo kicked his chin and lunged at someone hurrying out of their way. Stone cracked his knuckles and stretched his neck.

Then Iago fully ruined the image by waving at us enthusiastically, and I couldn't help but smile. I was pretty sure that Clove legitimately swooned, like that Aladdin GIF. It was definitely audible.

The boys stopped when they got to us, already arguing about what they were going to get to eat. As Ezra sat down, he was busy trying to convince Cairo to buy his for him.

"If you get sushi, I will," was Cairo's answer.

Ezra hung his head back. "Fine. Grab me whatever," he sighed.

Cairo's eyes shone with victory as he left to get his and Ezra's lunch. Once his back was turned, Ezra winked at me, and I laughed. Iago and Vaughn were debating burgers, while Stone was eyeing off the fancy salad place.

Vaughn leant down to me, kissing my cheek under the pretence of whispering in my ear. "You want anything?"

"Burger sounds great, thanks."

"Perfect. Be right back."

Iago looked to Clove in question, and she shrugged in coy agreement. "Yes, please," she said, and he gave her a winning smile.

As the boys headed off, I leant into Clove and teased, "You two need to get a room already."

She went bright red as she smiled softly. "If only."

Ezra smiled at the exchange, but his eyes were tight as though he knew the real reason Iago pretended that he had no idea Clove was basically head over heels in love with him already. He said nothing, just dropped his eyes back to his phone as we waited for the others to return.

Cairo was back first, his eyes on me as he sat next to Ezra and passed him his packet of sushi. "Ladies."

"Cairo," I answered. "How's things?"

"Feeling fairly risky, Ms McCallan. I hope you know what you're doing."

Ezra's eyes darted between us like he was expecting some epic showdown as he scoffed his sushi roll.

"You didn't have to be here," was my response.

Cairo's eyes narrowed. "If you believe that, you're stupider than I thought." He paused for a second. "Which was already a fantastically low bar."

I wanted to retaliate, stick up for myself, just insult him in return, but Cairo kind of scared me. He was a loose cannon. You never knew what he might do in response to anything. Even when he was following Vaughn, and even knowing that touching me even in the non-sexual or romantic vicinity – although, I didn't doubt that pain and pleasure went hand in hand for Cairo – would get him in the deepest of shit.

So I said nothing, and I was sure Cairo took that as a win.

Vaughn, Iago and Stone all came back at the same time. Vaughn sat on the seat next to mine, somehow managing to position it so that his legs were on either side of my body and our chairs were right up close. I felt my cheeks heat and I fluttered that we were doing this.

Talk ebbed and flowed as we ate, and I noticed how much more involved Clove and I were than when we'd sat with Parker and his friends. Stone talked to Clove about football. Ezra and I bemoaned the latest assignment for English. Cairo and Clove were appalled at the closing of some shop they both loved. Iago found numerous topics of conversation that could get everyone talking, even if they were all disagreeing, like movies and TV and music.

Vaughn leant close to my ear while Iago and Clove were in heated discussion about the latest season of something I hadn't seen. "I could get used to this, darling."

I turned slightly to face him. "Get used to what?"

He ducked his lips back to my ear, his nose nuzzling my cheek as he leant against me close. "Us and our friends in public. Sharing food and laughter." He ran his hand across my lower back gently. "Being able to touch you."

I tucked my hair behind my ear as I couldn't help looking around in case there was someone who could dob us in.

Vaughn dropped a kiss to my neck. "Relax."

"Your life is literally in my hands, and you want me to relax?"

He nodded as he trailed kisses over me. "I do. I've got *you* in *my* hands. Everything is perfect, Maggie." He nipped my neck lightly. "Relax."

I took a breath and relaxed into him. His hand went to my thigh, and I felt his smile against my cheek.

"That's my good girl," he murmured as he nudged my jaw with his nose.

"You two are sickening," Cairo said, practically gagging, and Vaughn laughed before pulling his head from mine and looking at him.

"Jealous, Lock?"

Cairo scoffed. "Yes. If only I, too, was in the position to be suffering humiliating public displays of affection, my life would be complete." He rolled his eyes, and I looked down to hide my smile.

"No, no, baby," Vaughn told me, tilting my chin back up to make me look at Cairo again. "You want to laugh at him, laugh at him."

Cairo glared at me, as though both daring me to try it as well as warning me what awaited me if I did. With Vaughn basically wrapped around my body, I felt invincible and all Cairo's threats served to do was make the whole thing funnier and I grinned as I held Cairo's gaze. I felt Vaughn's pride as he put his arm around me and kissed my hair.

"There you go," Vaughn said, evidently pleased.

There was the smallest crack in Cairo's stony expression. Something that could have been misconstrued as the very barest hint of possibly even respect.

After we'd eaten and wandered and hung out and shopped and eaten again, Clove said she needed to head back to Hammersby for something with her family. I didn't want to stop hanging out with Vaughn, but I knew we'd have plenty more opportunities.

"I'll talk to you tonight?" I asked him.

He looked sheepish for a moment, then took my hand and said, "Can I give you a lift back?"

Clove nodded. "Yes, you can."

I looked to her. "What about you? You don't want to drive all that way alone."

"It's an hour," she said.

"I'll go with her," Iago offered.

"We can convoy and pick Iago up before you get the bridge to East Ham," Stone offered.

Clove tried very hard – and failed – to hide her pleased smile. "I could be persuaded."

Vaughn hadn't let go of my hand and gave it a squeeze. "We'll see you back there, then."

We headed for the parking lot and Vaughn stopped before the others. I looked at him pointedly. "You brought your bike?"

"It's still not my racing bike."

"I was less worried about that."

"What were you worried about?" he asked with a smirk.

"I was more worried about how I was going to fuck you more easily."

He stepped up close to me, put his finger under my chin as his other hand went to my waist. "Jesus, I love that mouth."

"And you might have been able to see what it could do if you'd brought the GT. It's much better than my hand."

He swooned. Visibly swooned and I laughed. "Next time. Promise."

"I'll hold you to that." I held my hand out for his jacket, and he smirked.

Looking around, I realised there was another jacket on his bike. A really ugly feeling welled up in me as I realised it was a lady's jacket.

"What's this?" I asked him, picking it up.

He looked me over with that sexy smugness. "That, love, is a leather jacket."

I rolled my eyes. "I know it's a leather jacket, Vaughn. Whose leather jacket have you got draped over your bike?"

He came over and put his hands on my waist as he looked down at me. There was a touch of mischief in his eyes. The kind of shit-stirring nonsense I was used to seeing in Iago, not Vaughn.

"You think some other chick's left her jacket with my bike, baby?"

I huffed, ignoring the butterflies in my chest that were making me worry that was exactly what it was. "That is not an answer."

His face broke into a wide half-smile that made the lapis lazuli in his eyes sparkle just the way I loved. "It's yours, Magenta," he said gently as he touched his knuckles under my chin, making sure

I wouldn't look away. "I can't have my woman on the back of my bike and not have her protected."

He'd got me a jacket. I didn't know the protocol for getting someone a jacket. It wasn't like it was plastered with Blood Rose patches or anything. It was plain black, double-breasted, with a belt around the bottom hem.

"You got me a jacket?"

He nodded. "Of course, I did."

I looked at him and couldn't have stopped the massive smile from spreading on my face. "You got me a jacket."

"Try it on."

I pulled it on and, as I went to do it up, I noticed something on the section of the inner lapel that would sit over my heart. It had been stamped into the jacket and foiled in dark pink.

VS♡MM

"That is unbearably cute, Vaughn."

He shrugged. "I do my best."

I finished doing it up and stepped back to spin around. "How does it look?"

"Like you were born for it," he said, all awed reverence.

I went up to him and wrapped my arms around his shoulders. "Thank you, Vaughn."

He seemed genuinely confused by my thanks. "For what?"

"The jacket, but also for making me feel like I finally belong somewhere."

"You will always belong with me," he said before he kissed me hard.

Needless to say, we did stop off on the way home, in a very out of the way place, and he learned that my mouth was very much better than my hand.

I spent every day of that week with Vaughn. Sometimes Clove and Iago joined us. Sometimes the rest of the Princes did as well.

That day was uncharacteristically hot for the time of year, so Vaughn suggested we go to his dad's property and maybe go for a swim. I'd done my due diligence and gone in the water to get Clove and Iago in there, then Vaughn and I had snuck out to leave them flirting and calling it play-fighting.

As we lay on the blanket in the dappled sunshine and our bathers, I watched the clouds float over us. "Vaughn?"

"Magenta?"

"How do you feel about whips?"

"I'm scared to ask what brought that question on," he chuckled.

I turned my head to find him looking at me with a wide smile. "Clove thinks I whipped you, and I joked that you probably wished I had."

His smile widened and that lapis lazuli sparkled at me. I didn't mind so much about being dazzled by it anymore. "Look, baby. If you want to play harder in the bedroom, then I am happy to play harder." He rolled onto his side. "But you know it's not a requirement, right?"

I rolled to mirror him and looked into his eyes. "I'm not sure if that's a really backhanded way of saying you'll deal with how boring I am, or if that's really sweet."

He snorted. "You're not boring. What about me says I can't get off without whips and ball gags?"

"No one mentioned ball gags except you, and..." I looked him over pointedly.

He inclined his head. "Fine. Your point is made," he acknowledged. "But all I need is you, and I'm at serious risk of getting over-excited and blowing my load too early."

I smiled. "You sure?"

He ran his hand over my hip. "You want to try whips or restraints or fucking furry foreplay, and I will try anything for you. But, just having you, I am happier and more satisfied than I have a right to be."

"You deserve to be happy," I told him.

"And how about your ex?"

Clove snorted as she and Iago dropped down beside us. "You know, they were never official?"

I sat up and glared at her betrayal as Iago spluttered.

Vaughn sat up behind me and said, "Oh, really?"

Clove nodded at him over me. "Really. She was just using him to tell herself she could resist you."

"Clove!" I hissed, like neither Vaughn nor Iago would notice my reaction.

"Pushing all your buttons was just a bonus," Clove added happily, and I groaned in annoyance.

Vaughn's arms tightened around me as he dropped his lips to the back of my neck. "Is this true, darling? You lied to me?"

"Seemed like a good idea at the time," I muttered.

He spun me around to face him and was looking at me with such a genuine smile that it took my breath away. "You wanted me so badly you had to fake yourself a boyfriend, love?"

I bit my lip as I looked him over. "I wanted you so badly that I've all-but thrown away a whole damned life – my so-called perfect future – just to be with you."

He took my chin in his hand. "Then we make a better one," he said before crushing his lips to mine.

Now was not the time to remind him that, if we got caught, he was dead ergo we didn't really have a future. Now was the time to bask in the feeling and just enjoy it for a little while before we had to deal with reality crashing in around us.

School went back on Monday and that was going to create a whole new butt load of trouble. But that could be future Maggie's problem, because present Maggie had a Halloween Party at Kenicki's to plan for.

Clove had convinced me to go as Sandy from *Grease*.

"It's symbolic," she'd decided.

"Of what? Me changing myself for some guy as I'm drowning?" I'd argued.

"No. Of you becoming who you're supposed to be. Without anyone dying," had been her counter.

Still, I'd given in when Clove's final argument had been Vaughn's face when he saw me in a skin-tight pleather cat suit.

Clove and Iago slipped away again as Vaughn kissed me and things heated quickly. Until he pulled away to nudge my nose with his and stare into my eyes.

"I used to hate the fact your mum had you three weeks and your old man only got one."

I smirked. "Why?"

"Because seventy-five percent of the time, there was only a slim chance I'd see you outside of school."

"And now?"

He dragged me onto his body. "Now," he said with a smile in his eyes. "Seventy-five percent of the time, we're less likely to get caught."

"And coming here where no one will catch us has nothing to do with that?" I teased.

He jumped up and held his hands out for me. "Speaking of no one catching us… I have a sudden urge to show you a specific tree deep in that copse."

I let him pull me up, grabbing a towel as I did.

"What is that for?" he asked as he dragged me to the trees.

"For the ground. For the tree. I'm all for sex in all kinds of places, but that doesn't mean one of us should get dirt in their arse or scraped up by some bark."

"You're a planner. Good to know."

I shrugged, all coy. "I do my best."

He laughed as we disappeared into the tree line.

CHAPTER TWELVE

It didn't take Parker long to move on. As in, the next Monday, when I walked into school acting as downcast as the newly broken up was supposed to look, his tongue was down another girl's throat.

I couldn't say I didn't feel something about it. After all, there was still a part of me who still remembered him as the sweet, caring, doting almost-boyfriend. The part that needed reminding of the way he reacted when we broke up, the things he'd said, and the fact that he'd tried to hit me. Even though I *had* hit him first.

I also couldn't say that it didn't backfire on him tremendously. There was me, studious, kind, hard-working Maggie, all sombre and reserved. Then there was him, basically dry humping Lettie against her locker.

The majority of the school decided pretty quickly that Parker had dumped me for a girl who was a gold-digging dipstick at best, and I was heartbroken about it but putting on a very brave face in the face of their indiscretion.

I didn't see there was any reason to set the larger populace of Hammersby Bay to rights. If anyone asked me, I didn't confirm it, but neither did I deny it.

"I'd rather not talk about," I'd say.

"It's between Parker and I," I'd say.

"I guess we just weren't a good match after all," I'd say.

And, all the while, Clove and I were giggling about Parker's comeuppance, and the fact that I had a damned sexy, much more exciting, new boy-toy.

By Wednesday, Vaughn and I had fallen into a pretty easy routine of ignoring each other the same as usual during the day – except via text – and making up for it if and when we could after school. Although that second one was still only a theory. He even had the other Princes interacting with me less than usual. I was both impressed and terrified by even Iago's relative silence and lack of shit-stirring.

Meanwhile, Parker had clearly been on defence for his actions.

"Did you really cheat on Parker?" Kayla asked as she came up to me in the corridor. "Because I *know* he was with Lettie after the Storms game."

I looked to Clove, wondering what the hell I should say. How did I play this? Victim? Victor? Did I want to be pitied or Parker to be pitied, or just want this over with? It honestly depended how he was going to play this. He was obviously going for victim now that his 'moving on' had backfired on him.

I smiled at Kayla as pleasantly as I could. "Uh, no. Parker was the one who wanted to keep things open and not make anything official. I guess I just didn't realise how open he was being about it." I shrugged.

Kayla frowned a little. "You guys weren't official?"

"I mean, we'd never talked about it, and I was pretty sure he was hooking up with other people, yeah."

"Huh. That's funny. Because Parker told everyone you'd been official and exclusive since like the start of Summer and you totally broke his heart by cheating on him."

"What other lies has he been telling?" Clove asked.

I forced a smile and shrugged again. "I don't know. Maybe he's confused?"

Kayla nodded. "Confused or delusional," she muttered. "Anyway, thanks. I'll see you in bio."

I nodded to her as she walked off.

But she wasn't the only one who was hearing rumours. And plenty of them were not afraid to ask me to sort the fact from fiction for them. Everyone but one person.

When I got in that afternoon, it was just Freddy home as the parents were still at work. He was sitting in the kitchen, stuffing his face as he was wont to do. Until he saw me and just frowned.

"Nope," he said, sliding off the barstool at the bench, picking up his plate and stalking to his bedroom.

Even at eleven, he was taller than me and faster than me. I skidded to a stop as his bedroom door slammed shut in my face. I heard the lock click.

I banged on Freddy's door. "Come on," I whined. "Talk to me, Fredster!"

"No!" he yelled, his door still firmly locked.

"Mum and Dad are going to be pissed if they find out that this door is locked!" I tried on him.

"Good. Then I can explain to them I don't want to live in a house with someone who betrays me."

I sank down on the floor, resting my back against the door. "It's not like that," I told him.

"How is it not like that?" The closeness of his voice sounded like he was in a mirror position. "You dumped him."

"I think you'll find he's quite happy to tell people he dumped me."

"But why? Why did anyone have to dump anyone?"

What the hell did I say to him? If I told him that I fell for someone else, he'd want to know and he was eleven not stupid; if I told him I couldn't tell him who, he'd know it was someone I wasn't supposed to be with – he knew Dad's rules as well as anyone in Hammersby. East or West. Not to mention, Freddy would know that, if things were over with Parker, then I was with that person I wasn't supposed to be with. I didn't want to lie to my brother, but I also didn't want to risk him, in his hurt, telling Mum or Jonathan anything that would definitely get back to Dad.

"Parker was supposed to help me train to play football," I heard him say quietly.

I sighed. "I know, dude. I know. I'm sorry."

And I was sorry. I wanted Freddy to have everything in life that he wanted, just the way Dad wanted that for me. But I couldn't do that by being with Parker. Maybe Stone could help him instead?

Oh, shit.

I had to snap my lips shut before I let that one slip.

"You guys were perfect together, Mags. What happened?" Freddy asked.

I banged my head on the door a little in annoyance. If Freddy had reacted like this, the guy who always had my back, how would everyone else react?

It wasn't like Vaughn and I had planned on shouting it from any rooftops. We knew we had to stay secret. But was I just spiting myself? Had I made the wrong decision? Should I have just stuck it out with Parker until I got over this obsession with Vaughn?

Well, no. Turned out Parker was a bit shit and I'd probably dodged a bullet with that one.

But what did I really think I was doing? Did Vaughn and I have an expiry date? Were we just going to keep hiding it until we had like four kids and Dad would have no choice but to keep his grandchildren's father alive? Did this end with Vaughn's untimely death?

I flopped forward and rested my head on my knees in frustration.

"What have I done?" I muttered to myself.

Did I regret Vaughn? Not really, but I realised I hadn't thought much about this beyond enjoying the moment. Which was good and all, but...

While I waited for Freddy to eventually talk to me, I texted Vaughn.

Maggie

What are we doing?

He took longer to reply than I'd expected, and I wondered what he was up to.

As I waited, I ran through any number of worst case scenarios: Vaughn was done now that he'd got what he wanted; I felt so guilty that I told Freddy anyway, and he told Mum, and she told Dad, and he killed Vaughn; I got radio silence off everyone because Vaughn was playing me and the others all found out anyway and even Dad was like 'you should have known better' and I spent the rest of my life alone.

So I was in a real cheery mood when Vaughn finally replied.

V

I can't speak for you, but I'm helping your dad with something. Hence the slow reply. Sorry.

Well, I felt slightly better. Maybe.

Maggie

Well, I'm sitting on the floor outside Freddy's room wondering what the hell you and I thought was going to come of this.

V

Are you having second thoughts about us?

Just the idea of the 'us' being over made my heart twinge in a really uncomfortable way, so I knew the answer to that one easily.

Maggie

No.

V

Then what's wrong?
Talk to me about it.

Maggie

I'm just wondering how we thought this would end?
Do we just choose a time to walk away?
Get complacent and then Dad finds out and kills you?
Or are we running away from our families to never see them again but at least be together?

V

You have had way too much time to think about this, huh?

Maggie

Freddy won't talk to me! He never doesn't talk to me. He

yells at me, and he tells me all the things that are wrong, but he just won't talk to me!

V

And you're wondering if you made the wrong choice.

Maggie.

No. You're the right choice. I just want to know that it's going to be worth it.

V

I don't plan on walking away. I don't want us to choose that this ends when you go to uni or whatever cutoff date we could pick. I don't want to leave our families, even if it meant walking down the street holding your hand. Sorry, but I'm not doing that to you.

Death and you deciding you're done with me are the only things that will part me from you at this point.

So, unless your dad gets real cool about a bunch of stuff real quick, I don't know, baby. I don't know the answer other than I want to be with you. If that's not enough, I understand.

Was it enough? I wanted it to be. The alternative was so painful, I couldn't really even bring myself to think it. I dropped my phone in my lap as I rested back against the door again. I had to be with him; there was no other option that didn't make me feel sick. But the uncertainty didn't sit well with me. I was going to have to find a way to either ignore it, let things sort themselves out, or decide how I wanted to sort it out.

For now, uncertain in secret was going to have to do. I refused to risk talking to Dad to take that uncertainty away, so I was going to have to live with it.

Maggie

It's enough. It's more than enough.

V

I will never get enough of you. Whether I die today or in seventy years, I'll always want one more.

Maggie

One more what?

V

Touch. Taste. Smile. Laugh. Joke. Sight. Even an insult.

Maggie

Are you fully whipped or something? 😜

V

Fully. I am yours.

As far as reassurances went, that was a big one. That made it all worth it. I didn't need to work everything out right now. We could just enjoy the time we had without worrying what the future looked like. What mattered was that we both wanted one. Together.

I was typing a reply to him when Freddy opened his door and I tumbled backwards onto his floor. Freddy took one look at the remnant on the smile on my face and his expression went from 'okay, I'll hear you out' to 'I'm not going to like this, am I?'

"There's someone else?!" he asked, more incredulous than I think even Parker had been.

I winced sheepishly. "There's not *not* someone else...?"

"What does that even mean?"

"It means it's new and I'm not ready to talk about it yet."

He crossed his arms as he frowned at me. "You dumped Parker for some random dude?"

I shook my head noncommittally. "I wouldn't call him random."

"How well do you know him?"

I inclined my head. "Better than I'd like sometimes." Which told him plenty about the whole situation.

He uncrossed his arms. "But you still chose him over Parker?"

"But I still chose him over Parker."

Freddy breathed out deeply. "I guess I can hold off on my football aspirations for your heart."

I smirked as he helped me off the floor. "Thanks, little brother."

He shrugged, all self-conscious now. "It's fine. You'd do the same for me."

We went back to the kitchen and ate way too much food. We'd coaxed Mum into joining us in our inadvisable pre-dinner feast and she was licking her fingers as Jonathan stormed in the front door.

For a man with very little trace of a temper, he was miffed.

"Those…" Jonathan growled in frustration, which always hid a curse word when Freddy was around. "…Blood Roses!"

"What happened?" I asked, very tempted to ask specifically what my father and my boyfriend had done now.

Jonathan ran his hand over his chin. "They've taken over half the..." Another groan. "...docks for their shipments. We can't get a single cop in there, even the ones we think are on their payroll."

"You've got to hand it to them," Freddy said. "They're shady criminals who all deserve to rot in jail if not Hell, but Maggie comes from pretty smart people on both sides."

"Thank you, baby," Mum said to him as she ruffled his hair.

"No disrespect to him as your dad, Mags. That's a whole other kettle of fish," Jonathan said with a nod on my direction. "But as a criminal, Blaise is a bloody nuisance whose too smart for his own good."

"That's the worst insult you could come up with?" Freddy teased.

Jonathan nodded. "In front of you, yes."

"Can you arrest someone if you're told they killed someone?" Freddy asked.

Jonathan looked at him quickly, all thoughts about my dad and his cleverness off his mind. "Why?"

Freddy shrugged. "That St Jude kid in my class says his brother and his friends killed someone."

I didn't doubt they had, whether Freddy was talking about Ezra and the Princes, or the twins, or any other number of the St Jude progeny. I was also quite sure that didn't narrow down exactly who was dead or when it happened.

"Uh, no. No. That's not enough, Fred."

Freddy sighed. "Shame. They might leave Maggie alone if there were in jail for a while."

Now, Jonathan and Mum both looked at me. I held my hands up in innocent defence.

"That is probably not what it sounds like. The Princes–"

"The what?" our parents said.

"Their nicknames. It's a whole… Never mind. My point is, they talk to me as much as Dad allows and no more. Sometimes they give me a lift to and from school where we sit in sullen silence."

Jonathan nodded again. "Okay. Good."

Mum put a hand on his arm. "I can have a word with Blaise. Make sure he reminds the boys to behave."

"Maybe when it comes to Maggie," was Freddy's sarcastic reply as he crammed toast in his face.

So, maybe Freddy *would* get over me ending things with Parker for someone else. Eventually. But even he wasn't going to be okay with who that someone was if he ever found out.

Maggie

Jonathan would like you to be less clever.

Dad

Oh really? And how's that?

Maggie

He was hoping you might invite some employees to your new party so he'd find out who was pulling double shifts.

Dad

I look after my own. I think we'd all rather they be at home with their families than at a party they're not needed at.

How's the new term treating you?

Maggie

As fine as when you asked yesterday. Thanks 😊

Dad

Good. Think about what you want to do next weekend, yeah? I was thinking ribs.

Maggie

You know I will never say no to ribs.

Dad

A whole week of ribs?

Maggie

I think it's an experiment worth conducting.

Dad

🤣 All right. It's on.

Maggie

Perfect.

Dad

Love you ❤️

Maggie

Love you, too ❤️

CHAPTER THIRTEEN

The next week, Clove and I were headed to my locker at the end of recess.

"Oh. My. God," Clove sighed as her steps faltered, and I turned to see what she was staring at.

I'd expected it to be Iago in his unnecessarily tight sport uniform or with a new haircut or a new tattoo on display or something.

It was not.

She was staring at my locker. The reason she was staring at my locker had me also unable to move and staring at my locker.

Attached to my locker door was a rose.

The colour could only be described as blood red.

"Someone's got an admirer," Kaley said with a wink as she passed.

I could only nod, dumbfounded.

"Well?" Clove whispered.

"Well, what?" I whispered back.

"Aren't you going to see if they left a note?"

I shook my head.

"Why not?"

"It has to be Parker."

Clove frowned. "Why would it be Parker? Could it not be…anyone else?" The way she said 'anyone' was obviously code, and any passing idiot would guess we knew who the alternative was.

I shook my head again. "He wouldn't do this," I whispered.

"Well, I know how we can find out," she said, then strode to my locker and took the rose off it.

She found a tag and read it. I assumed it was good news based on the fact that a smile spread over her face before she brandished the rose at me.

I hurried over to her, half-slinking and half-skipping like I hoped no one would notice and snatched it out of her hands.

From a Prince to his princess. Beauty despite Thorns. V

"I think it's obvious Parker didn't leave it," Clove pronounced proudly.

It *was* obvious that Parker hadn't left it. The Prince of Thorns clearly had. Or someone wanted me to believe he had. It was quite likely the Prince of Thorns himself wanted me to believe he had. He had mentioned roses the week before.

I saw Parker coming towards us. He saw what was in my hand and his victorious, superior smirk turned to a displeased grimace.

"Well, I think we're about to find out," I muttered to Clove as Parker angled towards us.

"What is that?" Parker growled at me.

I held up the rose, looked at it, then looked at him. "For a minute, I thought it might be me sticking my tongue so far down Lettie's throat that it risks cleaning her arsehole. But no. Silly me. It's just an innocuous rose." I brandished it a little to really drive the point home.

Clove coughed, barely covering a laugh. Parker was less impressed with my sass.

"So much for not dating someone the next day, huh?" Parker said, ignoring Clove.

"That's rich coming from you. I saw the pictures of you and Lettie from the Hut over the weekend." The term dry humping would have applied if more clothes had been involved.

His smirk was so ugly. How had I been attracted to him? "Jealous, Maggie?"

I pretended to think about it. "So jealous that I was dating someone else *before* that?" I asked, sarcastically enough that I could have been confirming his suspicions or was just mocking his insane theories. "Obviously."

As the bell rang, his lip rippled into a snarl. "You will be."

I nodded as I took Clove's arm and started walking away. "Sure, Parker. I'm sure I will."

"You'll beg for me back, Maggie!" he called after me. "But whores don't get a second chance!"

I whirled around, ready to punch the idiot again. But there were a lot of people hovering. I couldn't tell if there were more appalled by me or Parker. If I wanted it to keep being Parker, I was going to have to play it smarter than just breaking his nose.

"You dumped *me*, Parker," I said, affecting a watery waver to my voice. "You didn't want *me*. You don't get to turn around with someone else and call me a whore just because you regret it. You were everything to me, Parker. And now I'm just the girl with the broken heart."

I saw Iago down the hall and momentarily panicked that he'd bought into my act, but he covered a smirk more expertly than Clove and inclined his head at me in a tiny show of kudos. I had to school my expression not to smile back at him.

Parker was looking me over like he was suddenly rethinking the whole thing. I could see it in his eyes; had he misunderstood what I'd been saying last week? Or was I lying now to just be a dick after he was one first. It was that second one, for sure, but I enjoyed watching him second guess himself.

"Maggie…" he said softly.

I sniffed dramatically like I was holding back a torrent of tears and shook my head before sweeping off towards the library where Clove and I had our free lesson next.

"Maggie!" he called after me and I heard Iago strongly encourage him not to follow me.

"That was brutal," Clove whispered.

"Too brutal?"

"After what he said?" Because of course I'd told her EVERYTHING about that night. "Not brutal enough."

I smiled at her. "Good."

News spread fast of the showdown between me and Parker in the hallway and I had to pretend that I was feeling all sniffly and fragile after it as people stopped by to express their disgust with him. Given the things a couple of them said about him, I was starting to feel bad about what I'd done. But then I remembered everything he'd said and done since I'd told him we should just be friends and I felt a little less bad.

V

Heard you won a smackdown.

Instinct made me look up and I saw Vaughn was sitting over the other side of the library.

Maggie

Jealous? 😛

V

That I missed it. You're fucking fierce.

Maggie

Dreamer tell you?

V

He gave me the FULL play by
play.

Not knowing what to say to that, I changed the subject.

Maggie

So... Someone left something
on my locker today.

Clove and I watched him check his phone. The corner of his lips tipped as he typed something out. He looked up at me pointedly just as my phone vibrated.

V

Did they? How rude was it?

Maggie

It wasn't rude at all.
It was actually really lovely.

V

So, I'm not going to need to
beat anyone?

I gave him a shrug.

Maggie

Not so much, no.
Thank you.

He gave me a wink before going back to his phone.

Clove nudged me. "Subtle as a goddamned sledgehammer, you two," she whispered, and I nudged her back.

I didn't care just then. I wanted more Vaughn. It felt good to feel good after Parker made me feel like shit.

V

What are your plans for the
weekend?

Maggie

Why?

When he looked at me again, I gave him an expectant, questioning frown. He just smirked and bent down to his phone again.

V

I was thinking we could take a trip.

Maggie

A trip?
What kind of trip?

V

The kind that involves you, me, and nothing but wilderness for miles.

Maggie

Does this trip also include a tent?!

V

It might.

"He wants to take you *camping*?" Clove whispered, as confused as me as she peered over my shoulder.

Maggie

You want to take me camping?

My eyebrows rose at him to show him exactly what I thought about that plan. But his face was set in grim determination. He barely took his eyes off me as he typed his reply and hit send.

V

I want you to myself.
I want to bury myself inside you and not have to be thinking about who might catch us.

I want you somewhere you can be as loud as you fucking want and no one will hear us.

"Okay," Clove breathed. "That actually sounds *really* good."

I smiled at her, then bit my lip so Vaughn wouldn't see how much I'd liked that and I'd lose any bargaining power I might need.

Maggie

And do you have a tent?

V

I'm capable of purchasing one.

Maggie

And sleeping bags? Lanterns? Food?

V

It was my idea. You just let me sort the details. All I need from you is a decision that preferably involves your arse on my bike on Saturday afternoon.

Clove shook me in excitement. "Give him your arse!" she squeaked. "Do it!"

A couple of kids looked at us at the noise, realised it was probably nothing to interest them, and went back to their work.

Chewing my lip as I locked eyes with Vaughn, I hit send.

Maggie

My arse is yours whenever you want it ;P

On the other side of the room, I saw him swallow hard. He sniffed as he put his phone in his lap, looked around the library once – his eyes avoiding me – then picked his phone back up.

V

Do not tempt a man. It's already taking far more willpower than I have to not drag you behind these stacks, bend you over, and make you cum so hard you see stars.

I exchanged a look with Clove. She clearly worked out what I was thinking by the look in my eyes.

"Okay then," she said with an approving chuckle.

I very slowly put my phone on the table, stood up and wandered over to the stacks. It didn't work if I looked back at him, so I just dragged my hand over the nearest shelf as I entered them and hoped he was going to follow.

He caught up to me as I was trailing a hand over the absolute back shelves – the ones no one used so they didn't even light back there, which made it perfect for hook ups – like I was looking for something. He spun me as he pressed me back into the wall and claimed my lips with his. He was breathing so hard that it made me laugh.

I put my hand on his chest and pulled my head back. "Did you *run* after me?" I asked.

He shook his head. "Always."

"You're that desperate for sex?"

"I'm that far gone for you."

"Jesus, Vaughn…" I breathed.

He shook his head again before he kissed me again, saying against my lips, "We can take our time on the weekend. But if you want this now, we don't have time for emotions, baby."

I nodded. "Okay. No. I want this now, Vaughn."

He groaned into my mouth as he lifted me up. I wrapped my arms around his shoulders and my legs around his waist to free his hands to grab the condom out of his pocket. Not that he didn't have me pinned to the wall with his body alone.

He rubbed over me as he kissed me hard. His lips trailed down my neck and my head fell back against the wall. "Vaughn…" I breathed as my fingers went to his hair. "I am *so* wet enough. Cock. Now. Please."

His groan was even deeper this time and I felt it rumble from his chest between us. He got the condom on, slid my pants aside and slid into me in one thrust. I grabbed his shoulders, digging my nails into his shirt, as my whole body tightened around him.

"Fuck, Maggie," he breathed hard as he pounded me even harder. "Remember our first night?"

I nodded as I clutched onto him. "Definitely."

"This is good, darling. But you remember what it was like when we had all night?"

I nodded again as I felt that little coil in me start to wind so damned tight. It was going to be hard and fast, my excitement as much because of him as the thrill that someone could find us at any moment.

"Oh, my God, Vaughn. Yes, right there. Harder. Please."

He obliged and it was neither the first nor would it be the last time I counted myself unbelievably lucky. Vaugn's hand slid between us and found my clit. He only had to rub over it twice before he had me cumming on his cock. I pressed my face to his shoulder to muffle my moan, my nails digging into him deeper as my legs tightened around him. But he was still relentless. He slid out of me, dropped my feet to the ground, and spun me before thrusting straight back in.

I braced my hands on the wall and his fingers reached around and played with my clit again.

"You got one more in you, Maggie?" he asked as he trailed his lips over my neck.

I nodded as I more whimpered than made a noise of agreement, having to bite my lip to stop from being any louder.

"Tell me, darling. Tell me what you want," he demanded, the fingers of the hand not on my slit digging roughly into my waist and sending tingles of excitement all over me.

"Fuck, Vaughn…" I wrapped my fingers around the hand between my legs and gently coaxed him to wrap it around my throat instead. He tightened it slightly and I rested my head back against him as the pleasure zinged around my body. "Yes, make me cum."

My whole body contracted as I came hard again. I felt myself squirt and then Vaughn's smile against my cheek. He wrapped one arm around my stomach and braced the other hand against the wall by mine as he pounded me harder and faster until I felt him tense, and he throbbed inside me.

"Fuck," he breathed as he slid out of me. "I will never get enough of that."

I righted my pants and turned to him. "Sorry about that… I wasn't thinking–"

He quickly dealt with the condom, pocketing it before tucking himself back in. He didn't look *too* wet. "Never apologise."

"I mean, it's not ideal for…keeping on the downlow."

"I don't fucking care as long as you enjoyed yourself."

I looked down as I smoothed my skirt. "You know I enjoyed myself. Twice!"

His fingers played under my chin as he tipped my face to his with a sinful smirk. "I want you to spend the next couple of days thinking about what's just happened here, and remembering how much better it is when I can take my time with you."

I pressed against his body. "Just so long as I'm not the only one thinking about it."

He licked his lip slowly as he shook his head. "You won't be." He looked me over. "Well, you look a little fucked. Sorry about that."

I bit my lip and shook my head. "Never be sorry for giving your woman a right fucking."

He leant into me as he rearranged his trousers. "This was supposed to *stop* me going to next lesson with a boner."

I pouted dramatically. "Was I not good enough?"

"You're too good. You're getting me hard again. Go on, get back to Clove."

I laughed as I reached up and pressed one more kiss to his lips before hurrying back out to my desk.

"Oh, yeah. Because no one could possibly know what you've just been up to," Clove huffed, all sarcastic humour, as I dropped back into my chair.

"Is it that bad?" I asked her.

She shook her head. "You're flushed and your neck's probably going to bruise a little, but otherwise you did well."

I smirked as I looked at her. "I'm not sure I ever thought I could be excited about a camping date."

She gave a small squeal of excitement. "Yes, but you know any date with Vaughn is going to be amazing."

I huffed as I took in her words. "I'm dating Vaughn Saint."

She bounced her eyebrows at me. "Yeah, I think it's more accurate to say that Vaughn Saint is dating you."

"I think so, huh?"

Vaughn took his time sauntering back to his desk, like nearly the whole rest of the lesson. He was very careful not to look at me as he picked up his books, then headed out. But I got a text from him a moment later that just read;

V

It would be so easy to fall in love with you.

♥

Maggie

What do you mean 'would be'? 😉

V

I mean you're not ready for that to be anything more than hypothetical yet and that's fine.

Maggie

I don't know. I might have already fallen.

V

Me, too, Maggie. Me, too.

CHAPTER FOURTEEN

It was Saturday. Trip day.

Date day?

Camping day?

Whatever it was, I was excited. And Dad totally noticed.

"You're in a good mood, sweetheart," Dad said, and I tried really hard to keep the goofy smile off my face.

"I guess I'm just really looking forward to the movie tonight. You sure you don't mind we're going tonight?"

Dad smiled. "Sweet, when your favourite cult movie series is playing at the Orion, you get dressed up, you get all your mates, and you go and make a big night of it. You don't worry about missing one night with your old man."

I grimaced, still feeling guilt. "Are you sure you're sure? I feel like I keep making plans on our days."

And I did. Mainly because Dad was more lenient and had less questions. In fact, I wouldn't put it past him to know exactly what sort of teenage debauchery I was getting up to and he figured it was so tame compared to what he knew the Roses my age were doing that he was willing to allow it. Even if he knew about the camping trip, it was undoubtedly far less bad than anything he did at my age that he probably counted himself lucky.

"I would rather see you live your life to please you than to please me. That's what makes me happy, Maggie. If that means we miss hanging out a couple of nights, then yeah I miss you, but I know you're having a good life."

There was a very large part of me who hoped he already knew about Vaughn and that was his way of opening the conversation that he could be okay with it. I was too chicken shit to follow through. though.

"That's why you have your rules," I said instead, forcing a smile I was ninety percent sure he saw right through.

He nodded. "That's why I have me rules. So you get the life you want."

Again, I felt like that was a pointed message. But I convinced myself I was reading into it. How would Dad know? Unless he'd hacked my phone or actually did have surveillance on it, I couldn't see how he would. Vaughn and I had been careful. I mean, he'd dropped me at Dad's the afternoon before in the GT and we'd done such a decent job of pretending we still hated each other that Dad had slapped him upside the head for whatever slight he assumed Vaughn had made against me.

"Besides," Dad said. "You're fucking glowing today, sweetie. I could never deny you something that made you so happy."

I had to look away or I was so sure that he'd see on my face and in my eyes the exact reason I was so happy. And I wasn't all that bothered by him knowing there was a new guy. We'd had a talk about Parker, or the lack of Parker in my life now. Dad wasn't the one who'd worry about me falling for another guy so quickly. Mum would, and I certainly had to pause about it.

Vaughn consumed me now. He'd gone from a guy I hated to someone I knew I didn't want to live without in what felt like a ridiculously short amount of time. Then again, if I was doing this whole being honest thing properly, I had to acknowledge that maybe I'd never wanted to live without Vaughn. Before, it had been fighting with him. It had been an integral part of my life. Because I wasn't the only one off-limits to the Roses, Vaughn as a Rose was off-limits to me. It was just that Dad had probably never considered that was a rule that needed to be enforced.

I wondered if maybe there'd always been something between us, and it had simply taken one kiss to make both of us realise it. We'd hidden behind hate and (very poorly) masked the sizzle between us. Vaughn had admitted, the night we started dating, that he'd wanted me even back then. And I'd never lied to myself about being unreasonably attracted to him.

"This new fella of yours going, too?" Dad said and I grinned at him.

"You always see right through me."

Yeah, I felt guilty about lying to him. About hiding something so important from him. Hiding some*one* so important to me. But the fear that I would lose Vaughn so soon after getting him overrode my guilt. Dad couldn't know. At least not now.

"Is he good to you?" Dad asked, with a self-satisfied smile at his 'detective' skills.

I nodded. "Really good. He treats me well. He cares about me. He kind of took me by surprise."

Dad's smile softened. "I'm really glad, sweetie. What time do you need to leave?"

I looked at my phone and realised it was already ten in the morning. "Couple of hours."

"Wanna do something for brunch?" he asked.

I rolled my eyes at him in humour. "When do I *not* want to do brunch?"

"Ribs for brunch is probably overdoing it, right?" Dad asked as he stood up and headed to the fridge.

I actually had to pause for thought. "People probably have feelings about it…"

"We could add eggs?"

I nodded. "That would make it more brunch-ly."

"More bunch-ly it is." Dad grinned and we set to work.

A daddy-daughter brunch session was just what I needed to feel better about abandoning him that night. Especially with me leaving at midday under the guise of Clove and I getting ready for the movie marathon. Luckily, we'd seen the whole series a thousand times between us so missing out on it wasn't going to be noticeable if Dad asked me anything about it the next day.

When Clove arrived to pick me up, I grabbed the leather jacket Vaughn had bought me, my phone, backpack and keys, and headed to say goodbye to Dad.

His eyes darted to the jacket in my arms and frowned. "What's that, darling?" he asked, feigning nonchalance.

I swallowed and went with the first lie I could come up with. "Uh, Halloween costume I got attached to."

He stood up and held his hand out. I put the jacket into it, and he looked it over. "Good quality. Riding quality." His eyebrow rose and I knew what he was thinking. I mean, he wasn't wrong, but shit.

I shrugged. "Clove and I found it at the op shop."

Luckily, it was all done up and he didn't unzip it and accidentally see the addition Vaughn had made. It wasn't like it was that coded a message. Anyone who knew Vaughn and I, and saw the message, would probably know exactly what it meant.

Dad nodded to me. "Put it on and let me see it on you, then."

I huffed self-consciously, "Oh, that's okay."

Dad looked at me pointedly. "The least you can do, if you're leaving me home alone tonight, is let a man pretend for five seconds that his only child belongs in his world."

I paused. "Are you sad that I…don't?"

He shook his head. "Not at all. You're you and you're perfect. But I do like to imagine it from time to time, knowing that you'll always be safe from it."

Well, if that wasn't a mixed message…

I pulled on the jacket and zipped it up. Dad looked me over and a smile spread over his face.

"Oh, Mags. You look beautiful. Like that jacket was made for you." I heard the wistful longing that turned 'that jacket' into 'this life', and my heart hurt a little. For two reasons.

"Thanks, Dad." I gave him a hug. "I'll see you tomorrow."

"Tomorrow. Love you."

"Love you, too."

He walked me outside to where Clove was waiting for me.

Our convoluted plan involved Clove picking me up from Dad's – to my deepest gratitude – and dropping me at Kenicki's where I was getting onto the back of Vaughn's bike, and he was taking me to our camping spot.

"You girls have a brilliant night," Dad said through the window to Clove.

She nodded. "We will, Mr McCallan."

Dad smirked at her. "Blaise, Clover."

She gave him another nod. "Blaise. See you tomorrow!"

"See you then. I'll put something on for you. Let me know when you're on your way back."

"Will do."

"Bye, Dad."

Dad waved as we headed off and Clove looked back at him in the mirror.

"You think he knows?"

I shrugged. "He knows there's a new guy. I failed to hide that. But I *think* he believes us about the movie marathon."

"Iago agreed to come with me."

I blinked and tried to feign nonchalance. "Oh, really?"

"Really."

"Just the two of you? Up in the back row of the practically empty theatre? I wonder what might happen."

She snorted. "I wish. But unlike you, I won't be spending the night getting railed by the love of my life. I'll be sitting next to him while he's completely oblivious to how badly I want him."

I never had the heart to correct her. Whether she was hiding behind ignorance, so it hurt less, or she really didn't know the feeling was mutual and he was just keeping her at arm's length, I didn't want to make it hurt more than it already did.

Clove pulled into the Kenicki's parking lot, empty in the middle of the day which had made it feel like a pretty safe place to meet as well as somewhere not too far out of Clove's way when she was already pretty far out of her way.

Vaughn was already there, leaning on his bike with his arm's crossed as he waited for us.

"Where is the gear?" Clove asked him as she got out to say hello.

Vaughn smiled as he came over to me. "It's waiting for us." He gave me a kiss and said, "Hi."

I don't know why I blushed. "Hi."

He wrapped his arm around my back. "Back here tomorrow?" Vaughn said to Clove.

"Yep. Just let me know what time you're heading back," she as she waved to me and headed back to her car.

"Can do. And Clove?"

She paused. "Yeah?"

"Thank you. So much."

Vaughn's voice was so tender and sincere, and Clove looked him over with a soft expression. I knew that was the point she wasn't just supporting me and my choices, but the moment she was on Vaughn's side as well. On our side.

As she got into her car, she gave him a nod. "You are most welcome. But you know what will happen to you if you hurt her."

"I have no doubts that you'll go straight to Blaise."

"I am going straight to Maggie's dad," Clove agreed.

Vaughn's arm tightened on me. "I won't hurt her," he promised, then his tone went cheeky. "Unless she asks."

I nudged him as Clove laughed.

"You ready to go?" he asked me as we waved goodbye to Clove pulling out of the parking lot.

I looked at him as he got the spare helmet for me. "Definitely. Let's camp."

He laughed. "You don't have to sound so excited about it."

I shrugged. "You are literally the only reason I could be excited about camping."

"You're excited about me?" he teased, and I shoved him playfully.

"Let's go and I'll show you just how excited I am."

"Fuck. Yes, please."

When we got to his dad's property, there was a big tough box by the river.

"Planned ahead, did you," I teased as I put his spare helmet down.

He inclined his head as he ran a hand through his hair. "Not as much as I'd have liked. I had a whole thing planned and was supposed to have time to set it up before bringing you out here, but I got called in."

I nodded, trying not to feel too weird about knowing he was working that morning. "Fair enough."

"Fair enough?"

"Fair enough."

"You know what my life is."

I couldn't look at him, more from my own awkwardness than anything. "I do. It's not the life… It's just us talking about it."

He lay his fingers under my chin and tipped my eyes to his. "Do you not want to talk about it?"

I chewed my lip. "I don't *not* want to talk about it. It's just weird still. So many years only hearing anything by accident or being crafty, and now you're just…" I shrugged. "I think I like it. It just feels…naughty."

He wrapped me in his arms and smirked. "Everything about us is naughty, baby."

The smile rose unbidden, but I loved it. "How about your plans for tonight?"

"My plans for tonight have been slightly derailed, but we've still got plenty of time." He pulled out the picnic blanket and lay it out. "Tent first."

"That is a picnic blanket," I pointed out with a lot of sass.

He glared at me as he went to the box, but there was humour tugging at his lips. "You be quiet, or I'll show you what you'll get for sassing me, darling."

I dropped onto the blanket. "I get the feeling I'll enjoy whatever 'punishment' you have planned." I used air quotes and all. He got the bag for the tent open and looked a bit confused. "Want some help?"

"I can do it. You just relax."

I looked him over but was quite happy to let him for my own amusement. I sat back, my legs crossed in front of me, and my arms braced behind me, as I watched him struggle with the tent. After a while, I couldn't keep quite much longer. He needed to be teased.

"Might I remind you that you said, and I quote, 'I can do it. You just relax.'?"

Vaughn huffed as he looked at me through his hair. "Do you think you can do better?"

I pulled myself up. "Are you doubting me because you think I'm an East Ham priss or because I'm a girl?"

"Can it be both?" he asked with a grin that made his words an obvious joke.

"I'll have you know that Clove and I were Scouts. For a couple of years. Plus, I'm a woman so I can automatically read instructions better than you."

Vaughn laughed, picked them up, and passed them to me. "Fine. You read. I'll do the manual labour."

"Are you being sexist again?"

"It's pronounced 'sexy'. And no. This is a point of pride now. I will *not* let a tent beat me."

As I walked him through the instructions, he kept glancing up at me like he wanted to say something.

"What?" I asked. "Just say it."

He shrugged. "No. I just… I didn't know you were a Scout."

"I'm sure there are a lot of things you don't know about me, Vaughn."

"Like what?"

"Are we playing twenty questions now?" I laughed.

"No." He smiled. "But I want to know you. I want you to know me. Where else is going to be more perfect for that than here?"

"And here I thought you just wanted to fuck me senseless all night."

"I might not be able to multitask as well as you, but I *can* achieve two things in one night." He pushed the last guide rope into the ground and stood up. "Will that be satisfactory for her highness?"

I smirked. "Very much so."

He gave me a sassy nod as he wandered back to the box. "Lovely."

As Vaughn pulled a string of fairy lights out of the box, I got up and put my hand on his arm. He looked at me in question.

"You *could* spend all night setting up what you think will be the perfect date…or…?"

"Or?"

"Or we could just *have* the perfect date?" I suggested. He eyebrow rose in question. "We don't need *things* to have the perfect date, Vaughn. We just need us."

He huffed a rough laugh. "You're right. Sorry. I just wanted this to be worth it."

"Vaughn, we're together. Of course, it's worth it."

He breathed out heavily. Like he was relieved. Was he worried about my commitment to this? Did he think he wasn't really enough for me? What was going through his head?

I lay my hand on his cheek. "I appreciate that you want this to be special. I didn't expect it from you. You are so much more than I could ever have imagined, and I imagined you were pretty good. *We* are so much more. Whether we're sneaking around or together with no one to catch us."

The lapis lazuli in Vaughn's eyes was bright with humour. "Just what did you imagine about me?"

"That?" I asked, incredulously. "That is what you decided to take from that?"

"Oh, I took it all. But that's the bit I want to know more about right now. I've got time to explore the rest of it later." He stepped up close to me. "What did you imagine, darling?"

A shiver rippled over me at the depth of his voice. The pure seduction. I wrapped my arms around his shoulders and reached up to him. "I imagined exactly how well you'd fuck me. I imagined you'd be possessive and a little obsessive and deliciously dark and sexy. But I didn't expect just how sweet you'd be."

His arms tightened around me. "You thought it would be all rough and no love?"

I shrugged. "I didn't think there'd be *no* love. I just didn't realise you'd be way better at expressing it than…other people."

"Police Chief's wankstain for example?"

I took a breath. "For example."

"Don't tell me he didn't treat you right, baby," he begged as he ran his nose over my cheek.

"Not until it ended. But no one else has treated me the way you do. No one else, even Clove, accepts all of me the way you do. You don't degrade my dreams or plans. You don't expect me to live in two worlds. You want me to have one."

"Why wouldn't I?" he asked softly. "I want you to have the life you want – I want you to be a teacher and respectable and confident – but I wish that life and that world can include us." He kissed me gently. "I want us to have it all."

My heart clenched and fluttered and soared. "I want that, too."

"Maybe one day we can find a way to get it. But today is just for enjoyment. For dating. For being together like it's fucking normal because you deserve that."

I held him tighter. "And do you have an itinerary or are we playing this by ear?" I joked.

"Why? What did you have in mind?"

"I seem to recall you wanting to put my leg over your shoulder?" I teased.

He groaned as he crushed his lips to mine.

He didn't put my leg over his shoulder that day, but we did pretty much everything else.

VAUGHN: SIX

Fucking hell.

Why couldn't we do this all the time?

I mean, I knew why not. Because then it would be over. But this was fucking perfection. And not just because I'd lost count of how many times that we'd had sex in the last twenty-odd hours. Not like it was some heinously ridiculous number, but it had been an impressive amount considering we'd also eaten too much, and we'd talked and laughed, and just sat by the fire and watched the stars together.

It had been amazingly domestic in its simplicity. It was an almost unfair glimpse into how our lives should be together. If we could be a real couple in the real world and not worry about a forbidden love that would end in death if her dad found out.

I wasn't sure how I was supposed to go back to life after this. I'm not sure I wanted to. Maggie had asked me the week before if we were supposed to abandon our families to run away and be together. I couldn't say the idea wasn't tempting. If we could always have this freedom. But I'd meant it when I told her I couldn't – wouldn't – do that to her. I didn't really want to do it to me either. I might not have had what the East Hammers considered a conventional relationship with my dad, but I loved him, and I knew he loved me. Until Maggie, he and the club were all I had.

Now, it wasn't so much a matter of me being afraid of taking away the future she wanted by being with her, but the realisation that she could give me a life I'd never even considered before. And the fear in the knowledge that I'd lose that at some point. She gave a whole new meaning to the word family. The idea of family wasn't just an obligation anymore but yearning and aspiration.

Working out how this ended without me dead in a shallow grave was going to take no small effort. It also wasn't just up to me. We had to get around Blaise and I could understand if she was more than a little reticent to approach him about it. But for now, we had each other and I'd take whatever I could get.

Maggie stretched against me as she woke up, rubbing her arse against my morning wood like she knew exactly what she was doing.

I dropped my lips to her very naked shoulder and mumbled, "What time do you want to be back?"

"Mmm. How about never?" she said as she snuggled into me.

I tightened my arm where it lay over her stomach. "I am definitely a fan of that option."

She laughed and rolled over, those beautiful grey eyes searching mine. "Dad won't expect me home until after lunch at least. By dinner is fine."

"And what's Clove's schedule like if she's dropping you back?"

A bit of sadness crept into her eyes. "Part of me wishes this was easier. That you could just pick me up and drop me off like a normal boyfriend."

I really hoped it didn't show on my face just how my heart reacted to her using that word. But, based on the slight smirk that lit her eyes, she'd noticed.

I shrugged, somewhat defensively. "You've never called me your boyfriend before."

"Was it the wrong word?"

I shrugged again, more coy this time. "I've lost count of the number of times I've had to remind you that what's between us is more than just dating, darling."

She nodded slowly. "Well, I don't see a ring on my finger–"

"Be very careful what you wish for, baby."

She tried not to smile and encourage me. She failed. "I think that would be a dead giveaway, don't you?"

"Emphasis on 'dead'?" I asked and she nodded. "Okay. No ring, then. I could still ask the question…" I sassed.

She pushed me onto my back and rolled over on top of me. Her entrance teased at my tip as her breasts pressed into my chest. Her lips brushed over my ear as she groaned, "Do not tempt a woman, baby."

God, I loved her.

I wrapped my arms around her and thrust into her. She was so warm and tight and wet. It was fucking perfection. Her whole body clamped around mine and her nails dug into my shoulder as she sighed in pleasure.

"Goddamn, Vaugh," she breathed as she rolled her hips.

I crushed her lips to mine and met her thrust for thrust before I realised I was bare. I grabbed her shoulders and froze. "Fuck, babe."

She frowned. "What?" Then her eyes went wide. "Oh."

I smirked as she pulled off me. "Oh."

She reached over for a condom and shifted back to roll it on me. Fuck, but I loved the feeling of her fingers on my cock. My head was back, and my eyes were closed as I felt her move, then she was sliding me back home again and my hands went to her hips. I felt her lay her hands on my chest and use the leverage to ride me. My fingers tightened on her hips as my eyes opened and I saw she was staring at my face with a smile to rival my own.

Oh. My. Fucking. God. She was beautiful. As in, it actually took my breath away. And this fierce, sassy, sweet but spicy woman was mine. Better yet, I was hers.

As her breathing got faster and shallower, her teeth caught her lip and she ground against me. I held her hips tight, holding her hard against me as she rocked back and forwards. Her eyes narrowed and her fingers pressed hard into my chest as her orgasm built. And they never left mine until I felt her walls clench on my cock. Her head fell back as she cried out my name and I felt her whole fucking body spasm.

I thrust into her hard and her thighs shook as she whimpered and nodded her approval. I rolled us over, bending her knee up to slide deep into her and her back arched off the ground.

"Fuuuck..." she breathed.

"You going to come again, baby?" I asked and she nodded.

I lifted up as I pounded into her.

"You want to rub it, baby?" I asked and she nodded again. I loved the way she couldn't speak while I was inside her. "Then rub it for me."

Her fingers went to her clit, and I felt her body shudder as we both pleasured her. Fuck, but it was sexy. Everything about her was sexy. She excited me the way no one ever had before. Her mind. Her sass. The look in her eyes. The way she bit her lip for me. The way her body responded to mine. The way she touched me and fucked me and drove me insane physically, mentally, and emotionally. It was the best fucking feeling.

As her walls tightened on my cock again, I couldn't hold on any longer. We both came, hard and fast, within seconds of each other and I dropped down over her to get my breath back.

She laughed as she pushed me off her and, as I rolled beside her, I laughed, too. She somehow always managed to make me laugh. Or smile. I actually couldn't remember being happy that much before her, let alone as happy as she made me.

Part of me wondered how in the hell I'd found myself here. Not just unintentionally spending the night with her, but actively planning a camping trip so I could spend the night with her again. On purpose. Being utterly addicted to everything about her. Craving her worse than I'd ever craved riding.

Me.

As Blood Roses, the boys and I had been brought up to have a very particular mentality. Compartmentalised. We had to be able to kill without hesitation. Likewise we had loyalty to the club burned into us. We had to be emotionless and deathly devoted, usually on the same day, plenty often in the same moment. They built us to be inhuman to many while ensuring we'd have the strongest of animal bonds with each other.

I'd lived my whole life that way. It had made it easy to live up to the name 'Prince of Thorns'. Outsiders were nothing to us. To me. I'd enjoyed watching – making – girls fall for me, getting what I'd wanted out of them, and then leaving them broken and bleeding in my wake. Leaving them with the memory of me carved into them while I forgot them easily.

But the idea that I'd ever thought I could do that to Maggie actually hurt. Viscerally. I hated myself for it.

A hate only made better by the smile she was currently giving me, and the knowledge that she'd gone into this as dishonourably as I had. Part of the reason I was head over heels for her before we'd slept together was because she'd said no. To spite me. To play the game. She'd wanted me to hate me, not love me. And the feeling had been mutual.

Love had never been part of either of our plans. And yet…here we both were.

Later that week, there was an uncharacteristic blip in Blaise's 'no business when I have Maggie' rule.

Some twat had been caught stealing from him and it was punishment time. As the unofficial heir, it was my job to be there as well. In the last year or so, it was usually my job to 'retire' the idiots. And my fists were nice and bloody until the idiot in question this time decided to mention Maggie.

"Do your worst, McCallan. I've already had my revenge."

I punched him again for good measure as Blaise drawled, "Really? What did you do? Sell some of the merch to a Monster?"

"I fucked your girl."

There might not have been many of us in the room, but there was an audible hiss as Blaise stood up. I felt a surge of jealousy in my chest, even knowing the guy was talking absolute bullshit.

He chuckled, blood dribbling out of his mouth from where he'd lost a tooth. "Right under your fucking stupid nose, and you never even knew."

I was starting to feel personally attacked, but it wasn't like he was looking at me, so I didn't think it was anything more than a very heavy coincidence. My heart still pounded. Both in fear and anger. I couldn't shake the jealousy. The rage. It wasn't the first time I'd felt it, but it was the first time it was simmering close enough to the surface that I wasn't sure how long I could control it. Most of the time, Blaise would get me to step in now and remind the perp of the rules. But it seemed Blaise was taking matters into his own hands.

He casually rolled up his sleeves. "I know this is just the fear of a man who's going to die wanting to go out with some dignity, but an admission is an admission. You all heard him," he said to the room at large. "He fucked my girl and Roses rules state that's grounds for immediate dismissal. Given you were heading for that anyway, I think we might add a little extra punishment in there." Blaise turned to those of us gathered. "A reminder that Maggie is not a joke. She is not a ploy or a toy or a tool. All right? You're not smart if you try to use her to get one over on me. You're a fucking idiot and will be treated as such."

I made myself watch Blaise dole out the punishment without flinching. But internally, I fucking collapsed in on myself. I knew there was far worse coming for me if Blaise knew half of what I'd done with his daughter. If he knew that, even seeing the reminder right in front of me, wasn't stopping me from thinking right then about seeing her later that night.

Because it didn't.

Blaise could have been laying into me right at that moment and it would have changed nothing. I'd still be all in with her. I *was* all in with her. Even with my death a certainty because of it.

I knew it wasn't a matter of *if* but *when* her dad found out about us. We'd slip up sometime. We'd get complacent. Fuck, being the least advisable thing, we'd probably get carried away and get her pregnant, and there was no way I couldn't front up about that.

So, us – Maggie and me – we had a limited time together. We both knew it. We both seemed okay with it, but that was the thing, wasn't it?

Seemed.

Because I'd just remembered her words on the night she'd come to my house. Her concern about what happened to her when Blaise did find out. Was it okay that, by being with her, I was basically making the choice for her that she'd have to go on without me, facing the consequences alone?

But then, walking away from her to save her that future would also be making a choice for her. And that wouldn't be okay either. The only thing to do would be to have an adult conversation about it. Which, when it came to Maggie, didn't worry me in any way at all.

Which is what I did when we snuck a moment later that night while I pretended that I didn't have the blood of a now ex-Rose staining my knuckles despite the extended shower I'd put myself through.

"Maggie?" I said slowly.

She looked at me expectantly. "Vaughn?"

I took a deep breath. "The night we got together…?"

She bit her lip, but her smile still shone through warmly. "What about it?"

Well, a million things. Nearly all of them fucking amazing, and I wished I could go back and do them for the first time all over again. But…

"You asked what happened to you after your dad ended me for touching you. It's probably safe to assume he'll do worse if he knows we're dating."

She nodded. "I did. And it is."

How did I put this that she knew I wasn't looking for a way out? That I was legitimately just asking her the question.

"Knowing there's basically no chance we'll last, do you still want to be with me? Or would you rather walk away now and save yourself the heartache?" It all came out in a rush because I wasn't sure I was strong enough otherwise.

"Vaughn…do *you* want to walk away?" she asked.

I shook my head. "No. Fuck, no. Never. But I want to be sure this is your choice. That we're on the same page. If you dad finds out, you're the one who's going to have live with the consequences."

She was chewing on her lip in a way that was neither turned on or amused by me. "I don't think that walking away now *will* save the heartache, Vaughn. It might even make it worse. Maybe. If heartache is guaranteed, then I'd rather enjoy the time we do have." She paused before adding, "As long as you're still okay risking death to be with me?"

"God, yes," I said with far too much emotion.

Her cheeks flushed as she looked away and my heart thudded. We'd said a lot of things to each other in the last few weeks. I couldn't speak for her, but I'd had a crash course in falling in love and no mistake. I'd fallen hard and fast for this chick, but suddenly that made me feel really awkward and self-conscious because I'd just completely given the game away and what if she didn't feel the same.

The air around us got really tense for a moment. Then, I realised that she seemed really awkward and self-conscious as well.

I took her hand and she squeezed gently.

"Did you just worry you were the only one feeling weirdly intense about us?" she asked with a hint of self-conscious humour.

I nodded. "Yes. Yep. Yeah. I definitely did that. Did you?"

She also nodded. "I did, yes."

I breathed in deeply, feeling way more relaxed again. "That's reassuring."

She squeezed my hand again. "It really is, huh?"

CHAPTER FIFTEEN

After school on Friday the next week, Vaughn was the one to drop me home just because we wanted a few minutes in person together, made easier by it being a back to Mum's day.

He drove the GT and, as usual, parked a couple of streets away after we'd driven around aimlessly for a while just to get a few more minutes. I was kissing him goodbye when we were interrupted by the last person that I'd expect to interrupt us.

"You dumped Parker Bates for Vaughn Saint!" I heard Freddy's voice and pulled away from Vaughn quickly.

"What are you doing?" I hissed at him as I put down the window.

Freddy leaned over to look into the car and his eyes bugged as he looked at Vaughn. "I was going to get some ice cream, but this is far juicier."

I rolled my eyes. "What's your silence going to cost for this?"

Freddy looked between us and said unhesitatingly, "I want to hang out with Vaughn."

"What?" echoed around the car as Vaughn and I expressed the same sentiment.

Freddy nodded eagerly. "I want to hang out with Vaughn. He's way cooler than Parker. Why didn't you just tell me you were dating him instead? I wouldn't have been mad." His eyes bugged even further to the point he looked like a cartoon character. "Do you think Stone Daniels would help me train for football?" he gasped with all the excitement an eleven-year-old could muster.

Vaugn chuckled as he leant over me towards my brother. "Tell you what. Keep our secret and yeah you can hang out with me, *and* I'll make Stone train you."

Honestly, Freddy swooned over Vaughn way harder than I'd ever seen Clove swoon over Iago. Which was bad enough, but Vaughn swooned over Freddy's swooning. Oh, they both tried to hide it and they both failed spectacularly.

"Oh, my God," I muttered as I climbed out of the car. "You two are so weird."

Freddy stood back. "I'm not weird. You're weird. You're dating Vaughn Saint, and you let me get all mad at you?" He batted my arm.

"You could have just not got mad at me!" I reminded him.

"Uh, no. I couldn't. Because you were ruining my football career." He legitimately pointed both hands at Vaughn. "But this is even better!"

"You'd rather train with Stone?" I asked him, incredulously.

He nodded madly. "Uh, yeah. Stone Daniels is amazing! He's so much better than Parker. But don't tell Parker I said that. But Stone is brutal on pitch!"

"If you're comparing all of us to Parker Bates, that's a pretty fucking low bar," Vaughn chuckled, standing up on the other side of the car.

"Don't you start," I warned him.

He shrugged. "I'm not starting anything."

"He's not starting anything!" Freddy jumped to Vaughn's defence.

I looked between them, totally bewildered. "What is happening? Why are you two ganging up on me?"

Vaughn grinned and it was so totally swoony and adorable and sexy. "Family, baby."

Jesus, but I was so very into that. Into the idea that my boyfriend and my brother would…

No.

God.

That was such a dangerous thought.

"Family wouldn't leave family behind," Freddy said pointedly.

I whirled on him. "You're leaving *me* behind!" I countered.

"You could come."

I smirked. "I don't want to."

"Neither do I, but Mum and Dad don't want to leave you with me while you're 'studying'."

"Take it up with Mum and Dad."

"I have. Many times."

"What are you two talking about?" Vaughn asked with a lazy smile.

"Dad's got business next week and I have to go with him and Mum, but *someone* gets to stay home," Freddy answered.

"Really?" Vaughn asked, looking at me like that was an interesting turn of events. "Home alone for a whole week?"

I shook my head at him, grabbed Freddy's arm and started walking home. "We can talk about this later."

"I'm holding you to that," Vaughn said.

"What about my ice cream?" Freddy said and I ushered him home.

"I'm sure there's some in the freezer."

"Bye!" Vaughn called and I waved at him over the back of my head.

Freddy was far more excited. "Bye! We'll hang out later!"

"Yes," Vaughn promised him. "We will!"

"Stop it!" I hissed at Freddy.

"Stop what?"

"We're supposed to be on the downlow. You guys yelling at each other from across the fucking road isn't keeping this on the downlow."

"Who's going to notice? Mrs Partridge? She's too busy pushing Cotton around in his pram."

I rolled my eyes. "You cannot tell anyone. Okay? Like, his life is literally in Blaise's hands here. I know you don't know much about this stuff, but it's not like a joke or hyperbole. Dad will kill him if he finds out. You have to keep the secret."

He nodded. "I will. I promise. Your dad will really kill him?"

I swallowed. "He's done it before, and *that* guy just *hypothetically* asked me out. Vaughn's gone way beyond hypothetical."

"Woah…" Freddy breathed. "That's brutal."

"Then why do you sound so excited by that?"

"Because it's cool."

"It's not cool, Fredster. It's terrifying."

"Well, it's that, too. But I'm eleven. It's cool." He gasped. "Have you guys had sex?"

I spluttered. "Excuse you?"

"What? It's a legitimate question."

"It's a question, but not one you should be asking."

"Why not?"

"We've covered this. You're eleven."

He snorted. "You so have."

"Oh, my God…" I muttered as I shoved him into the house. "Why didn't you care about this when I was almost dating Parker?"

"Because it's better."

I rolled my eyes. "You think it's better I'm with Vaughn?"

He nodded. "Yeah. And you're happy now."

I looked at him. "What?"

"You're happy. I'm happy for you."

I actually paused. "Happy for me? You're really okay with me being with Vaughn?"

"Why wouldn't I be?"

Was Freddy just being eleven and naïve? Or was he just proof that other people could be okay with it, too? And, God, what did that thought do to me? I felt hope and terror and such a flood of emotions that I had to push the whole thing away because it was just too much in the moment.

I'd just had a week with Dad, so he was all for me house sitting for Jonathan and Mum instead of hanging out at his place. Part of me knew he had business he'd ignored for the week he had me and he could only put off for so long. But I appreciated the sentiment anyway.

Especially when it became very obvious that everyone else being away meant that Vaughn temporarily moved in. Not that it was on purpose, but we took full advantage of our privacy. Vaughn even parked in the driveway. My neighbours wouldn't necessarily recognise him and there was no reason for them to think that my parents hadn't okayed me having a 'friend' over for the week to keep me company.

On Monday night, I'd encouraged him to come inside with me after school and he hadn't left by the time we had to leave for school the next morning. On Tuesday night, it was looking very much like the same thing was going to happen, and I wasn't going to let him go to school in the same set of clothes for a third day.

"I could get used to this domesticity," Vaughn said as he leant against the laundry bench.

I snorted as I pulled his shirt out of the dryer. "Domesticity?"

He nodded. "Doing our washing together. Having dinner together. Sleeping together. I think I've seen our future, love."

"If this is our future, *someone* isn't going to be pulling their weight," I commented dryly.

He huffed a laugh and wrapped his arms around me. "Don't you worry, buttercup. I'll be ironing. And if you want me to cook dinner, you just have to tell me."

I span to face him. "I'm not sure what surprises me more."

"Ironing. Definitely. A man's got to eat."

I shook my head. "But a man can get takeout. I think I'm less surprised that you iron."

He looked down at me with nothing but humoured warmth and affection in his eyes. If this was our future, it didn't look so bad to me. The idea our future could be this made my heart flutter and twinge in the best and worst ways at the same time.

"Are you calling me vain just because I like to look good?" he spluttered, all fake indignation.

I nodded. "You are *so* vain."

He pulled me closer and dipped his face to mine. "It worked on you, though, didn't it?"

My eyes pinned to his, I bit my lip and ran my hand up his body. "Yeah, but who worked who? Really?"

He picked me up and propped me on the bench. "Oh, baby. *You* worked *me* something shocking." He ran his hands up my legs. "Addiction is nothing new to me, but you are my addiction now." His hands gripped my hips hard. "Everything about you is like it's made for me." He frowned. "No. That's not right. That sounds fucked up. I meant that in a much more…mutual kind of way. Like we've been so lucky to find that person we're supposed to be with." He grimaced. "Jesus, that sounds stupid, doesn't it?"

I shook my head. "Not at all. I know exactly what you mean. I won't be quite so wanky to say 'soul mates'–"

"No?" he teased. "Why the fuck not?"

I laughed. "Because you're probably not ready for that just yet," I joked.

He huffed a rough laugh as he pulled my body to his. "Maggie…" he started as he rocked his pelvis to mine. "There is nothing I'm not ready for when it comes to you."

I ran my hand down his naked chest and over his cock. He was hard and I throbbed for him. His eyes fluttered closed and his forehead leant to mine as I rubbed him through the towel that he'd slung around him after his shower while his clothes were washing.

"You really *are* ready, aren't you?"

Our faces nuzzled as I slipped my hand under the towel and stroked him. "I am always ready for you, Maggie. I always want you, and that didn't change just because I kissed you. But it's not just physical. It's like burying myself inside you feels like the only way to really show you how I feel." He shook his head again. "I don't know what I'm saying."

"You might not, but I like it. I like all of it."

"You do?"

I nodded. "I do. And I get it. There is so much I don't know how to put into words, but like this…" I gripped him slightly harder as I stoked him. "When you're inside me, when we touch, I don't need to find the words, because my body tells you the same way yours tells me. I don't need to make sense of it because it already makes sense. Which doesn't really make sense."

He laughed. "Okay. I'm glad I'm not the only one having trouble with the words. I thought I was just emotionally broken."

I slid my hand back up to cup his cheek. "You're not broken, Vaughn. You can't be, because you're here and you're trying. We're both here and trying together. And we're finding our way together."

'Until it ends', was what I wasn't going to add because I was deep in denial. Some could call it living in the moment. I wasn't quite so optimistic. I knew what I was doing, but I wasn't going to let that stop me from enjoying this – him, us – now.

"I don't have a condom on me..." he said slowly, and I laughed.

"How convenient that I have some in the bedroom."

"Less convenient because I could be inside you now."

I sighed. "That does sound quite nice."

Vaughn pressed his lips to mine as he picked me up and started carrying me to my room. "Laundry would have been fun though."

"We could have set the machine to spin."

He burst out into a loud bark of laughter, like I'd truly surprised him, and it warmed my heart. "That's something I've never tried. You think it works?"

I nipped at his lip. "I certainly don't think you need it."

"Oh, that's high praise. Thank you, darling."

I snorted. "Said as though you have no idea how good you are."

He shrugged as he dropped me on my bed. "I find myself compelled to please you. I'm driven to give you pleasure. It's all I want. Maybe I'm scared you'll leave me if I don't give you a reason to stay."

I pulled him down to the bed. “I could go with at least half the amount of pleasure before I’m even thinking about leaving, Vaughn,” I sassed, and he smiled.

“Good to know. Especially considering I can’t seem to hold on with you.”

“Is that good or bad?”

“Depends how you want to look at it. I think it’s good for the way I feel about you. But I dunno… Maybe it’s bad for you?”

I shook my head. “Oh, yeah, multiple orgasms are *the worst*.”

“I’ll do my best to restrict them, then.”

I nodded. “Thank you. I appreciate it.”

He laughed as he got back up and rifled for a condom. While he was up, I pulled off my shorts and scooted up the bed. He kicked his chin to me expectantly, and I obligingly took off my tee as well. His teeth caught his lip as he looked me over with a hunger in his eyes that made everything in me tingle. Then he wrinkled his nose and gave me a wink before dramatically ripping the towel off him and crawling into bed with me.

Half-tackling me into the pillows, he peppered me with kisses and held me tight. I wrapped my whole body around his and loved the feeling that spread through me.

“You know if you don’t want me here, you just have to say…” he murmured against my lips.

I gripped his hip harder with my knee. “Do you need a reason to not be here?”

He shook his head. “I don’t want one, but I will *need* one or I might never leave.”

I smiled. “I don’t plan on giving you one this week, then. Sorry.”

“Oh, no,” he said sarcastically, with a wide smile. “Damn. I might never forgive you.”

I slipped my arms tighter around him, and his arms tightened around me. "If you're going to *plan* to stay, then are you going to want to bring some stuff over?"

He looked me over. "Are you actually asking me to stay?"

"I'm just saying that I'm enjoying this time with you and, if you think you might end up continuing to not go home, then maybe you might want one of the Princes to get you some stuff to make yourself more comfortable. You can do whatever you want with that."

"More comfortable? You want me to bring my jammies and my toothbrush and take over one of your drawers, baby?" he teased.

But I nodded. "If that'll make you more comfortable, sure."

"Fuck, but I'm trying really hard not to want more of this, Maggie," he said as his nose trailed over my face. "I'm really trying not to want this all the time."

I hugged him even harder. "Me, too. But there is more. This week, there's more. This week, for the most part, we can pretend all we like that we don't have to be a secret."

"Maybe not at school."

"Maybe not. But here. In the car. And more importantly, with our friends, we don't have to be a secret."

"I really like that."

I couldn't not smile. "Me, too, Vaughn. Me, too."

I pushed him onto his back, took the condom from him, and made him submit to me for once.

CHAPTER SIXTEEN

On Wednesday, Clove drove to my house so she and Iago could get a ride with me and Vaughn so things would look less suspicious. Maybe Clove's car was in the shop? For what other reason would Maggie be getting a ride with Vaughn on a week she was at her mum's?

At least, that was the theory.

Vaughn held my hand the whole way, except when he was changing gears. When we got to school and the four of us were walking from the parking lot, Vaughn and I walked much too close to each other to the point that Iago appeared between us and put his arm around us both.

"What the fuck are you doing?" Vaughn growled, plucking Iago's arm off his shoulder.

"Giving you a reason to be weirdly close to her. Or have you got your funeral booked already?"

I shoved him off me as well. "Cheery."

Iago shrugged. "Practical. You two might get to play domestic bliss at home but try to remember you are *not* an extension of each other. You cannot subconsciously hold each other's hand. You can't whisper sweet nothings. You are relegated to eye fucking each other across a crowded room and pretending you both hate it as per usual. My blacks are at the cleaners, and I don't wanna have to rush them unnecessarily."

"Blacks?" Clove asked.

Iago nodded. "Funeral blacks."

I heard Clove gulp. "Oh."

"Oh," Iago said pointedly to Vaughn. "Understand me?"

Vaughn shook his head. "Understand you," was his deep, resigned answer.

Iago breathed out heavily. "I'm too pretty to die, guys. Let's not fuck this up for me."

"Because it's all about you?"

"Of course, it is," Iago said with a smirk. "This conversation would be a fuck load more serious and depressing if was about *you.*"

Vaughn huffed and a smile played at his lips, but all he gave Iago was a small nod.

I touched Iago's arm. "We'll see you guys later."

Iago nodded. "Later, ladies."

I looked at Vaughn through my lashes like a complete idiot who thought I was being totally inconspicuous. We exchanged a tiny half-smile, then Clove and I were heading off.

"Do you think he's looking at my arse?" Clove asked and I huffed a laugh that was full of relieving tension.

"Yes. Yes, I think he's looking at your arse."

She nudged me playfully with her hip. "You're welcome."

I couldn't help but grin, feeling so very lucky that I had such wonderful friends. Because there were actually multiple now. They just weren't who I'd thought they'd be at the start of the year. Instead of Parker's friends, they were Vaughn's. Well. It was Iago and maybe Stone. Possibly Ezra. Cairo would probably – definitely – kill *for* me, but that was obligation rather than fondness, I was sure.

Still, it felt good to have quality over quantity, even if I couldn't celebrate it in public.

That whole week, I'd felt good. Really good. I felt free and happy and settled and myself. So, of course it was ruined at lunch while Clove and I were at my locker.

"Maggie?"

My whole body froze. Clove and I shot each other a look. I knew she was even more displeased that Parker was talking to me than I was. But she was also the less confrontational of the two of us.

I turned to Parker with bored expectation. "What?" I asked him.

His eyes darted to Clove like he'd rather she wasn't there.

"Whatever you *think* you need to say, you can say in front of her," I told him.

It had very little to do with not wanting to be alone with him and everything to do with making him feel more uncomfortable.

He licked his lip. "Fine. I wanted to apologise."

I looked him over. "If that's true, why does it sound like you're kind of choking on the word?"

He took a deep breath and I saw that he was holding back that fury he'd lost control of the night I'd ended things. "Because I shouldn't have to be the one to apologise. I'm not the one who decided they wanted to go and fuck someone else."

I scoffed. "Excuse you? It's not like you were monogamous. I know you were hooking up with other people."

He blinked like he legitimately didn't think I knew that, but he rallied like a fucking pro. "But I wanted to be with you. You're the one who decided that this cock was worth ruining a good thing." He shook his head like he had to stop himself saying anything worse. "We can just put it behind us. No relationship is perfect."

Now I was blinking. "Relationship? Parker, you had your chance to be in a relationship with me. You had the chance to see me for me when no one else did, but you fucked it up."

"You hurt me," was his excuse. "I was going to make it official, Maggie, and then you ditch me for some random arsehole and have the fucking disrespect to tell me you'd rather go and be *his* piece on the side than be *my* girlfriend?" He looked around somewhat sarcastically. "And where is he now, huh? Where's this guy whose cock was so magical? He leaves you roses, but he won't touch you in public, he won't talk to you. Is he ashamed of you as well?"

As well?!

Okay, I couldn't pretend that didn't hurt just a lot. I couldn't pretend I didn't do a quick scan of the hallways like even just seeing him might make it hurt a little less. I knew Vaughn would have been proud to be with me in public if it were possible, but that moment in front of Parker would have felt better if I could see him. But none of the Princes were in sight.

I nodded slowly. "And you think this counts as an apology, do you?"

Parker took another deep breath. "I'm sorry. Okay? I'm sorry. We were both wrong. Let's put it all behind us and we'll move on. Things can go back to the way they were."

"Both wrong? How was I wrong? Because I didn't want to be strung along anymore? Because I chose someone else? Newsflash, Parker. I get to make those choices. I might be *just* the daughter of the leader of the Roses, but I'm also a human being – as weird as that might seem – and I get to choose who I fuck or date or fall in love with or just hang out with. Not you or anyone else who likes to have an opinion as to my worth based on my parents. Now, unless you have an actual apology for me after being a total dick, then you can kindly fuck right on off out of my life."

"You're making a mistake, Maggie."

"Grovelling is not an attractive trait, Parker. Go back to Lettie or whoever you're sticking it in this week. I have no interest in going back to the way things were."

"You want to be official? Monogamous? You want my ring?" Parker said and I saw a hint of desperation in him.

What drove it? Possessiveness? Obsession? Did he just want to own me, or did he really think he loved me?

I shook my head and scoffed, "No. You lost your chance, Bates. You showed your true colours. Even if you only said those things because you were hurt, you still said them, knowing they would hurt me. You don't deserve me, and you can move on without me."

I took Clove's hand and walked away from him.

"Wow," she whispered.

I smirked but wasn't sure how humoured it was. "What? No 'hello, Magenta'?"

She shook her head. "No. I think that was all Maggie. There's no real line between you anymore, and I love it."

Despite the ugliness of my unexpected encounter with Parker, I felt my chest warm. I liked that my best friend didn't see me as two people anymore. I was just me, the good parts of both my personalities that could live, unashamed, in the same body at the same time now. And I think that's what I was revelling in; Vaughn made me respect myself, made me see that the worthwhile people would respect me as well. And I was learning the strength to tell the rest of them – the people not worth it – to piss off.

I thought I'd been proud to be my dad's daughter, but I saw now there had always been an element of shame. Around these people. They'd made me ashamed and apologetic about who I was and the people who loved me. Well, I wasn't going to let them anymore. I was Blaise McCallan's daughter, and I was the only person responsible for my future. Not the fucking East Hammers.

It put a slight crimp on my happiness, until I saw Vaughn again that day. It was a simple brush in the hallway. Akin to those many weeks ago when he'd been trying to seduce me, but it wasn't just heat and desire that I felt in myself at his touch anymore. It was a different kind of heat, one that simmered in my chest, slow and steady and strong. It made me smile despite myself. It made my fingers linger against his.

"You holding up the corridor on purpose, princess?" Stone growled at me, clearly taking the job Iago had taken earlier that morning.

I cleared my throat. "I didn't realise the Princes owned the hallway now."

Vaughn's lip rose in a wicked half-smirk. "We own everything, sweetheart."

My heart twinged, but it hurt, and I reminded myself we were all playing a game here. Vaughn calling me the moniker he called all his nameless conquests meant nothing more than he was keeping our secret. He was just doing what needed to be done because I was letting our 'domestic bliss' – as Iago would call it – bleed into the rest of our lives. I was risking his life and then daring to feel weird when he was cleaning up after me.

But something flashed in his eyes that told me he recognised my reaction for what it was. He licked his lip, for all intents and purposes intimidating and threatening, but I knew him better by now. I knew he was regretful. I pulled myself together.

"You don't own the hallways, arsehole," I snapped as his fingers toyed with mine, safely surrounded by our friends and the passing students much too close for anyone to notice.

Vaughn used the moment to step closer to me. His fingers tightening against mine. "You want me to own *you*, Magenta?" he purred, and my eyes narrowed at him shrewdly.

"You wish, Vaughn," I scoffed. "But I don't touch Roses."

"Couldn't break Daddy's rules, could you?"

"Daddy doesn't tell me what to do," I purred right back, leaning into him. "You're just all beneath me."

He chuckled. "As you wish, Maggie."

Heat engulfed me, but I rolled my eyes at him and stepped back. "As *you* wish, Vaughn."

His eyes ran down my body then back up and I saw the heated desire in them. His lip caught in his teeth as he smirked appreciatively. He got to play this part in the game, and I didn't. I'd make him pay when we got home.

"Oh, yeah. I wish, princess."

I did my best to look unimpressed before Clove and I walked away.

"Nice save?" she offered, sounding very unsure.

"I'm going to get him killed," I told her. "I'm messing this up."

"You're not messing this up. Besides, he knows the risks and has told you a million times that he's more than happy to pay the price. He knows what he's risking."

"Yeah, but maybe *I'm* not happy to pay the price. I don't want to lose him."

"You love him," she teased, nudging me.

I nudged her right back. "I don't not love him," I admitted.

She threaded her arm in mine. "Maybe it'll all work out?"

"Maybe it will, but that requires me taking a risk I'm too scared to take."

"You think if you go to your dad to plead your case, he won't listen?"

I dropped my voice to a whisper. "He killed a guy for asking me what kind of date I liked. To only mention the one I know about for sure. Who knows what else he's done under the guise of giving me the life I want. I love Dad, but what the hell's he going to do to Vaughn if I go in there and say I might want to marry him and have his kids one day?"

"You want to marry him and have his babies?" she squeaked excitedly.

I rolled my eyes, but this time all fondness. "Maybe. One day. I'm very open to the possibility, provided everything goes well. At the moment, we're going well, but it's difficult to see me making it down the aisle when the man giving me away would kill the groom!"

"Mr McCallan loves you," she chastised. "All you have to do is tell him that you love Vaughn and voila he's helping you plan the wedding."

I wished I had her faith. I'd meant it when I'd told her I love my dad. I loved him so much and I knew he loved me. I knew he loved me more than his own life. It's why I was so worried that he'd only hear half my plea on Vaughn's behalf and then lose it before I could finish. Meaning I'd lose Vaughn before I could finish.

But, for Clove, I nodded. "Maybe you're right."

She smiled. "Exactly."

I shoved those thoughts aside for the rest of the day. I told myself they weren't getting in the way of the happiness I'd been feeling all week. And, for the most part, I succeeded. But when

Vaughn and I got the front door closed behind us that night, I pulled him close and kissed him hard.

"Baby, I'm sorry," he said against my lips.

I pushed his blazer off his shoulders as I shook my head. "Don't be. I nearly blew it."

"No, darling. You saved it." He untucked my shirt from my skirt. "Only thing better would have been if you *had* hit me."

"I wasn't going to hit you," I told him.

"You weren't?"

I stepped back. "No. I was surprised."

"I didn't mean to make you feel bad. I just–"

"I knew what you were doing, Vaughn. And I understood. But it did bring up some uncomfortable…thoughts. There was a bit of that going around today."

I was trying not to doubt him. The biggest parts of me didn't, but there was this niggling question in the back of my head at how easily he'd slipped back into the old game.

Suddenly, I was feeling horribly awkward and weird and just so not like us.

I cleared my throat and heard myself asking, "Do you need to go home?"

Vaughn's confusion was understandable. "You want to get rid of me, love?"

I shook my head as I bit my lip and looked him over, not wanting to do this; not wanting to push him away because I was being stupid and insecure. "No. I said you can stay and I… Just… Won't your dad wonder where you are?"

"It's cute you think this is the first time I haven't been home in a week," he chuckled.

Everything in me fell at his words and I wondered if I was being that stupid after all. Of course I wasn't the first. And despite his pretty words, I was unlikely to be the last. This was the Prince of Thorns after all. He dug in deep for that extra level of hurt.

"Magenta. Love," he said, his voice stern, and I looked up at him, hoping my face didn't show the hurt.

Vaughn looked me over carefully. His face was all annoyance, but those blue eyes sparkled with heat. He put his finger under my chin so I couldn't look away.

"Playing house isn't the only reason to not go home for a few days," he said, a message in the tone of his voice that I didn't quite understand. Not understanding made me feel stupider which made me defensive.

"Just be open with me for once. How many girls have you 'played house' with?"

He frowned. "Is it the phrasing you have a problem with, baby?"

"It's the question of your sincerity."

"You know how many girls. And you know the depth of my sincerity."

"Pretend I don't," I snapped, feeling petulant and unable to stop it.

His hand slid to my throat. "Let's not do either of us the disservice of you acting dumb now, Magenta. Eh?"

His voice was dark and dangerous. It was nothing like what he'd used on me the last few weeks. This was the Vaughn of the start of the year, the one who'd wanted to ruin me. But there was one difference; there was unmistakable love shining along with the darkness in the depths in his eyes.

I leant closer to him, a taunt and a challenge. "Dumb, Vaughn? You really want to call me dumb?"

His lips rippled in a snarl. "You know what I mean."

"Do I?" Another taunt.

There was a flicker of understanding in his eyes. A cockiness that stole over the thunderous expression on his face. But it was so brief, I knew that he was hiding it from me. His fingers tightened on my throat and tingles shot through me. "You want to play, baby?" he purred.

"I want to play, baby."

He lifted me up and wrapped my legs around his waist. "Fuck, I'm falling in love with you."

"Only falling?" I teased him, remembering a previous conversation.

He seemed to remember it as well. "You ready yet, baby?"

My heart fluttered as I looked into his eyes, so ready to drown in that lapis lazuli. So ready for other things as well. But if we said those words, we couldn't take them back, and if my dad…

It was going to hurt enough; I didn't want it to hurt more.

"Is it not enough to know?" I whispered and I saw his eyes soften.

"Yeah, baby. It's enough to know. For now."

"For now?"

He nodded. "You are mine, Magenta. If you think anything but death is going to get in the way of me telling you that I–"

I kissed him hard to cut him off and I felt his smile. Then I leant my forehead to his and sighed, my eyes still closed. "I can't hear you say that now, Vaughn. Especially when you try to put it in the same sentence as the reminder that just being with me could get you killed."

"I love you," he said quickly, and I did hit him then, gently as he pressed a quick kiss to my lips.

Because, sure I was annoyed, but I was even happier. "You arse," I laughed.

"I love you," he said again. "I love you. I–"

"Vaughn..." I said slowly and he looked at me questioningly. "I can't–"

"I know," he told me. "I know and I don't care. I wanted you to know in case–"

"If you want to remind me that I could get you killed one more time, I will never tell you how I feel."

"Oh. But, baby, I *know.*" He was all sexy cheek, and I knew I'd totally fallen.

"Exactly what is it you think you know?" I teased him.

His hands slid to my arse, and he squeezed it tightly. "Just how much you want me beneath you right now."

I bit my lip and felt his rough chuckle vibrate through his chest. "You are totally beneath me, baby."

"Not yet I'm not." He dropped me gently to the ground, turned me and slapped my arse. "I'll give you a head start, baby. But if I catch you..."

"If you catch me?" I asked as I started slowly backing to my room.

"If I catch you, Magenta... You're going to know exactly what it means to be mine."

Oh, I liked the idea of that. But it would hardly be fair. So I tried to make it to my room, but Vaughn caught me. His arm wrapped around me as he pulled me to him and I laughed as he pressed a kiss to my neck and we frog marched into the bedroom, where Vaughn kicked the door closed before throwing me on my bed.

VAUGHN: SEVEN

I was completely in love with this woman.

There were no two ways around it.

She wasn't just it for me, she was perfection for me.

I shouldn't have said it. I shouldn't have said it just after she'd told me not to, but I hadn't been able to help myself. How in the hell did you love someone, have them all-but tell you that the feeling was mutual, and not say it? I was new to the whole thing, but saying it just felt right and, based on her body's reaction after, it most definitely hadn't been wrong.

It was Friday night. We had two more nights of this, of us, before reality crashed back down around us. I'd asked her if she wanted to go out, but she had given me a resounding 'hell no' to that option so I'd offered to cook.

It was nothing fancy. Bit of casserole; beef and a few veg and a nice red wine gravy. Something Dad's mum had taught him, and he'd passed on to me. It was our comfort food. It was the fanciest thing *we* ever had, and I was sure the stepdaughter of the fucking mayor was eating far fancier feasts. But it was still going to be fucking delicious.

"How pissed do you think Freddy's gonna be that he had to go with the parents this week if he knows I was here the whole time?" I called to her as I diced the potatoes.

Yeah, I might have *really* liked the fact that her little brother wanted to hang out with me. Like, not even to corrupt him or teach him to ride or anything. Just hang. He'd apparently been bugging Maggie about just watching a movie or playing some console with me. Just really normal things and that made my chest warm. He accepted us, wanted us part of his life, and I was super chuffed by that.

Maggie didn't say anything to my question for a moment. But then came her sexily teasing, "A lot less if he finds out we had sex in the kitchen."

Wait. We'd had sex in the kitchen?

"We–? Oh, fuck me…"

I'd looked up at her voice, but the smile that had been threatening died a premature death as I took in the sight before me.

Little Magenta McCallan was leaning back against the doorframe. One foot flat against it, her arm reaching lazily above her head. But it wasn't just the sultry pose that stirred my cock. Not just the bedroom eyes or the way her teeth caught her bottom lip so damn sensuously.

Fuck, no.

It was the white lace lingerie that left precisely nothing to the imagination. It was the thong she wore under it. It was her hair tumbling down over one shoulder. It was, one hundred per-fucking-cent the undeniable primary school teacher in the streets, seductive temptress in the sheets vibe she was giving off as she looked at me over the rims of her glasses.

"That was kind of the idea, yeah," she said with a little laugh as she walked towards me.

Fuck, but her hips swayed with every step she took. I just wanted to grab hold of them tightly as I buried myself inside her over and over again.

Something was going on in my chest. That something that only Magenta McCallan had ever been responsible for. It was warm and bright. It made me wish for a different future than the one that lay before us. It made me want to hold onto her and never let her go. I didn't just want to fuck her, I wanted to make love to her. And I didn't even feel like an utter wanker for thinking it. It was too right to ever be shameful.

"Magenta…" I said slowly as I wiped my hands on the tea towel, unable to look anywhere but her and those hips that wouldn't quit.

"Vaughn…" she said equally slowly and questioningly.

"What is this, baby girl?"

She paused in front of me and ran her hand up my chest. My heart pounded under her fingers, and I was sure she felt it. She looked up at me and there was absolutely no doubt that I'd met my match in this woman. She was fucking perfect. She was sweet and spicy, strong and gentle, kind and fierce.

She *was* fucking it for me.

And the way she was looking at me, I knew she felt it, too.

"Baby *doll*, actually," she sassed me, and I felt the smile ripple unbidden across my face.

"Fucking hell…" I breathed as my hands went to her waist, so damned carefully because I could be convinced this was just some epic dream I was about to be rudely woken from.

Maggie leant into me, her pert curves pressing against my body and, if I wasn't already rock hard, that would have done it.

She slid her arms up to wrap around my neck, lifting her onto her toes as she looked, fearlessly, into my eyes.

"What's all this?" I asked her. My voice was gravelly, like she'd stolen it or something.

The smile in those bright grey eyes of hers was infectious. "Oh, this?" she said casually. "I'm just playing house, baby."

"If this is the way you play house, love, I don't think I ever want to stop."

I'd known since Tuesday while I watched her pull our clothes out of the dryer that I didn't want this to stop. I'd told her then that I was trying hard not to want this, but I'd lied. I wasn't trying to do jack shit.

I wanted this.

I wanted this life, this domesticity, and this simple enjoyment of that life with her.

And I sure as shit wasn't going to stop myself. The feeling was fucking epic, and I was going to hang onto it.

I didn't want her parents to come home and wreck this bubble we'd so effortlessly built for ourselves. Likewise, I knew we couldn't live in it forever. And there was still a big part of me that didn't really want to stay in it forever either. The part that wished we could hold hands while we walked down the street, laugh during dinner with our dads, and one day wear each other's ring.

There was something just so fucking nice about that. Wanting it. Feeling it. Knowing she felt the same, even if one of us wasn't saying it out loud. I'd be a fucking moron to stop it.

"Are you just going to look at me like you totally adore me, or…?" she teased.

"But I *do* totally adore you," I reminded her.

The heat in her eyes softened. "I totally adore you, too."

It meant enough to me that I felt that way about her – there was something gratifying and rewarding about loving someone so completely – but to know she felt the same way made it feel surreal. Just loving her would have been plenty for me, but her loving me felt like a dream come fucking true.

And I was turning into fucking Iago, talking about dreams.

I lifted her up on the bench and kissed her hard. Her knees hugged me tight as her arms went around my shoulders, her fingers playing with my hair as our bodies pressed together. I could feel the heat and softness of her skin beneath the lace under my fingers as they skimmed over her hips.

"Clove warned me about these," I told her as I toyed with the hem, and she smiled.

"Did she?"

"She did."

"And you didn't once beg me to see one?"

"Just how many do you have?"

"Wouldn't you like to know?"

I smirked. "Yes, I would. That's why I asked."

"Well, I don't know if this one has even had the desired effect…" she sassed.

I chuckled as I pulled her hips to mine roughly and I saw her eyes melt as her legs clamped around me tighter. "What was the desired effect, baby?"

She ran her hand through the front of my hair. "What are you thinking, baby?"

Oh, I loved it when she wanted to play games. When she teased me. When she really made me work for it. No matter what 'it' was; her smile, her sass, her fury, her body.

I ran my hand up her thighs, squeezing them roughly. I felt her squirm and arch into me. I dropped my lips to her neck and trailed kisses over her as I told her, "I'm thinking about you in a different kind of white lace, Maggie." My fingers pressed into her hips, and they rocked against me. "I'm thinking about burying myself inside you until you absolutely soak me." She closed her hands around my shirt and pulled herself closer to me as she tilted her head to give me better access. "I'm thinking about ripping that gorgeous little thing off your body with my teeth before I drag them over your skin."

"Vaughn…" The way she whimpered my name was hot and needy and only matched by the way she wrapped her arms around my shoulders and pressed herself against me. "I need you."

"What do you need?" I begged her as our lips found each other.

"I need you inside me, Vaughn. I need to feel you."

Jesus, I couldn't say no to that. Our kiss deepened as her hand skimmed down my body and over my crotch. The other one joined it, and she started undoing my jeans as she nipped my lip and I groaned against her.

"You're fucking amazing," I told her.

I felt her smile before she bit me again. "Show me how amazing I am, baby."

She reached into my jeans and ran her hand over me. I shivered and my cock twitched in her hand. She kissed me deeper as she slipped my cock out and angled her opening against my tip. She rubbed against me, and I felt how wet she was getting.

"My god, you're a fucking temptation," I murmured.

"Temptation implies you shouldn't have me, Vaughn. But we're safe here. There's no reason not to have me right now."

I took my cock out of her hands and guided it into her. We both leant against each other's foreheads and breathed deeply together as we both just enjoyed the feeling of me inside her. Then she rocked her hips against me as she kissed me, it was deep and slow and passionate and I fucking melted.

We didn't fuck. The only word I had for it was proper making love. And I would not deny it if anyone – most people, the other Princes – asked.

"Fuck, I love you," I told her as we moved together. I didn't mean to, it just slipped out.

I felt her nod against me. "Vaughn…I…" she panted.

I claimed her lips again. I didn't know for sure, but I could guess why she was hesitant to say it. I guessed it was the same reason that I felt compelled to say it; we had a limited time in which to say it – and, in my case, feel it – and we were handling it differently.

We wrapped each other up tightly. I was deep inside her and I felt like she wasn't nearly close enough. Like I could never get her close enough. I knew it was because I felt the pendulum swinging. She was mine but, more importantly, I was hers. I think I'd always been hers, but it had taken losing my goddamned mind and kissing her to realise I didn't have to hate her because I could have her.

God, I wanted to keep her. I wanted her to keep me.

Had I lost enough of my mind to actually tell Blaise myself? Was I mad enough to risk immediate death for a shot of doing this for real? Yeah, I kind of think I–

Maggie's walls clamped on me as she moaned my name and she fucking gushed all over me. God, I loved it. The feeling of it. The way she–

We both froze at the same time.

"Shit."

"Fuck."

I pulled out of her quickly and we both looked down. I was already reaching into my pocket and ripping open a condom. That might have been really stupid, but I could solve the problem and get back inside her.

As I stepped back to her, she smiled at me. I saw relief and humour and no less lust than before as she pulled me against her again. Her feet against my arse was all she needed to slide me inside her and things were a lot harder and a lot faster after that. I lifted her knee and thrust into her hard. She had one hand bracing on my shoulder and the other behind her on the bench to give her leverage to meet me thrust for thrust.

Our eyes were locked, and everything passed between us. What we didn't say. What I couldn't stop myself saying. What she couldn't. I saw it all in those gorgeous grey eyes and I felt alive for maybe the first time in my life.

The feeling was honestly better than racing. It was better than being lucky to get out of one of Blaise's pickles of my own volition. It was better than any chemical high Ezra had ever given me.

The world was fucking perfect.

"Oh, my God, Vaughn," she breathed as her movements started getting less smooth, more erratic, as she ground on my cock.

"You gonna cum for me again?" I asked her and she nodded.

"Mmhmm…" she moaned. "Yes, Vaughn. Right there. Please."

I smirked as I fully lifted her leg and put it over my shoulder while my other arm wrapped tight around her so she wouldn't fall backwards. I watched her eyes go wide, but then her head dropped back, and she took everything I gave her. She moaned with every thrust. She whimpered as her body shuddered and arched into mine. I kissed her leg, and she sighed my name.

She nodded at me.

"More?" I teased and she nodded again.

"More," she begged.

I took her. Harder. Faster. As deep as I could get.

"Vaughn," she panted. "Vaughn, I–"

She cried out as she came again and there was no way I was holding out any longer. I let her leg drop gently and we kissed as I came, holding each other tightly. Her whole body was wrapped around mine.

Two more nights. I had two more nights of this. And I wasn't fucking wasting either of them. If I had any hope of this ever happening again – maybe in a place of our own – then I needed to show her exactly what that future could look like. However I could give it to her. I wanted to show her a world where we could be there for each other, take care of each other. And that night was my turn.

I slid out of her to deal with the condom, pressing tiny kisses to her lips as I did and she laughed, warm and bright, as she kissed me back. I felt her sway after me as I stepped away.

"Why don't you get more comfortable, and I'll finish dinner?" I told her.

She was still sitting on the bench. "You think I'm not comfortable?" she asked.

I shrugged. "I think maybe that little sexy lace thing isn't really built for snuggling on the couch with your boyfriend and watching some cheesy rom-com."

"You're going to watch a rom-com with me?" she teased as she slipped off the bench, careful to avoid the small puddle on the floor.

I nodded. "I'm going to watch a rom-com with you."

"What's it gonna cost me? Action? Horror? Sci-fi?"

I rolled my eyes dramatically. "I'll go easy on you."

She exaggerated her hips as she walked to the door. “Okay. But just make sure it’s got cars in it. Fast ones. I like those.”

Once she was out the door, I actually physically swooned over her. “Jesus, marry her now,” I muttered to myself.

CHAPTER SEVENTEEN

It was our last night before Mum and Jonathan got back and I knew I was going to miss it. I knew I didn't want to it to end, even as I knew we couldn't just hide away forever. I just still wasn't brave enough yet to risk talking to Dad. But I was getting there.

Vaughn and I had fallen into bed after dinner and he'd been pulling out all the stops, the same way he'd been doing the last two nights. Between dinner and movie choices and being sweet and sexy, and telling me that he loved me… If this really was what our futures looked like – if this was what a real relationship looked like – I had zero doubts. It didn't negate the fear, but it was starting to be more important.

After our last round of sex, I was getting my breath back while Vaughn went to the bathroom. By the time he came back, I was still lying face down on the bed, my legs spread. I felt the bed shift as he climbed back on and hovered over me.

"Fuck, but you're the sexiest thing in the whole damned universe," he said as he ran a hand up my body.

I smiled into the pillows. "I'm sure you've had girls older and wiser and better than me."

I felt him nod at my back. "I've had older girls," he admitted as he dropped a kiss to my left shoulder. "I've had girls with more experience," he said as he kissed my right shoulder. "I've had girls who knew tricks even I didn't," he added as he kissed my left shoulder again. "But none of them compare to you, Magenta."

"You'll say anything to get laid again, won't you?" I teased, as my heart and stomach fluttered wildly.

Vaughn nudged my leg wider with his knee and lowered just enough that I felt his cock hot and hard right at my opening.

"There's something about you, love," he said, his voice low and husky, almost strangled. "Something special that's just for me. No. More like…" He paused like he was thinking. "Whatever 'it' is that brings people together. The spark. The connection. You're the only one I've ever seen it in. That I ever *want* to see it in." He ran his nose over my cheek, my jaw. "You started as a joke, love, but you are *it* for me, Magenta McCallan."

Overcome with emotion, I didn't know what to say to that admission. Nothing seemed enough to do it justice. So, all I could do was ease back and take him into me. His hand tightened on my hip as he groaned in pleasure and dipped his lips to my neck.

He thrust into me, slow and deep, our bodies pressed together, our fingers intertwined by my head. My heart beat hard and fast, my stomach tingled, and I had never felt closer to another person.

Vaughn flipped me over, slamming back into me. It was hard and fast. He was possessive and domineering, but between us was charged with emotion. All the things we hadn't said, maybe wouldn't ever actually say. But I felt it. And I knew he felt it, too. I had never been more sure of anything except what was between us in that moment.

I gripped him tightly and he held me just as tight. Our fingers dug into each other's skin. Arms and thighs and back and waist. Vaughn trailed kisses over my neck, my cheek, my collar bone. He interspersed the kisses with his teeth grazing me gently and it took very little time for my already sensitive nerves to tingle and fizzle and the coil in me to tighten until I was teetering on the precipice, and it was going to snap.

"Yes, Vaughn."

"Magenta. Love, I'm not wear–"

"I know," I told him. "Please don't stop now."

I felt rather than heard the groan rumble through his chest. He lifted my leg higher as his teeth grazed my shoulder again. My back arched into him as I got closer and closer. He kissed me tenderly, passionately, and he came moments after me.

He rolled us so I was snuggled against him and gave me a damned cocky smirk. "You trying to get one kid out of me before your old man does me in, love?"

"I didn't see you stopping," I reminded him, my lips brushing over his.

He gripped my arse tight, rolling me over to straddle him. "Because, unlike you, the idea isn't a joke to me."

"You want to make me a teen mum?"

He smirked. "I want there to be no question you're mine."

"And a kid would do that?"

"A kid. A ring. A house. I'm not fussy."

"So you're going to get me pregnant, lump me with a mortgage, and then leave me at the altar?" I sassed.

"Not by choice, love, no."

I looked him over. "Is that really the life you want, Vaughn?"

"Only if I can have it with you."

I didn't know what to say to that, so all I could say was, "I wasn't trying to get pregnant…"

He nodded. "I know, love."

"I was just… It was just supposed to be…"

He nodded again, humour in his eyes. "I know, love. I know."

"Exactly what is it you think you know?"

"Everything you'll never say out loud."

I chewed my lip as I tried to decide if this was it. Maybe it would hurt worse if I never said it. What if Dad found out tomorrow and I'd never told him–?

"I love you, Vaughn," burst out of me in a flood of words and emotion, and he actually stopped dead.

He looked up at me with wonder in his eyes. "Maggie…" he breathed.

I swallowed. "I…" I licked my lip. "I love you, and I just…" I took a deep breath. "I thought it might hurt less if I never said it. But now I feel like maybe it will hurt more if I don't."

He wrapped his arms around my waist. "If we only have a limited time together, then I don't want to waste it."

I chewed my lip as I debated the sense in telling him that I was thinking about talking to Dad. But I didn't want to get his hopes up. Or freak him out. It was one thing to say he was ready to die for me, but if that death might have been around the corner, then maybe he'd be a little less willing, and I wouldn't blame him.

I shook my head. "I don't want to waste any more time either, baby."

His smile was soft and gentle. "Okay. Not wasting time it is." He gripped my hips and drove back into me.

"You are insatiable," I laughed.

He nodded. "Maggie, I will never get enough of you, baby. I want your mind. I want your sass. I want your smile. I want your body. I want all of you."

"You have all of me," I told him honestly.

"All I am is yours," he said.

"God, I love you."

"Say it again."

"I love you."

"One more time?"

I laughed. "I love you."

He sighed happily. "I love you."

CHAPTER EIGHTEEN

On Tuesday, I was missing Vaughn. I felt like the stereotypical teenage girl with a crush raging out of control. It was both ridiculous and amazing, and I loved it and hated it.

But Clove, as the bestest best friend anyone could ever have, was doing her darndest to take my mind off it while also making me feel much more normal about the whole thing than I was sure I should.

"So, formal?" Clove said and I looked at her.

"Formal?" I questioned her question.

She nodded. "What are we doing? Stag? Or are you and a certain someone going to try to go together without anyone noticing?"

I snorted. "I'm not sure how that would work. Or that he's the formal kind of guy."

She nodded. "Stag it is."

"He might still ask you," I suggested.

She shook her head. "No. He won't. It's not going to happen and I'm going to have to accept that."

"Well, we've got each other at least."

"Want to go into Everdale on the weekend and go looking for a dress?" she asked.

I sighed. "Yeah, I guess putting it off isn't going to make our date prospects any better."

She chuckled as she hugged me. "No. I don't suppose it will."

On one hand, I was lamenting life being so awkward and difficult and complicated. On the other, the way Vaughn made me feel was totally worth it. Being with him was worth it. What was missing out on one dance together?

It was clearly not the philosophy we were all operating on.

"Go to the formal with me," Parker said as he sat down at my table in the library later that day. It was not a question.

Did he know Clove and I had been talking about it just earlier that day? Weird timing. Then again, the formal was less than three weeks away now and those who were worried about saving face were probably getting desperate.

I looked him over, not at all impressed with the soft smile or the attempted charm in his eyes. "Why would I do that?"

"Because we belong together, Maggie."

"Do we?"

"You know it. I know it. So why put off the inevitable?"

"Parker, you're delusional."

"Delusional?" he asked, a twitch in his eye pretty much making my point for me. He scoffed. "I think I've been pretty patient with you, Maggie. Okay? I've forgiven you for this little blip, and for punching me. I think it's time to be done with this little rebellion of yours."

I blinked. "Excuse you? Little rebellion?"

He nodded. "Yes. I've been lenient until now, but I think it's time we put this behind us now."

"What makes you think there could ever be an 'us'?" I asked him.

"The Police Chief's son and the mayor's daughter. It just makes sense, Maggie. We'd be a power couple in this town. We could rule the whole fucking thing together."

I scoffed. "I have no interest in ruling anything or being a power couple."

Parker's eyes got this ugly, knowing glint in them and it froze my blood. "Really? Well, why don't we see what options you have left to you when your little boy-toy is finally rotting in jail?"

I frowned. "What are you talking about?"

"It would be a shame if my dad was to turn up to the Laneway this Friday, wouldn't it? Imagine if he found drugs on some of the riders?" He mock-gasped. "I can't imagine anyone getting out of that one easily."

Bile rose in my throat, but I stamped it down. Parker was just peacocking, surely. He couldn't know anything for sure.

"Go to the formal with me," he said again. This time there was a definite order in his tone.

"No, Parker. You can't blackmail me and bully me into being with you."

"Why not? I wouldn't be the first, would I?"

Fuck. What did he know, and how did he know it? But I was going to play it cool. If he was fishing for information, I sure as shit wasn't going to give him the answers he was after.

"I don't know what you think you know or what you're insinuating is going on, Parker. But I'm not going to go to the formal with you. You can threaten whatever you like, but I don't see why I'd care if your dad went to the Laneway on Friday night or not."

"Is that the story you're sticking to?" he asked me, that feral snarl rippling across his face.

I nodded, hiding all my discomfort. "It's the truth." Because it would be. Whether Parker followed through on his threats or not, I could warn Vaughn and he could just not go to the Laneway on Friday. He hadn't gone the previous Friday while we'd been playing house. I didn't see why he couldn't just miss that week as well.

Parker looked me over. "I sure hope you like fucking in a cheap-arse trailer, Maggie. Because he's going away for a long fucking time."

My heart pounded too hard in my chest, and I covered my trepidation with derision. "I'm sure that would mean more if I knew what you were talking about, Parker. But sure. You tell yourself whatever you need to so you can sleep at night."

He shrugged and just walked away, all nonchalant and casual.

Meanwhile, I was trying not to hyperventilate.

I needed to warn Vaughn and I needed to do it now.

"You can't race on Friday," I told him when he finally picked up his phone.

"Um, hi?" he chuckled. "Why not?"

"Because Parker has something planned."

He scoffed. "Am I supposed to be scared of that weak piece of shit?"

"He's getting his dad involved and it sounds like someone's planting drugs."

"Where are they going to plant drugs? On who? What? Where would the little wankstain even get them? You're worrying about nothing, baby. I'll be fine."

"Vaughn–"

"Mags," he said firmly. "I will be fine. There is nothing that idiot can do that will–"

"No!" I snapped. "No, Vaughn. What if you're not?"

"Then the lawyers will do what we pay them to do. If he's planning to plant drugs, then it'll be a walk in the fucking park for them. I'm not going to stop living my life because your ex is a dickhead."

"Because you don't have any dickheads in your past," I argued.

"The biggest dickhead in my past is me, darling. You know that."

"Not if you think your future is my future. You want to be together? Then we're going to have to deal with each other's pasts, our presents and whatever they throw at us in the future. And I'm telling you, mine is coming to bite us in the arse on Friday."

"Babe, chill–"

"Do not 'babe' me, arsehole," I warned him, pushing all my annoyance into my voice. "And do not just dismiss me because–"

"Mags, I love you. Okay? But I have more experience in this world, and I know what I'm doing. You don't have to worry."

"Just because you say so?"

"Because I know so. Don't you trust me?"

"Don't *you* trust *me*?"

"Look, where are you? This really isn't a conversation to have over the phone."

"No. You're not going to get your hands on me and seduce me into giving in this time."

"When have I ever done that?"

"You do it constantly. The fact that I let you does not mean I'm going to let you this time."

"Then having this conversation in person should be fine."

"No. You clearly don't want to hear what I have to say." And I hung up on him.

I ignored his calls and his texts. I ignored him driving past Mum and Jonathan's. I even ignored him at school. Which turned out to be a bad plan, because Parker spent the rest of the week trying to get close to me. And he did it every time a Prince was around. I was starting to think he wasn't sure which of them I was with. Which meant he was possibly going after them all.

Parker fell into step with me on Thursday as I walked down the hallway, dropping his arm around my shoulder, and I immediately looked around to see which Prince was nearby that time. My blood ran cold as I saw one of them was Vaughn.

I pushed Parker off me and glared at him. But the damage was done. Iago had a hand on Vaughn's left arm, and Stone had a hand on his right. And Vaughn was watching Parker with absolute murder in his eyes.

"Well," Parker said happily. "That answers that question now, doesn't it?"

And he sauntered off merrily. I flicked a look to Vaughn, frowning hard, before turning and heading for somewhere private. I wasn't sure if I wanted him to follow me or not, but I suspected he would. So I found myself in the very back stacks of the library in the semi-dark. It didn't take Vaughn long to join me.

"What in the fuck was that?" he growled, but I knew he wasn't angry with me.

"That," I said as I whirled on him, "was my past working out who to direct his father to. And you gave him exactly what he wanted."

"He had his hands on you. What did you want me to do?"

"I don't know, Vaughn." I shoved against him. "Maybe not give him the ammunition he was looking for?"

He wrapped his fingers around my wrist. "I'm not going to give into that little arsewipe, baby. If I did, I wouldn't be the man you love. You just have to trust me."

"Just…" I grumbled. "Put your hands on me, Vaughn."

He smirked. "Why? You ready to give in?"

"I need you to remind me how much I love you before I walk away from you being a jerk. Unless that's what you'd prefer."

I watched him swallow hard. "What the fuck are you saying?"

"I'm saying you either kiss me now or you might not get to kiss me for a while."

His hands went to my waist as he stepped up close to me. "You going to blackmail me into not racing tomorrow by withholding your kisses?"

"Why not?" I huffed. "Parker's trying to blackmail me into going to the formal with him."

"He's doing fucking what?"

"That's why I need you to not race."

"You planning to give in if I'm arrested?"

I stepped away from him. "No!"

"Then what's the problem?"

I opened my mouth, then closed it again. "Seriously?"

"What? I'm going to be fine and you're not going to the formal with him. We win, baby."

I shoved him again and walked out.

"Maggie!" he called, but I shook my head and he didn't follow me.

VAUGHN: EIGHT

I fucking itched. I was restless. My whole body thrummed with too much energy, and I had nowhere to fucking put it.

Maggie had walked away from me, and it was…not the best feeling in the world.

Why hadn't I just fucking kissed her when she'd asked me to? Why had I argued? Why the fuck did I get all pissy about something I had no reason to think was going to happen and give her a reason to be angry with me? But jealousy got the better of me. Jealousy got the better of me and instead of fixing a few days of awkwardness, I made it worse.

And I only had myself to blame.

It was taking all my insignificant willpower not to fall back on my usual coping mechanisms. Not to drink and race and fight and fuck my mood away. That last one was pretty easy when all I wanted was Maggie in my arms.

But she had to know I'd be fine. I couldn't miss the race and there was nothing her idiot ex's dad could do to me for just racing. We weren't illegal. We might have trod the line pretty closely, but the only thing the cops could ever do to us at the Laneway was give us a couple of parking tickets and maybe slap us with having a non-road-worthy vehicle if I rode my racer out of there.

Drugs? Where the fuck were they going to get drugs and how were they going to pin them on any of us. It was a fucking joke, is what. She was worrying over nothing, and I wasn't going to feed into her unnecessary concerns and let them grow.

There was only so much willpower I could muster, so the boys and I were at Kenicki's. We were outside having a vape and enjoying the cooler air against my restless anger.

Then a fucking prissy convertible was pulling into the lot. I knew who owned that car.

"What the fuck's he doing here?" Stone asked.

I shrugged, feeling cocky and confident. This was our home turf. Whatever the punk was here for, we could send him home with his tail between his legs.

Parker Bates walked right up to me, leaving his friends in the car. There was a feral look in his eyes.

I knew that look. I *felt* that look every time I thought about him and Maggie. Felt it every time the idea of losing her crossed my mind. It was enough to make a man insane. And Parker Bates was clearly insane. I'd have felt sorry for him if he hadn't tried to hit her.

"Stay away from my girl, Saint," he gave me his best imitation of a threatening growl.

I kept my composure somewhat better than Iago, who spluttered a laugh so violently that he spat out his beer. Ezra chuckled behind us.

I huffed a laugh. "Or, what?"

I could see the fear in Parker's eyes, but his jaw was set. This fucker wasn't going anywhere. "Or you'll regret it."

I pretended to think about it. "Yeah, nah. I don't think so, mate. She's not something I see myself regretting." I leant towards him to really drive my point home, and whispered like it was a secret, "Maggie's not your girl."

He drew himself up like he was actually going to fight me right here. "Maggie *is* my girl. She's not yours. She's *my* girl."

I gave him a haughty smirk while Iago doubled over, pissing himself laughing. I caught Ezra's smile out the corner of my eye. "You know," I said, tapping my chin. "Actually, you're right. She's not my *girl*. She's my…old lady."

He knew what an 'old lady' was to us and that pissed him off, just like I hoped it would. "You stay away from Maggie, or I'll *take* you away from her." At the look in his eyes, I actually believed him and some of my unbridled confidence started cracking.

The fucker was actually threatening me? Over Maggie?

And look, I understood. If she walked away from me now and I found out she was with someone else, I'd burn this whole fucking place to the ground. But I'd also let her go. I – me, Vaughn-fucking-Saint, the heir to the Blood Roses – would let her go. I'd let the next wanker put his hands on her and fuck her and do whatever she wanted him to. If it made her happy.

And yet here was this pathetic Police Chief's wankstain, standing up to me over her.

Would that make me more respectful of her wishes, or was he fighting harder for his love?

I did not like that he'd made me ask myself that question. It put a whole lot of other unpleasant thoughts in my head. Thoughts like, if he was willing to attempt to intimidate me, if he was willing to threaten me to my fucking face on our fucking turf, what else was he willing to do? How far was he willing to go for her?

How long until he won her back?

Oh, fuck. That didn't sit well.

Because I wasn't going to pretend that I wasn't fucking paranoid about what I was to Maggie. I had no doubt she believed she loved me. I was sure she did. For now. What if this – what if I – was just a teenage rebellion? Just a bit of fun before she finally realised who she was meant to be and where she was meant to belong. And that neither of those answers involved me.

Now, who was fucking weak?

But I couldn't help it.

There was a strength in Parker standing in front of me now, willing to risk the wrath of me and the rest of the Princes with me. Had I not been so stuck up in my own arse, I'd have wiped the fucking floor with him. Had I not been very aware that he was looking for a reason to put me away, I wouldn't have hesitated to give him the epic beat down he was just begging for.

Iago had no qualms about that or in maintaining his intimidating mask. He was still bent over, laughing at Parker's threat while he cradled his beer by his knees. He slapped my leg as he fought for breath. "Oh, fuck," he chuckled. "Do you hear this idiot? He thinks…" He was overcome with another bout of laughter. "Fucking hell. Oh, Bates-y. That's hilarious. You think you can…?" There he went again and even Cairo scoffed behind us.

While he was busy, Parker and I glared at each other. Something hardened in me as we faced off. I wasn't going to be weak. This fucker wasn't going to make me weak. My love for Maggie wasn't going to make me weak. I would rise above this shitstain and remind him that Vaughn Saint always wins. Beating him would ensure he had nothing Maggie could ever want. Even that fucking white picket fence, the pearls, the dog, and the two-point-five kids in East Ham. If anyone was going to give that to her, it was going to me.

My rage that Parker thought he could get in the way of that completely overrode the logistics. Blaise would kill me? Fuck that. I was Vaughn Saint. I was fucking invincible. If Blaise couldn't touch me, Parker and his dad had no fucking hope.

I felt the calculating, condescending smirk tug at my lips as I looked Parker over and the dude had the decency to pale a little. "While Magenta wants me, the only thing that could take me from her is death, Bates," I growled, much more impressively than he was trying on. "You man enough?"

Parker swallowed hard, and he was obviously done. "Just you wait, Saint," he threatened as he backed away. "You'll get yours. I'm going to make sure you go away for a long time. Then, she'll have no choice but to find comfort in familiar arms."

I stepped forward, ready to one-punch this arsehole, but Iago grabbed me. I heard his bottle crash to the pavement beneath us in favour of getting both hands on me. *Oh, now the Dreamer's laughter stops.*

Parker nodded knowingly as he stopped back up. "You touch me, Saint, and you're just making my job easier for me. I've got witnesses, too." He threw his arms wide. "But I'll give you one free shot. And remember, I know just how tight and warm that little cunt is, Saint. The feeling of those hands, those lips around my cock. The way she moans *my* name as I cum inside her. You think you can stop at just the one?"

Blood rushed in my ears, and I saw fucking red. Now it wasn't just Iago's hands on me as I fought to get to Parker. I was going to put him down. I was going to fuck him up. I didn't give a fuck who he was, who his daddy was. He was going into a shallow grave, and I was going to smile the whole fucking time I was putting him there.

"I will fucking kill you, Bates!" I snarled as I thrashed against my Princes. It took all four of them to hold me back and even that wasn't enough to stop me fighting.

I accepted Maggie had a past – didn't we all? It wasn't the fact he'd had her that *really* pissed me off – not that I liked it – but he'd talked about my old lady. She deserved better than that, and I was very willing to follow through on my threat with my fucking fists.

But I'd just given him the reaction he wanted. Again.

"Have a good race tomorrow, Saint," he said, his confidence soaring now he knew I wasn't going to touch him. For now.

He sauntered off back to his car where his idiot lackies waited for him. We watched them tear out of the carpark and, even then, it took a good minute or two for the boys to let me go.

I was vibrating with anger, but not quite so far gone that I was going to get on my bike and follow. "Something has to be done about that fucking arsehole," I growled.

My boys looked between each other.

"We can't kill him, V…" Iago pointed out, almost apologetically.

"Not pre-emptively, at least," Cairo added.

"I dunno. I could slip a little something into his coffee," Ezra offered with a shrug.

"You into poisoning people now?" Stone rumbled.

"It's all chemistry, my bro."

Iago rubbed his eyes and shook his head. "Without a sanction and a fucking good alibi, we're not poisoning the fucking Police Chief's fucking son. Look, dude is serious, obviously. Maggie already warned you that something's going down tomorrow, and he's just confirmed it."

"I'm not backing down now," I snapped.

“No one’s asking you to,” Iago snapped right back, in no mood for me taking my mood out on him.

“Fucker thinks he smart, we need to be smarter,” I said, trying not to lose it on the people I relied on. Maggie didn’t deserve to be talked about like nothing more than a piece of arse, and my boys didn’t deserve my wrath.

“What do you wanna do?” Cairo asked.

“I wanna fucking kill him,” I said, stretching my neck.

“Aside from that,” Stone pointed out.

“I’m racing. But we need more security. Maggie mentioned something about planting drugs. If anyone other than Daniels or I touch my bike, Lock’s up.” Cairo and Stone both nodded. I looked to Ezra. “I need you on recon and intercept.”

“Aye, aye, boss,” was Ezra’s reply.

“And someone’s going to need to keep an eye on Maggie and Clove.”

“If he fucking touches–” Iago started vehemently, then stopped abruptly. “I’ll watch the girls.”

It was a testament to how much we loved the idiot that no one – even Cairo – took that moment to make a comment on his outburst.

“We are fucking beating this arsehole,” I reminded them.

“Without killing him,” Iago reminded me.

I shook my head noncommittally. “Sure. Without killing him.”

“For now,” Cairo promised, a chilling half-smirk touching his lips.

CHAPTER NINETEEN

The parking lot at the Laneway was packed. Like, more so than usual, and I wondered what in the hell was going on.

This was more than just a normal race night. How much had Parker planned?

Clove had to park much too close to the tree line than we liked, but what other choice did we have? I had to go and try one last time to talk some sense into Vaughn. Except, just as we got out of the car, hands grabbed me.

"It's best you stay out of it tonight, Maggie," I heard Parker's voice in front of me.

"What are you doing?" I hissed at him, struggling against whoever held me.

"Stay still," I heard Nick say. I decided not to oblige.

"This is ridiculous," I told Parker as I wriggled. "What are you hoping to achieve?"

I heard Clove yell and looked over to see Rich stalking towards her. Oh, this was some bullshit.

"Leave her alone!" I yelled as Rich grabbed Clove, and I thrashed harder against Nick. "Parker! This is between you and me. Leave Clove out of it!"

"Yes, Parker," came the deadly calm tones of none other than the Prince of Dreams himself. "Leave Clove out of it."

Parker's smug victory turned to regretful terror as Iago stepped out of the shadows. Gone was the mischievous jokester I knew and in his place was a Blood Rose enforcer, full of fury and retribution.

"*You*," he said, pointing at Nick. "You are going to want to let go of Maggie."

Nick's hands were very suddenly anywhere but on me. Iago gave him a nod before turning his attention back to Parker.

"This is some class A bullshit, Bates." He scratched his ear absently as he took a step towards Parker. "You know, this is almost the kind of stunt I'd pull."

"I'm not a criminal!" Parker cried. "I'm saving her from the criminals!"

As my heart twinged, Iago scoffed. Clearly Iago and I had a very different idea of how tonight could end.

"Maggie doesn't need saving from anyone. Least of all by some prissy wanker she kicked to the curb."

"*I* dumped her!"

"You tried to hit her," Iago snarled, making it very obvious what he thought about that.

"She hit me first." He wasn't wrong.

"Good on her."

"By now, my father is rounding up your little gang of degenerates," Parker sneered at Iago. "Who are you more loyal to?"

"Keeping you away from Maggie and Clove conveniently lets me be loyal to everyone." His eyes snapped to Rich. "Are you particularly stupid?"

Rich stepped away from Clove. Iago gave him a nod as he backed away further.

"Maggie, come with me," Parker implored.

I shook my head as Iago herded Clove and me behind him. "No, Parker."

"You're choosing a Blood Rose over me?"

"I would choose all the Blood Roses over you."

"How fucking delusional are you?" Iago scoffed.

"But, Maggie, I love you."

Iago took a threatening step forward. "No, you fucking don't. If you loved her, you'd let her be happy. You'd do everything in your power to give her the life she really wants. The life she deserves. You wouldn't be fucking up her life for her."

I heard the visceral pain in Iago's voice at those words and I suspected he was thinking about Clove. Or at least his misguided sense of duty when it came to her, if that's even what was keeping him from her.

"I'm not leaving without Maggie," Parker said, and I had to applaud his nerve.

"I suggest you walk away, Bates."

"Not without Maggie."

Iago pulled a gun and pointed it at Parker. "I'm about done asking nicely."

But Parker was doing a brilliant job of holding his own. "She belongs with me," he said. His voice only wavered a little.

Iago was clearly fed up with the Police Chief's son. He re-angled his gun and fired a shot into the ground beside Parker's feet. Parker jumped and glared at Iago. But Iago was giving him a cold, calculating smirk.

"If you don't want to be benched in a shallow grave for your last season, then I suggest you and your cronies get the fuck out of here."

Rich decided to take that advice and took off through the trees.

"Or what?" Parker asked. "You'll shoot me? Like they'll never trace the bullet back to you."

Iago's eyes narrowed and I was afraid of him. I didn't know how Parker was still standing there. "I'm not afraid to go fishing for it after it's done its job."

"And the witnesses?" Parker sneered.

Iago huffed, ejected his clip onto the ground then threw his gun away. "Fine. You leave me no choice," he said as he rolled up his sleeves. "But I'm warning you, this is not my forte. So, I have no idea how this is going to go."

On his way past Nick, Iago punched him in the face and Nick dropped to the ground in surprise. Parker started backing up, but Iago wasn't playing anymore, and he caught Parker easily, grabbing hold of the front of Parker's shirt.

"You are not going to enjoy this, Bates," he warned. "I'm not going to enjoy this. It was supposed to be my night off for fuck's sake."

"My dad will–"

"Your dad will what?" Iago laughed. "Be incredibly embarrassed by you and do nothing because you sent him in with a dodgy bust while you kidnapped your ex? This doesn't end well for you. Still choosing not to walk away?"

Parker clenched his jaw, and I didn't know why he didn't just walk away. How proud was he that he'd let Iago give him a beating? Iago West. The bare-fucking-knuckle fighter who was so good that the bruising on his knuckles was the only regular sign of his particular extra-curricular activity. And he hid it pretty well with tattoos.

"I would like to point out that this is really not my skillset," Iago said calmly to Parker as he threw his fist into Parker's face a couple of times. "They trained me to keep going until the other guy was unconscious. I don't do specific levels of beatings to really drive home the exact right message. They saved that for Saint or Lock. *I'm* not the subtle torture guy."

He dropped Parker to the ground and cocked his head. There was something so very inhuman about Iago in that moment. Like he was confused about how breakable and fragile and mushy humanity was, and he just couldn't get his head around it. Parker got two more hits to the face.

Iago crouched down to closer to Parker's level. "I don't want to risk you forgetting what's happened here tonight, but likewise I'm just not sure that you've really understood the gravity of the situation, Bates." He wiped his hand over his chin, heedless of leaving blood all over it.

Parker's eyes widened. "I've got it," he stammered.

Iago didn't look convinced. "Have you, though?" he asked, and Parker nodded quickly. "Tell me exactly what it is you think you've understood, arsehole."

Parker swallowed heavily. "Maggie's done with me. She will never be mine. I fucked it up with her and deserve everything I get. I'll tell them all to back off."

Iago smiled as he stood up again. "Huh. That went better than I thought." He looked back to me and, despite everything that had happened that night, I couldn't help smiling at the gentle self-pride on his face. "Seems that we've solved one problem, then."

I nodded. "And the other problem?"

He shrugged. "I dunno. My phone's been buzzing like mad." Before he checked it, he hauled Parker to his feet. "Now get your arsehole friend out of here before I change my mind about my benevolence."

Parker nodded hurriedly, scrabbled at Nick, and they ran off through the trees. Iago made sure they were gone before he pulled his phone out. His next words were a string of very colourful and creative swears.

"What?" I said, my heart in my throat.

I watched Iago's jaw twitch. Something was wrong. "They got him."

My, "What?" was slightly more panicked that time.

Iago nodded, dragging his tongue over his lip as he looked over his phone again. "Fuck. Idiot. How?" he muttered, then he looked at me again. "Chief Bates has him in lockup. Lawyer reckons he'll be out Monday morning. A raid off information provided by Parker at the same time he tries to kidnap you is going to look mighty circumstantial. A few nights in solitude aren't going to hurt V."

I was livid. "No, but *I* might hurt him once he gets out."

Iago looked at me with sympathy. "Mags, you have to understand, he had to do it."

"Why? Why did he have to do it?"

Something crossed his face and I had to wonder how much they'd planned. "You weren't there last night, okay? Things were said. Little shitty Bates said… It could have got pretty ugly. Tonight is the fallout."

"So he was off ignoring my concerns while I was getting kidnapped?"

"Why do you think I'm here? Okay? We had contingencies in place. We had a plan for everything." He looked at his phone. "Mostly."

"So that makes it okay?"

He looked back at me. "He's gonna beat himself up about it enough. You don't need to add to it."

"Don't tell me what I can and can't do, Iago!" I snapped, then huffed. "I'm just grateful I didn't have the guts to go to Dad before this stunt."

In the wan light, I saw Iago's jaw drop, all thoughts about whatever went down with Vaughn forgotten. "You fucking what?"

I nodded, feeling overly cocky and huffy. "That's right. After last week, I was getting up the nerve to tell Dad I fell in love with Vaughn. Well, fuck that for a joke. Or maybe I'll still tell him, and he'll deal with Vaughn for me!"

"Mags, you don't mean that," he said gently.

"Don't I?"

"You don't," Clove insisted, pale and a more than a little shaken but determined not to let me be stupid.

I deflated. "Okay. Fine. Maybe not. But how could he do this to me, Yago? He just completely dismissed me. I warned him, and he thought he knew best!"

"Yeah, all right. We were cocky. But it's just one weekend in jail, Mags. Aren't we all allowed one slip up?"

"It's not about the jail time!" I cried, then took a breath. "I am not in the solution-oriented stage right now, Yago. I'm in the emotions stage, okay? I don't want you to problem solve my relationship, I want someone to tell me that I was hard done by, and I deserve some ice cream."

Iago nodded. "You always deserve ice cream, Maggie." His eyes darted to Clove and something unspoken passed between them. "I'm going to walk you back to the car and then you're going to get out of here. Plausible deniability and all that. I'll let you know when I hear he's out."

I was still angry, but I couldn't stop thinking about what Iago had said about one slip up. Maybe Vaughn *was* allowed one slip up. But maybe I was also allowed to be angry about it. I guess I'd see whether I was still in the emotions stage or the solution stage by the time Vaughn was out of jail.

Clove and I went back to her house, where there would be less questions or scrutiny if we locked ourselves in her room. All things considering, she was holding up well. Little shaken, like me, but no real worse for wear than before we'd been grabbed.

But then, neither of us seemed inclined to sleep, so we left the television on all night until we couldn't keep our eyes open any longer.

CHAPTER TWENTY

I spent the whole weekend pacing my room and the only one in the house I could tell about my anxiety was Freddy. So the poor guy heard way more than he should, but at least I had some physical support.

Iago texted early Monday morning.

I

He's out. Easy bail.

The bail might have been easy, but the conversation Vaughn and I were about to have would not be.

Maggie

Is he coming to school?

I

I don't know.

Why?

Maggie

Because I need to have a

conversation with him.

Where is he now?

I

Heading home.

I waited for him in the parking lot at school during first lesson, suspecting that he was going to be late if he had to go home, presumably shower, then change. I'd already set up my backup plan; if it went badly, then I was taking Clove's car and Iago was going to get her home safe that afternoon. Clove's car keys weighed down my pocket, and I tried to remind myself they were not proof things were going to go badly. They were simply a contingency. I wanted this to work out and I was optimistic that Vaughn did, too.

Eventually, he pulled into the parking lot. Vaughn parked his bike, and his eyes were on me by the time his helmet was coming off. There was a hesitancy between us that I don't think I'd ever felt before. We'd been angry and antagonistic and sarcastic and sexy and sweet, even comfortable silence, but never this weird uncertainty.

"Morning, darling. Shouldn't you be in class?" he said with his usual charming smile as he stepped over to me.

Seriously? No apology? No 'sorry, I didn't let you know I was okay all weekend'? He was just going to act like nothing was wrong?

"You fucking cockwomble!" I yelled as I shoved him.

I could see him trying not to smile. "Cock-what?"

"Add any word after that you want, Vaughn. I'm too mad to care."

He seemed to know I wasn't messing about. "Baby–"

"You'd be fucking wise not to 'baby' me right, now, Vaughn," I growled.

"Maggie…" he said gently. "I'm fine. That wasn't my first weekend behind bars, and it won't be the last."

Did he really not know why I was mad at him? Did he really think I'd been concerned that he might be uncomfortable for a couple of nights in jail when I knew for a fact that he slept out on his dad's property with a lot less than a fire and a tent?

After everything – everything we'd talked about, everything we'd risked, the things we'd said to each other, that we felt – had it honestly not occurred to him why I was angry with him?

Was this hiccup something we could get through? A misunderstanding we could avoid in future because it had now happened once? Or was this proof our whole relationship had been just one long con? Maybe worse, nothing more than a mistake?

I was more inclined to believe the former, but this was a man who was willing to die to be with me. He was a self-saboteur. Knowing him, he was pushing me away on purpose. Because I got too close. Our intensity scared me, too, but I wasn't about to let him fuck up the best thing that had happened to either of us.

"One prick and you'll bleed," I muttered sadly, completely unintentionally.

Vaughn frowned. "What?"

I sniffed back the tears. "It's right what they say about you. The Prince of Thorns. He who bleeds anyone who dares get too close."

He bristled. His shoulders tense and his jaw tight. "If you knew me so well, how did you *expect* this to end?"

"I'm not sure I *did* expect it to end," I admitted.

I was woman enough to admit I was in over my head with Vaughn. For Vaughn. I loved him. Completely and utterly loved him. There were a thousand and one reasons why I shouldn't, but I still did. I didn't even know rightly why or when it had happened, but that didn't matter because even without him telling me I was beyond certain the feeling was mutual.

I had no ideas how to get around the whole 'my dad would kill him' situation to let us do it properly without outright risking Vaughn's life, but that was fast becoming irrelevant. I wasn't doing this thing unless we were equals. I wasn't going to have a relationship this…serious and intense and all-consuming with a guy who wouldn't listen to my fears or take my feelings into account. I couldn't – wouldn't – be with someone who just dismissed me the way he had simply because he was so overwhelmingly arrogant about his abilities and my supposed naivety.

I took a breath. "I hoped we'd find a way through," I continued. "A way to really be together. Maybe even actually get married where my dad gave me away."

Everything about him softened, like he'd sort of deflated in awe and confusion. "You did?"

I nodded. "Yeah." I forced myself to keep going despite the look of hopeful optimism growing in his eyes. "But I can't do this if you're just going to dismiss me. I warned you Parker was planning something, and you didn't care if it got you killed. We're supposed to be in this together, Vaughn. You told me you'd risk death to be with me, but that's nothing like risking leaving me behind just to feel superior over someone who isn't even really my ex." I breathed against the heat in my eyes. "You had me, Vaughn. Why wasn't that enough?"

I saw him fighting his conditioning. I watched his mouth twitch between a snarl and neutral as he tried to control the instinct to lash out and fire back with something to hurt me worse than the realisation that he'd hurt me. I watched the look in his eyes harden as his jaw clenched, right along with the fists at his sides.

"What are you saying, darling?" he asked, forcing his voice to stay calm even through gritted teeth.

"I'm saying I don't know how this is meant to work."

"What?"

"Our relationship. If you won't dial back this flirtation with death."

He scoffed, but it was humourless. "You want me to stop racing? Leave the Blood Roses? Be someone I'm not? Maybe you *should* just go back to your ex."

I was going to try very hard not to rise to the bait. "No. I want you to be exactly who you are. That's who I love. But I want you to stop the ridiculous risks. I told you Parker's dad would be there. It wasn't just a risk. It was a certainty, and you still had to go. What's the point of pursuing me and making me fall in love with you, just to be taken away from me?"

"So what? Are you just going to walk away from this? From us?"

"I *am* going to walk away, Vaughn, to give you *one more* chance. If this is something you think you can do – let us be equal, give us a proper shot, and make sure you always come home to me – then good. But really think about it, Vaughn, because it tears me apart to live with this fear anyway. Living with the fear *and* you wilfully taking stupid risks might kill me."

All fight left him.

He didn't need to fight his conditioning and his instincts anymore because they just…died.

"Magenta… I–"

I shook my head. "You think about it, Vaughn. You think about it and let me know what you decide. Decide if this – us – is really what you want, or if you want to perpetuate this whole self-sabotaging idiocy thing that they beat into you."

"And you think I can just get over it like that, do you?"

I shrugged. "I don't know, Vaughn. But we got this far so, the way I see it, the only one standing in our way is you."

I pulled Clove's keys out of my pocket and took my sweetarse time stalking over to it. Tears were hot in my eyes, but I would not give him the satisfaction of running away. Let him think that I could live without him, and my heart wasn't cracking at the idea that he might not make the decision I wanted him to.

Climbing into the car, I didn't even think. A Blood Rose had broken my heart, so a Blood Rose was going to be the only thing to help it. Not long later, I found myself at Dad's. As I closed the front door, the emotions I'd so far held at bay broke free. A single tear slid down my cheek and I sank to the floor.

"Maggie?" Dad said as he ran in and dropped to my side, already looking for wounds or hurts. "What's wrong, darling? Who hurt you?"

I sniffed as he wrapped me in his arms. "I can't tell you."

"You can tell me anything."

I shook my head against his shoulder. "Not this."

He pushed me to arm's length and looked me over. "Yes. You can."

The tears were starting to leak, and my bottom lip trembled. "I…" had no idea where to start.

"Is it a boy?"

I spluttered a watery chuckle at the combination of terror, fury, and discomfort on his face at the mere idea. I wiped my eyes and nodded.

"Yeah, it's a boy," I told him.

Dad might have had a lot of feelings about the concept of romance and me and boys, but he was also my dad, and he was going to pull up his big boy pants and be there for me.

He cleared his throat and gave a nod. "Okay. Uh… Right. Can I…? Can I do anything?"

I shook my head. "I think it's over?" I said sadly.

Gone was the terror and discomfort. All that was left was fury. "What!" he roared. "What sort of idiot breaks up with my daughter?"

God, I loved the man.

"You don't know that he broke up with me," I told him.

"Well he made you cry, and I'm going to rip him apart."

"Please don't rip him apart, Dad. He might come through for me, and being in one whole piece might be better for that."

Dad frowned. "The man doesn't get a second chance."

"The man is what you made him," slipped out and we both looked at each other in surprise.

"What?" Dad asked, his voice scarily quiet.

I blinked innocently. "What?"

"Maggie, darling… You didn't?"

I breathed deeply. "I tried not to, Dad. I swear. I kept my distance like you wanted me to. Like I should have. But he… I…"

"Are you in love with him?"

I looked down. "Uh…maybe…"

Dad swore heavily and creatively. "Who is it? Who've I got to kill for touching you?"

"I told you I love him and you're still planning to kill him for touching me? I'm not telling you."

He fixed me with his most intense, terrifying stare. The one that had even the St Jude twins shaking in their massive boots.

"Maggie…" he said, warning heavy in tone.

"You can Blood Rose Boss me all you like," I told him. "He knew the risk, and he still wanted me. Maybe it's the only reason he did want me. Knowing what you'd do to him. But I won't give him the satisfaction of you killing him."

Dad nodded and scrubbed a hand over his chin. "Fucking Saint, then."

I blinked again. "How did you know?"

"I've basically raised that mangy dog from the useless wee pup his mother walked out on. I know there's been something different about him. I see the change."

"What change?" I asked.

Dad shook his head. "If I didn't know him better than I knew meself, I'd have missed it. But the idiot's been… I'd have called him happy. As much as Vaughn could ever look happy." Dad looked at me. "It was you. And you love him, too?"

I nodded. "I really do. And I know the rules, but please, Dad. For me, can you please not kill him?"

"You love this mongrel piece of shit enough to beg for his life?"

I rolled my eyes at his attempt at injecting humour into the situation. "I'm actually being serious here, Dad."

He dropped all vestiges of humour and nodded his promise that he was going to be a good boy and take this seriously. "Sorry, darling."

"I know the rules," I started again. "I know it's 'touch me and die'. I get that. And I know where it comes from. I do. And I haven't given up ideas about that life. I'm finishing school, I'm getting my teaching degree, but I also want him."

"Sweetheart, he's got you sitting in the hallway crying your eyes out and you still want him?"

I nodded, feeling those tears threatening again. "Yes. I'm not crying because he was mean to me or treated me wrong or hurt me. Not really. Nothing unforgivable. He made a bad choice that affected us both. So, I'm here because I gave him an ultimatum and then walked away, and I don't know what he's going to choose."

"What's the choice, darling?" he asked softly.

"Us. Him and me. I don't want him to be anyone other than who he is, but I want him to choose us over something as stupid and insignificant at getting on over on my ex-not-even-boyfriend."

Dad nodded solemnly. "And if I kill him, he can't make that choice. He can't choose you."

"Exactly."

"And that's what you want? You want him to choose you?"

I was losing the ability to control the tears forming in the corner of my eyes, but I nodded. "Yes. I want that life we had planned for me, Dad, but I want Vaughn in it. By my side."

"Sweetheart, I want you to have the fucking world. But what if you can't have both?"

"Why can't I?"

"You know why."

The tears bubbled over, and I gave him a very watery, "Pretend I'm stupid."

He sighed as he bundled me into his arms. "Because he's a Rose, darling."

I sobbed as he held me, my arms wrapping around his.

I felt him nod against my head. "Sh. It's okay, Mags. My darling girl. I've got you. I can't promise you a future with him, but I can promise you that Vaughn will not die by my sanction. Not for this. If he makes the wrong choice, we'll have another little chat."

I couldn't help but splutter a wet laugh as I wiped a sleeve over my eye. "Thank you."

He shook his head as he hugged me tighter. "Everything for you, sweetheart. Everything I can give you. Can I ask what this stupid choice that caused all this was and what it had to do with Parker?"

That dried up my tears and I pulled away from him slowly.

"Oh, no. Mags..." he breathed. "Please don't tell me I owe the Police Chief's son a beating."

I shook my head. "No. Iago did you proud."

Dad looked only mildly surprised by that. "If you're going to tell me this is some kind of reverse harem thing..."

I choked on some spit. "Uh, no! God, no!" I cried through coughing. "No. Definitely not that. Jesus Christ, Dad." I shook my head. "No. I'm a one-man kind of woman." As a rule. "Besides Clove would put Stone and Cairo combined to shame if I touched Iago."

Dad chuckled. "Our sweet little Clover got a dream of her own, eh?"

I nodded. "Yeah. The feeling's pretty mutual, but either neither of them realise it or *someone* is playing very dumb."

Dad shook his head in amused surprise as he leant back against the wall and put his arm around me. "Anything else I need to know about those Princes?"

VAUGHN: NINE

It had been two days since she'd basically ended things. And I had no one but myself to blame.

Why the fuck had I let Parker Bates and his little, futile show of strength get to me? What? The guy had been willing to stand up to me so that automatically meant he'd win her back? Of course that wasn't fucking how it worked.

At least I knew I'd got to him as well. Why else would he have sent Daddy in to arrest the big, bad guy? So I wasn't alone in my wallowing about losing her. The thing that made it worse was the fact that she still wanted to be with me, and I'd fucked it up. Like she'd said, I was the only one standing in the way of having what I wanted. What we wanted.

And I didn't know how to get it back.

I wanted to do this whole equal thing. I wanted to make sure I went home to her. I wanted us to be in each other's decisions. I just also didn't know how to show her I meant it. Was she going to just accept words if I gave them to her? Why would she when my actions had just backed up what she'd thought about me at the start of the year?

The last two days had been torture. I'd watched her tear out of the school carpark in Clove's car, and no one heard from her for the rest of the day. Or, if they did, they weren't telling me about it. Then there she was on Tuesday, pretending like everything was fine.

It was what she'd done at the start of the term after she'd ended things with Bates. She'd held her head high, but maintained her demure demeanour, her smiles for everyone. Then, they'd sympathised with her. Now, I heard the whispers.

Bates had clearly thought about outing us before Iago's warning on Friday night. He'd let enough slip to enough people that other people were asking the question; was the mayor's stepdaughter dating the heir to the Roses?

It killed me to watch her answer their questions with the same blank, fake politeness and pleasantness as she'd answered their questions about her breakup with Bates. I was keenly aware of coping mechanisms, but post-Bates it had been a distracting tactic as much as anything, so people didn't find out about us. Now? Now she just seemed like that prissy little princess I'd thought of her all those months ago. She wore the mask, the one that I hated she wore for them. The one so she'd fit in with people who wanted her to fail.

The rumour that she was dating me was one step closer to failure to them.

And I couldn't fucking do anything for her. I couldn't remind her that she was better than them. Assure her that they were all fake arseholes who didn't deserve her. I'd typed the message out a hundred times and deleted it a hundred more. She didn't want to hear from me. In case there was any doubt, Clove had made that obvious.

"Unless you've got the right answer, she doesn't want to know right now. She needs some space. She's giving up a lot for this, Vaughn," Clove had reminded me. Not that I needed the reminder. "She wants to do this properly. She wants to marry you and have lots of sex and, hopefully, babies and have dinners with her parents and let the whole world know she's yours. But she won't do that with someone who's not as all in as her. Not just for what she's giving up or you're both risking, but because that's what she deserves."

Clove's cheeks had been flushed bright red in embarrassment, but her voice hadn't wavered once in fighting for her best friend, and I'd had to applaud her assertiveness. Clove was the quieter of the two of them. She was all talk with Maggie but couldn't really walk the walk. Which I had no problem with; she was innocent to the world of the Roses and Maggie wasn't. Clove wasn't fake, she just needed the practice to voice what went on in her head. We all started somewhere, and this year was her start.

But she hadn't been wrong.

I tried not to let my fears get in the way of finding a solution, but I was dragging my heels about it. I wanted to go to her and tell her that I was all in. That I'd been all in since at least Rizzo's, if not earlier. But it didn't feel like enough. And I couldn't win her back for good if it wasn't enough.

So I put on my own mask – my game face – and I went about my life like I wasn't an even more broken shell of a man on the inside. Which, as I found out on Wednesday evening at the clubhouse, was one of the poorer ideas in my long list of bad ideas.

I smirked to Chord with an insinuating nod. "You should have seen the way she squirmed for me."

Blaise suddenly pulled his gun and pointed it at me. "You and your fuckin' smart mouth, Saint."

Wait, what?

Oh, fuck.

He knew.

How did he know?

How *long* had he known?

And why the hell was he only doing anything about it now? Chord and I were talking about one of the Monster's girls, not Maggie. Why did Blaise choose now–?

Oh, I knew why.

Blaise did *not* appreciate my cocky bluster about fucking over a girl, even a Monster, when I'd just, albeit unintentionally, fucked over *his* girl. I could see why that might piss him off.

He nodded, his smile kind of insane. "Oh, yeah, fucker. I know you touched her."

There was an indrawn hiss around us, because everyone knew he wasn't talking about the Monster, and I swallowed hard.

"You moron!" someone called.

I kicked my chin in acknowledgement, except it was a little late for that.

Death was staring me in the face, and I fully deserved it. Weirdly, I didn't lament my end. Maggie was worth it. I'd die a hundred times over just to have the time that I'd had with her. That I'd had and fucked up so, really, I deserved whatever Blaise was about to do to me twice over at least. The only thing I did regret was that I wouldn't get to say goodbye to her. I wouldn't get to apologise. To tell her how much I loved her and how much I wished I hadn't been so stupid.

Blaise waved his muzzle at me. "Get the fuck in the office," he snapped.

Frowning in the most epic confusion, I preceded him into the office. He closed the door behind us and pulled the shades down.

"Sit the fuck down," he snapped, still waving the gun around.

I did what he said, and he dropped into his seat, fixing me with a terrifying combination of disappointment and fury. “Blaise…” I started.

He shook his head. “No. No. Nothing out of you for a minute.”

I inclined my head and pressed my lips together as he just kept staring at me. I didn’t know if he was trying to intimidate me into revealing all my secrets or just some wanky admission or apology, or if he was too pissed to have the words.

Finally he took a breath. “Were you looking for a death sentence?”

I licked my lip. “It’s the least I deserve.”

Blaise released a deep breath. “And I promise to give you one…if you don’t go crawling back to my girl on your fucking hands and knees and grovel like your fucking arse has never grovelled before.”

I blinked. “What?”

“You fucking heard me.”

“Why do I get a pass?”

Another very deep breath and his hand twitched like he really did want to sink a bullet in me but was holding off for some reason. “The only reason you’re not rotting in a shallow grave is Maggie.” He paused and I gave him a nod to show him I was listening. “She fucking begged me to keep you in one piece because she seems to think you might make a good choice for once in your life, son.”

Shit.

“I found her on Monday, fucking crying on the floor in the hallway and she still wouldn’t give you up without a decent fight.”

Double shit.

“And she told me every little detail.”

Triple shit.

"Blaise–"

"Do not 'Blaise' me, boy," he snarled, pointing the gun at me. "I would like nothing better than to empty this clip into your fucking head, then grab another one and aim it between your legs. You knew the rules. You enforced the fucking rules. No one touches Maggie. What the fuck made you think you were so special that you got to ignore the rules?"

I swallowed and put aside all the defiant shit that tried to force its way out of me from sheer habit. If I wanted to walk out of that room and back into Maggie's arms, then I was going to have to throw absolutely everything on the table and hope it didn't make him double down on his desire to kill me.

"Maggie did," I said quickly. "She… She wanted me. She…" I scrubbed a hand over my chin and realised it had been a while since I'd shaved regularly. "Okay, it didn't start with good intentions." I held my hands up, fully expecting the bullet. Blaise shifted in his seat but inclined his head for me to continue. "I was a cocky piece of shit who wanted to be the one to ruin her. Okay? I admit it and I'm sorry. But it's not like she came into this totally pure either. The night she gave into–"

"I do not want to hear the rest of that thought, Saint."

I inclined my head. "No. Right. Good point. Look, the fact is that it was just hate to start with. For both of us. I kissed her to mess with her. Then, she kissed me to hate me. We…" I slunk in the chair as I rubbed my finger over my lips and huffed a rough laugh. There was no humour in it. "By then, I was already in love with her. I'd kissed her once and argued with her fucking a million times, but I would have – still would – die just to hold her fucking hand." Another huff. "I messed up, man. I know that. But I love her, and she loves me," I shrugged, "and–"

"And she gave you an ultimatum that she's *still* waiting for an answer on."

I swallowed again. Hard. Daddy McCallan was, understandably, fucking pissed. "I don't know how to answer her."

He nodded his head at me. "*That* is not a good answer."

I sighed. "I want to tell her I'll always choose us. I want to tell her that I will always come home to her. But how do I do that? How do I make my words mean more than my stupid fear-driven actions?"

Blaise's hand twitched. His mouth rippled like he was making a decision. Finally, he put the gun down and sat more comfortably in his own chair. "When Isabel got pregnant, we thought about giving it a go. We were attracted to each other enough for the sex to be…" A very 'fuck, it was good' expression flickered over his face. "We thought, why not see where it went?" He scrubbed a hand over his jaw as he sat forward. "It didn't go well. We failed at the first hurdle. We told everyone Maggie was nothing more than a one-night stand so Isabel and Maggie could walk away.

He looked at me pointedly. "Our hurdle was the nature of a Rose's life. Isabel couldn't settle with the knowledge I could be taken from her any day. Any time. She couldn't give it a chance, and I accepted that. Without her all-in, it was difficult to really establish anything real between us and I felt no real pain in it ending. But there was still Maggie.

"Isabel wouldn't even think about an abortion, and I was more than happy to support her however I could. Her body, her choice. I offered to walk away as well. Keep them both safe. But then Isabel called me for the delivery. They wouldn't let anyone else in for some stupid fucking reason and she needed someone. The minute Maggie was in my arms, Isabel saw how much I already loved her. She couldn't, in good conscience, ask me to walk away from that."

He took a deep breath, ran his tongue over his lip, and fixed me with an even more level stare than he'd levelled so far.

"Seems to me, son, that you and Maggie passed that first hurdle with flying fucking colours. She knows who you are and she knows, at least enough, what this life is like. She's seen you race. She knows enough of what I ask you to do for me. She knows you are next in line for this seat. And she still wants her life to be with you."

My chest was tight. It twinged in what was both a really uncomfortable but also amazing kind of way. "She does?"

I saw the dad in him as he rolled his eyes. "You really are a fucking moron," he sighed, then his expression softened. "You really are what I made you. But yes. She wants a life with you, Vaughn. And you know me, I will quite literally kill to get my princess the life she wants. Now, killing you would do the opposite. You can see my conundrum here."

I nodded quickly as I sat up straighter in my chair. "Yes. Yeah. I can see that."

"Good. So I think you know what you need to do about it, yes?"

My chest fluttered nervously. "But how do I–?"

"You do your fucking best," Blaise said, getting sick of talking. Or maybe my stupidity. Or both. "You do as she's asked, and you stick to the calculated risks, not the stupid ones. You use your fucking head. You've got her, son, don't fuck it up just because I ruined you."

"What if I ruin her?" I asked quietly, only voicing my fear because I wasn't afraid to be vulnerable in front of him now.

"Then you should have thought of that before the two of you fell in love."

"Will she forgive me?"

"Son, she's already forgiven you. But she's only going to give you one chance. Fuck it up again and you won't be so lucky. Once is a teachable moment, Saint. Twice is wilful stupidity." I nodded, then he amended quickly. "Unless you're unfaithful. In which case, once is a death sentence."

I couldn't help my smirk. "What if it's consensual?"

He closed his eyes for a second. "That is literally the definition of unfaithful. What are we *doing* to you younger generation? If it's consensual, it's faithful. You do not need to be making insinuations about my daughter's kinks. I only promised her you wouldn't die for touching her, so do not bait me." He opened them again and looked at me. "You have one last chance, son. My daughter loves you and, while I want to string you up and take my slow arse time peeling your skin from your body, I trust my daughter. If she loves you and wants you in one piece, then I'm obliged to acquiesce and give you the chance to be worthy of her. But do not fucking let me down, or it's a whole new game. Understand me?"

I nodded quickly. "Understood, Blaise."

He inclined his head. "Now get the fuck out of here, go and find Iago and come up with some ridiculously outlandish plan to get her back."

"Iago?"

"Grand, sweeping romantic gesture? Let's not pretend that this isn't right up his alley, huh? And we'll also not pretend that you don't need all the help you can get."

"I'm going to try not to take offence at that."

"You and I are cut from the same cloth, Saint. It's why we get on so well, it's why I'm preparing you to take my place. We understand each other in a way that no one should really understand another person, because we are the same. I know your weaknesses and I know your strengths because they're mine. The Roses are a family, son. And we should never be afraid to ask family for help."

I nodded as I stood. "Okay. I'm sure Iago already has like ten options."

Blaise nodded. "Just don't let him get too carried away. I'm not dealing with another fucking fireworks permit this week, okay?"

I snorted. "Okay."

He kicked his head to the door, but he was smiling. "Go. There are far worse arseholes I could have for a son-in-law."

I paused, with my hand on the doorknob. "You giving me permission to ask her for her hand, then?" I teased.

The smile lingered in his eyes even if it dropped from his lips. "Too soon, Saint. You come back when you've won her back and we'll talk about it, otherwise you don't come back at all."

I swallowed hard. "I'll be back."

"Good man."

As I headed out, I grabbed my phone from my pocket. I was so busy texting Iago that I almost missed the huge cheer that went up at the sight of me being alive. I grinned as I ran a hand through my hair somewhat sheepishly.

"He's immortal!" Chord called.

I shrugged. "Turns out love does beat death."

"Oooo!" went off around the garage and I shook my head.

"Shut up."

I hurried out to my bike as I finished my message to Iago.

V

Need help.

I

Always.

Murder? Mayhem? Debauchery? Public drunkenness? Or just some minor breaking and entering?

V

Winning Maggie back.

I

cracking knuckles

You have come to the right place.

Let's win back your woman.

V

My old lady.

I

Your old lady.

CHAPTER TWENTY-ONE

Freddy and I were sitting on the couch, pretending either of us were really paying attention to the TV.

"Sorry about… You know," he said.

I nodded. "Yeah."

"It sucks."

I nodded again. "Yeah."

"Do you think it's going to work out?"

I sighed. "I don't know, Fred."

"I hope it does."

"You do?"

"Yeah."

"I appreciate that. Thanks."

"Appreciate what?"

"That you didn't just write Vaughn off, or worse be bitterly disappointed in my life choices. It kind of feels like you're the only one."

Freddy gave me a hug. "You're my big sister. I'll love you no matter what life you choose. As long as you choose the one that makes you happy."

I huffed a small laugh as we pulled away. "I don't know if I get to choose that one. That one has Vaughn in it and he's currently being a bit of a twat. It's kind of up to him now to choose my happily ever after." I took a deep breath. "Or, I'm going to have to find another one."

"But you don't want to?" Freddy guessed.

I shook my head. "Not really."

"But you will?"

"If I have to."

Freddy didn't seem to be the only one who wasn't as disappointed with my life choices as I'd expected them to be.

I was at Dad's the next afternoon, just for a bit because I needed to see him what with everything going down. Mum and Jonathan could think I was with Clove all they liked.

"I've been talking to Vaughn…" Dad said as he walked in.

I nodded, suddenly wary. "Okay."

"He's working on it."

I nodded again. "Sure. Glad he's made that clear to everyone *but* me."

"Give him time, darling. This is new territory for the both of you."

"Just because it's new doesn't mean the answer shouldn't be obvious."

"Not everyone has the freedom to be so single-minded in their desires and how they flaunt the rules to chase them, Mags."

I turned to him and he was looking at me pointedly. "I'm sorry, Dad. I know that I've disappointed you."

"Oh, darling," he said with a head shake. "You're not a disappointment. Sure, I wanted another life for you. I wanted you to have everything you wanted. Everything good and clean and safe. Your mother's life. It never once occurred to me that *you* might want *my* life."

I sighed. "I… I think I understand it better than the one I'm *supposed* to live in," I admitted. "It's easier. I don't feel like I'm playing a role. I'm just Maggie, who *is* Magenta. One whole person, not two personalities I can't seem to reconcile. I didn't think I should want to be part of your world, but I know now I don't want to be kept outside it anymore."

Dad nodded. "Then I'd best start training you."

"For what?"

"To lead the Blood Roses after I succumb to a violent death."

I frowned at him. "Thanks for the imagery, Dad."

"Darling, I don't want to go out any other way."

And I knew it, but his death wasn't my only problem with the idea of me taking over after he died. Wasn't one of a few problems with that idea, actually.

"But Vaughn's supposed to secede you," I said quickly, wanting to move on from the certainty of my father's death, even if he had brought it up to break some tension.

He waved all concerns away. "Vaughn would follow you through the gates of Heaven itself, Maggie. I don't think he's gonna have a problem sharing the throne with you."

"Sharing?" I squeaked. That was honestly not something I'd ever thought about. Until now.

Dad nodded. "Lord and Lady Saint, co-leaders of the Blood Roses. I gotta say, I kind of love it."

"Maybe we'll hyphenate," I joked.

And only then did reality really hit me.

I wanted to be with Vaughn. For real.

Not in secret. Not with the safety net of it all ending when Dad inevitably finds out. Without the thrill of hiding it keeping things interesting. With all the worry of being public and real life interfering and having to actually work at it.

I wanted to marry him in front of all our friends and family and have lots of sex and (hopefully) babies.

Part of me knew I'd always wanted that. I'd basically told him that when we'd… Had it been a breakup? But even wanting, I hadn't known how to get it. I didn't think I was going to get it without taking it. So maybe that's what I'd have to do. Take it and the rest of the world be damned. Provided it was still what he wanted as well.

Dad's eyebrow arched, like he'd literally seen the epiphany blossom over my face. More like smack me over the head.

"Oh, really?" he asked, all coy.

I nodded. "St Callan has a nice ring to it. Like St Jude, but with slightly less psychopathic tendencies."

"Hopefully a lot less."

I gave him a wide smile. "Is it okay if we hold off on the whole training me up thing, though?"

Dad cocked his head at me.

"I know where this is coming from, and I appreciate it. All this hinges on if Vaughn actually gets his act together, but I want to try to have my life *and* Vaughn. My plans still haven't changed, and I don't see why I can't go home to Vaughn while I'm living them. Cairo's mum–"

"Is getting out," Dad interjected quickly.

I frowned. "What?"

He nodded. "Why do you think I've been so worried about this, darling? I guessed you've been looking at Celia and thinking you can live the respectable life *and* have the bad boy. But Celia can't do it. I don't think she ever *wanted* to do it, but Rocky…made her. She loves Cairo more than anyone else in his life is probably ever gonna be capable of, but he's old enough now that he doesn't need her protection and she's getting out. They've separated, she's moved in with someone else."

"Cairo never said…" I whispered, wondering how the hell I felt so sorry for a guy I was pretty sure couldn't feel anything.

"He wouldn't have. That's not the way these boys were raised. It's not your business so you don't need to know. My point is that you can't look at the Lockworths and think they're defying the rules for love. They have never been like that."

"Then I make my own path. I make my own rules. I'm going to teach at Hammersby Primary and I'm going to live with Vaughn. And if the world doesn't like that… Well, it can fuck right off. If they try to make an issue, then I'll consider inheriting from you."

Dad smirked. "I'm glad you've got a backup plan, sweet."

I took a deep breath. "Both plans rely on Vaughn making the right choice."

"Vaughn's made the right choice, Maggie. He's just overthinking how to make sure you believe him."

"He could just try telling me?" I suggested.

"You know, darling? I mentioned that to him, and he seemed to think that wasn't enough."

I nodded. "Or he's playing us all."

Dad shook his head and I'd never seen him more sure about anything. "I put the fear of his fucking maker in him, he's not playing anyone. He wants to get it right, and I'm actually going to allow it."

"And if I'm left for the next…year without him saying anything to me?"

"Give the man some time. I only spoke to him yesterday. Iago's on it."

A thrill of trepidation – good and bad – ran through me. "Iago's involved?"

Dad nodded. "Oh, yes. If you think the Prince of Dreams isn't planning to make all yours come true, then you don't know him half as well as you think."

It would be incredibly stupid to think that Iago wouldn't have made himself involved with some kind of grand apology gesture. And he was going to throw his own over the top flair onto it. "Ugh, he's like the world's most annoying older brother I didn't even want."

"And yet, you love him, and you're stuck with him."

I nodded. "Yeah. Both of that."

"It's the formal on Friday, isn't it?" Dad asked and I nodded. "Well, isn't that that time that all you dramatic teenagers make your big romantic gestures?"

I snorted. "Sure. Why not?"

But there was absolutely no sign that Vaughn was going to do anything, let alone at the formal, and I spent more time than I really should have trying to convince myself that Dad wasn't wrong.

CHAPTER TWENTY-TWO

Was this the senior formal I'd hoped for and more? Yeah, not really.

A few months ago, I'd thought I'd be here, all respectable and envied as Parker's girlfriend. Then, I'd hoped that maybe Vaughn and I could enjoy the night together. Somehow. But neither of those things seemed likely to happen, and I wasn't going to let that get in the way of Clove enjoying herself.

Clove and I both pushed all thoughts of boys aside and focussed on us. Because, naturally, Iago was also absent. Which I would berate him for later. The least he could do while he was pretending not to be in love with my best friend was act like the flirty friend that he felt he could give her.

So, Clove and I were dancing and chatting and flitting around acting like everything was fine. For the most part, it was. I wasn't going to let any boy ruin *my* night either.

But then, Clove was elbowing me fairly violently actually. I turned to her in exasperation. "What?" I huffed, but she was staring at the door, her jaw pretty much resting on her not insignificant cleavage.

"Wow," she breathed.

I frowned. "Yago's he–?"

No. Nope. Oh, wow. Nup.

That was not Iago standing in the doorway under the streamers and balloons in his dark grey suit trousers and vest, complimented by a black shirt with the top button undone and black boots. His left hand was in his pocket and his right scrubbed over his chin as he looked around. His eyes found me, and I saw them drop down and back up as he took me in. He chewed his lip with an uncertainty I had never seen in him before.

My heart fluttered nervously, but not traitorously. It knew what it was doing, and I couldn't be mad at it.

There was only one reason why Vaughn was here; he was choosing us, and he was going to do it at the formal after all.

I wasn't going to let him win that easily, but I also suspected he'd win more easily than he should. Despite Dad's assurance he was going to choose us, I was still angry with him, and he was seriously going to have to show me that he was in this, but I also just wanted this to be a blip in our past that we could tell our grandkids about one day.

Because he was here, and looked fucking lickable in his finery, and that was a pretty big first step.

I heard Clove's squeak and realised Iago had stepped up beside Vaughn. Unlike his friend, Iago didn't hesitate. He came straight over to Clove, complimented her, and asked her to dance. She was also not wasting any time. Which left me alone as Vaughn walked over to me.

I'd be a naive idiot if I believed no one was watching the very obvious tension between us as he beelined for me. I was sure we looked right out of some cheesy teen movie – which, I won't lie, I kind of loved – our eyes locked, our body language awkward. If there was anything that would confirm the rumours Parker had started spreading, it was this exact scene.

"Maggie…" Vaughn said carefully as he stopped in front of me.

I took a breath. "What are you doing here?"

He looked around lazily, like he didn't give a single shit that everyone was watching. "It's my senior formal, too."

I chewed my lip to stop myself blurting out something stupid. "Great. Well, have a good night, then," I told him and started turning away.

He caught my hand to stop me. As I looked down at it, I was sure I heard people's indrawn breaths around us. But I tuned them out. The room was dark, music made it difficult to hear a conversation you weren't directly part of, and I could pretend they weren't there well enough.

"What are you doing, Vaughn?" I asked him.

"Big romantic gesture?" he offered, his face furrowed in uncertainty.

The whole image – him in his suit clearly willing to do whatever it took to win me back – made my whole body flutter. But he was going to have to do more than look pretty if he wanted this to work.

"Here?"

"No," he said like that was absurd. He shook his head. "Come with me?"

"Why would I go anywhere with you?" I knew Dad had been championing him, but he didn't.

"That's a fair question. But I am trying to make it up to you, baby. I'm trying to apologise and I figured here, potentially in front of everyone, was maybe not the place to do that."

That was actually a pretty fair answer.

"Please, Maggie. Come with me. Let me explain. Talk to me. Argue with me. Fucking hit me if you want. Just, please give me that one last chance."

I looked to Clove and Iago.

"He'll keep her safe and get her home. You know she'd rather spend the night with him while we talked than you spite both of us to stay here with her."

I had to admit, that was also a fair answer.

Damn him for planning ahead.

I nodded once. "Fine. I'll come with you."

He breathed out heavily in obvious relief. "Okay. Thanks."

Our hands still clasped, we walked out of there and to his waiting GT. He opened the door for me, helping me and my floor-length skirt to get in. Once he was in and we were driving, we didn't say anything for a while.

"Did you envision words occurring during this talk?" I asked him.

It took him a tense couple of heartbeats to get going.

"I'm sorry," he finally said. "I'm fucking sorry. I messed up."

"You think?"

He sighed. "I… He was willing to go to war against me for you, darling, okay? I did us both a disservice and I freaked out that, if he'd go that far, it was just a matter of time before he won you back. He gives you the option of a different life. A good life. The life you've always wanted. I'm the option that gets you the life you don't want. What if I was just a passing flirtation? A minor rebellion before you realised where you belonged?"

My heart caught as I remembered Parker calling me fickle. "You think that badly about me?"

"I think that badly about me. What do I have to offer you, really?"

I blinked, done with making him work for it. If we were going to survive, we both had to work for it. "Um. How about everything, Vaughn? Happiness. Safety. Home. I belong with you. I belong with the Roses. With you, I belong in the rest of the world because I'm not afraid to be me anymore. I don't have to choose between Maggie and Magenta. I'm just one person, and I finally love her. You give me that. No one else."

He breathed out deeply. "I fucked up, Maggie. I know that. You said you couldn't do this without us being equals and I want that. I want you to be part of my decisions. I want to be part of yours. I won't… I'm not going to let my insecurities take me away from you. Maybe I was looking for a way to end this now because I thought it would help you move on? I don't know why, like you said, I pursued you, made us both fall in love, and then fucked it up. I was an idiot. An idiot, scared to lose the woman he loved. And I just… There are not enough apologies in the world to begin to make it up to you."

It was a pretty damned good start, but I couldn't say anything. I was sure I'd cry if I tried. I wanted to throw my arms around him and kiss him. I wanted to make him really know how I felt about him in ways words just couldn't quite cover.

"Baby? Maggie? Why aren't you saying anything?"

"I really hope we get where we're going soon."

He snuck a look at me in panic. "Why?"

"Because I need you to kiss me, Vaughn."

His breath was shaky as he released it. "We're almost there."

And we were. Vaughn pulled off the road and into what I now recognised was his dad's property. I was blown away by what I saw before me.

There was our tent. Our picnic blanket. There was a bonfire ready to be lit. A table. Fairy lights strewn around on poles and running off some fearsome batteries. There was a cooler and a grill set up.

"This is what I wanted to do when we camped out here," he told me.

I climbed out of the GT and just shook my head. "It's beautiful."

"It was the biggest gesture Iago could persuade me to go for. The biggest gesture that didn't involve public displays. For once, I didn't shut him down on any of them, but I wasn't sure you were ready for this to go properly public yet. Rumour's one thing, confirmation is another."

I looked at him over the top of the car and bit my lip. "There is *way* too much distance between us," I told him.

For a second, I was sure he'd misunderstood me. Then his eyes went shrewd, and a smirk lit his lips. "I can fix that."

He slammed his door shut and was around to my side in moments. He pressed me against the car as our lips met.

It had been a week since I'd touched him like this, and yet it felt like so much longer. This feeling in me settled, and I only then realised that I'd spent the last week feeling an anxiety like the whole world was ending only for it to now be just right and absolutely fine.

Vaughn mumbled something that might have been 'Sorry,' against my lips as his hands started ruching my skirt up my legs. Once it was high enough that I had full range of movement, he lifted up and coaxed my legs around his waist.

"You do look gorgeous, by the way," he said between kisses that were just getting more frenzied. "The dress. Beautiful."

"I wasn't expecting you to fuck me in it," was my defence.

He shook his head. "I don't have to."

I felt him start to pull away and clamped my legs around him. "Don't you dare," I growled.

"You watch yourself, Miss McCallan, or, instead of telling my boss you took me back, I'm gonna have to ask him for you hand."

He was here with Dad's approval? If he asked, I was pretty sure I'd say 'yes' right there.

"Whose ring did you think I was wearing while dressed up in those sweater sets, darling?" I asked as I dragged my teeth over his lip.

"Fuck. What have I said about testing a man?"

I shrugged, all coy. "Last time, it got me squirting on your cock in the library stacks."

"My God," he whispered as he reached down to undo his trousers. "I love you. So much, Maggie."

I breathed in deep as he slid into me and corrected him. "Magenta."

"Magenta?" he clarified as he thrust into me hard.

I nodded as I clawed his back and bit my lip. "Yes, Vaughn."

He smiled. "I love you, Magenta."

God, that sounded so good. I hugged him close as he thrust deep and strong. "You're not adding 'Saint' to that yet?" I teased.

"Don't. Fucking. Tempt. Me. Darling," he said, punctuating every word with a deliciously punishing thrust.

"Would you prefer 'Mr McCallan'?"

I heard the humour in his voice. "For you? Yes. Now, stop making me think of my ring on your finger or this is going to be embarrassingly quick."

I held him tighter. "What? You get off on the idea of me in a white dress, pregnant with your–"

Vaughn growled as he snaked a hand around my throat and crushed his lips to mine, kissing me even harder than he pounded me. As his other hand slipped around the back of my neck, the one at my throat went to my clit and rubbed fast and light. Pleasure zinged around me as I came hard and fast, at the same time as him.

He thrust lazily a few more times before pressing his forehead to mine. "You want more satisfaction? Stop being so fucking sexy."

I laughed and his eyes opened to look into mine. There was a really big smile in them.

"Does that really turn you on that much?"

His hips pulsed against mine again gently, making him rub up against everything so damned nicely. And he nodded. "Yes, Maggie. The idea of you in a white dress and…" He bit his lip as he groaned appreciatively and pressed deep into me. "…pregnant with my baby. It's *such* a turn on." He ran his nose over mine. "Can you feel me getting hard again?"

I nodded against him. "Mmhmm."

We rocked together again. "You're going to want to get out of that dress before I rip it off you," he warned me.

I smiled. "Do you just want to get me naked, Vaughn?"

The cheeky smirk in his eyes made my heart tingle and my stomach flutter and my clit throb. "That is just the silver lining to me not ruining your dress, darling."

I ran my nose over his now. "Then you might want to get out of me and let me down."

He shook his head. "See, I don't love the sound of that."

I gripped him tightly as he thrust deep into me. "Me either," I admitted as our lips found each other again.

He thrust again. "But I also don't want to ruin your dress."

"You could control yourself."

"I could, but I could also drag my teeth over your nipple."

I nodded. "I see the conundrum."

"You do?"

"I do, because I do love the sound of that."

The pleasure was growing in me again, and I held him tightly.

"Maybe just this and then… Fuck, Vaughn."

He nodded. "I know. Okay. Good idea."

We paused the conversation in favour of concentrating on the job at hand. Once that was done, Vaughn helped me out of my dress on the way to the tent. I shivered and he smiled at me.

"Baby, I'm going to keep you warm all night."

"Promise?"

He snuggled me under the blankets before stripping off himself and joining me. "I promise," he said when I was back in his arms. "And I promise to talk to you, to listen to you. I want this to work so much, Maggie. Your dad has actually sanctioned us now, so we can really make it work, if you want."

"He has?"

Vaughn nodded as he coaxed my leg over his hip. "He said if I won you back then he wasn't going to kill me."

"How kind of him," I huffed sarcastically.

"He said you fought for me."

"Of course, I did. I love you. I want to be with you."

"Even though you walked away?"

"Not forever."

"Did you mean what you said about maybe getting married one day where your dad can give you away?"

I nodded. "Yeah. Is that okay?"

He nudged my nose with his. "So very okay."

I rolled us so I was lying over him. "So where are you taking me for our first date?"

"Does the camping trip not count?" he asked with a laugh.

I shook my head. "Our first formal, official, in public date."

He looked me over. “Where do you want to go?”

I leant down over him, so my chest was flush with his. “You’ve got me so now you’re going to stop wooing me?”

“Do you need another big romantic gesture, baby?”

I bit my lip as I looked into his eyes. “No. Not really. You are entirely enough.”

“But you still want a public date.”

I nodded. “I still want a public date. I want many public dates. Like, I’m thinking Jonathan’s Christmas party, public date.”

There was a hint of panic in his eyes. “That is a *very* public date.”

“Are you rethinking this?”

He shook his head. “Fuck, no. But I will need another suit.”

I leant my lips to his. “I’ll take you shopping tomorrow.”

“Oh, goody. Can’t wait.”

I trailed my lips down his neck and bit him playfully. “I promise I’ll make it worth your while.”

He rolled us so he was on top again and slid into me. “Sounds like a deal then, baby.”

VAUGHN: TEN

"Will you fucking stop fidgeting?" Blaise growled at me as he pulled into a park.

I fidgeted again, pulling on my shirt collar. "Sorry."

"Don't be sorry. Be fucking still."

"You be fucking still," I snapped, then stiffened.

But Blaise only chuckled. "Fucking my daughter sure has made you looser," he pointed out.

I shot a look to him out the corner of my eyes. He nodded.

"Oh, yeah. I meant that the way it sounded, pretty boy."

The corner of my lips tipped up, unbidden and a full smile broke out on Blaise's face.

"I'm fucking terrified," he told me, and I really appreciated the honesty. "We're both doing this for Maggie, remember."

I nodded. "For Maggie. Look, I know we look good, but these fucking penguin suits."

Blaise nodded as we climbed out of his Dodge. "Yeah, but the women go fucking nuts over them."

Maggie had suggested that to me the night of the formal, yeah. She'd also suggested our first official date be her stepdad's Christmas party where I would need another suit that she'd promised to buy for me. Threatened, more like. But I didn't know how the mayor was going to take his only daughter inviting a

Blood Rose to his fucking posh Christmas party. And, yeah, maybe I was looking for an excuse to get out of it.

But before that, we had to get through dinner with the mayor, his wife, and his kids. It might have been a little bit of an ambush. Isabel and the mayor were expecting Blaise for a pre-holiday family dinner out. I tried not to think too hard about what it meant that I was turning up; it was all good things I was currently too nervous to wish for.

"You know you look good," Blaise chastised as I took a huge inhale of my vape. "But you could lose the 'I'm gonna murder everyone in the building' look. It might get my daughter into bed and make the Monsters shit themselves, but I don't think it's gonna win over the mayor and the rest of his family."

I tried to relax and failed. "How do you do it?"

"Do what?"

"Turn off the club leader thing and just be her dad. Not want to murder all these judgemental arseholes and show them what we're capable of."

He inclined his head as we walked for the front door. "Ah. It's a gift, son. One you'll learn now you've got to walk with one foot in each world."

"Oh. Like Mags' been doing for years," I realised.

"Just like Maggie's been doing for her whole damned life. She's a natural. I learnt it to try to make things work with Isabel. Maggie just did it. Like she knew. She was two different people for so long. I saw it. But now. She's not two people, but she still knows how to balance each part of her to suit where she is. She's going to end up ruling the fucking world without even trying."

Blaise paused at the door. "Ready?"

I shook my head. "Fuck, no."

He grinned. "Good."

He pulled the door open, and we walked in. I'd fallen into growly-gang mode as a self-defence mechanism, and I couldn't fucking get out. This was the guy who killed a guy for touching his boss' daughter, not the guy who was trying to win over said daughter's parents. But this whole schtick wasn't me. I wasn't the penguin suit, nice restaurant kind of guy. I didn't belong here, and I didn't want to. This place was for arsehole East Hammers. But I could have done without the reminder they thought I was inferior in this place. And that made me want to be superior in all the ways I'd been brought up to be.

But I was pretty sure that pulling a gun in here wasn't going to win over the mayor.

"Blaise?" came a woman's voice and I looked up to see a woman the spitting image of Maggie in twenty-odd years standing up with her head cocked and eyebrows furrowed in question. Blaise went to hug her, and they obviously said something to each other to make her look at me in confusion.

They were going to fucking kick me out of here. And I might be about to do something to deserve it.

"Vaughn!" Freddy cried, giving me a huge, welcoming smile that I couldn't have helped returning if I'd wanted to.

He wasn't the only one. As I stopped by the table, Maggie took my hand with so much happiness on her face that I felt the choking knot of tension in my chest start to ease.

"Sit, ye mongrel," Blaise barked, clapping me on the shoulder before taking the seat two away from Maggie, leaving the one between us free.

I dropped into it, all the tension melting to a sliver. Maggie kissed my cheek surprisingly casual before picking up her napkin and laying it on her lap. Her mum looked me over with shrewd interest while the mayor was obviously trying to work out what he'd missed.

"Uh, Blaise…" he said, that mayoral politeness plastered to his face.

"Jonathan," Blaise answered, looking up from the drink menu.

Jonathan shot a look to me, hiding under a smile. "You haven't introduced your guest."

"He's my guest," Maggie said, putting her hand on mine.

It was way too high on my leg, and I jumped before sliding it towards my knee. Her mum saw the interaction and humour lit her eyes. She guessed or knew why I was here. She could tell the effect her daughter had on me. She also knew I was only here because of that daughter. And she wasn't afraid to show me that she could see through me as easily as Maggie or give me shit for it. I had a feeling I was going to like Isabel.

"Vaughn, this is Jonathan, my stepdad. Jonathan, this is Vaughn, my boyfriend."

Jonathan did his best to hide his surprise. "Oh. Boyfriend? What happened to–?"

Isabel elbowed him none too gently and I saw Blaise wasn't the only parent she took after. "Vaughn, have you got your patch yet?"

Jonathan had been sipping his wine. He choked on it a little.

"Uh…" I started, unsure how much we were supposed to give away here.

Maggie had hinted that there was some code that made this all work. Some set of unwritten and unspoken rules. And I had no idea what they were. Yet.

"Issy," Blaise chuckled. "At least get some whiskey in him before you interrogate him."

"I'm sorry!" she replied, acting the innocent. "But if he's sleeping with my daughter, I deserve to know how deep he is."

Blaise looked over the top of his menu at her. "Love, you are too pretty to play that dumb. You know how deep he is."

Her eyebrows bounced. "He is Brent's son?"

"You know Dad?"

She looked at me scathingly, but more like she felt sorry for me being so stupid. "Of course, I do."

"This is all very lovely," Jonathan said. "And I think Blaise has got the right idea. Whiskey all round?"

"Yes!" Freddy cried.

"Not you, dumbarse," Maggie teased, but there was all love in her voice.

Freddy's expression dropped and I couldn't help but smile.

"Boyfriend, then?" Isabel said to Maggie and me while Jonathan and Blaise were ordering whiskey.

I had a feeling there was going to be a fight about who paid at the end of this. I hoped Blaise wouldn't mind me sitting that one out.

Maggie nodded, her hand still on my knee. "Yes. Problem?"

Isabel looked at me before shaking her head. "No. Should there be?"

Maggie held her mum's stare easily. "No."

Isabel nodded. "Then good." She sat back as she picked up her cocktail. Something clear with a garnish. "How long have you been together?"

"Long enough that, yes, I hid it from you," was Maggie's answer.

She nodded. "You broke up with Parker for him."

"I was never actually dating Parker," Maggie reminded her.

"And he tried to hit her," just popped out of me and the whole table turned to look at me. I wasn't going to feel self-conscious about that. I shrugged. "What he did."

"He hit you?" Jonathan hissed.

I shook my head, feeling the pride tugging on my lips. "He *tried*," I emphasised, and I saw Isabel's eyes mirroring the pride.

Jonathan frowned. "That explains what happened at the Laneway." He shook his head. "Well, at least if a Rose is going after revenge, it will mean less paperwork."

"And how do you figure that?" Blaise asked, but the exchange was companionable, as though it was just the usual familial ribbing.

Jonathan gave him a small smile, almost like he was trying to hide it. "A Rose would have succeeded and not been caught."

"Did he get in a lot of trouble?" Freddy asked.

"For bad information and attempted kidnapping?" Jonathan asked, sarcastically. "No, not at all." Still very sarcastic.

"And suddenly my kids aren't the biggest problem this town has," Blaise said, clearly stirring shit.

Jonathan hid his humour behind his whiskey, and I picked up mine. I had no idea if this was going to stay jovial, or if someone was about to say something they couldn't take back.

After Jonathan had some more control over himself, he pinned me with a look. "Now, Vaughn. May I ask what your intentions are with our daughter? Or has Blaise tortured that out of you already and I'm just late to the party? I'm sorry to say my methods of interrogation are less…" He pointed to Blaise. "…and more…" He motioned to the whole restaurant.

I smirked. "Well, Mr Mayor–"

He actually cringed a little. "Jonathan, please. Even Jonny would be preferable to 'Mr Mayor'."

I nodded. "Jonathan." Then, realising this wasn't an answer just for him, I looked to Isabel and Blaise as well. "I'd quite like to marry her one day. If she'll have me."

Maggie batted my chest, and I wasn't convinced that it was all playful. "Vaughn," she hissed. "Not cool."

I shrugged. "They asked my intentions. You want me to lie to them at our first dinner?"

Maggie pushed her glasses up her nose and nodded as surreptitiously as she could. "About that, yes."

The adults laughed.

"You're serious about her then?" Isabel asked.

"Don't ye think I've done this dance, Issy?" Blaise asked.

She rolled her eyes. "Yes. And I'm sure you had your gun out like a big strong man and everything. But does it hurt to have him say it again? If he means it, it can't be that difficult."

This whole scenario was reminding me of something. It was like a movie or something. There was the super cool biological dad, who still gets along fantastically well with the mum even if there isn't a shred of romance between them anymore, and then there's the just really nice guy stepdad who was doing his damnedest not to be intimidated or jealous.

I nodded quickly, taking Maggie's hand under the table. "I'm very serious about her," I told them. "I'm a Rose, Mrs Green…" Oh, I saw how much she liked that out of me. "Isabel. And I haven't been a good guy. But I just want to do right by Maggie."

"What if that means walking away?" Isabel asked me, direct and fucking fierce.

"Mum!" Freddy and Maggie cried while Jonathan and Blaise chimed in with, "Isabel!"

But I wasn't going to shy away from her piercing gaze. "If it's the only option."

Maggie pulled her hand from mine. "What?"

I was going to get to that, but I was busy winning this showdown with her mum. "But the only time that will ever be an option will be if Maggie asks me to."

"What if it's better for her?"

"Mum!" Maggie cried again, but Isabel and I were busy.

I shook my head. "I won't make those choices for her. No one will but her."

Isabel stared me down for a few more moments and I was starting to panic that hadn't been the right answer. But finally, she sat back and picked up her own whiskey. "Good boy." Then she took her eyes off me and looked to Maggie. "Fine, darling. He's clearly good enough, but we have to be smart–"

"Yes," Blaise said, sarcastically humorous. "The kind of smart that involves a very public family dinner with Maggie's new beau."

"Whose fault was that?"

"Now, children," Jonathan teased before Blaise could jump in again. "Let's think about how we can make this work. Because this isn't just politics, this is Maggie's happiness."

I'd never had a reason to like the mayor. He seemed to scream everything that was wrong with the stuck-up wanker East Hammers. But he was just a guy who loved his daughter and wanted her to be happy. I couldn't' fault that.

Jonathan leant towards us. "If this is going to work, you're going to have to come to the Christmas party, Vaughn."

I kept my mask on, but inside I was even more jittery than after one of Ezra's bad batches. So much for him being reticent and me getting out of it. "Christmas party?" I clarified, leaning back all nonchalant. Maggie saw right through me.

Jonathan nodded. "I know enough to know what Blaise's sanction means with the Roses. Well, mine –and Isabel's – will go a long way with the East Hammers. So, what do you say?"

Fuck, the lengths people were willing to go to for my old lady. It made me love her even more.

I swallowed hard and nodded. "Sure. Of course. Anything for Maggie."

"Everything for Maggie," Blaise agreed, clapping me on the shoulder again.

Even Isabel smiled at me. There wasn't a shred of insincerity on her face. I could tell, because there *was* trepidation. She wasn't again this – in theory – but she was wary. I couldn't blame her for that. Blaise McCallan and his unofficial heir were sitting at the fanciest table in Hammerby's swankiest restaurant with the mayor and his upstanding family. I'd been holding Maggie's hand and smiling with her brother. And there were already questioning eyes on us.

Whether Isabel was more worried I'd hurt Maggie or their reputation, I didn't know. But I was willing to believe it was the former. After all, this was a woman who had fought the stigmas of all these arseholes for the last eighteen years to keep Maggie and her dad together. Her prejudice was obviously not having Roses in Maggie's life, it was only how we'd affect that life. I could respect a woman like that. Easy.

"Good. It's agreed. Vaughn and Blaise will come to the party, and we'll be one happy family," Jonathan said with a nod. As far as I could tell, he was also completely sincere. He honestly just wanted us to be one happy family.

A twinge cracked through my chest, but I liked it. I had family in my life. I had my dad. I had the Princes. I had the Roses. And now I had Maggie. And with her came the Greens, the mayor to boot. Who'd have thought I'd even think of the fucking mayor as family?

I watched Maggie and Freddy exchange a look before Maggie looked to Blaise to get his reaction. But Blaise was grinning from ear to ear.

"Nice family dinner, then nice family party," Blaise said casually. "What's next? Nice family wedding?"

Maggie was the one to choke on her drink this time, but I smiled around mine. I pinned Isabel and nodded. "Here's hoping."

Humour tugged at her lips, and she gave me the slightest nod as if to say, 'well played, Vaughn'.

The rest of the night went fucking easy compared to that.

CHAPTER TWENTY-THREE

So, yeah. Vaughn and I were officially, in public dating. We were sanctioned on both sides of Hammersby Bay. By the people who mattered, and those that didn't could deal with it.

We spent the rest of the week making the most of it. We walked down the streets of West and East Hammersby together, holding hands or our arms around each other, or even kissing. We didn't hide anything. In Hammersby, they looked at us with a combination of interest and disapproval. We didn't let that discourage us. Especially not when Stone was more than happy to growl at anyone who looked like they were going to make a comment, and Cairo liked to pull his knife out and play with it pointedly in front of people who stared too long.

Maybe I could learn to like Cairo.

On Thursday, we were up at Everdale. Clove and I had a few more bits of shopping to do before Christmas and Vaughn had been dragging his heels about his new suit for the mayoral Christmas party. Which I totally understood, although I'd already bought two new dresses and had my eye on a third in my excitement.

But it wasn't just the whole being allowed out in public with my boyfriend that I was enjoying, it was also just the Christmas season in general. And much to Cairo's intense annoyance, Clove and I had dressed accordingly for some holiday shopping. We were, though, currently taking a break for some lunch.

"Where's Clove?" Ezra asked as we sat down. Vaughn was already shoving burger into his face and his very fine arse hadn't yet hit the seat.

I looked to the seat beside Iago and realised Clove wasn't there. I frowned. "She was right behind us."

Stone pulled open his wrapper. "Maybe she wanted something else?"

I nodded. "She was talking about those gingerbread biscuits they only make in the holidays." She talked about them all year, but she had more specifically been talking this morning about getting enough to last the year. "She probably just decided to get them now and catch up."

It seemed the most logical conclusion until Iago suddenly looked up, and I could practically see his ears prick like a dog.

"What?" Vaughn asked.

Iago shook his head, frowned, looked over to the juice bar, then his lunch fell from his hands, and he was running.

"Shit," Vaughn muttered as he dropped his burger, then was out of his own seat and running after Iago through the food court as quickly as he could between the throngs of holiday shoppers.

I turned. "What?"

Cairo put his hand on my arm. "Don't," he warned, and I flashed him my confused expression. He shook his head. "Whatever they're dealing with, you need to stay put."

"Monsters?" I asked.

Cairo shrugged. "Probably. Just don't give them another thing to worry about."

Worry about...

"Clove!" I yelled, standing up. How stupid did I want to be? Of course the only thing that would have Iago running off like that would be Clove. In danger. With a Monster?

Cairo's hand on me was much firmer as he forced me back to sitting. I knew he'd hurt me if he thought it would help me. "If you truly love any of them, sit the fuck down and do not become a liability."

My heart thundered in my chest with concern for Clove, but I knew Iago and Vaughn would die to keep her safe. And knowing how little they looked forward to death, I felt like she was in pretty good hands. So, I took my mind off my worry by glaring at the Prince of Agony.

"Why do you say that like you don't believe I do?" I asked him.

Ezra snorted. "Just go ahead and bust open that can of worms."

Cairo shot Ezra his own glare. "Like you can fucking talk."

Ezra shrugged, affecting a fake pout. "The *doctor* said I'm broken. What's your excuse?"

"You're both fucking broken," was Stone's deadpan addition.

Cairo looked like he was going to launch himself over the table for a moment, then got control over himself. He'd just opened his mouth to retaliate when a fight broke out behind me. I had no doubt Iago and Vaughn were involved.

"What the hell did you get yourself into?" I whispered.

As though Cairo knew I was desperate to check on Clove, his hand tightened on my arm again. Just that simple action and I could see why they called him the Prince of Agony. It was in his restraint and exactly what I knew he was capable of because of it.

"Bravery will not help them," he reminded me.

I couldn't take my eyes off the direction of the others, but I kept my mind busy from imagining the worst. "It's not bravery,

Lockworth. It's stupidity and I know that but love really does make you stupid sometimes."

"Yes," Cairo drawled sarcastically. "Really selling me on this love bullshit, Maggie. You will convert me in no time."

I huffed. "A hundred bucks says, for your arrogance, you fall worse than the rest of us."

"Fucking cursed now," Ezra chuckled.

I pointed a finger at him, still anxiously watching for any sign of Vaughn, Iago or Clove. "You watch yourself or I'll curse you, too."

"I can't feel, Mags," Ezra said loftily, like it was a badge of honour. "I'm not falling in love."

I chewed my lip as the commotion started dying down. "If you're willing to risk it, that's on you."

"Fuck," Cairo muttered. "Please say it isn't so."

Then the crowd was parting and Vaughn, Iago and Clove were walking towards us. Vaughn and Iago both had a few more marks on them than they'd had when they left. And Iago had his arm around Clove, who was white as a sheet in her sexy Santa outfit.

I rushed over to them and hugged Clove tightly. "Are you okay?"

She nodded. "I'm fine. Little rattled, but fine."

"I'm taking her home," Iago said.

I looked between them. Something sizzled. Something new. Iago had his 'I'll murder the fucking lot of them' face on and I was sure I saw him twitching like he had to physically stop himself from running back there and doing just that. Clove, I noticed, kept herself closer to him even than usual. It was like they were both pulling comfort from each other after whatever had happened.

I stepped back and nodded. If she needed Iago now, I could get caught up later. "Okay. Sounds good. Be safe."

Iago took Clove's hand somewhat absently and nodded. "Will do."

I looked to Clove. "Call me later."

She nodded. "I will."

Vaughn and I gravitated to each other as we all watched them head out.

Stone was the first to ask. "What happened?"

Vaughn indicated I sit and then sat nice and close beside me, one leg on either side of the bench. "A Monster thought Clove was fair game. West wiped the fucking floor with him."

"Is she okay? Did they touch her?" I asked.

Vaughn shook his head as his arm wrapped around me, like he needed the comfort as well. "No. Lot of threats and intimidation but I don't think they actually got hands on her."

Ezra smirked. "They're fucking tonight." We all looked at him in surprise and he shrugged. "What? Did you see them? Wound so fucking tight. Adrenalin flooding their systems. Relief and survival. There's no fucking way he's resisting her today."

I looked him over. "For someone who says he can't feel, you sure seem to know a lot about it."

Ezra winked at me. "Mimicry is the only way to pass for normal, Mags. And mimicry requires an awful lot of study. I don't feel, but I'll wager I know more about emotions than the rest of you."

Maybe he was full of bullshit. Maybe he wasn't. Maybe he had spent so long studying others so he could pass for 'normal' that he knew us better than we knew ourselves. Either way, he wasn't wrong.

Clove texted me the next day to tell me that she and Iago had in fact exploded in sexual combustion. Not that we could tell when we saw them together next; Iago was acting like nothing had happened.

But that is a whole other story.

CHAPTER TWENTY-FOUR

Vaughn was in his new suit, looking unnecessarily dapper and gorgeous, and we were an official couple at the mayor's Christmas party. The elite of Hammersby Bay were in attendance, and some extras. Extras being the Princes and my dad.

But those elite didn't say a word against them. They fawned all over my dad like he was the mayor himself. They laughed at his jokes, and I was pretty sure that a whole bunch of them actually fall for him a little bit. Not in like the romantic way, although there were a few I wondered about, but for his charm and his character. They all walked away from him looking like they couldn't remember what was so bad about Blaise McCallan after all.

Even Vaughn's dad was in attendance, and it was the first time I officially got to me my dad's right-hand man, let alone the father of my boyfriend.

"Pleasure to see you, Mags," he said with a nod, and I gave him a shy smile.

Vaughn was tall. Brenton Saint was just as tall, and his muscles were much thicker than his son. Where Vaughn was sleeker, Brenton was a tank. Was Vaughn only going to get even bigger as he got older? I could work with that. The beard though? Not sure how much I'd enjoy that.

"Same to you, Mr Saint."

He spluttered and let out a full belly laugh. "Oh, Mags. No. You know it's Brent. Let's not stand on ceremony just because you're doing my boy."

My cheeks went bright red, I was sure of it. And Even Vaughn coughed into his drink.

"Jesus, Dad," he muttered.

Brent shrugged. "What? We gonna be children about it?"

Vaughn rolled his eyes. "Can we get to maybe the first anniversary before you fully douse her in our lifestyle and conversation? Little class, please?"

Brent clapped his sone on the back with enough force to rock him. "Mags brings the class to our family, V. Let her teach it to us before we start bumbling around with it." He shot me a wink and I looked down to hide my smile.

"I need another drink," Vaughn mumbled before he pulled his hand from mine gently. He pressed his lips to my hair. "Want anything?"

I shook my head. "No. Thanks."

Once he was out of ear shot, Brent's presence was burning at my side.

"Questions or comments?" I said to him. "Disapproval?"

"Why would I disapprove?"

I couldn't look at him. "I just figured you probably think I'm not good enough for him."

"You not…?" Brent breathed out. "Magenta McCallan, don't you dare. Fucking hell, you two have it bad for each other if you think… You don't need to be some arbitrary level of 'enough' for my boy, Mags. You make him happy – happier than I have ever seen him or realised he was capable of – and that's enough for me."

I snuck a look at him. "Thanks, Brent."

He wrapped an arm around me. “Thank you. And welcome to the family.”

I laughed, feeling that bubble of happiness explode like a firework inside me. But it fizzled a little when I saw Parker walking past. He’d heard what Brenton said. He had to have known that Vaughn and I were official and sanctioned and public now. And he clearly had thoughts.

“Hands off my old lady before all I can smell on her is you,” Vaughn said, but there was humour in his voice.

Brenton stepped back with his hands up. “Of course.” He patted Vaughn’s arm gently. “I’m off to find Blaise.”

We nodded and watched him go.

“Vaughn Saint,” came a familiar voice from behind me and Vaughn actually grabbed at my hand like he needed the comfort.

We turned to find the Police Chief behind us. “Chief Bates,” I said with my politest smile.

He gave me a nod. “Maggie. Nice to see you.”

“You, too.”

Then his eyes were on Vaughn as he cleared his throat and rearranged his belt almost self-consciously. “How’s things?”

Wait, what?

Vaughn nodded. Both men were stern and serious, but there wasn’t a whole lot of hostility I could feel. Between them. Parker was standing behind his dad and there was a lot of hostility there.

“Fine. Yourself?” Vaughn replied.

Chief Bates inclined his head. “Good. Good. Not getting yourself into trouble?”

“I promise you’ll be the first I call when I do.”

Oh, my God. Was that a hint of a smile on the Police Chief’s face? What was happening tonight?

“I’d appreciate that.”

"I would hate to make your job harder."

Chief Bates coughed like he was hiding a laugh. "Very thoughtful. Well, I'll leave you to your night. Happy Christmas." He nodded to me. "Maggie."

I nodded back. "Chief Bates."

He left, leaving Parker standing in front of us. He looked between us, hatred smouldering in his eyes. But the other thing about his eyes was the bruise still blushing a brilliant shade of purple after being kissed by Iago's fist.

"Maggie," he said through gritted teeth, and I honestly wondered if this was him pretending to play civil.

I gave him a nod. "Parker."

Parker looked at Vaughn and I saw his nostrils flare. "You convinced the mayor to let you date his daughter, then." It wasn't a question.

Vaughn scoffed as he put his arm around me, and I was going to allow the show of possessiveness. "I convinced Blaise McCallan to let me date his daughter, yeah. I also convinced the mayor to have me at his fancy party. Problem, wankstain?"

Parker shook his head quickly and I was pretty sure he was remembering the night Iago put him in his place. "Not at all."

It was lies, but it was nice that he was playing the part. I guessed. I didn't need or want his approval, but knowing he wasn't going to make more trouble for us – hopefully – was nice.

"This is really the guy you want to be with?" Parker said to me, as though this was the sentence that would break the spell that had been cast over me and I'd suddenly come to my senses and realise that Parker was my soulmate.

I lay a hand on Vaughn's chest and leant into him. Playing his role perfectly, Vaughn took hold of the one on his chest and tightened the one around my waist.

"Yeah, I'm sure," I told Parker.

"Tough shit, sir," Vaughn added, and I tried not to snort in humour.

Parker was visibly pissed off about that, but I got the impression he wasn't going to do any more than use his nasty words about it. And nasty words, I could deal with. "Well, a bad choice is still your choice," were Parker's lofty parting words before he stalked away, his shoulders bent in clear defeat.

"If I never see him again, I think I could very easily live with that," I said.

Vaughn hugged me. "The lawyers have made it very clear to the Police Chief that harassment on the part of his son's bruised ego will not be tolerated. So, as long as I keep my nose clean, I'm golden."

"You really think you can keep your nose clean?" I scoffed and he smiled down at me.

"We've got enough ammunition on Parker's little stunt that I can afford a little smudge and still be fine," he assured me.

"Oh, a little smudge," I teased, and his grin widened.

"A little smudge," he agreed.

"And does that include brown nosing my dad?"

He dropped his lips to my jaw, and I felt his smile. "Brown nosing your dad means we can be together," he reminded me.

I shook my head. "Uh, no. Keeping me happy means we can be together because Daddy wouldn't do anything to hurt his little princess." I put on a fake pout and a burst of laughter escaped from Vaughn.

"How *do* you fool these idiots with the little innocent act? You're so fucking foxy, darling."

"My mind or my body?" I teased.

"Uh, both. Definitely both."

I looked around quickly. "Do you think we've been here long enough?"

Vaughn also looked around. "I hope so because, if you're suggesting we leave, there is no way we're coming back."

"You hated it that much?" I'm not sure why that made me a bit sad.

He shook his head. "No. I'd stay here all night if you wanted me to. But once I get you out of that dress, it's not going back on until at least tomorrow afternoon."

"It's Christmas Eve tomorrow, Vaughn."

He inclined his head. "And we don't have anything on until dinner."

A thrill ran through me at his words. Especially the 'we' part. It just sounded so good.

My eyes darted to Clove and Vaughn's lips went to my neck like he knew I needed the encouragement. Well, maybe not needed, but wanted.

"You know the boys will make sure she's fine."

"She and Yago are barely even talking."

He shrugged. "I don't see a difference."

I glared at him. "Exactly."

"What do you want me to do about it, love? Huh? I can set Lock on him until he admits he loves her, or we can let it sort itself."

"We've been leaving it to sort itself for years and look where that's got them."

"They fucked. You know…" He nipped at the lobe of my ear playfully. "…as well as anyone that's the best way to get things started. Leave their relationship to them."

I sighed as my head tilted to give him better access. "Was that Iago's policy when it came to us?"

The huff of Vaughn's laugh skipped over my neck and goosebumps spread over me. "No. But he doesn't have a death sentence hanging over him."

"Neither do you anymore."

I felt his head shift and saw he was looking up at my dad, who was watching us. Dad's eyebrow rose in a very shit-stirring 'you all good there, Saint?' expression. Vaughn nodded back to him before taking my hand and dragging me out of there.

"So, assuming that everyone's parents are going to be going home at some point tonight and it's fucking cold, where are you planning on taking me tonight, baby?" I teased him.

He watched me pull my jacket on, then handed me my helmet. He was wearing a very sexy smirk. "I was going to spring for a room at the country club but even Iago thought that was too wanky."

I inclined my head. "Oh, so there is a limit to his grand gestures?"

"It seems there is."

"So, what's the plan?"

"It was heavily suggested to my father that he not come home tonight."

My eyes bugged. "You told your dad not to come home so you could fuck me all night?"

He grinned cheekily and God damn, it was sexy. "Your dad suggested that mine crash at his place tonight."

"That is not better, Vaughn. That is definitely not better."

Vaughn laughed and the sound did things to my stomach that were too nice. "What's the point in pretending? They know we're having sex."

I cocked my head at him, and he huffed as he pulled on his jacket.

"What?" he asked.

"You said 'having sex'."

He shrugged as he ran his hand through his hair. It was getting long on top. "Your point?"

I chewed on my lip in that way I knew he really liked, knowing my eyes were shining with cheek. "You didn't call it fucking."

He wrapped an arm around my waist and pulled me to him tightly. "Your point?" he asked again, heavily intimating he wouldn't be asking a third time.

"I think the words alone made my point for me."

His eyes glittered with the fairy lights that decorated the parking lot. They looked like true lapis lazuli now. "How many more times do I need to remind you that what we are is more than just dating, darling?"

"However many times I need to hear it to remember it." I shrugged, but it was all saccharine coy. "I just seem to keep forgetting."

His nose nudged mine playfully. "As long as you don't forget that you're mine."

I shook my head. "Oh, I think that's kind of burned into the very fabric of my being now, baby. I think it's been woven through me since that day I was born."

He pressed his forehead to mine and growled, low and soft and needy. "I love you."

I ran my hand over his chest firmly and was surprised when he winced. "What did you do?"

"Not what you're thinking," he assured me. As he started undoing his shirt, he continued. "I was going to show you when we got home."

I really like the way he kept saying that. Home. We didn't live together, and I was sure we wouldn't for quite a while, but maybe home wasn't just the place you slept. Although, if those holidays were anything to go by, then I didn't doubt that Vaughn and I would end up spending most nights together. But maybe, just maybe, home was actually where your heart was and, in that case, home would be wherever Vaughn was.

What I also like was what I saw when Vaughn pulled his shirt aside. I mean, yes, the body was droolworthy, and it made me quite literally drool far too often. But no. It was the way my name was emblazoned on chest with a heart.

Magenta

"Vaughn…" I breathed, my fingers itching to touch it through the clear medical plaster. It was obviously fresh. "A tattoo is permanent."

He looked down at me through his hair, the softest smile playing at his lips and mirrored in those beautiful eyes. "So are we."

He kissed me hard. It wasn't the first nor would it be the last time I melted against his kiss. For his kiss. Only now, unlike our first kiss, I didn't make myself pull away for the stupidest reasons. I pulled him closer.

"If you don't want me to fuck you on my bike right here, then you'll get that sexy arse on it and let me take you home," he said through kisses that were getting mighty desperate.

I did have to make myself pull away from him, but it wasn't the sex on the bike that was putting me off. I nodded as we stared at each other, both breathing heavily.

"Okay, but you better fuck me on your bike when we get there."

"Fuck," he sighed as he climbed onto his bike like he wouldn't be able to control himself if he didn't. "Do not make me propose right now, baby."

I laughed as I got on behind him and wrapped my arms around him. "It's Christmas, baby. Maybe if you make a wish, it might come true."

I felt him shiver as my hand slid down his stomach and between his legs. He started the bike and shook his head. "I am stronger than this," I heard him tell himself before we peeled out of the parking lot.

But that strength only served him until we'd parked in the garage and got the door closed, and then he showed me all the ways he could have me on his bike. I had never seen him so excited.

VAUGHN: ELEVEN

Dad cleared his throat, and I looked up from my phone to see him hovering in the kitchen, making it look comically small against his hulking frame.

"You heading out soon?" he asked, gruffly.

Oh, shit. He was about to get into some emotional bullshit. That was his emotional bullshit voice.

I nodded. "Soon," I said slowly, a question.

He inclined his head as he dropped onto the seat in front of me and cleared his throat again. "Maggie."

My blood ran cold as I shifted in my seat. "Blaise is okay with it. It's sanctioned. We're sanctioned." Why was I still defending us to people? This was my dad, for fuck's sake.

Dad coughed. "No. Fine. I like her. I wasn't…" Another cough.

"Will you just fucking spit it out?" I sighed as I put my phone down and looked right at him.

I watched his eyes widen in surprise, then the smile hiding in his beard. "You're gonna need to nut up now, son. Provide."

"And if she wants to provide?" I huffed, knowing how she'd feel about the apparent sexism in that statement.

Dad smirked like he knew what I was thinking. "Then fucking good for her. But just like you can't expect her to sit home and look pretty, you don't get to fucking sit home and look pretty either."

I nodded. "What's your point? I'm supposed to get a 'real job'? I think it's a bit late for higher education aspirations."

His smirk grew. "Mortgage free."

I blinked at him. "What?"

"You can ignore any other piece of advice I have for you but listen when I tell you that no rent or mortgage changes the whole fucking game. You want to give your woman a life like that?"

"I want to give her a lot of things. I'm focussing on the ones that are obtainable at this point. Thanks for bringing that up, though. Financial impotence sure was what I was after just before a New Year's Eve party with said girl and all our friends. Ta."

Dad scoffed, all humour. "I want you to have the riverfront."

"Sorry. What?"

"The riverfront. I'm gifting it to you and Maggie. Do whatever you want with it. Build on it. Sell it for the money to get what you want. I don't care. All that potential doesn't belong in the past, Vaughn. It belongs in the future. Bright and warm and loved. Everything I want your future with her to be."

I was so stunned, the only thing I said was, "I've been saving, but I don't know if I've got enough to build."

"Then you're lucky it has an upkeep account with more than enough for even the most ridiculously lavish mansion with fully imported materials, aren't you?"

"How? Why?"

Dad reached his hand over the table, and I took it. "You're my nest egg, son. And now we have Maggie, too."

We have Maggie.

It seemed I wasn't the only Saint who was in all on this. Dad didn't just accept me being with Maggie because Blaise had sanctioned it, but because he was happy for me.

Dad cleared his throat awkwardly again as he pulled his hand back. "I can't imagine the shit you two went through to get here," he started. "I don't doubt you went into it with less than honest intentions and I'll forgive you for that. Maggie's no idiot. Forget Blaise's rules, if she's willing to have you, then you've earned it. But that doesn't mean you can get complacent now. All right?"

I nodded. "No. Okay. I won't."

"I mean it, V. Sneaking around is exciting. It's exciting enough that fighting for your love could have been the easiest thing in the world. But love takes work, son. Work I want to believe you want to do, but you have to make sure you fucking do it. Never let things fester. Talk. Argue. Whatever it takes. As insignificant as it feels, communicate. Make sure she knows you will always hear her, make sure she'll hear you. Love's not fucking roses all the time, and it's not meant to be. People are messy and love's messier, but that just makes it so much more worth it in the end."

I felt like I knew that already, but it never hurt to have the people older and wiser than you confirm it. None of the adults in my real life had ever pretended to have all the answers or have all their shit together. Not like the teachers at Rosewood Hall or the East Hammers' parents. But I knew there were things they did know better than me, and I wasn't going to throw away good advice when I heard it.

I inclined my head to him. "I'll remember that. Thanks, Dad."

Dad gave me a nod, cleared his throat again and stood up. "You guys have a good night. Kenicki's?"

I nodded noncommittally. "At some point. The girls want to go to the Hut for a bit, too."

Dad's nose wrinkled but his eyes were bright. "You are fucking whipped," he teased.

I fought a smirk to maintain *some* dignity. "Shut up, old man."

As he left, I heard the fondness in his chuckle and a huge weight eased off me. I actually rubbed my chest at the sensation, wondering what the hell I'd done in my dark past to deserve this ending.

The Princes were at Kenicki's with Maggie and Clove, and it was almost midnight.

Iago and I had snagged a booth. Stone was off getting lucky with some East Ham cheerleading girlfriend of one of his teammates that he'd coaxed away from the Hut when we'd finally left. Ezra had begged a dance with my old lady. And Iago's eyes were locked on Clove where she danced *very* closely with some idiot. The way his eyes had been the whole fucking week, to say nothing of the years before that.

"This is your own fault," I told him as the guy's hand slid over her arse and Iago's hands fisted around his beer bottle like it was someone else's neck.

"What's my fault?" he asked, his voice casual as he took a sip of his beer.

"You're still playing that card?"

"What card?"

"Clearly." I rolled my eyes. "If you think she didn't tell Maggie what happened after the food court, and Maggie didn't tell me, then you're a bigger idiot than you thought I was for pursuing Maggie in the first place."

Iago vibrated with the sheer force of keeping himself in his seat and acting nonchalant. "Fine. We had sex. What does that prove?"

"That you *are* a bigger idiot," I muttered.

Iago huffed but it was humourless. "I saw what happened to you. It was exactly what I was trying to avoid with her. One taste and you're done. Done worse than you already were before that taste."

I laughed. "You're whipped."

He snarled, and I knew he was angrier with himself than with me. "I've been whipped for years. Now I'm obsessed as well, so thanks for that."

"Are you blaming me?"

"Yes."

"Why is it my fault?"

"Because you went and made me forget I can't have her!" he hissed harshly. "You and your fucking domestic bliss. But she's not Maggie, V. She's too fucking good for this world."

I was going to try very hard not to take offence at that. "You saying Maggie's not?"

"I'm saying Maggie will end up running rings around all of us. She'll probably end up leading us, and you know it. She's made for this world. Clove's not, and that's fine because that's who she is and she's fucking perfect as she is, but it does mean that I can't have her. I can't drag her into our shit. She deserves better than that."

"Mate, she *wants* you to drag her into your shit. She's wanted that for probably longer than you've wanted it."

He shook his head. “Don’t do that,” he begged, his voice raw with emotion and I could see how much he felt for her. “You think I don’t know that? All of that? Why do you think I’ve kept my distance? Pretended I had no idea how she felt. She’s all I want, and I can’t fucking be with her.”

I nodded loftily, like I was agreeing with his self-sabotaging bullshit. “I’ve recently learned that there’s a lot to be said for just giving your woman what she wants. And if all she wants is you, then it seems pretty fucking simple to me.”

“Don’t be a fucking arse,” he growled, and I was surprised at that side of him. I knew it was there, I’d seen it plenty, but it had never been directed at me before. “I’m not you, V. I make other people’s dreams come true. Mine don’t. She’s better off without me.”

I knew better than to keep pushing him. Especially while his narrowed eyes were focussed on Clove with her tongue down that wanker’s throat. I was more likely to get a knife to the gut than a thank you for butting in.

I also knew what Clove was doing by making Iago watch. She might not have been as assertive as Maggie as a rule, but she wasn’t the kind of girl to sit back and let *her* dreams go unanswered. I’d seen it the day she chewed me out over Maggie. She was finding her feet in our world, and it was only a matter of time before both of them were firmly planted and she got what she wanted. I was sure of it.

I was looking forward to how dumb Iago was planning to play before he finally accepted that, though.

Maggie dropped into my lap and put her arm around my neck.

“Ezra treat you right?” I asked.

She laughed. “Perfect gentleman until some random girl caught his fancy, then he dropped me like a bad fart.”

A little bit of sunshine broke through Iago's bad mood, and I again thanked anyone who'd listen for her. She was utter perfection, and I had no doubt I was the fucking luckiest guy in the world.

I saw Maggie's eyes dart to Clove surreptitiously. "And what have you boys been talking about?"

"Idiocy," Iago mumbled before getting up and stalking off.

"He okay?" Maggie asked.

I sighed as I wrapped my arms around her. "Yes and no. He thinks he can't have her."

"Oh, so the opposite problem you had then?" she teased, and I grinned.

"Something like that."

She looked to Clove again. "And she's determined to prove him wrong."

"Don't tell me," I guessed. "One taste and she's hooked?"

Maggie chewed her lip. "She knows he wants her now, and she's not going to let him ignore her anymore. This is either going to end in two broken hearts or a love story possibly more epic than ours."

"More epic than ours?" I scoffed. "Impossible."

As she looked me over, her eyes fucking shone with happiness and love and, once again, she blew me away. "I love you, Vaughn Saint."

I nudged her nose with mine. "I love you, Magenta McCallan."

"Still not 'Saint'?" she teased, and I was rock hard just at the thought of it. I would totally take McCallan, so long as we wore each other's ring, but Magenta Saint sounded a damn sight better than Vaughn McCallan. Actually, both were pretty good. Maybe we could hyphenate.

"If you're that keen to be Magenta Saint, darling, you just have to ask."

"Maybe I will. One day."

"Maggie!" Clove called happily as the countdown began and I held Maggie tighter to stop her jumping off my lap.

She laughed and leant into me.

I didn't think I was an overly superstitious kind of guy, but I wasn't about to risk it either. If you were supposed to be with the first person you kissed after midnight for the rest of the year, then I was going to make sure I kissed her as soon after midnight as possible. And I'd do it every damned New Year until I was dead.

If I had any say over that, it was going to be a fair few fucking years away.

After all, I had a whole life with my old lady ahead of me.

And the first thing I was going to do was marry her. Right after I kissed the living hell out of her.

CHAPTER TWENTY-FIVE

The next term back at school, Iago took up following us around making gagging noises. Cairo looked like he might actually be sick. Ezra found it amusing. And Stone didn't give much away about what he thought about it.

Clove was unbelievably happy for me, even if her own happy ending was not going the way we'd hoped. Yet. I knew something had happened at New Years, but no one was talking about it. Which made me think that it was the right kind of something and neither of them wanted to jinx it. That, or they were in the denial phase of hooking up; if they didn't talk about it, then it couldn't be happening and there wouldn't be any repercussions. I knew all about that.

Now, when the Princes of Rosewood Hall walked down the corridor and Caitlin would prefer to face plant the door frame than one of them, I was at Vaughn's side, his arm around me. Parker and his new girl were pressed against the wall to get out of *my* way.

It was a stark contrast to the start of the year when I'd thought I was in the right place, with the right person. Looking back, I felt like a naïve idiot. But wasn't that the point of life? Learning and growing and getting to where we were supposed to be by whatever path we had to take.

Parker had been a path I needed to take to show me that I didn't *just* want the East Ham life. I needed to see that future ahead of me to know that it wasn't all I wanted. All I needed. Without him, I wouldn't have found the right path. The one that led me not just to Vaughn, but also to accepting myself for who I was. All of myself. With no more shame.

"You should learn to ride," he told me when we walked into my dad's after school one afternoon.

"Me, ride?" I clarified.

He nodded. "Why not?"

A thrill ran through me. More nervous that excited. The idea of riding on the back of Vaughn's bike was crazy enough when I wasn't doing it. I don't think I could stomach being in charge of one. "I could kill myself."

"You could fucking love it."

I smirked. "I'm not agreeing to anything until you make an honest woman out of me."

As a ruse, a stalling tactic, it was perfect. I wasn't saying no. I was actually saying yes. But giving us both some time. Because the actual time was going to be a few years' away because there was no way he was going to…

"Marry me."

I blinked.

Vaughn hadn't even hesitated.

"What?" I asked.

He nodded, like it was the most obvious thing in the world. "Marry me."

"As far as proposals go–"

"It suits *us*. Stop stalling and say 'yes' already. Get the formalities out of the way so I can fuck you senseless."

I fought a smirk at the cockiness of my man. "Who says I'm going to say 'yes'?"

"We both know you're going to say yes, love. Magenta Saint is your destiny, the same way *you* are mine. I know you want to do school and university and all that, so I don't expect you to marry me tomorrow. But you will wear my ring. I'm not going to let there be any confusion about who you belong to."

"And what about you?"

"What about me?" he asked.

"You think I'm going to let there be any confusion about who you belong to?"

"Then you'd better hurry up and marry me, so you can get a ring on my finger."

"You can wear a ring before we get married."

I saw the victorious smirk on his eyes. So much like our first night together when I'd let slip that fateful 'we'. But he didn't gloat this time. Straight away.

"I *could* wear a ring before we get married," he agreed slowly.

I wrapped my arms around him and smiled. "I could also hurry up and marry you."

He inclined his head. "We could do both."

"Both is good."

He pulled me closer. "Both is very good," he murmured against my lips, then kissed me hard.

Dad was at work, so Vaughn and I had the place to ourselves. In the week after Christmas, my parents had all sat down and decided that we had to run some sensible PR campaigning. Even if that didn't involve actual publicity, we had to make things look on the up and up. We had to find a way for it to be obvious that the mayor approved of my relationship without them spending too much time with Roses or making it look like I'd been kicked out of East Ham, which meant we had to balance things. So, I it was agreed all around that I'd spend two weeks with Dad and two weeks with Mum and Jonathan. Instead of the one and three from before.

Dad also didn't have to ban all work while it was my weeks with him. There was a rule about a Roses' state when they arrived at the house – light on weapons and blood splatter – but otherwise the business door was getting a lot more bang for its buck and I didn't have to hear anything more about Old Finkle's dog.

"When's your dad coming home?" Vaughn asked me between kisses.

I shook my head. "I don't know. There was something about the docks?"

I felt Vaughn smile against me. "Then we've got fucking hours."

He lifted me up and propped me up on the bench. "Bold, Saint," I pointed out.

He was all humoured, cheeky, animalistic sexiness as he ripped open his shirt, then his hands were on his belt as he said, "Oh, you have no fucking idea, McCallan. I'm going make you squirt everywhere in this damned house if it kills me."

"Tonight?" I squeaked.

"Challenge?" He grabbed my hips and pulled me to him hard.

"Dad promised not to kill you for touching me," I laughed. "That might be taking it a little far."

As he leant into me, his fingers ran over my clit. "Oh, but Daddy wouldn't do anything to the man making his little princess so. Fucking. Happy."

Well, I couldn't deny that Vaughn was expert at making me…happy. He kissed me as he played with me until I'd taken his lip in my teeth and was groaning his name. His kiss turned fierce as he slammed his full length into me. My back arched into him, and I cried out his name.

On my dad's kitchen bench was not a place to be gentle and I wouldn't have wanted him to be. There was plenty of time in the rest of our lives to be romantic and sweet as well as sensual. It's not like we hadn't done it before, but today was for hard and fast and as many orgasms as we could fit in before Dad got home and we had to keep our hands to ourselves for a few hours.

Vaughn and I picked out engagement rings. For Valentine's Day. It was both the most cliched wank and just so nice. We spent the whole time taking the piss as well as taking it utterly seriously.

His was a thick black thing with a big black diamond. Mine was gothic-inspired with thorns and roses and a big honking diamond of the highest cut and clarity that Vaughn could organise on such short notice.

The next weekend, we lay on a blanket under the stars at his dad's property. No more was it out of necessity. It was desire. It was just for the sheer joy of it. The weather was finally getting warmer – during the day at least – but we'd dressed for the weather and Vaughn had a fire roaring beside us. His arm was under my neck and our fingers toyed with each other, finding our new rings and running over them absent-mindedly.

He pressed a kiss to my hair. "Dad's made me an offer."

"That sounds ominous."

He huffed a chuckle, but it didn't sound very humoured. "He's kind of sick of this place being left to history. He'd rather its future was bright and warm and loved."

"Would he now?"

I felt him nod. "Dad said we could have it."

I half sat up to look at him. "What?"

He smiled at me, but I saw the hesitation in his eyes. "He said we could have it. We can build a house on it. We can sell it and buy somewhere we want. But he wants it put to good use."

I sat up properly and looked around. Not that I could see much past the fire just then. "All this, for us?"

Vaughn sat up with me. "All this. Just for us." He put his hand on my stomach lightly. "And maybe whoever else might choose to join us in the future."

I smiled at him. "Bright and warm and loved?" I guessed.

"Bright and warm and loved," he agreed. "What do you say?"

I wrapped my arms around him and smiled. "You know my answer, Vaughn."

"Does it hurt a guy's ego to hear it out loud?" he teased.

"It might hurt a girl's if she thinks he doesn't trust her."

"I will always trust you."

"Then you know my answer, Vaughn."

Turn the page to find out what's coming next for the Princes of Rosewood Hall.

PRINCES OF ROSEWOOD HALL

The Princes of Rosewood Hall each have their own story to tell.
Releasing in November 2024-2027.
Look for them on pre-order November 2023-2026.

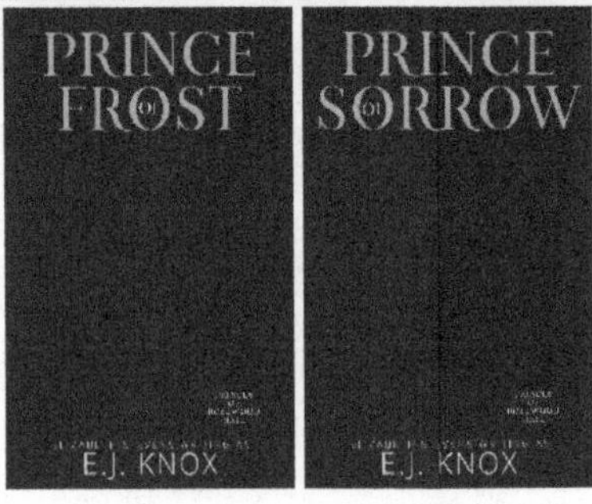

REIGN

If you liked *Prince of Thorns*, you might also enjoy *Reign*. A New Adult darker, high school, bully romance. Get it here: https://books2read.com/u/4D6Qa7

From Elizabeth Stevens, writing as E.J. Knox, comes…

A King. An Heir. And the unwilling pawn with the power to win or crush a Royal coup.

Beckett Maxwell reigns over Rivermont Academy with his loyal court: the Royals, their courtiers, their harem. He doesn't have time for a nobody like me: a scholarship student and daughter of faculty to boot. I'm the lowest of the low in a school full of highs.

One year everything's going fine. Enough. The next, I'm some pawn in a Royal power struggle. Well, I won't have it. They can bully me, they can torment me, they can make my life miserable. But I will not be used in one of their twisted games.

But when the fox is lurking at the door, sometimes the only safety is in the arms of the lion. Beckett might actually be the lesser evil in this case. And I can't deny there's something between us. Something I wish wasn't there.

The closer we get, the further he pushes me away, but something keeps pulling me back. When it comes to Beckett Maxwell, I'm a sucker for punishment.

But I'll only bear it so long. If Beckett wants his claim on me to stick, then he might need to choose between his crown and my heart.

GODS & ANGELS

If you liked *Prince of Thorns*, you might also enjoy *Gods & Angels*. A New Adult darker, high school, bully romance. Book 3 is out soon! Get it here: https://books2read.com/u/38yaGw

From Elizabeth Stevens, writing as E.J. Knox, comes…

A ruthless god. A sinful angel. And the princess between them.

My life is perfect. My life is planned. My life isn't mine.
Promised to a man I love. A man I hate. Not even a man. A god.
Apollo Callahan is that and much more.

My life is broken. My life is fractured. My life isn't free.
Craving a man I hate. A man I need. Not even a man. An angel.
Valen Kincaid is nothing I could ever want.

Though the Saints rule the hallowed halls of Saint Benedict's College, they're anything but saintly. Behind closed doors, they call themselves the Sinners. Sex. Fast Cars. Drugs. Money. The odd assassination or two. Nothing is beneath them, except the next in a long line of women. Can one little princess, searching to break free from her prison tower, bring these mighty lords crashing to their knees?

The stunning first book in the Sinners of Saint Benedicts series.

LITTLE NYMPH

If you liked *Prince of Thorns*, you might also enjoy *Little Nymph*. A New Adult darker, enemies-to-lovers, mafia romance, perfect for fans of *365 Days*. Get it here: https://books2read.com/u/bW0GdW

From Elizabeth Stevens, writing as E.J. Knox, comes...

Forbidden lust, a marriage pact, and the dangerous secret that could ruin it all.

My job is simple; protect Olive. Whatever she needs. Including spending the summer with the family of her intended fiancé.

Mav Vitali is anything but simple. Olive's future husband. Heir to his father's crime empire, he's as deadly as he is gorgeous.

I have one job. One. Goddamned. Job. My life is hers. So, of course I fall head over heels into lust at first sight with Mav.

I could have resisted – he's an arsehole, after all – if the feeling hadn't been mutual. And it takes just one inadvisable kiss for him to decide I will be his at any cost. Luckily, Olive's had more spark with a wet towel but, when a stalker comes after her, we've all got other things on our minds.

To save her, I'll have to team up with the man I love to hate. As the stalker grows closer, so do we. But what price will we pay to be together?

PRINCE OF THORNS

Thank you so much for reading this story! Word of mouth is super valuable to authors. So, if you have a few moments to rate/review Maggie and Vaughn's story – or, even just pass it on to a friend – I would be really appreciative.

Have you looked for my books in store, or at your local or school library and can't find them? Just let your friendly staff member or librarian know that they can order copies directly from LightningSource/Ingram.

If you want to keep up to date with my new releases, rambles and writing progress, sign up to my newsletter at https://landing.mailerlite.com/webforms/landing/y1n6q2.

Follow me:

THANKS

I am honest to goodness running out of people to thank without sounding like a broken record in these pages, but that's the life of a hermit writer for you. The main difference this time has been working out how to get comfortable with a broken toe.

Firstly, I'd like to thank Melody of Paradise Cover Deigns for the absolutely stunning cover. This book only exists because I saw the cover and HAD to have it, so kind of needed a story to go with it. I cannot wait to see the rest of the series.

Thank you also to Kaity and Riker for all your help, and for working out this was actually, accidentally a motorcycle club book. Special thanks extra to Kaity as well for being as excited about Vaughn as I am, and her fantastic beta reading abilities, as always.

Thanks to the usual suspects who keep me alive, provide me with Freddos, and help me human.

And the final thank you to Vaughn himself. You are amazing and I'm going to miss you a lot. Still, I'm looking forward to playing with Iago next!

MY BOOKS

You can find where to buy all my books in print and eBook at my website; www.elizabethstevens.com.au/.

ABOUT THE AUTHOR

Writer. Reader. Perpetual student. Nerd.

E.J. Knox is the Darker/Bully Romance penname of bestselling author Elizabeth Stevens. E.J. is the name to read if you want darker/bully romance in the Mature YA/NA crossover space. Think high school, college, and academy. E.J. brings my usual wit, banter, and repartee in good old enemies-to-lovers showdowns between alpha males and the sassy heroines strong enough to knock them down a peg or two. There'll be fake-dating, love triangles, kidnapping and danger, second chances, and more.

Born in New Zealand to a Brit and an Australian, I am a writer with a passion for all things storytelling. I love reading, writing, TV and movies, gaming, and spending time with family and friends. I am an avid fan of British comedy, superheroes, and SuperWhoLock. I have too many favourite books, but I fell in love with reading after Isobelle Carmody's *Obernewtyn*. I am obsessed with all things mythological – my current focus being old-style Irish faeries. I live in Adelaide (South Australia) with my long-suffering husband, delirious dog, mad cat, two chickens, and a lazy turtle.

Contact me:

Email: ejknox@elizabethstevens.com.au

Website: www.elizabethstevens.com.au/ej-knox

Twitter: www.twitter.com/writer_iz

Instagram: www.instagram.com/writeriz

Facebook: https://www.facebook.com/elizabethstevens88/

Made in the USA
Las Vegas, NV
28 March 2024

87895236R00236